Protectors of Humanity

4 Books in 1

Rebecca Proenza

PROTECTORS OF HUMANITY BOOK 1 Magician Ways.
PROTECTORS OF HUMANITY BOOK 2 Damnation Land.
PROTECTORS OF HUMANITY BOOK 3 Disorder Reigns.
PROTECTORS OF HUMANITY BOOK 4 Family Wars.

Published by: Proenza Productions LLC

Cover design by:
Aleena J Valentine Lopez

Edited by:
Arielle Hebert
Liam Richards
Alexander McCarty
William McCarty

Dedication

Special Thanks to the real Proenza family.

To my father for helping me grow up to be the person I am today. If it wasn't for you, I might not be the same woman.

To my brothers for always being there for me, and for putting up with my shenanigans growing up, and helping me grow up.

To my grandmother for all of your help.

To my late grandfather for seeing me and not my troublemaking.

To my grandparents for your continued support.

To my aunts and uncles, thank you for being like other parents to me, and for your wisdom.

To my cousins for always making life a little more interesting, and for taking an interest in me for more than just the family reunions.

To my mother for everything you have done.

To my sister for always being there for me.

Special thanks to the friends who were with me to Hell and back.

All the amazing artists I have met in my life.

To my good friends at Sphere Of Compassion, for all you've done to help me. Thank you.

To my convention friends who have been nothing but supportive, thank you.

Thank you to everyone I can call my friend.

Special thanks to Victoria University in Melbourne, Australia, and the FIU study abroad program for giving me a chance to explore the land down under. Another thanks to the friends I have made there, and my roommates/flat mates.

Thank you to the kind people of Boston who helped me.

To Jill for your knowledge on Boston's people, culture, and places.

To Nina for your vast knowledge on Salem and Paul Revere's house.

To Hannah and Evan for your knowledge on the Paul Revere museum.

To Assunta for your knowledge of the church and what used to be of little Italy.

About the Author

I have always been a weird person. Loving dark horror stories and very happy stories, there was almost no in between for me. I've had a passion for writing since I was very young, writing the first draft of the prologue for Protectors Of Humanity at the age of eight. I grew up in South Florida, living there all my life. I got my undergrad at Florida International University in English, and a Master's in Creative Writing. I encourage everyone to do what they love and finish what they start, because you never know who you will inspire. All my stories have a focus on mental health and maintaining positive relationships, but they do have fictional elements with different genres. Horror, science fiction, urban fantasy, coming of age, and some comedy. Having autism myself, I hope anyone who is labeled with a "disability" reading this will not let their labels define them. We are all so much more capable than what society deems us. Follow your dream and you'll be amazed where it leads.

Book 1

Magician Ways

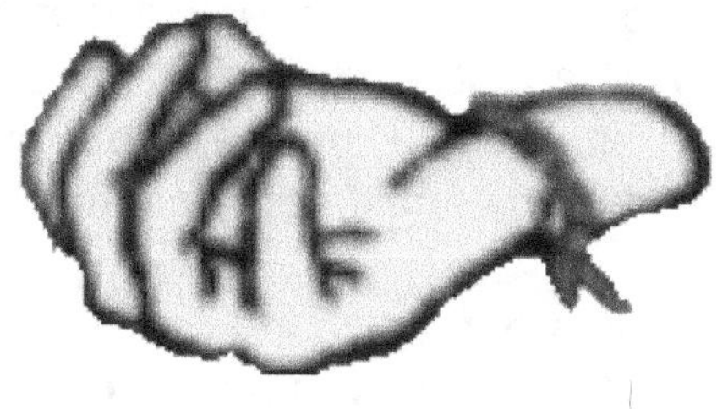

Prologue

Begrudgingly ending my nap, I leisurely open my eyes as blinding rays of sunlight pierce my eyelids that I quickly close shut tight. Where's my hat? The black fedora that I put over my face before falling asleep must have fallen off. So much for blocking out the sun! How long have I been napping? My iPod was still playing music on shuffle mode, so I couldn't have been out that long. I cover my eyes without sitting up and completely open them. I wait about a minute for my eyes to adjust to the bothersome sunlight. I sit up, take my hand off my eyes, squint, and search for my hat. Thankfully, I find it right next to where my head was.

Duh!

I put it on and look around.

My oldest brother is sitting with my parents, aunts, and uncles. They're all still on their beach chairs, but had moved into a circle. They're probably talking about whatever it is adults talk about. I look toward the lagoon with my other older brother and sister splashing around with some of my older cousins, playing a three-way chicken fight. My brother and some of my cousins that were not playing were splashing water on the six players like crazy, probably trying to distract them. My sister is on top of my cousin, dominating him as usual.

I hope the red rope bracelet I made her doesn't get ripped off like my necklace did last time I played Chicken Fight in the pool.

My younger cousins are building sandcastles better than I could ever make. They have a three-story sandcastle with windows, a big wall, and a moat. My cousin Joseph is running back from the shore with a blue pail, with water splashing out of every side. He gently pours water in the moat. My cousin Aliya looks up and sees me staring at them. She jumps to her feet and waves frantically to me with both hands. I shyly wave back with one hand. She gestures for me to come over and join them.

"Soon," I mouth to her.

She cocks her head to the side, confused.

"Soon!" I yell, cupping my hands to the side of my mouth.

She smiles wide and gives me a thumbs up.

I look at the other families. There are three teenagers skim boarding on the shoreline. Two boys, probably around sixteen or seventeen. Or maybe fifteen. It's hard to tell. The girl of the group looks about fourteen, and very pale. Paler than me!

"Hey, Bec!" It was my oldest brother, Tom, calling me.

"You alright?"

"Yeah," I tell him.

"You want to come sit with us?"

"No, thanks," I say, standing up. "I'm just going to walk around for a bit. Plus, you guys will just bore me to death!"

He playfully sticks his tongue out at me and says, "You don't need us for that!"

I laugh and shake my head. Then I make a heart with my hands.

"Hate you," I mouth to him.

He makes a heart back and says, "Hate you, too."

"No you don't!"

It's his turn to laugh and shake his head.

I blow him a kiss and I turn away.

I shuffle my feet toward the back of the lagoon and look at the other people. There is a couple a good distance away from the chicken fight playing in the water with two babies. The babies are in two separate floaties, with the parents still holding them close. There is a woman close to my parents, but something about this woman seems strange. She's under a large umbrella reading a magazine, and she keeps glancing around. She's wearing black sunglasses, a big straw hat, a scarf, a light jacket, and... basically her entire body is covered with clothing. It's as if she's hiding from the sun. I suppose I'm wearing a jacket and hat too, but I'm not hiding from the sun.

A gust of wind blows hard and knocks my hat off. I quickly catch it before it can blow away. The umbrellas that were planted weren't so lucky. I see my father run after one and catch it just before it hits the shore. I look to see that the chicken fight has been broken apart. The wind destroyed their balance. Then, my brother is pulled under the water by something. It happened so fast, I'm not sure if he ducked under the water, or if one of my cousins is playing a trick on him.

One by one everyone disappears below. The screaming is unbearable. This definitely isn't my cousin! I watch helplessly as my family get pulled under. With despair, I notice that the couple with the babies are gone. My sister is the last one standing.

I run towards her with my arm outstretched.

She nearly makes it out, but then...a tentacle? Yes, a red tentacle comes out of nowhere, wraps itself around my sister's waist, and pulls her right back in, all while she screams until she's pulled under into the depths.

Did...Did I really just see that?

I can hear my mother and aunts screaming the names of their children. A creature that's the size of a toddler steps onto the shore. It scans the beach with its large green buggy eyes. It opens its mouth and screeches, revealing red blood dripping from three rows of teeth. It flails its red tentacle appendages as it shrieks.

This can't be good!

One of the skim boarders foolishly walks up to it, his skim board raised over his head. I feel like yelling at him to not be stupid and get away from the thing, but my lips won't budge.

He hesitates when he's next to the tentacled toddler like creature. The board quivers in his hands as the toddler faces him.

"It's kind of-," was the last thing he ever said. The toddler thing spits a light green liquid on his face and the boy screams as his skin slowly melts.

This thing spits acid!

The toddler jumps on the boy and starts to eat the parts of his face that are melting, all while the boy screams and begs for help. When the acid reaches bone, the screams stop. The boy falls before his bones become liquid.

God almighty! Did I really just see that?

Three more of these creatures emerge from the water. They have a few differences, but they all have the buggy eyes, and they're full of hate and hunger.

It's not until the toddlers charge the beach that everyone starts reacting. They were just too fast and they caught up, ripping every human being to shreds.

A scarlet one lunges at my mother and pins her arms to her side with its three legs, and decapitates her in a single bite. Through her newly opened wound, the toddle digs his own head inside to feast on her.

I'm petrified. My legs don't work, so I can't run. Too afraid to even think of breathing the wrong way, or I'll be next.

A white toddler is feasting on a different person. Its head writhing around and gnashing it's teeth like a shark. It then...sets itself on fire?

No, it's the teenage girl who was skim boarding that caused the flames.

The great white toddler is being roasted as blue flames erupts from the teen's hands as she incinerates it.

Wait, what?

Yes, there is actually a ball of blue fire in her hand.

I'm dreaming!

Wake up!

The red one sticks his long neck into my uncle's stomach and devours his internal organs. It glances up at me with its emerald eyes and we lock for a split second. It knows I'm unable to run.

"I'm going to kill you," it seems to taunt me.

I can't scream. I can't move.

Why can't I wake up?

I never noticed that it started to charge at me.

The creature is almost on me when it explodes. Its body, yellow blood, and freakish organs splatter, hitting my chest and drenching my arms. Standing about twenty feet away is the woman I saw hiding from the sun. Her hand is glowing white on the arm stretched out toward where the creature was. Her hat has blown off and her skin is turning red. The glow in her hand then vanishes. She locks eyes with me for a quick second before turning to charge the third toddler. She rips it in two, letting the body wiggle on the floor.

What am I watching? Why can't I wake up?

The girl is still roasting the great white toddler. When she finishes, she looks up at me.

"Help us!" she shouts, then she runs to the three-legged one and snaps its neck.

I can't move. I can't even open my mouth to speak to her. Even if I could, nothing would come out anyways.

I can't wake up!

I hear a strange shriek. I look to see that the woman has killed the green toddler. I look around. I can't tell if anyone besides the three of us survived. All I see is blood. Yellow and red puddles are scattered across the lagoon. Organs both human and other are scattered on the sand, along with body parts.

My body finds a little strength. I am drawn towards the back where sand becomes grass. My legs aimlessly take me there. More bodies lie scattered. I recognize my brother's face among them. My heart crumbles.

He can't be dead.

Tom *can't* be dead!

I see another body. It's headless, but I know it's my father. I'd recognize those tacky shorts anywhere.

No!

I need this nightmare to end!

I look toward the horizon. I see that the waves are bringing small pieces to the shoreline. I drag my feet there. I look at them, and I instantly regret it. It's human body parts. I see a baby's foot and a small ear. There are several hands. One of them stands out to me.

A hand that has a red rope bracelet around it. I'd recognize that bracelet anywhere. I made it three years ago.

"Ash..." My sister is gone.

More limbs and organs come out of the water, then another hand comes into view. This one has a silver ring on it. I remember that ring, a class ring, a ring I tried to throw away once as a prank and the owner ended up having to dig through the garbage on trash day to find it.

"Jake..." I start to cry.

My siblings, my mother, my family, they're all gone.

This...isn't a dream.

I start feeling dizzy, and my vision goes fuzzy.

"Mom!" the girl calls out. "What are you..."

I don't hear the rest. I grab my head and try to breathe, but everything starts to spin. I fall on my knees and see the girl running toward her mother, and the mother reaching out to me.

I blackout before I hit the sand.

Chapter 1

Two Weeks Earlier

The dismissal bell rings and my friends and I throw our hands into the air. I didn't bring any papers like my classmates, only a small black bag with my house keys, my iPod, my crappy cell phone, and one pencil with a green eraser topper. That's more than what some people brought today! Seventh grade is finally over. Summer break is going to be a blast!

***

"So, I'll see you tomorrow for my sleepover?" I ask my friend Mabel, standing outside her stall in the girl's restroom. I study myself in the mirror after washing my hands.

"Definitely," she says. "Is John coming?"

"You know it's not a party unless I invite John! Besides, he lives five houses down from me. It'd be a crime for him not to come!"

I stare into my own eyes. I always loved my heterochromia, and the different emotions they tend to portray. My right green eye sparkles like an emerald happily while my left hazel eye glosses over a little desperate to leave. My long dirty blonde hair is tied back in a high ponytail, almost reaching my butt.

"Excellent!" Mabel cheers, walking out of the stall.

I take out my ponytail and my curly hair falls down further. I mess it up a little before straightening my black jacket. I put the hair tie around my hand, and smile again. I'm so happy to leave!

I move my wooden Star of David out from under my shirt, and turn away from the mirror to face Mabel.

"I have to go catch my bus. See you tomorrow!" Mabel gives me a quick hug, then runs out of the restroom.

The stupid busses. Just another stressor we will not have to deal with for the next two months.

As I exit the school, I see John about to board our bus and I cut the line and grab his polo collar.

John's a year younger than me. He's a little on the overweight side, about a head taller than me, has short brown hair, and dark brown eyes. He's not the cutest or most handsome, but I love this kid to death! Not *in* love; there's a huge difference.

"We're not riding the bus today," I tell him as I yank him away. "We're walking." Despite being half an hour walk from our houses, the bus takes forty-five minutes. Go figure.

"Come on!" he cries out in protest. "I'm tired!"

"We did absolutely nothing today but party."

That's middle school life for ya.

"Fine," he says. "I can't win an argument with you anyways, so I'm not even going to try."

It's true

No one can.

***

"So, it's tomorrow," I tell John as we walk into my house. "You're coming," I say sternly.

"Alright, but I'm not wearing Ash's bra again."

Long story.

"Is that you?" my mother calls from inside.

"Yes, Mom!" I call back as John and I take off our shoes.

"How was your last day of school?" she asks me, appearing from the kitchen. She has her hands facing up and there's juice all over them. She's probably cooking.

Page 8

"Great," I tell her. "We did nothing but party!"

"Sounds fun. I'm making dinner. Steak and potatoes."

"Uh, mom. I don't eat meat."

"I know, I'm making you a salad and some garlic bread."

She knows me so well.

"John, are you staying for dinner?" my mom asks him.

"Damn right!" he says. "I'm having some of that steak!" He then clears his throat. "Thank you, ma'am."

"Where's Dad?" I ask.

"He's working, he won't be home until Monday."

My father's a pilot and he's always out flying. He's almost never home, which is good when I want to do stuff like have a sleepover. I love my dad, but he's *very* strict.

"Did he leave this morning?"

"Yes."

"Good," I say and smile. "The sleepover can't happen when he's home!"

"Be nice to your father."

"I will . . . When he's home."

***

"So then what happened?" Mabel asks me.

"We ran as fast as we could."

It's the night of my sleepover. I'm playing dreidel in my room with Mabel; John; my brother, Jake; and Mabel's cousin, Josh. I invited more of my friends, but their parents found out that tonight is a mixed sleepover, so they left us several hours ago. That's fine though, I'd rather have my best friends sleeping over.

The five of us are sitting in a circle in my room with pennies in front of us. John is by far beating us. I think he has thirty pennies, but it's hard to count with him flaunting them in our faces. It is about two thirty in the morning, and none of us are even close to being tired. We are all in our pajamas with messy hair. I'm telling them a story about how John and I messed with our neighbors' Christmas decorations last year. All the time we would switch the neighbor's decorations and watch how the neighbors would get angry and confused. There was one year when we completely stole our next-door neighbor's decorations and put it back on their lawn the following year.

"What do you two do when I'm not looking?" Jake asks.

"How badly do you want to know?" John smirks.

Jake hesitates for a moment. "Not that badly,"

We all start laughing.

"You two get into some crazy adventures," Mabel says, spinning the dreidel. She lands on hay, takes half the pile, and the rest of us throw in a penny.

"Hell yeah, we do." John spins the dreidel, lands on gimel, and takes the whole pile. We all groan and throw in a penny. He passes the dreidel to me while wiggling his eyebrows.

"How have you guys not been caught yet?" Mabel asks.

I spin the dreidel and land on shin. I sigh and throw in two pennies. I only have eight left, pathetic compared to John's pile.

"Don't know, don't care," John says. "I'm just glad it hasn't happened yet!"

"Does Nancy know?" Jake asks John.

Nancy is his mom. She's a very cool mom, but she's very stern with her six kids. Especially John, since he's the youngest.

"Actually, yes," he states. "She tells me which houses to hit."

"I would not have expected that from your mother!" I say laughing in shock.

The wink he gives me tells me he's joking, but not fully.

"She hates the Perez's next door to you, so she's fine with us ransacking their house."

"Just be happy mom and dad don't know about any of this," Jake says to me, taking the dreidel. He lands on nun and passes it to Josh.

"Hey, Mabel," I say, "remember the all-nighter we pulled in the pool?"

"Yes!" Mabel exclaims happily. "We were so pruny!"

Her sea-blue eyes shine excitedly. "We had to dive under the water every five minutes because of the mosquitoes and wasps!"

"And when my dad caught us showering together in the morning!" I laugh.

"Yes! Imagine what was going through his mind!"

"He probably thought we were lesbians or something!"

We start laughing uncontrollably.

"Why wasn't I there?" John asks.

"You had a family thing," I say, remembering when his uncle came up from Colombia.

"Speaking of family things," Jake says, "you know our family is coming down on Monday for our reunion?"

"What? No, I didn't," I say disappointed.

Those blue eyes of his give me a concerned look. Always my over-protective big brother.

"You don't like your family?" Josh asks me.

I don't really know Josh all that well, but I hang out with him every time I go to Mabel's, so he's basically part of the group.

"It's them who don't like me," I explain to him as John passes me the dreidel. I didn't even realize we made a rotation.

"Why don't they like you?" Josh asks me.

"It's because I'm not blood. My parents adopted me when I was a baby. They knew nothing of my birth parents or why they had given me up, or if they died, or what happened to me. They don't know my real nationality, but I consider myself American. My dad's side of the family always hated me because I wasn't one of them. My mother only has one sister, and I almost never see her, but she doesn't show me any love even when I do. Only my parents, siblings, and younger cousins really care about me."

"They don't hate you," Jake assures me for the twentieth time. "At least Tom is coming down as well."

"He is? What a relief!"

Tom is my other big brother, the eldest of the four. He's twenty-three and lives with his girlfriend in Tallahassee, so we don't get to see him much. When we do see him, it's always a blast.

"Can you pipe down?" We all turn around to see Ash standing in the doorway where the bathroom joins her room with mine and Jake's "I'm trying to sleep, I have work tomorrow."

I haven't even noticed we were loud.

"Sure, Ashley," Jake mocks.

"Don't call me that," she snaps. "That's a name reserved for bitches!"

Page 11

Jake smirks at her.

She looks down at her hand and twirls the red rope bracelet I made for her sixteenth birthday. She never takes it off.

"Don't make me tell mom about the-" Ash starts.

Jake interrupts, "we'll be quiet!"

"Hey, Bec," Mabel says as Ash leaves, "can you show Josh that magic trick with the three cards?"

"What trick?" Josh asks.

I look at Jake. "Wanna get me my deck?"

He stands up and gets me my deck of cards that are on my nightstand. From the deck, I grab the ace of hearts, the eight of diamonds, and the queen of clubs from the top. I'm holding the three cards face down, and move the rest to the side.

"Alright, Josh," I say, "so in life, you have options, you can have this," I flip over the ace, "that," I flip over the eight, "and even more of this." I flip over the ace again.

"Wait, what?" Josh asks, staring at the ace of hearts.

"Now," I continue as I shuffle the three cards in my hand, "life can sometimes be backwards, so you can have that," I flip over the eight, "this," I flip over the ace, "and more of that instead." I flip over the eight again.

"How the-" Josh starts, but I continue my trick.

"So, in life you can have some of this," I flip over the ace, "some of that," I flip over the eight, "but not a lot of the other," and I flip over the queen.

"Wow," Josh says. "How long did it take you to perfect that?"

"I don't know," I say smiling. "It just came easy to me."

Chapter 2

I'm baking cookies with Ash in the kitchen on Monday when the doorbell rings.

I look at the clock. 12:34. Our relatives aren't supposed to arrive until two.

"Na-ah," Ash says shaking her head "It's *way* too soon!"

"Maybe it's not them," I say, using the roller to flatten out our homemade cookie dough. "Perhaps it's John dropping off my skateboard."

He borrowed my skateboard the other day, and I called him an hour ago asking him to drop it off.

"He would have called," she pointed out. "You know he doesn't ring the doorbell!"

I hear the door open followed by a greeting.

It's them. Well, some of them. It's my dad's little sister, her husband, and her two little kids. Aliya runs up to Ash and hugs her, and Joseph runs up to me. The adults might not approve of me, but the little ones sure do. Then they switch and I embrace Aliya.

"Hey, guys," they say to us.

"How have you been?" Ash asks them.

"We're good," Aliya tells us.

"Are you making cookies?" Joseph asks.

Always to the point.

"Yes, we are," I tell him, using a candy cane mold to cut a few cookies out of the dough. Jews making Christmas cookies in the summer. Talk about unconventional.

My uncle walks up to me and gives me a shy hug. "Hello."

"Hello, Uncle Dominic."

"When are the cookies going to be ready?" Aliya asks, hopping up and down.

"In about an hour," Ash tells her.

"Aw!" she and Joseph both whine.

"How about we play hide and seek after we pop the cookies in the oven?" Ash asks them with a grin on her face.

"Yay!" they both cheer.

***

More of our relatives come in throughout the day. There are about thirty or forty people in our house. Ash and I didn't make enough cookies. Our driveway is loaded with cars, and it's hard to get around the house. The first day is just everybody getting here. They stop by to say hello, then go to their hotel. How they all managed to book the same hotel, I have no idea. My mother said it wasn't hard to do.

"I'll show you one day," she tells me.

The next day, we went down to Miami. Once in the city, we all split off into little groups. I was with Jake, Ash, Tom, and his girlfriend Roxy. It was great hanging out with our brother again. I didn't realize how much I've missed him.

Tom and Roxy take us to this one place to eat in the city for lunch. I look like the odd ball out at the table. All three of my siblings have straight dark brown hair and blue eyes, while I have curly blonde hair and mixed eyes. I'm sort of glad Roxy's blonde too; we need more blondes in the family.

"And Chuck couldn't sit for an hour!" Tom was finishing up telling us a story while he and Roxy paid the bill.

We are all laughing.

"Wow," Jake says. "That's insane!"

"So, Bec," Tom asks me, "you and John do anything crazy lately?"

Page 14

"We found a canal," I told him.

"Where?" Ash asks. "There are no canals here, only the lake."

"Yes, there is, right behind the development," I tell her. "I can show it to you if you don't believe me."

"We believe you," Roxy says. "What did you guys do there?"

"We just rode our bikes along the canal and explored the forest, and played with a dead goat's body."

"Now I don't believe you," Ash says as the waiter brings back Tom's card. "There are no forests in Florida, and why would there be a dead goat?"

"Could you bring me my side of garlic?" I ask the waiter.

"I'll go get it for you now," he assures me.

"Thank you so much!" I look back at Ash. "Well, this was a forest. Like I said, I'll show it to you. I'm sure the body's still there."

"Well, I know what we're doing tomorrow," Jake jokes as we stand up.

Once were outside, Roxy turns around. "Hey, Tom, do you think you can convince your dad to let us go to the beach? I really miss the beach."

"I can try and convince him to squeeze it in," Tom tells her, slipping his hand into hers. "You know how my dad is with his schedule."

"Aw." I pop a piece of garlic the waiter brought me in my mouth. Most people say it's too strong, but I love the taste. I always keep some peeled cloves in my pocket and eat them from time to time. Except today I couldn't because we ran out. Most kids have their mom buy them candy or nuts, then there's me. "The beach sucks!"

"You live in South Florida," Roxy points out. "How can you hate the beach? You're surrounded by it!"

"I just don't like it." I tell her. "I burn easily, it's hot, dreaded sand is everywhere, even if you're standing the whole time it still gets in your bathing suite. and on top of that birds like attacking me! And-"

"And there's too many people," Ash says, mockingly in my voice.

I make a face at her, and she smiles to show me that she's only joking.

"Maybe it wouldn't be so hot if you take your jacket off once in a while," Ash tells me.

Page 15

"Then I'll burn!"

"Then wear sunscreen!"

"I do, but I have to reapply it every twenty minutes."

"I'm sure that's exaggerated," Roxy states.

"No, she's pretty spot on," Tom tells her.

"Really?" Roxy asks amazed.

"Yeah," I tell her, "it's a curse."

"Are you secretly Irish?" Roxy asks me.

"That is a high possibility," I smile at her.

"So, Ash," Tom asks, "how's college going?"

"Great, actually," she tells him. "I'll have my associate's next term. Thank you, dual enrollment!"

"That's amazing!" Tom exclaims. "It's great that you're finishing up so fast, it took me forever to get my associate's. Know what you're majoring in?"

"Psychology," she tells him.

"A bipolar girl helping other bipolar girls?"

"I'm not bipolar!"

"Well, you can get mad out of nowhere," I tell her.

"Doesn't mean I'm bipolar!"

I stop walking and stop in front of a window. I look inside and see all these different kinds of hats on display.

"Let's go inside," I tell them, and I dash inside the store before they can say anything.

There are maybe a hundred hats inside, all different styles. Caps, beanies, fedoras, skullies, and more. I take off my green and pink camouflage cap and grab a black skully. It's way too big on me and keeps falling off. I take it off and grab a baby blue fedora with a fake red flower. I walk in front of a mirror and try it on. It looks quite nice on me, but clashes with my green demolition derby T-shirt.

Fedoras are my favorite.

"Need any help?"

I turn around. There's an old woman standing there in dress clothing and a Donna name tag.

"No, thank you," I tell her. "I'm just looking."

"Alright," Donna says. "Just let me know if you do."

"I will, thank you," I look back in the mirror and model the hat.

In the mirror, I see her staring at me. Her eyes slightly squinting like she's studying me. Figures she'd think I'd rob the store!

"Like it?" Jake asks me from behind.

"It's nice," I tell him, "but the flower throws me off."

"Try this one," he hands me an aqua fedora with a black stripe.

I try it on and look in the mirror. It looks really nice on me.

"You really have the head shape for hats," Ash tells me. She then runs to the other side of the store and grabs me a black fedora with a white stripe on it.

I hand her the aqua one and try on the black one. It complements my pale face very well and it even matches my outfit. Actually, it can match any outfit I throw on, and my blonde locks clash in a good way. The gold and dark colors go great together, and it's a gorgeous hat.

"I love it, Ash," I whisper.

"Then get it," she tells me.

I check the price tag. Fourteen dollars. Little pricey for a hat, but it is Miami. I only have a dirty quarter and my inhaler in my pocket.

"I can't," I sigh. "I have no money."

"Then get a job," she elbows me.

"If you can find a place that would hire a twelve-year- old that looks nine, please tell me," I joke back with her.

Jake and Tom both grab the hat at the same time.

Tom looks at me. "I got it."

"We'll go half and half," Jake tells him.

"Can't argue with that," says Tom.

Chapter 3

Being with my family isn't god awful like it usually is, so I'm pretty thankful for that, but you can only spend so much time with your family before you want to yank your hair out.

At least that's how it is for me.

I called John up and we took a day to go to the skate park. My dad wasn't comfortable with us going alone, so he had Jake accompany us, along with two of my cousins who also like skating. We usually come alone, but that's when father is on a trip. It took a lot to convince him to let me come here today to get away from the family. I wasn't going to ruin it by arguing with him about the boys.

"Fucking prick," John mutters from under his breath.

"John?" Jake snaps. "Your language!"

"Did you not see the look that guy gave me? It's because I'm fat, isn't it!"

"Just turn the other cheek," Jake tells him. "He's not worth it."

John sighs. "Fine."

"Let me try teaching you the kickflip," I tell Jake.

"What's the point?" he pouts, "I'm going to be a doctor, I don't need to know how to ride a skateboard, it's not going to save my life, or anyone else's life!"

"It's good to know a few tricks," I tell him while demonstrating my kickflip. "Plus, Sean and Aiden are having fun," I say, pointing to my cousins on the half pipe.

"Don't you want to join them?" I gently kick my board to him and turn it upside down with my foot. "You try."

Jake puts his left foot under the board.

"Is that the foot you're most comfortable with?" I ask him.

He sighs and puts his right foot under, "You used your left foot," he pouts.

"I'm ambidextrous," I explain. "It doesn't matter which foot I use!"

"Doesn't that only apply to hands?"

"It goes for both."

"Scientifically speaking-" Jake starts, but I interrupt him.

"Scientifically speaking, who cares."

He sighs and puts his left foot on top. He grabs my hand and then he grabs John's hand after he offers it to him.

"Now just jump and turn the board as fast as you can," I explain. "Like how I showed you earlier."

He does as I instruct, but he lands on the side of the board and almost falls over. Luckily, he was holding our hands.

"Try again," I instruct. "You can do it, big brother!"

"You're thinking too much," John explains. "Just feel it in your lower body and push."

Jake chuckles.

"Not that way!" John snaps.

"What?" I ask after a couple of seconds, completely lost.

"Nothing!" they both shout.

I just roll my eyes. I take a garlic clove from my pocket and shove it in my mouth. "All right... Try again, you can do it!" I say as I grab his hands again and chew on my garlic.

Jake takes a deep breath while I reposition the board with my feet. When it's ready, he tries again and does the kickflip successfully.

"You did it!" I cheer while giving him a big hug.

"Yeah," he beams proudly. "I did it! Fuck yeah!"

"You ready to try the half pipe?" John asks him.

"Hell no!"

***

I'm practicing my violin later that night when Ash comes into my room from the bathroom.

Page 19

"You're getting better," she tells me.

"Thanks," I tell her, "I haven't really been able to practice much since the reunion started, and this isn't an easy piece."

"Is it your favorite?"

"No," I get out my folder that's behind my book of songs and find my favorite. "This one is." I turn over the book and show her the sheet music.

"Can you play it for me?" she asks.

"Sure," I say, "but I only know the first half."

"That's fine."

I put my violin in position and play it for her. The song lasts about two minutes. I had to play a lot of legatos, so my arms were tired by the end of it.

"Nice," she says when I finish.

"Yeah, it makes me think of our ancestors." I sigh. "I need a break."

"Come on," Ash says sitting on the floor. "Let me braid your hair!"

"Why?" I ask puzzled.

"Because you never let me do your hair anymore!"

"I don't even do my own hair!" I laugh and sit down in front of her, with my back to her so she can braid my hair.
I feel her slide all my hair through one hand and try to get the knots out, then separate it into three strands.

"I hate your room," she says.

"Me too, kinda, but Jake won't let me decorate it how I want to. I would make everything colorful, playful, and have stuffed animals everywhere!"

She laughs. "Sounds like something you would do."

"That would be my dream room. I'd have curtains one color, each wall a different color, all my furniture a different color, and my violin stuff in the corner."

"Sounds fun. How was the skate park today?"

"It was cool," I tell her as she starts to braid my long hair. "John and I taught Jake how to do a kickflip today, I learned how to grind today, and John got into a fight with a guy who kept giving him dirty looks."

"Is that why you guys got home early?"

"Yeah. You should have seen it, things almost got really ugly."

"Why was the guy giving him dirty looks?"

"I don't know. He called John a faggot and John started telling him off. What's a faggot? I hear it a lot but no one ever told me what it means."

"It's basically a bad term for homosexual," she explains, "Although it can have another meaning to mean a highly annoying person, but it's mostly used in the first context."

"But John's not gay."

"As far as we know," she smirks.

"He's not!"

"Well, I'm glad John stood up for himself and didn't let anyone treat him like crap."

"Well, you and Tom are always telling us to watch our backs and always defend ourselves, no matter how hard things get."

"Damn right! Promise me that you will always defend yourself no matter what?"

"Of course," I promise. "It's how you guys brought me up."

"What? Me and the boys?"

"Yeah," I tell her, "The three of you are always telling me to watch my a-"

"Yes!" she says, cutting me off. "We do say that a lot, don't we? All right, you have a hair tie?"

I gasp. "You're done already? How? My hair is so long!"

"Yep," she tells me. "I just need a hair tie to tie it up."

"I have one on my night table."

Ash stands up while still clinging to the tip of my braid, so I'm forced to stand with her. We go to the night table and she finds the red one I always use and ties my hair. She pulls on it a bit, causing me a little pain, but eventually she has it all tied up.

"Go look in the mirror," she instructs me.

I run to the bathroom and stand in front of mine and Jake's sink. She gave me a high ponytail. The top hair tie is light blue. I don't even remember her putting it on me. My hair doesn't look messy at all, it looks really nice. I turn to the side and examine my new braid. It's braided down all the way to my lower back. She left a good portion of

Page 21

my hair unbraided. She always did that when we were younger and it would really bug me. Now it's not so bad.

"It looks nice, Ash," I tell her. "Thanks!"

I was never into girly stuff like doing my hair, make up, or even dressing nice for that matter.

"Any time, little sister," she smiles at me. "Now you can impress Josh!"

I gape at her and give her a little push. "I don't like Josh!"

"He likes you," she informs me.

"No, he doesn't!" I insist. "We don't even know each other that well!"

She smirks at me. "Suit yourself."

"Girls!" our mother calls from downstairs. "Dinner's ready!"

"Come on," Ash tells me. "Let's go show mom your hair."

"Alrighty then!"

We exit the bathroom and enter Ash's room. Her bed is not made, and she has school books and clothes all over her floor. Her desk is a mess of papers and pencils, and her television is on.

"You should really clean up in here," I nag her. "Honestly, you're a girl, you're not supposed to be messy! Jake's cleaner than you are!"

"You're one to talk," Ash shrugs as she turns off her TV.

"I'm not messy!"

"Yeah, but you do leave your books everywhere."

"Well, Jake won't let me put them on the bookshelf."

She pokes me in the ribs and I laugh, then she playfully pushes me out of her messy pigsty she calls a room.

Chapter 4

"Dobroe utro," I hear my grandmother calling from my bedroom door.

"Dobroe utro, baba," I say, half yawning.

My mother's side of the family is Russian, so I grew up fluent in the Russian language.

"Vstavay," she tells me. "Mi sorerayemsya na plyazh."

It isn't until after she leaves my room, when I sit up in bed and rub my eyes, that I realize what she said.

"Wake up, we're going to the beach."

I lie back down and groan. I lift my feet and push up on Jake's mattress above me. He's a heavy sleeper, and I'm pretty lazy in the morning, so this is how I wake him up usually.

"Wakey wakey eggs and bakey!"

I hear him groan and roll over. I sigh and rattle his mattress with my feet.

"I'm up! I'm up!" he says groggily.

"Get dressed, bozo," I say in a glum manner. "We're going to hell."

"Grand Cayman?"

"No, the beach."

***

My father's packing the cooler when I approach him. He's wearing a black T-shirt, and the tackiest orange shorts I have ever seen.

"Dad, can we talk?"

"What is it?" he asks matter of factly, not taking his eyes off the bottles of water he's placing in the cooler.

He takes family planning very seriously.

"I was wondering if I can stay with John while you guys are at the beach." We have plans to go bowling.

He stops what he is doing and gives me a dirty look. "Absolutely not!"

"But, Dad, I-"

"I don't care! Your family is here, and not for very long. You are going to spend time with them. I already let you go to the skatepark with him. Wasn't that enough for you?"

"Yes. No. I mean, Dad, they don't like me. We live to piss each other off!"

It's only after I say it that I realize it's a pathetic excuse.

"Bullshit!"

"And you know I hate the beach!"

"I don't care, you're going. End of discussion!"

"What about my violin lesson?"

"I called your teacher yesterday and canceled the lesson, now go get dressed."

And that was the end of that.

***

We arrive early at the beach. Only, it isn't a beach. It is a small fresh-water lagoon inside a park with sand instead of grass. There's only one other couple there at the moment, who are sitting at a distance. Jake, Ash and all the teenage cousins run in the water, while Tom, Roxy, and the other adults set up the chairs and place all the coolers.

This is going to be a long day, I think to myself and I take out my black Pikachu towel and laid it out on the sand. Technically, it's Ash's towel, but my cousin hid my SpongeBob towel before we left.

Like I said, we live to piss each other off.

I lie down on the towel and stare up at the sky. I study the lady-bugs and ice cream cones in the cloud shapes.

Sadly, clouds never stay the same shape for long, so the lady bug transforms into an alligator head.

I am overwhelmed with heat exhaustion. My mouth starts to dry, my neck is starting to feel wet, and every cloud looks like a lake. I'm wearing a T-shirt, khakis, and a light jacket because I didn't think it would be this hot. At least I am lowering my chances of skin cancer, and making sure my skin doesn't turn red speedily like it always does, although I already feel my face start to burn.

I go to my mother and grab the SPF 75 from her and rub some on my face.

I take my iPod out of my pocket once I'm back on my towel, and put my headphones in. I play my favorite artist on shuffle mode. I take off the fedora my siblings got for me, put it over my face to block out the sun, and fall asleep.

***

Begrudgingly ending my nap, I leisurely open my eyes and a ton of sunlight comes rushing in. I quickly close them shut. My fedora that I put over my face before falling asleep must have fallen off. How long have I been napping? Well, it mustn't have been very long because I still want to go back to sleep! My iPod is still playing my music on shuffle mode. I put my hand on my eyes and completely open them. I wait about a minute so my eyes can be used to being open.

Then I sit up, take my hand off my eyes, and search for my hat. I look left and right and I find it right next to where my head was.

Lovely, there's no wind.

I sigh and put it on.

Where is everyone? I look around.

Tom is sitting with my parents, my aunts, and my uncles. They're all still on their beach chairs, but they moved into a circle. They're all holding drinks, mostly beer, and they all laugh in unison. They're probably talking about whatever it is adults talk about. My father is doing most of the talking, as usual.

I look towards the water. Jake and Ash are with some of my older cousins playing three-way chicken fight. Jake and some of my cousins that are not in the chicken fight are splashing the six players

Page 25

like crazy. Probably trying to distract them. Ash is on top of one of our cousins. She's slashing at our cousin Red. Jake splashes salt water in her eyes. She only has enough time to cover her eyes and flick him off before she's knocked over and the last four remaining players go at each other. Ash lunges for Jake and pulls him under the water.

My younger cousins are building sandcastles better than I could ever make. They have a three-story sand castle with windows, a big wall, and a moat. They have a bunch of seashells decorating the castle. It looks very pretty. My cousin Joseph is running back from the shore with a blue pail, with water splashing out of every side. He then gently empties the pail into the moat.

I remember sand castles enough to know that the water seeps down into the sand, so you never really have water staying in your hole or moat for very long unless you dig down deep enough. My cousin Aliya looks up and sees me staring at them. She quickly stands up and waves frantically to me with both hands. I shyly wave back with one hand. She gestures for me to come over and join them.

"Soon," I mouth to her.

She cocks her head to the side confused.

"Soon!" I yell cupping my hands to the side of my mouth.

She smiles wide and gives me a thumbs up.

I look at the other families. There are three teenagers skim boarding on the shoreline. Two boys, probably around sixteen or seventeen. It's hard to tell because they have older faces, but no hair on their chests. Maybe they're fifteen? They're very prepubescent. The girl of the group looks about fourteen. She has sunglasses and a hat, and she's very pale, paler than me. I never thought that could be possible, but this girl has a skin color that you can find on the walls of an art museum.

"Hey," it was Tom, calling me. "You all right?"

"Yeah," I tell him.

"You want to come sit with us?"

"No, thanks," I say, standing up. "I'm just going to walk around for a bit. Plus, you guys will just bore me to death!"

He just playfully sticks his tongue out at me and says, "you don't need us for that!"

I laugh and shake my head. Then I take my thumb and two index fingers and shape them into a heart.

"Hate you," I mouth to him.

He makes a heart too and says, "Hate you, too."

"No you don't!" I say.

It's his turn to laugh and shake his head.

I blow him a kiss and then I turn away from him. I walk towards the back of the lagoon and look at the other people.

There is a couple a good distance away from the chicken fight playing in the water with two babies. The babies are in two separate floaties, but the parents still hold them close. The mother is closely watching the younger baby, a little boy probably not even a year old while the father is messing around with the older baby, a girl about two. She looks at the man and says something to him, probably to be careful with her.

There is a woman close to my parents. She seems normal enough, but something about this woman seems strange. She's under a large umbrella reading a magazine, but she keeps glancing around. It's hard to tell what she might be thinking. She's wearing black sunglasses, a big straw hat, a scarf, a light jacket, and... basically her entire body is covered with clothing as if she's hiding from the sun.

I'm wearing a jacket and hat too, but I'm not hiding from the sun.

Am I?

She looks over at the three skimboarding teenagers. She's watching them very closely. I think the pale girl is her daughter, judging from the fact that they both have pale white skin.

I look up. There's only three small clouds in the sky, and none of them are covering the sun. That's Florida for you. You're cloud watching one moment, and the next moment they're all gone.

Oh, what I wouldn't give for some shade right now!

A gust of wind blows and knocks my hat off. I quickly catch it before it can blow away.

Thank you, Florida!

The umbrellas, however, weren't so lucky. I see my father run after the umbrella and catch it halfway towards the shore. I look towards the water to see that the chicken fight has been broken apart.

My teeth start to chatter from the strong wind gusting against my mildly sweaty body.

Half my cousins start laughing, the other half start booing. Then, my brother is pulled under the water by someone. It happened so fast, I'm not sure if he ducked under the water awkwardly, or if one of my cousins is playing a trick on him.

One by one everyone in the water is quickly pulled under by something, and the screaming is unbearable. I can't stand to watch it, their look of fear, and then the quick yelp for help as they're soon silenced by the Atlantic Ocean.

This definitely isn't my cousin!

I watch my family get pulled under, and I notice that the couple and the babies are gone, but the floaties still remain.

My sister is the last one standing. I run after her with my arm outstretched to try and pull her out. She nearly makes it out on her own, but then... a tentacle? Yes, a red tentacle comes out from the depths, wraps itself around my sister's waist, and pulls her right back down under. She screams until she's pulled under.

Did I really just see that?

I feel my heart start to hurt.

I can hear my mother and aunts screaming the names of their children who were in the water.

A creature that's the size of a toddler, comes out of the water. Its huge green bug eyes are scanning the beach. It raises its two small red tentacles that it has instead of hands.

Is this the thing that pulled them under? A thing like this shouldn't even exist.

Judging by the size of the tentacle that pulled my sister, I think it can grow and shrink- Why am I analyzing this?

Shouldn't I run, or grab a stick, or something?

It looks around, opens its mouth to reveal three rows of sharp teeth that are caked with blood, and screeches.

This can't be good!

I can't seem to move as I watch my family die. I can't do anything as the girl sets fire to one of the toddler creatures. I can't function as the woman tears the last one apart. I can't tell if anyone besides the three of us survived.

All I see is blood. There is some orange blood from where both bloods have mixed. Organs both human and other are around the lagoon, along with body parts to match, most are human though. With great effort I develop enough courage to walk towards the end of the lagoon. I recognize my brother's face among them. My heart aches a little.

He can't be dead.

Tom can't be dead!

I then see my dad's body with no head. I immediately know it's him. I'd recognize those tacky shorts anywhere.

No!

I really need to wake up now!

The waves bring in body parts, as I get closer to the shore, one of them stands out to me.

A hand.

A hand that has a red rope bracelet around it. I'd recognize that bracelet anywhere. I cautiously walk up to it and try to pick it up. My hand immediately jerks back at the cold flesh.

How can this be a dream if I can physically feel?

"Ash..." My sister is gone.

More limbs and organs come out of the water, then another hand comes into view. This one has a silver ring on it. I remember that ring, a class ring, a ring I tried to throw away once as a prank and the owner ended up having to dig through the garbage on trash day to find it.

"Jake..." I start to cry.

My siblings, my mother, my family, they're all gone.

This... isn't a dream.

Before I can process this, I start to feel dizzy, and my vision grows fuzzy.

"Mom!" the girl calls out, "what are you..."

I don't hear the rest. I grab my head and try to breathe, but everything starts to spin. I fall on my knees and see the girl running towards her mother, and her mother reaching out to me.

I blackout before I hit the sand.

Chapter 5

My eyes snap open. The first thing that registers is the taste of dirt in my mouth. I was just in the sand, how is there dirt in my mouth?

I have several blankets on and I'm soaked in my own sweat. Why are these on me?

"Stay under, child," I hear a woman's voice say. Two hands keep me from throwing the blankets off. "You nearly died from sickness so your body's going through a lot right now. You should be better in the morning."

She releases my hands, and I look around while staying under the blankets that feel like lava. It's nearly pitch-black outside, with only the stars to give me light. There are thick trees everywhere. Some of the trees don't look familiar. Maybe I was taken to unfamiliar territory. I hear crickets chirping in the bushes, and flies buzzing around in the air.

How did I get here?

"Mom."

I didn't say that!

"Yes, Audrey," I hear the woman say. "I'm over here."

"I didn't find much for us to eat but there's a creek where we can fish."

Wait, I recognize her. It's the girl from the beach who was skim boarding. She's holding the head of a...is that a deer?

The poor animal.

"It won't take long to cook something up. Is she okay?"

"She'll be fine tomorrow if she relaxes to-"

"Mommy!" I sit up screaming. "Daddy! Tom! Jake! Ash! No!" I stand up, throwing the blankets in every direction, and I start running to God knows where. Tears are pouring down my face as I run. That couldn't have happened. It's not-

Someone grabs me. I start screaming and tugging my arm away. I feel myself being lifted so I start screaming louder, punching my kidnapper in the chest. No one is around to save me.

I look up to spit at my kidnapper's face, but I realize that it's the woman from the beach. I remember seeing her right before I blacked out. She has straight blonde hair and soft grey eyes. She's very thin, but has a nice muscular body, like a model. She's also very tall and has big feet.

"Get away from me! Put me down!" My screams of bloody murder are useless. My head starts to spin and I fall into her.

"Calm down, young child," the woman says, having the same soothing voice I heard before when I was under the blankets. "We'll explain everything."

"Mommy!" I cried. "I want my mother!" More tears pour down my cheeks. I bury my face in the woman's chest.

I cry for what feels like forever. She gently strokes the back of my head and holds me close. The crying continues until I feel her stop walking and lie me down back under the blankets. I didn't even realize she had picked me up.

"Is she okay?" I hear the young girl ask.

"She will be in time, Audrey," her mother says. "She's in shock, and she might have the instailk. She will recover. I'll make sure of it."

I wipe all the salty tears from my face and sit up with the blankets still around me. I don't say anything for a while. It could have been an hour, three hours, or five minutes. I can't tell.

The young girl eventually sits next to me. "I'm Audrey." She has short light brown hair, grey eyes, a round face, and a friendly smile. She looks about two years older than me. She extends her hand out to me and I shake it.

"Are you thirsty?"

I shake my head.

"Hungry?"

I shake my head again.

"Audrey," her mother says, "give the child her space, she's traumatized enough."

"So, you're not going to kill me," I say as Audrey sits next to her mother.

"Of course not!" Audrey says, appalled. "Although most of us will be shocked if they find out that you didn't help us with the demons."

"Is that what those things were?" I say looking at the woman, then back at Audrey. "And what do you mean most of us?"

"You know," the woman says, "how we protect the humans from them."

"Humans?" I'm confused. "So you guys aren't human?" I try and force myself to stay calm, but I can't hide the shake in my voice. "So you guys are dangerous?"

"Why does everyone think-," Audrey starts to rant, but her mother holds up a firm hand and she stops. "Never mind! Never mind."

I'm silent for a moment. I didn't really process what she said.

"So....what?" Her words of not being dangerous come back to me. I start to breathe easier. "Not human? What are you?"

"Magicians of course!"

"A magician is a job though, tricks that people play to entertain people." I raise my eyebrows. "Um..." I think of Audrey at the beach with the fire in her hands. "I guess magician means more to you guys than cards, smoke, and mirrors. And you guys are not human at all?"

"I'm half human," Audrey says crossing her arms, not meeting my gaze.

Her mother stares at the floor and clears her throat.

The temperature seems to drop ten degrees. I take one of the blankets and put it around my back and shoulders. I don't take my eyes off them, but they don't set their eyes on me.

"So... half human."

She nods. "Just like you."

"What?"

Audrey starts to laugh, and then she meets my gaze and immediately stops.

"You didn't turn red immediately in the sun."

"What are you talking about?" I ask.

"Mother, she doesn't know who she is."

Page 32

My teeth start to clench. I force myself to breathe. They saved my life, but who are they?

"You're a magician," the woman says. "Though there's a high possibility that you are a half magician."

"No no no no no no," I stutter. "I'm no magician. I mean, I can do one little card trick, but that's only one. I lived with my human family for..." I stop dead in my tracks.

"What is it?" Audrey asks.

"I..." I stat to say, but I can't bring myself to say it out loud. I start to cry again.

The woman nods. "We're a species that can blend in with humans. It's highly possible that you were raised by humans and didn't know your identity until now. We age a little slower than humans, so we can never stick around a place for long. We must stay hidden. I'm deeply sorry for your loss. We're here to help you. Part of that is helping you come to grips with all this. You need to understand all of this, so I will try to tell you as much as I can."

"Wh-why must y-you...we stay hidden?"

She looks down, takes a deep breath, and looks up at me. She's clenching and unclenching her fist.

I take a quick look at Audrey, she comes up to me and starts to rub my back.

"We used to co-exist with humans," her mother says.

"We would protect and help them anyway we could, and they would give food and shelter in return. About two thousand years ago, the humans became suspicious and started to mistrust us, especially in the United States and several parts of Europe. They tried burning us, staking our hearts, poisoning the food with..."

She drifts off and purses her lips together. She turns her head and starts to stare at the rock adjacent to me, but then her eyes slowly become unfocused.

"Mom?"

"Sorry," she whispers. She clears her throat and looks me back in the eye. "We were forced into hiding, but some humans, drages, help us from their ignorant brethren. Nothing has changed on our part though. While the humans have forgotten of our existence, except in

Page 33

Vegas, and the drages who help us, we still protect them. We take only what we need to survive."

"Vegas?" I ask.

"You know that saying 'what happens in Vegas stays in Vegas?'"

I nod.

"Well, we use our powers there a lot because of a lot of demons there, and some Magicians get jobs as entertainers and use their powers there."

"Powers?"

"Yes, every magician has powers, we call them tricks. We can't do everything though; every ability has its limits. A magician loses their tricks when their skin is in direct contact with sunlight. We use energy from nature, but mostly by the light of the moon since the sun is too strong for a full magician. A half magician can still maintain their powers during the day, but too much and it takes a toll on them. To restore them, fulls must stay away from light for a few days. Half are not affected by sunlight, and there are some things a full magician can do that a half magician can't."

"Like what?"

"You'll find out soon," Audrey smiles. "Everyone is different. Your powers will probably be much different from mine."

I blink a few times, not sure if I heard her right. Did she say my powers will be different? "I'm sorry, what? I have tricks besides maneuvering three cards?"

Her mother squints her eyes at me and crosses her arms. "We don't know what they are yet, and odds are you probably have no idea what they are."

I sigh. I try to stand up, but I'm forced back down.

"Stay child," the woman says, sitting next to me, "you need to rest."

I start to get a really bad hunger headache. I pull a clove of garlic from my pocket, but the scent of it seems to make me more dizzy. The woman grabs the garlic clove with a terrified look, and throws it as far as she can.

"Garlic is very bad for you right now!" she tells me, practically shaking. "It can weaken you further, any solid food can. You must stay with liquids and rest."

"Why am I sick though?" I ask. "I was fine earlier."

"The instailk happens randomly when a magician is young. Kind of like chicken pox for humans."

"So, it's contagious?"

"No... It comes and goes suddenly. It has to do with an imbalance in your body. Not like chicken pox, forget I said that."

I search my jacket pockets. I have three garlic cloves left.

I'll save them for later.

"You'll get used to traveling with us." Audrey tells me.

"What?"

"Yeah, it's a lot of fun, except when we have to track down-"

"I want to go home!"

"You're one of us now," Audrey told me. "We're not able to blend in with humans very well."

"I did for twelve years."

"Yeah, but, you were probably a baby living in the human world."

"Human world? Am I in another dimension?"

"No silly. I meant human society. We're not the ones who made the dimensional hop."

"What do you mean by that?"

"Audrey," the woman snaps, "do not overwhelm her!"

"Too late," I assure her.

"Well we can't take it slow forever," Audrey states. "If a demon comes around and she's still taking it slow, she's chopped liver!"

My family was chopped liver. I start to cry again.

Audrey pulls me into a hug. "The poor girl is going to need therapy for the rest of her life!"

"I'm so sorry, child," the woman says. "I know this is difficult for you."

After several minutes, I slow my crying and try to process what they are telling me.

How can I travel with them? How can I learn magic tricks? How can I go on? How can I fight...demons?

Page 35

"Demons, like from exorcisms and stuff like that? O those things on the beach?" I ask.

"Demons come in many forms. The powerful ones can even possess human beings. Those you saw were little ones, babies we believe."

"Are they the things that killed my family?" I ask again.

I picture my brother's body and my brother's hand on the shoreline. A few more tears pour down my face, but I don't go into a sobbing rage like before.

"Yes, they're nasty little things. They cause havoc, murder large amounts of humans and other living creatures; they're careless and hate anything that lives besides their own species. They've been trying for millennia to wipe out several races, but we've always stopped them."

"So, all they do is kill and eat?"

"Yes."

"And you supposedly stop them?"

"We are stopping them." She smiles.

"How many magicians are there doing this?"

"All of us."

"Numbers?"

"Several thousand. We have a few hidden colonies around the globe."

"How do you guys fight them?"

"Oh you know, extra strength, magic, improved senses," said Audrey.

"What kind?"

"You know, senses, like hearing-"

"I know that, I meant magic. Is that the tricks your mom mentioned earlier?"

"Our magic-"

"Audrey, we will explain all that later," her mother says before turning to her daughter. "We don't want to throw everything to her at once. It might make her illness worse."

"Fine," she pouts and crosses her arms.

"One more question," I say. "What was that thing you said about going into a different dimension? Magicians don't live in another dimension, do they?"

"The demons do." Audrey says. "There are a total of eight dimensions, humans are the dominant intelligent species of dimension eight. Demons dominate four dimensions, but they originate from dimension five. It's our job to keep them only at four, or else they will wipe out every living creature in all known dimensions in the universe."

Did she have that memorized or something? Sounds like a bad horror movie script.

"Are they trying to occupy all eight?"

"Yeah, those greedy little bastards," Audrey adds.

"We should let the child get some sleep," her mother says.

"We're not in Florida anymore, are we?" I ask her matter of fact-ly, wiping some tears from my face.

There was a long pause.

My sister used to twirl her bracelet at awkward silences like this. Ash.

"No, child," the woman tells me. "We're not."

"Where are we?"

"Don't worry about that," she tells me.

I have a feeling she's hiding something from me, but I don't mention it. I'm on their good side right now and I want it to stay that way.

"So, you're not going to kill me after all?"

"Of course not," says the mother.

"Welcome to the team," Audrey says with a grin.

"Just one more question?" I ask.

The woman looks at me kindly. Audrey raises an eyebrow.

"I never got your name," I told her.

"I'm sorry, I forgot to mention it with all the information I was giving you. I am Emma, and this is my daughter Audrey."

"What is your name?" Audrey asked me.

"Rebecca Proenza," I tell them. "Bec for short."

Chapter 6

"What exactly am I?" I ask Emma the next night. My cold went away shortly after I woke up. I was still confused on everything, so I decided to ask again.

"You're a magician," she tells me.

"What does that mean?"

"You're one of us."

"I don't understand what that means."

"We don't have to get into all this right now," she tells me, moving my hair out of my face.

"I'd like to know more now please."

"Very well," she sighs, then cocks her head and stares out into the distance. She smiles and looks at me after several moments. "Have you ever traveled to a different time zone?"

"My mother took my sister and I to Paris last year," I tell her. "It was a wonderful girl's only trip. My brothers were pissed that they couldn't go."

Emma laughs. "Paris is wonderful. Do you remember the hour difference, and how long it took you to get used to the time zone?"

"Yeah," I admit. "It took me half of the trip to fall asleep on time because I was so used to our time zone. Ash, my mom and I would be up at three in the morning just talking, then Ash and I would run to the lobby barefoot and get Orangina and snacks from the vending machine with the Euro coins we had." My heart starts to ache a little.

"Using your tricks for the first time is the same way," Emma explains. "Your body is so used to not using them that if you were to use them right away it would not feel right to you. It will take you a few months until your body is ready for it. Just like when you exercise for the first time, your muscles are sore. Everything I tell you, everything you do with us, it will be just like the time zones. It will take you a while to get used to everything that is happening to you."

"That makes sense," I say, piecing everything together. "What about the demons? Why did they kill my family?"

"They hate anything that's not a demon," she explains. "Like the Nazis hated anyone who wasn't German. You know about the Holocaust, right?"

I take out my wooden star from under my shirt and show it to Emma. "Believe me, I know."

"Would never have guessed." She gently handles the necklace. "It's beautiful. Wood?"

"Yes."

"Who gave it to you?"

"My grandmother," I tell her. "I wear it every day. Do magicians have a religion?"

"Not really, but you're more than welcome to practice yours," she says, not taking her eyes off my necklace.

"So you don't believe in God, or an afterlife?"

"We believe in the here and the now," Emma says frankly. "Although, most humans believe us to be wiccans. Wiccans are nature loving and believe in mother nature, whereas magicians wield magic and don't believe in any deities."

"Wow," I say in disbelief, but who am I to judge their beliefs, or lack of beliefs. "So, what's the demon's end goal?"

She lets go of my necklace and looks into my eyes. "They want to wipe out all life and take control of all eight dimensions. Right now they are targeting this dimension. They know we are a threat to them, so they hunt us along with the humans, but they seem to aim for the humans first. As magicians, we are the sole protectors of humanity, so when we found out about the demons, we made it our life's mission to wipe them out. If humans knew of all this, then they could stand a chance, especially with their tech."

"Then why not tell them?" I ask.

"We've tried. Some take action when necessary. Other ignorant humans have aimed at us, other times chaos was erupted, most just don't believe."

"So why are we the sole protectors?"

"Think of it this way, some of them protect and house us and take care of us, the few that know of our existence and help us how they can. You eat cows, use their skin, and drink their milk, they help you live, so wouldn't you want to protect them for as long as you can?"

"Actually, I'm a vegetarian."

She nodded several times, extremely slowly. I twirled my thumbs around each other, waiting for her to continue speaking.

"This whole sunlight and tricks thing makes us sound like vampires."

She chuckles and shakes her head. "The story of Dracula was actually based off a famous magician, and then the stories of vampires were born after Nosferatu. We do not suck blood though."

"Then how come almost every vampire story I've ever heard has the vampires killing humans for their blood?"

"Humans always twist their stories. They over exaggerate everything."

"Believe me, I know," I told her. "That's why I don't pay attention to rumors!"

"Ever heard of Hercules?" she asked me.

"Yeah, but what does a demigod have to do with..." I realize what she is trying to say when she smirks at me and pokes me in the stomach. "He was a magician!"

"Indeed he was, way before my time. The best magician this world has ever seen. Most people see him as a mythological story, but he was real. A rare magician who excelled at all the magic types."

I was amazed. Every Hercules story I've ever heard said he was a demigod, except for one version that said he was a straight God.

"So, Audrey said magicians practice magic. Is that what you guys were using to fight on the beach?"

"Yes, every magician has the ability to use magic. Full magicians are the strongest."

"So, what can I do?"

"Depends on how much you train and how focused you become, and how much control you have."

"Are you going to train me?" I ask excitedly.

"Of course," Emma told me, smiling wide at my eagerness. "Whenever you'd like."

"Let's start now!"

Chapter 7

Several steps echo out into the night.

Seventeen-year-old Richard was walking home from his girlfriend's house. Someone has been keeping an eye on this kid for a few nights.

He was up in a tree, and if someone was to look up, they'd only see a black shadow with two eyes.

When Richard walked under the tree, the stalker used its enhanced abilities to leap to the next tree. Richard looked around, hearing the rustling leaves, but thought nothing of it as his phone rang.

"Yes, Mom, I'm on my way home," he said into his phone. "About ten minutes." His mother was talking to him, but the stalker didn't pay attention to her words, just her son's warm O positive.

The stalker smiles, revealing inch-long fangs.

When Richard walked past the tree, the stalker teleported down and was not far behind the boy. Richard's steps were slowing as he put his phone back in his pocket.

He was feeling very uncomfortable. He didn't know if it was because he felt like he was being watched, or because he hasn't eaten since he was released from school.

Richard turned around to look at the dark street and many houses extending out behind him. He put a hand on his stomach and kept on walking. The creature followed the boy, hovering inches from the ground.

The creature made a noise with its tongue, sounding like a deck of cards was being shuffled, and Richard spun around to see a black shadowy figure. The shadowed figure lifted its head, revealing a green eye, a hazel eye, and fangs.

Richard's eyes widened, and he began to run away screaming.

Richard was fast, but the shadowed creature was much faster.

It sank its fangs into the teenage boy, and started drinking his blood. Richard screamed, praying that his neighbors could hear him cursing bloody murder.

The creature threw the boy on the ground, and Richard landed on his elbow.

"Are you going to kill me?" Richard cried.

The creature drew its hand back and used its finger nails to cut open Richards stomach. His blood was pouring out of his flesh. Richard's skin went pale, and he was too weak to get up.

The creature went to Richard's stomach and was sucking up all of his blood. It then shoved its hand inside where it made the incision, and ripped the boy in half until the spine snapped. The creature took out several organs, and made them disappear one by one with a snap of the finger and a flick of the wrist. Richard's blood stopped flowing.

The creature finished drinking his blood, stood up, and laughed. The laugh was like an evil queen from a fairy tale.

It sounded strangely female.

The creature's shadowy complexion started to shimmer and fall off her body until she looked like a regular human.

Long, curly, blonde hair was revealed, an evil smile with apple cheeks, and a young child's face with murder in her colorful eyes, one green, one hazel.

It was me!

I stared at the dead Richard, and laughed like the evil queen, then...

***

I shoot up screaming and flailing, fall out of the hammock I was sleeping in, and hit my head on the hard grass floor.

We're camping in a forest in Colorado, no idea which part though. They don't tell me much.

Page 43

It has been a month since I found out I was a half magician, a whole month since my life changed forever.

This is the sixth time I've had a similar dream. Every dream I'm a different monster. Last time I was a werewolf, today I was a vampire.

"You okay?" Audrey asks me when she notices I am rubbing my head after falling out of the hammock. I must have woken her up when I fell.

"I've felt worse," I tell her.

Audrey has been helping me train, and the lessons are always brutal. I always feel terrible afterward. I was very eager at first, but now I feel sore.

"You want to continue training?" Audrey asks.

"No! I mean, you want to go for a walk? The sun won't set for another three hours Besides, we're already awake."

"What about my mom?" she asks.

Emma's on the floor covered with five blankets and a pile of leaves.

"She'll be fine," I tell her.

Audrey worries about her family. She has cousins all over the world, and she always worries. I guess magicians and humans aren't so different after all.

Audrey agrees and we leave.

***

"So, then what happened?" Audrey asks me.

I was telling her a story about the time when the police caught me and John putting soap, laundry detergent, and baking soda inside our neighborhood fountain.

"We didn't want to get arrested, so we ran as fast as we could to the edge of the lake close by and found a paddle boat."

"What'd you guys do with that?"

"We borrowed it, and paddled away."

"You didn't need to hotwire anything?"

"It works on foot power. What's there to hotwire?"

Audrey starts shifting from foot to foot. "It sounds like you and your friends had some crazy adventures."

Page 44

"You should have seen us bowling."

I was supposed to have gone bowling like John and I wanted instead of the beach. What if John was there that day? I picture his severed leg lying next to my sister's severed hand. I shake the thought out of my head and continue my story.

"Have you ever bowled from the middle of the lane? Or bowled with three balls at once? We don't do regular bowling, and have been kicked out of at least four bowling alleys."

"I haven't even been inside a bowling alley. Is it dangerous?"

"No! It's a public place where people take a ball and knock some pins down." I never had to explain what bowling is. It amazes me that she doesn't know. "I haven't really done anything here except train and learn spells. Do magicians do anything for fun?"

"Fun?" Audrey looks like she never heard the word before.

"Have you ever done anything enjoyable and crazy?" I ask her.

She doesn't say anything for a while. She looks off into the distance and tries to think.

"Fighting doesn't count," I tell her when it looks like she has an idea. She looks out into the distance again.

"I used to climb trees with my cousins, play Bilcaton, go swimming...we were always outdoor kids. We never sat inside with TV unless we were watching news channels, we never stole, or vandalized, or anything like you did."

"You're too good of a kid. I need to take you bowling like John and I used to do."

"I have an Uncle named John," Audrey tells me.

That was random.

"I'm sure if he's anything like my old John...enough said."

"Well, you're going to meet him next week. My mother's two older brothers and my cousin live in a trailer park in Pennsylvania."

"Where? It wouldn't be near Eagle Lake by any chance, would it?"

"Yeah! Exactly there. You know of it?"

I nod and look away from her. "My cousins used to have a trailer up there, but they're all dead now."

"All of them?" she asked me.

"We had a very small family. My mom had one sister with no kids. Their dad had one brother with a kid. Their mom had a brother, but he died young. My dad had a brother and sister, each with two kids. Their dad had a sister with three kids and one of those kids had a kid."

"Did you have any siblings?" Audrey asked me.

"Three. Two older brothers and an older sister. I've always wanted a younger brother, but I never got one. I was stuck being the youngest, but I loved it." I was suddenly getting sad talking about them. I feel some tears creeping up on me, but I held them back.

"Well then I guess you might run into your cousin's trailer this year."

"Yeah...I guess so. Do you have any siblings?" I ask her.

She suddenly looks sad. "No, but I've always wanted one. The closest thing to a sibling I have is a younger cousin. My mom was pregnant some years ago, but the baby died."

"I'm sorry to hear that."

"Thanks," she says sadly. "It was awful."

I remember the couple that had the two babies in the floaties. They're gone now, too.

I nod my head, and develop the courage to ask her a personal question. "Audrey, who was your dad?" Audrey is a half, so her father was probably a human.

"Don't know," she says way too quickly, "my mom never told me about him, but I know he was human."

"You've never met him?"

She hangs her head and avoids my gaze. "No," she seems so sad, like I just pinched a nerve. "He's probably dead now, so it doesn't matter."

"Have you ever asked her about him?"

"Yeah, but she never wants to talk about him."

"I never met my real dad before either."

She looks up at me and suddenly seems so curious "What do you mean?"

"My parents adopted me when I was a baby," I explain. "It was a closed adoption so I never knew who my birth parents were. I have no idea if they're dead, or if they just gave me up for whatever reason. All I know now is that one of them was a magician."

Page 46

She gives me a hug. "That's so sad. Losing them too, that's even worse!"

I hug her back and enjoy the warm embrace. "Thanks."

"You must miss your family so much."

"I miss my mother and my siblings very much," I tell her. "My father was always working so it didn't even feel like I had one sometimes, but when he was home he was a good father. My older cousins and everyone else hated me because I wasn't blood. Still, I never wanted this to happen to any of them."

She lets go of me and gives me an angry look. "Those bastards. You know what, they can go to hell," she grabs my hands. "No offense. If they're not already there. You're a part of our family now and I'm glad you're here."

I squeeze her hands, not sure how to feel about her words. "Thanks, Audrey?"

I appreciate her saying all this to me, except the last thing. I know she and Emma really do care about me, but do I really want to be a part of another family only to have them taken away from me again?

Chapter 8

That night we head to Emma's car which has no license plate.

"Aren't you worried about getting pulled over by the police?" I ask, staring at the back of the car.

She snaps her fingers and a license plate appears, but it has six zeros.

"That'll definitely alert the cops that it's a fake," I say.

"It's different for every human that sees it," she explains. "It helps other magicians know who around them is a magician as well."

"That's so cool," I exclaim. "So magicians see the zeros while humans see an actual plate number?"

"Correct."

"Cool! What else can magicians do?"

Audrey climbs in the passenger seat, Emma in the driver's seat, and I sit in the middle back seat.

"Every magician is different," Emma tells me as she starts the car.

"Different how? And what can you do?"

"I'll explain all this later."

"Boo!"

"Bec!"

"Sorry! So, how long will it take us to get there? Twenty, thirty minutes?"

"Longer."

"How much longer?"

"Two days."

"What!"

***

"Tell me one trick you can do?" I plead as we pull into Eagle Lake.

"Well, I can teleport," she tells me.

"Can all Fulls teleport?" I ask Emma.

"Not all," she tells me. "Only physical magicians can, but not all physicals can teleport, and not many teleporters can travel long distances."

"What's a physical magician?"

"I'll explain later."

"Why can't you explain now?"

"Because one, you will find out later on your own, and two, I get lost in here easily so I need to concentrate."

After five minutes of driving around we reach the right trailer. All of the trailers had signs in the front with their state or country, and the family name.

'The Paris's, Minnesota' the wooden sign said.

"Your name is Paris?" I ask as we get out of the car. I start stretching my arms by bringing them over my head.

"Yes," Emma says. "I didn't tell you?"

"Nope. Oh, and Minnesota?" I ask Audrey and Emma.

"You have a problem with that?" Emma asks me, giving me a direct look with a straight mouth.

"It just seems like an uncommon place. There's not much to do there. I have never heard of anyone wanting to move to Minnesota and–"

"Uncle John!" Audrey screams when she sees her uncle open the trailer door. She runs up and embraces him.

"Hey there kiddo, it's been two years and you haven't grown an inch," he says, rubbing her head.

Audrey only looks fourteen, she should have grown. Then again, Emma did say that magicians age slower. How long do magicians live? There is still so much I don't know.

"If you want to talk about not growing, look at JP."

"He's been growing slowly. Besides, he's still very young."

"And I'm not?" Audrey gave her uncle a puffed lip, dark-eyed look.

"You're just regular young."

Emma and I walk toward the door to meet up with Audrey and John.

John was a bald, six-foot-tall man with gray eyes like Emma and Audrey's. He was wearing a ripped white T-shirt and orange dungarees. He has the facial expression of a stalker who is squatting in a bush using a pair of binoculars to spy on someone he loathes.

"So, what is your version of young?" I ask, butting in. "How old are you anyways?"

It's been how long and I didn't ask for her age until now?

"Eighteen and a half," Audrey tells me. Usually when people put in the half, it either means they want to seem taller or older.

I look at Emma and give her a look that says it's her turn.

"Never ask a woman her age," she says.

"Why don't I start with a 'hello' instead of my age?" her brother laughs. "I am John Paris. It is very nice to meet you. Has my baby sister been giving you trouble?"

I shake my head. "She's usually kind to me, but she beats me up in training even though I'm still new to all this. I'm Bec."

John laughs and gives Emma a hug. "You really should go easy on the girl," he says, inviting us inside.

"I like your brother," I announce as I take my shoes off, forgetting about his stalker look.

"You don't have to take your shoes off," John tells me.

"But I'm entering someone's home," I tell him. "I have to take my shoes off."

He laughs again and has us sit down.

His trailer is equipped with a kitchen, living room, three bedrooms, and a small bathroom in the back.

I sit on the couch next to Audrey after taking a peek in the back, and Emma sits on the couch next to ours. I see the patio has a grill and a shed, and there is a trampoline in the back. It was just like my cousins' trailer, except that my cousins had a much bigger trampoline and an inflatable swimming pool. There gone forever, I'll never see them again. I look back at the trailer. I don't know why I expected them to be living like hobos.

John goes into the kitchen and gives us each an Aquapod water bottle with a dark red liquid inside.

"Would you like some?" John asks me.

"What is it?" I ask.

"Wine."

"I'm too young for alcohol," I tell him.

"You eleven?" he asks.

"Twelve," I say, "but I look nine."

"Nine by human standards," John laughs, "but you look eleven by magician standards."

"Even by magician standards, I still look too young!" I pout.

John laughs again. "Would you like something else to drink?"

"Do you have root beer?"

Audrey leans in and whispers to me, "Soda makes us very hyper. Along with anything that has too much processed sugar. We can't eat or drink any of them or else we get really sick."

"Basically everything that is good for parties?"

Audrey nods, "Only the ones humans have."

"That explains a lot."

I try not to remember my John, but fail. "Water would be fine then. I'm still learning everything."

"That's okay. You're new, it's understandable. How long have you known?" he asks as he sits on the chair in front of me.

"One month," I tell him.

He drops his jaw a little and he stares at me with puppy eyes.

I'm a baby to these people!

"How fast do magicians age and how long do they live?" I ask no one in particular.

"We age only a little slower," John tells me.

"How old are you?" I ask him, taking a sip of water that he just handed me.

"I guess around sixty-five."

I tried not to spit my drink out, but failed horribly. When I was able to breathe again I announce, "I forgot to tell you guys my most important rule, never make me laugh while I'm drinking something or else you'll have an early shower!"

"Understandable," Audrey says, wiping water off her face. Apparently my head turned a little in her direction. I mostly showered John who was right in front of me.

"You look like you're forty," I tell John.

John shrugs. "I get that a lot."

"Do halfs and fulls age the same?"

"Fulls age a little slower than halfs, but not by much though."

"How long can magicians live anyway?" I ask.

"Nobody knows," John tells me. "Almost all of us die in battle. I heard some of us dying of old age, but never really asked for their age."

"I see. That didn't freak me out at all!" I say sarcastically.

"So, Bec," John keeps on talking. "My sister told me a little of what happened, but I didn't get the whole story."

I'm silent for a moment.

John turns his head to Emma and blinks at her a few times.

I stare at my fingerprints.

She sighs. "Her adopted human family was killed by demons. I saw her and I immediately knew she was one of us, but she had no idea who she was until I told her."

"I'm so sorry that happened to you," John says very sympathetically. "Think of it this way, now you can avenge their deaths."

I look back up. John now stares at me like I'm an abandoned kitten. I look at Audrey. She looks back at me, her sea blue eyes heavy with concern.

Wait, her eyes aren't normally blue. I take a closer look and see that they are gray once again. I think about Mabel and shudder a little bit.

Just then, the whole trailer goes quiet, except for faint footsteps. A nine-year-old kid comes out of one of the small bedrooms. He has brown eyes and dark brown hair. He has pale skin like all the others.

"Hey, uncle John, when does my dad get back? He's been gone for five days now."

"A couple weeks, I think," John tells him.

The little boy looks annoyed, but this turns to happiness when he sees Emma and Audrey. He runs up to Audrey, jumps on her lap, and wraps his arms around her neck.

"Hiya, cousin!"

"Hey JP, how've you been?"

"Fine," the little boy says with a smile, he then looks at me. "Who's the blonde girl?"

"Bec," I tell him. "You can say I'm the newbie. What about you?"

"I'm Jean-Peter, but nobody calls me that, so it's just JP for short."

"Alrighty then," I say. "I'm going to guess you're a full magician?"

"Half," he says. "Do you always start conversions like this?"

I hang my head a little and avoid his gaze "No, I just...I'm Bec."

He laughs. "You already said that!"

"Alrighty then," I say again.

JP laughs again, "You really are a newbie, aren't you? You look around my age though, how new can you be?"

You know how they always say first impressions are everything? My first impression of this kid was that I thought he was cute, in a baby brother sort of way. Audrey and John are cool, and Emma is motherly.

I guess their first impression of me was the opposite.

They probably think I'm being super annoying.

***

"Keep it going!" Emma shouts.

Audrey, JP, and I are standing in a triangle. For this training session Emma is having us throw rocks at each other with telekinesis as we dodge them. It makes me think of a dodgeball game, except with rocks, it's three teams instead of two, and Audrey keeps lighting hers on fire.

"Watch it, Audrey!" I shout as I duck as fast as I can. "You're going to burn me!"

"Hey!" she shouts back, smiling wide while telekinetically juggling three rocks and lighting them on fire one by one. "No pain, no gain! Besides, if you don't like it, then hit me back!"

So far all I've been able to do is keep the rocks from hitting me, but I can't seem to lift one on my own, let alone throw one at Audrey who keeps on laughing. So far I can't do any magic besides deflecting, but that's ninety percent just me moving out the way. Emma keeps telling me that I'll get there.

"Oh! I will—"

"Bec! On your left!" Emma shouts.

I turn my head just in time to lift my hand. I meant to catch it, but I mentally stopped the rock that JP threw at me.

"Yea-!" I lose my concentration in my short celebration and the rock immediately falls. "Aw."

I extend my hand and mentally throw it back at him, but it doesn't budge. I think about lifting it, but it only shakes on the ground. I concentrate harder and it rises two inches.

I smile proudly, only for it to be wiped off my face by a fire rock that hits my right cheek.

"Ow!" I glare angrily at Audrey. She only smiles wickedly and throws three more at me. They stop, but it wasn't my doing.

"Give her some time, Sweetie," Emma tells her. "She's new, you shouldn't be hitting her in the face. That's abuse at this point in her training."

"Sorry, mom!"

"Don't apologize to me!"

"Sorry, Bec!"

I grunt and stomp on the floor.

"You'll get the hang of it soon," Emma says in an appeasing tone. "In the meantime, let's try something else."

I sigh and nod.

Emma extends her hand towards Audrey and a rock flies towards me. "Catch it!"

I lift my hand and the rock stops.

"Keep it there," Emma instructs. "Audrey!"

Audrey uses her telekinesis and throws a rock at me, but I use my other hand to stop it as well. JP throws a rock at me, but I move to the right to avoid getting hit.

"We're not doing that exercise right now," Emma says calmingly. "Right now you're just catching them."

She nods at JP, and he throws another rock. I don't have any free hands, so I duck when it gets close.

"I can't!" I plead. "How do I stop it?"

"You're smart," Emma tells me. "Use your mind."

I take a deep breath, and I nod at JP to throw another rock. I put all of my concentration into the rock he throws, and I stop it mere inches from my face. I smile proudly, but then I realize that I've dropped the other two rocks. I kick one of them several feet. I try to do the same to the other, but I just kick the grass around it.

"Try again," Emma instructs. "Put your focus into all the rocks."

I nod and she quickly throws a rock. I lift my hand and stop it with my telekinesis. Then Audrey throws one and I stop it with my other hand. I transfer the rock to my right hand as JP throws a rock at me, and I use my left hand to stop it. I transfer the rock as Emma throws hers at me. I keep doing this until I have fifteen rocks in my hand.

"Good," Emma tells me. She then picks up a large twig and it lights up white. She crushes it in her hands and several seconds later it turns into a small rope. She calls me over and ties my hands behind my back.

"Now try it with your mind," she tells me.

"I was," I tell her. I try to wriggle one hand out, but they're together real tight.

"Before you had your hands to guide your mind. Now try with only your mind."

"Alrighty then."

She nods to Audrey and JP, and they both throw two rocks at me.

"Whoa!" I shout as I throw myself on the floor. All four rocks passing where my head was.

"Not all at once, kids," Emma tells them. "She's still in training."

"So are we!" Audrey calls.

"Yes, but you've been training longer," Emma tells her daughter. "Now, quiet!"

JP throws a rock and I put all my concentration into stopping the rock. When I see it's not working, I move to the left to avoid getting hit.

"Try again," Emma says calmly.

Audrey throws a rock and I try again, only to move out of the way again.

"What am I doing wrong?" I ask her.

"Stay calm," Emma instructs. "The worst thing to do is to get worked up."

I close my eyes and take a deep breath. JP throws a rock once I'm ready, and I successfully stop it. I smile, and nod at Audrey to throw a rock. I stop it mere inches from my face. Pretty soon, I'm juggling ten rocks with my hands tied behind my back.

"Don't get cocky!" Audrey yells playfully.

"What?" I ask playfully. "Jealous?"

Audrey and JP share a look, and they smirk at each other. Then they each pick up a rock and throw them at me simultaneously.

"Is that all you got!" I shout, juggling the twelve rocks.

They each pick up two rocks, Audrey lighting her two up with blue fire, and launch them at me full speed.

I catch three of them.

The other fire rock hits me right in the nose, and I feel my cartilage snap.

I drop all the rocks and shout.

I can feel the blood quickly dripping out of my nose and down my mouth. It stings and hurts so much, and the booger blood tastes nasty!

Emma unties the rope from around my hands and cups my face in her hands.

"That looks bad," she says in a soft tone. She then takes my right hand and gently presses it to my nose. "This is the perfect chance for you to try something else I think you might be able to do."

"Might be?"

"Try and heal yourself."

"I can do that?" I ask, amazed. I remember reading a book series where a girl had healing powers and I thought it was one of the coolest powers ever.

"Maybe, I'm not sure. I still need to see what type of magician you are."

"Which you still haven't explai-"

"Concentrate on your nose getting better. Let the energy build until it has nowhere to go but out of your fingers and into your nose."

I do as she says and I feel my arm turning into ice.

"Now, you should feel a cold sensation in your arm. Do you feel it?"

"Yes!" I say very excitedly. "I do! Is it healing?"

"Not yet," she says "Now, you should feel the energy building. Let it out slowly, all the time thinking of your nose getting better."

I concentrate as hard as I can on my nose being as it was before, and I start to feel my nose turning into ice.

"You're doing it!" JP shouts excitedly.

"How come she gets it on her first try!" Audrey complains.

"You'll learn eventually, Audrey, if you even can,"

Emma tells her. "It's just that she's probably better with physical magic then mental magic."

"I feel it!" I shout. The cartilage and bones are snapping back into place, and the blood is lessening its flow. Once my nose is back in place, I still feel the blood flowing.

"The blood is still coming out," Emma says.

"Gee," I say sarcastically. "I didn't notice!"

Audrey and JP start giggling.

"Do you want my help or not?" Emma asks, getting stern.

"Yes, ma'am," I say apologetically. "Sorry, old habits die hard."

"Now, concentrate on closing your wounds and stopping the flow of blood."

I do as she says, but nothing changes.

What was I thinking of before? My nose being back the way it was.

I picture my mother's body on the floor. I force myself to change my thought and pretty soon the blood stops coming down my face and the icy feeling disappears.

Page 57

"Good," Emma says, smiling proudly. "How do you feel?"

I give her a big hug. She seems surprised, but hugs me back anyway.

"I can do magic! I can do real magic! Thank you, Emma!"

She laughs and lets go of me. "You're quite welcome, Bec. Now all we have to do is figure out your strengths and weaknesses."

"Can I try healing again?" I ask her eagerly.

"Are you sure?" she asks.

"Definitely!"

"All right," she says.

That's when she breaks my finger and I scream bloody murder.

"Heal it."

Chapter 9

My fingers keep slipping. I reach out as far as I can but it was no use. I stretch out my legs to reach farther. I get a better grip, but then I slip and fall out of the tree I was climbing. I land on my feet right where Audrey and JP are standing.

"Are you sure you know how to do this?" JP asks, freaked out at the sight of me twenty feet in the air, jumping like a monkey from branch to branch without using any magic.

"Of course I do," I tell him.

"Then why are you wearing a helmet?" Audrey asks.

"Because I like helmets," I tell her, tapping the black helmet that was tied on my head that I found by a tree near a trailer on the other side of the park. "You just can't fall and you'll be good. Didn't you guys used to climb trees?"

"Yes." JP says.

"Then go!" I laugh.

"But-"

"Look JP," I say, cutting him off, "you've climbed trees before. Have you ever gotten seriously hurt? Especially considering the fact we're...eh well you know."

"Well, we're supposed to be training." JP tells me.

"Well, we can work on our hand-eye coordination. What about you Audrey?"

She just looks at her younger cousin, and then puts on a poker face.

"That's it, you two need to start living on the edge!"

"We fight you-know-whats," Audrey says.

"That doesn't count," I tell them. "You need to take risks that don't involve fighting for a living or using your tricks. You need unsupervised fun. Try to sneak out; get your adrenaline pumping; do something that others wouldn't even think of doing." I cup my hands and kneel down. "JP, put a foot on my hands and I'll lift you up."

He reluctantly does as I tell him. I lift him up and he grabs a thick branch. Man, this kid is really short! No wonder he needs a lift.

"Okay, now use your upper arm strength to pull yourself up," I instruct him.

"I know how to do this." While he's doing that, I look at Audrey who is playing a thumb war with herself.

"Your turn," I tell her. "Jump up and pull yourself up."

She looks at her giggling cousin, standing up on his branch with the leaves tussling.

They are still a little uneasy around me. I don't blame them, I can seem insane to them at times, annoying at others.

I can tell that they are trying to warm up to me.

"No magic tricks, no training," I remind her, and she extends her arms. "We're kids. We deserve a little fun every now and then."

***

Two weeks passed since we first arrived at the trailer. It has been almost two months since I discovered that I wasn't fully human. Life is not as bad as I thought it would be, but I still miss my human life. Even if most of my family was ashamed of me, I miss them all. Especially my mother and siblings. I also think about my old John and Mabel. They probably think I'm dead.

"Hey Audrey," JP calls. "It's our old tree house."

The three of us are walking around outside by the lake next to the club house. Their tree house was covered by a lot of leaves, but it is still large enough to be noticeable.

"I thought you two weren't tree climbers," I tease.

"That's not climbing."

"We have several layers of magic that we hide from humans," Audrey tells me.

Page 60

"What's the limit to our magic?" I ask.

"Depends on the magician," she tells me.

"Like..."

"There are four types of magic," she explains. "There is physical magic, like shape shifting yourself. This shouldn't be confused with changing an object; that's something all Magicians can do. There's time magic, like seeing the future. There's elemental magic, like creating fireballs. Lastly there's mental magic, like reading minds. All magicians can do magic like lifting objects with a wave of a hand, but a magician can excel in more than one type of magic."

"So pretty much we all have telekinesis, but how can we tell which type of magic we excel in?"

"It's just what you were born to do," she tells me.

I remember the fireballs she created on the beach and how she lit the rocks on fire in one of our training sessions.

"Are you elemental?"

"Yes," she smiles at me.

"Do you use magic for anything besides fighting?"

"Depends. Lighting fire for food, Flooding an empty pool for swimming, yes. Freezing someone I don't like, no."

"Before your mom was saying something about physical magicians."

"Yeah," she tells me. "My mom's a physical magician, so she can do stuff like teleporting and shape shifting."

"So I can heal, does that mean I'm a physical magician as well?"

"Probably."

"How come she didn't want to tell me all this?"

"She was afraid you would focus too much on what you want to know and not what you can actually do." She runs for the tree.

"There are usually a lot of humans here," I inform them, following not far behind. "How do you get up there?"

"We have a rope ladder," JP says. I didn't even see the ladder until he grabbed it. "This place is protected with magic".

As I pull myself up the rope ladder, I notice how small their tree house is. It looks like only four people can fit inside of it. As I pull myself inside, I was proven wrong.

Page 61

They must have used magic to pack an apartment inside here!

The tree house has a kitchen with a mini fridge, and a small freezer. There's a small area with seven bean bag chairs, each a different color of the rainbow, set in a circle so people can talk to each other. There's even a small window so you can see the whole park. A small coffee table is in the center with a small wooden box full of blue flowers, maybe daisies, on it placed atop it.

"Let me guess, the magician's touch got to this place as well?" I ask, panting after running around the whole tree house.

"Yeah," JP tells me. "Aunt Emma did it for us."

"This is nice," I say. "How'd she get it to be bigger on the inside?"

JP cracks a smile "You haven't seen anything yet!"

"I haven't seen anything?"

"Yet."

Audrey walks towards a wooden wall in the kitchen, and waves her hand in front of it. A control pad with four buttons appears, each a different color.

"How is all this technology inside here?" I ask them, opening their mini fridge that was packed with fruits, vegetables, and a whole bunch of food that you would find in a healthy person's fridge.

A vegetarian's delight!

Because of Jake, there were always chicken nuggets in our freezer back home.

Jake.

"It's all powered through magic." Audrey explains.

"We have these appliances here and we have them working through all the spells we have on this place."

"Did you spell the fridge?" I ask them "There is a lot of food in here for such a tiny fridge."

"No, the fridge isn't distorted inside. JP just knows how to make space," Audrey says, "but it is spelled to not have the food spoiled."

"What's the difference between a spell and a trick?" I ask.

"Spells are...a little more of a process. Where tricks are fast, spells take more time and are permanent."

"Aren't tricks permanent though?" I ask.

She moves her head from shoulder to shoulder. "Not all the time."

She pushes the yellow button on the pad that appeared, and the walls turned inside out before spreading farther out.

A stove, a microwave, an oven, a toaster, several cabinets, and counters appear as the wooden walls flip inside out. I open one of the cabinets, and there were a bunch of canned foods like beans, vegetables, and soups. Another cabinet has plates and bowls with forks, knives and spoons.

I open the freezer up, seeing a bunch of frozen meats, frozen pizzas, and a lot of other frozen foods that you put in the microwave or oven. There were even homemade ice pops. "Ten people can live here for twenty years and never go hungry." The freezer is much smaller than the fridge, but there is twice as much food inside of it.

"We have it all for emergencies," JP explains.

"Sometimes we just hide from the grown-ups here."

"Why hide from them?"

"You never hid from your parents?"

"Yeah, but that was to avoid lectures or chores. Plus, your parents don't do anything."

"Try lectures, chores, and training!" Audrey chimes in.

"Don't act like you didn't have fun beating me up!" I laugh.

"Wait 'til you get more advanced, and my mom can get pretty mad sometimes. Best to hide and let her calm down."

"True."

I smile at them and sit on the freezer lid. It was low and strong enough for me to actually do that.

"How do you get stuff from the not-bottom then?"

"Telekinesis." JP says with no tone in his voice.

"Duh!" Audrey adds.

"So, what are the other three buttons?" I ask, changing the subject.

Audrey presses the blue button, and leads us into the bean bag chair area. The roof opens up to reveal the open sky, with barely any leaves in the way. This is weird considering that the leaves hide this place from all angles.

"Damn," I say. "You must love it here at night"

"Especially when humans light up fireworks," Audrey says.

"Can't an elemental magician make their own fireworks?" I ask.

"No fireworks, no bombs. Just the elements, and TNT is not an element."

"Boo!"

JP smiles and walks over to the button panel. He pushes the blue button again, and the wooden roof quickly slides back into place.

"Is there a glass ceiling there or just a big hole?" I ask.

"There's a force field that prevents things from coming in," Audrey says. "So, you're kind of right about the glass."

JP pushes the orange button on the wall, and the floor pushes the three of us in the air, and then flips like the walls did, revealing a large hole in the floor. We fall through it, coming back outside right next to the tree.

We slowly fall back to the ground when I notice the floor moving back into place.

"That was awesome!" I tell them as I walk up to the tree and kept looking at the tree house."

"That's our emergency exit," Audrey says.

"But there was a red button as well. Wouldn't that be the emergency one?"

"That one is only in case of extreme emergencies," Audrey tells me. "We've never had to use it before, and we hope we never do."

"Do powerful demons really come over here?" I ask.

"There are worse demons than the demons you've encountered," JP tells me.

Thinking of what some of these creatures did to my family, I did not have the courage to ask him how much worse.

Chapter 10

There's an intense heat in my hands. The pain is unbearable, but I keep it in my grasp. With my hands close to my chest and parallel to the floor, all the heat is transferred into my right hand. When I shoot my right hand forward to release a plasma bolt, I fly back several feet and fall to the ground.

"Well, at least there was actually a plasma bolt this time," Emma says one night, watching me from several yards away.

"Well I'm still not used to doing magic," I tell her. "The biggest trick I ever did before becoming a magician, I mean, discovering that I was a magician, was a card trick with only three cards."

Emma shakes her head and walks off a little bit. We were still at the trailer park in Pennsylvania. I've been training at night, and hanging out with Audrey and JP during the day. I'm just living the typical life of a magician in training.

"How does that card trick go?" Audrey asks me, sitting on a boulder nearby.

"Oh, you just take three cards, and you pretend that the person is-"

"Would you pay attention?" Emma snaps.

"Someone's being pushy," I comment.

Emma closes her eyes and sighs.

"Sorry," I tell her. "I have a hard time easing up a little."

"I'm sorry too," she whispers, "It's just that you should be more progressed in magic by now."

"It's only been about three months," I remind her.

"I know," she says. "It's just that others usually progress faster. What if the demons attack tomorrow? I can't have you killed on me."

"That's why you're training me."

"Maybe she's not an elemental magician," Audrey says. "Mom, you keep training her on elemental and physical things, but maybe she's a mental magician."

"Or time," I add.

"Maybe you are mental. It's not likely you'd be a time magician," Emma tells me.

"How come?"

She sighs and stares off in the distance. "Let's take a small break."

"Understood ma'am!" I even give a pathetic salute.

She nods and starts to walk, but then she turns back to me and says "How do you think you're handling everything?"

"You mean training or-"

"Everything."

I shrug my shoulders. "I can't answer that right now."

She nods and walks off into the forest.

"What was it like living like a human?" Audrey asks me when Emma was out of earshot.

"It's nothing special," I tell her. "Humans work hard, learn something new every day, grow up, families, typical things. When you're young, you go to school to learn. When you get older, you pay for a special school called college."

"Never been to school," Audrey tells me. "What's it like?"

"Long and boring," I inform her. "But honestly, it depends on the teacher."

"Huh, I guess we're not that different then."

"There are a lot of religions and beliefs, ethnicities-"

"What's ethnicity?"

"Yeah, this is going to take a lot of explaining."

"I got time."

"And plenty of it too. How long can a magician live again?"

"How many times are you going to ask that question?"

"Until I receive an answer."

"Oh, big words."

Page 66

"Using sarcasm against me?"

"Maybe," she smirks.

"You're learning well, old grasshopper."

"Hey! I'm considered a child, eighteen might be an adult for a human but for a- Uncle Freddy!" Audrey starts bolting past me. I turn around and see her hugging a man who looks younger than John. I'm guessing this is Emma's other brother. He has scruffy black hair and a very short beard. Looks nothing at all like his brother, but a lot like his sister.

He picks her up and spins her around. Audrey is giggling like a five-year-old. Tom used to do that with me and Ash a lot.

I stand up and walk toward the small reunion.

"How have you been?" her uncle asks.

"Great! You should have been back weeks ago!"

"Something came up," he tells her.

"Like what?"

"Adult stuff," he tells her, and then he looks at me. "You must be the young Bec, my brother told me what happened to you. I'm so sorry."

I force a smile and say, "what's done is done."

He extends his hand and I shake it. "I'm Frederick Parris by the way."

I didn't give him my name because he already knew it. I instead I give him a friendly, "Nice to meet you."

Frederick has a warm, comforting smile. He is polite, caring, and I could tell he is naturally a good person. I liked Frederick right away, and I could tell that there were not going to be any problems between the two of us.

***

A week later, I can't sleep. I'm sitting in the dark, eating an apple that JP and I brought back from the tree house. As a vegetarian, I always loved eating fruits and vegetables.

Apples were my favorite, especially the green ones. My mother would always have to buy me two bags of apples growing up because I was always eating them. When we went back to the tree house and

Page 67

saw that they had green apples I put several in my jacket pockets and started eating one right away.

I am chewing really slowly, because the crunching is very loud, and I don't want to wake anyone up. It probably won't, but the paranoia is always there. Just like that paranoia when you're home alone and you hear the house make a strange noise, you can't help but automatically think that someone is in the house.

While tasting the sour of the apple on my tongue, I remember my mom John, Mabel, Jake, Ash, and everyone else that I cared about in my life.

I never had a favorite sibling, but sometimes I felt that I was closer with Jake than with Ash. After Tom left home and I barely got to talk to him except over the phone.

"I love you, you are my sister and I love you. I'll always love you. Never forget that." I remember Jake telling me several years ago in our room. Jake and I used to stay up late just saying what's on our minds.

"Can I ask you something?" I said to Jake one night when I was ten. We were trying to fall asleep in our room, but there were too many bright lights outside due to the police sirens. It's hard for me to sleep when there are lights around. To this day, I still have no idea what happened outside that day.

"Sure, what's up?"

"Can you sleep with the sirens?"

"No," he told me. "Now what's your real question?"

He always knew what was on my mind. "Do you like middle school?"

"What makes you say that?"

I thought about what to say. "You make it seem like it's bad, and I have to go there next year. I skipped a grade, so there will be a lot of people older than me. I have always been gifted in smarts, but I'm not good with people. I mean, I've had the same two best friends since forever."

"It's middle school. Middle school is the bitch in everyone's life."

I chuckled at the phrase. He always knew how to make me laugh, even if I didn't want to. Jake moved to the bottom bunk and embraced me.

"It's very bland and no fun at all, like you at dancing parties."

I had to laugh at that one. I never was big on dancing. I've always been a singer. My mother had a lot of Hispanic friends, and they always invited us to parties. I would always stand by the fruit and clear the platter.

"So I don't dance. I like to shake my voice, not my hips."

Jake and I were laughing for a bit. My brother always made me feel better.

"You remember how when you would always go to the next grade and you'd be a little frightened?"

"Yes," I said, starting to see his point.

"Well, it's the same transition into middle school. Sure, it's not as fun in elementary school, but you get more freedom. Plus, you never walk in lines ever again."

"No more lines?" I asked getting really happy.

"Why would I lie to you? You're my sister and I love you."

"I love you too."

"Never forget that."

Just then, Tom slowly opened our door. Summer was about to end, and Tom was getting ready to leave us again.

"Oh, you guys are awake," he said when he saw us quietly laughing.

"Yeah," Jake told him. "Bec can't sleep with the sirens."

Tom looked at me. I put on an innocent face and said with a three-year-old girl voice. "I'm really tired, but there's too many lights."

Tom crawled into my twin bed. It was starting to get hot, so I threw off our blanket and let the cold air cool off my body, but only for a few seconds because both of the boys embraced me from both sides. It was a small bed, but we all fit.

"I love you both," Tom told us.

"I love you guys too," Jake said.

"As do I," I told them.

"I'm really going to miss you guys when I leave again," Tom says.

"You leave a lot," I said. "We're never together anymore."

"Aren't we together forever?" Tom asked us.

"Forever together." Jake and I said simultaneously.

Page 69

Tom smiled at our word play and repeated, "forever together"

"Maybe we should wake Ash up and have her come hug us," I joke.

"Yes!" Tom shouts softly. "I'll go wake her!" and he gets off the bed.

"Tom!" Jake calls, "We won't fit here!"

I snap back into the present and suddenly realize that I am close to tears. No water was falling, but they are threatening to fall. My brothers and sister have always been an important part of my life when I was living like a human.

I always felt safe around them, I learned so much from them, and I grew up with them, and now they're gone. As quickly as I came into their life, they were taken out of mine. I look down at the apple I was eating and whispered "forever together".

I guess this life is now my middle school, seeming scary but in the end it's just the next step in life.

We still had to walk in lines though.

Chapter 11

"This is bad," Fredrick says, coming into the trailer's living room one day. John, JP, and Audrey were hanging around and talking about nothing in particular while Emma was having me do push-ups before he came in.

"When again is our life good?" I ask, sitting and rubbing my arms.

"What happened?" John asks.

"There's going to be an opening in New York, next week." Frederick tells us.

Everyone looked horrified for a few seconds, and then there were several attack plans that were shouted out one by one. I didn't understand any of them.

"What's an opening?" I asked.

"Demons are going to cross over into this dimension." Frederick tells me without giving me a look that was calling me a moron, like several of the others were.

"How do you know there's going to be an opening?" I ask.

"Some full mental magicians have the gift of knowing about openings," Frederick explains to me as best as he could. "Do you know about...psychics?"

I nod my head.

"You know how they have the special ability to feel certain things?"

I was starting to understand.

"Well, some full magicians can feel openings."

"So, are you a mental magician then?" I ask him.

"Yes," he tells me. "Some mental magicians have this ability, but all half magicians do not."

My smile vanishes.

"Sorry, Bec," John tells me. "This is serious, we don't have time for a life lesson right now."

"Do you know exactly where in New York?" Audrey asks her uncle.

"Not exactly," Frederick tells her. "My readings would be more accurate if I had another teller."

I guess that's what psychics are called in magician language.

"So what do we do?" I ask.

"We're going to New York!" JP exclaims happily. "Aren't we, dad?"

Frederick smiles at him. "Of course we are, can' let those demons go on another rampage."

"Are we going upstate or in the city?" I ask, hoping someone would say upstate. I used to go upstate a lot in my earlier childhood. My mother's parents lived there so we always went there to visit them.

"What about the twins in the city?" John asks. "We can stay with them."

"Yeah, family reunion!" I hear Audrey and JP exclaim.

Great. Another family reunion.

"Plus, Deonna's a teller, she can help," John adds.

"Who is this girl of which you speak of?" I ask in a stereotypical psychic voice.

"One of our cousins that live in New York," Audrey says. "We haven't seen them in years. It'd be nice to know what they've been up to."

"Wow, back when I was living with my human family, we talked to our cousins every other day, every week if we were busy." I tell them. "We used to see them three times a year. How come you guys don't see your relatives as much?"

"We have responsibilities to the universe, and to humanity," Emma tells me. "We don't really have time for our family."

"What if you guys died tomorrow? How would your families handle it?"

Page 72

I would give anything to see any of my family members one more time.

There was a silent pause.

"You should make time for them," I tell them sternly.

I should have spent more time with mine.

"Maybe after we take care of the demons we could drop by and see our cousins more," Emma says.

"Agreed," John says. "We'll leave tomorrow."

***

We get to Manhattan the next night and we're standing in a place where I thought nobody could live in.

"They live here?" I ask.

"Yeah," Emma tells me. "So?"

"But, no one lives here," I state. "It's kind of impossible."

"Did you just seriously say that?" Audrey asks. "You've seen many impossible things almost every day with us, and you say that this is impossible."

We were all standing outside the Statue of Liberty in New York City. It was past two in the morning, but there were still a lot of lights and cars alive in the city. They don't joke when they say this city never sleeps.

"Our cousins live under this statute," JP tells me.

"You mean the Statue of Liberty," I correct him.

"Yeah," JP says apologetically.

"For the past several years," John adds, then his tone gets a little sadder. "Since their parents passed away."

"Who were their parents?" I ask.

Everyone fell silent for a bit.

"Our sister," Frederick says.

I just pinched a nerve there.

"I lost my sister too," I tell him.

I stare at the Statue of Liberty for what felt like minutes.

I hear some mumbling, and a secret trap door is opened. It wasn't like a wooden latch in the ground like people use to hide underground. It was an actual door, and it opened into a secret underground stairwell. It

Page 73

was dark underneath, but Audrey and JP had a fire in their hands that they used to light the way.

"That's never been registered in the books before," I mumble amazed.

You would think that after living a life of magic for three months I'd stop aweing at everything.

JP looks back at me and smiles, and they start walking.

I stay back for a few seconds. I hold out my hand and focus on my own flame. I get a small spark. I smile wide and focus again.

"Come on, Bec," I hear Frederick call out.

With that, I give up on summoning my own fire and started down the creepy steps into the unknown.

***

At the bottom of the stairs, we come across a wooden door. It looks just like it belongs in a Renaissance era film.

Someone knocks on the door three times, but I don't know who because I'm in the back of the group. There was a sound of opening at the door.

"Uncle John! Audrey!" I hear a girl happily screech. She was greeting everyone, and I see her face when she hugs JP.

She was about sixteen, I think, but who knows with magicians. She was pale, had long straight dark hair, almost as long as mine. She's about six inches taller than me. She's dressed in a messy T-shirt, shorts, and has knee high rainbow socks on.

When she lets go of JP, I notice she gives me a cold look with her black eyes.

What's with this girl? I haven't said a single word to her!

I give her a cold look back, which I hope I'm doing right.

My mother would not approve, but I remember my sister's words to not let anyone treat me badly. Looks like I can finally use her teachings.

The girl makes a silent scoff and then smiles at Emma. "Who's this?" she asks with a voice that said 'go fuck off'.

What's this girl's problem? I've been here for three seconds and she acts like our families have been feuding for centuries!

Page 74

"This is Bec," JP tells her with a smile. "She's the newest member of our family."

I smile at him when he said that. Good thing someone likes me.

JP introduces me. "Bec, this is our cousin Deonna."

I nod at her.

She just gives me a cold look. Someone's being a little snob! She turns back to her cousins, aunts, and uncles and says with a smile "Well, come in everyone. I'm so glad to see you all again. It's been a really long time. JP, you've grown!"

"Good thing somebody's noticed," JP says, gloating a little bit.

Behind the Renaissance door, I take off my shoes and look around. The area looks like a small, fifties apartment. There was a couch, two large chairs, and a coffee table in what looked like the living room. There's an open doorway that leads to the modern looking kitchen. I couldn't see much because there were only three torches that lit the area.

"You don't have to take your shoes off," Deonna snaps with a shake in her voice.

"She always does that," Emma informs her.

I smile. "It's a Russkie thing."

Deonna has everyone sit down, and they are all catching up. I sit on one of the chairs by myself, feeling very uncomfortable with the situation. Five minutes into their conversation, I hear a door open followed by faint footsteps behind me.

"Hey, Darren!" everyone else says cheerfully, facing the direction of the footsteps. I refuse to turn around to look at him. If he was as rude as the dark haired Deonna, I want nothing to do with him.

"This is a lovely unexpected surprise," the boy says.

Audrey and JP stand up from the couch and run toward his direction, probably to hug him.

"How have you been Darren?" I hear JP say.

"Pretty good!"

"Is Deonna giving you a hard time?"

"Oh yeah!"

Hearing him say that makes me smile. JP and Audrey are cracking up.

Everyone else stands up and Darren walks over and hugs each of them. I turn around and look at him. He's Deonna's height, and his hair is just as dark and straight as hers. It was long for a guy, reaching his neck.

He turns around to hug Emma, but he ends up staring at me. I stare back into his black eyes. His hair covers his ears and cheeks, but it's obvious he and Deonna have the same face. The look in his eyes said that he was kind, that he wasn't a bitch like his twin sister. He was actually very handsome looking.

"Hello there," he says to me with a shy smile.

"Hey," I smile back at him.

We stare at each other for a while. I wasn't uncomfortable or anything, but I wasn't used to being looked at for this long.

"Darren, this is Bec," Frederick announces when it was clear no one else was going to introduce me. "She's the newest member of our family," he says, quoting his son.

"Nice to meet you," he says. "So, you're a magician? Never mind, don't answer that. It's kind of obvious. Well, welcome to our... uh, family." After nearly choking on the last word, he looks down at his hands.

"Shy one, eh?" I ask him.

He just looks back at me.

I smile at him. "You'll warm up to me eventually. Audrey threw a rock at my face, and now we're besties. Right Audrey?"

She starts to stammer a little.

Darren laughs, then looks at everyone else. "So what event brings this pleasant surprise?" Darren asks the others. Perhaps they forgot to call saying that we were stopping by. "We haven't seen you guys in years."

"There's probably going to be another opening." Well doesn't Emma know how to get straight to the point.

"I got the same feeling, but I don't know where or when, just that it's soon." Deonna says. "I heard from Allen that there was an opening in a Melbourne suburb just last month."

"Yeah, what gives?" Darren adds. "Wasn't there also an opening in Miami about three months ago?"

I try not to show any emotion when he says that. Has it really been over three months since I saw my father dissolve before my eyes, three months since I saw my sister's severed hand with the bracelet I gave her?

"I agree," I hear Frederick say, disrupting my train of thought. "We should do that if we want to save as many lives as we can."

"Say what?" Everyone looks at me. Did I say that out loud? I must have gotten lost in my painful memories. How long was I spacing out? "I mean, the new girl needs some clarification please. I'm not sure what you mean."

Valid excuse.

"You heard what we said," Deonna snaps at me. "There's no need for the slow girl to have a review."

This girl is a real bitch, and even though I was just shy of thirteen, I had a bitch mode as well, and this girl was testing my patience. Why was she being like this?

I can hear my mother's voice in my head to be nice, so I try. "I just wanted you guys to-"

"Don't try to defend yourself," she interrupts me. "We all know that you're a little problematic wannabe with no   intelligent thoughts or-"

Yep. It's been activated.

I can hear Ash in my head now, defend yourself.

"Oh, I'm sorry, I had no idea that some problematic wannabe herself knew every detail about my life. Go ahead and tell me more about myself," I leaned my ear closer to her. She stayed quiet. "That's what I thought! Isn't that why you called me one? Guilty conscious I suppose."

"That's enough both of you!"

I reverted back to my normal self when I heard Emma yell at us. "Bec, you haven't even been here for ten minutes and you're already picking a fight with someone you don't even know."

"She's the one who had an attitude with me for no reason! I wasn't about to keep quiet and let her talk that way to me."

"You have to learn how to turn the other cheek in a situation like this."

"My siblings have always taught me to defend myself no matter what, to never go down without a fight. Why should I listen to your advice over my dead family's? You back down once and they walk all over you. I came into this world kicking and screaming, and I'm prepared to keep on fighting just like that." I tell her, remembering something Ash told me once.

"Go wait outside!" Emma snaps at me.

"No!"

"Rebecca, go outside! Practice your magic, curse my name, look at the stars, I don't care, just get out of my sight and calm down. Now!"

Whenever anyone shouts Rebecca at me, it's the Hispanic equivalent of saying the full name with the middle name and everything, or throwing the chancleta. My mother was the only person to ever call me Rebecca, but she didn't do it all the time, and I almost never got in trouble.

I gave Deonna the finger, my mother was probably frowning upon me right now, and I left the way I came in.

"And as for you, Deonna," I hear her start, but I don't stick around to hear what she says.

***

When I get outside, I lie on the ground next to the water, and look up at the sky. In Manhattan, you do not see many stars. I sit up and I use my magic to get rid of some of the light. Usually Magicians use this spell when they want to hide in the shadows or take shelter from the sun, but I'm using it for astronomical reasons at the moment. It didn't get rid of much, but it was better than nothing. I still don't know how to use it well.

Emma taught me that trick last week in case I ever need to make a quick getaway or blend in the shadows. Who would have guessed I'd be using it to get away from her?

Audrey did say her mom could be scary when she is mad. Turns out she was right.

"Nice trick."

I turn around to see Darren standing there, concern in his black eyes.

Page 78

"Thanks, it's an easy spell." I tell him.

He sits down next to me. We're both quiet for a moment.

I can't look at him, mainly because he looks identical to his sister and I didn't want anything to remind me of her.

Also, according to my old friend John, I'm an open book and I don't want Darren knowing what I'm feeling right now. I don't even know how I feel.

"I'm really sorry about my sister," Darren tells me after several moments of silence.

"Don't be," I tell him. "It's not like you made her say that."

"I know, but I can't help but feel embarrassed when she does stuff like that. I don't know why she's so hateful towards people."

He doesn't look at me when he says that last part. I can tell he's lying, but I don't say anything about it.

"Even if she doesn't know them?"

"Yeah. Where'd you learn to talk like that? You seem so sweet."

"I heard my sister say something like that once."

I turn my head to look at him. He's studying me. He stares into my eyes as if he was trying to pick a lock guarding my mind. I guess I'm not as open as John thought I was.

John.

My old John.

He has to think I'm dead.

He smiles another shy smile at me, and I smile back. I'm secretly very glad that Darren is not at all like Deonna.

"If you ever need to talk about anything, you can always talk to me."

"Thanks Darren, but I'm not much of a talker."

"You'll warm up eventually," he says, using my own words against me. I could tell that Darren and I might become close one day.

"I'm glad you're not like your sister," I tell him.

"Thanks," he says, "me too."

"Glad to see you're feeling better."

We jump and turn around when Frederick speaks.

"Does everyone in your family have a habit of appearing out of nowhere like that?" I ask rhetorically.

"You were surprised?" Frederick asks. "My apologies, but you really should be more alert. You never know what might be lurking out in the night."

"Thanks for the tip," I say with only a little bit of sarcasm.

"Are you getting to know our new friend, cousin…I'm sorry, I still don't know what to refer to you as. I know your name is Bec, but…I'll be quiet."

"Bec is fine," I say smiling.

"You getting to know our new Bec?" Frederick asks Darren.

"Yeah, well, a little, I think." He really isn't good with words. "I was trying to see if she was feeling okay.

Obviously she was upset, so I- Wait, friend? So she, is she adop-"

"Calm down," Frederick laughs. "You'll swallow your tongue again."

"Again?" I ask.

"That was in a demon fight," he says embarrassed "I was trying to-"

"Say no more," I smile. "I understand."

Darren smiles back at me, and gives me a surprise hug. I hug Darren back, and it ends up being a longer hug than I expected.

"Break it up you two," Frederick says jokingly. "Time for you to go back inside, Darren."

Darren slowly let go of me, and I start to feel my face blush.

Wait? I'm blushing?

"Yes sir," he says to Frederick, then he looks back at me. "See you later," and he walks away.

"So, how are you enjoying life?" Frederick asks me when Darren is gone.

I give him a look and say, "You tell me."

We were silent for a while, and then he finally speaks. "I really am sorry all this happened to you, you were brought into our bloody world by chance, even if you were not really supposed to stay with the humans. I know you feel forced into this, that God is playing a cruel joke on you." He held up my star around my neck when he said that. "But I'm sure things will get better. Sure, my niece can be a... why sugar coat it, she's a total bitch. That doesn't mean you should be down about all this."

I look at Frederick and smile. "My mother always told me that everything happens for a reason, that our life is planned. We can either fight it, or accept it. Try and change it for the better and everything will follow suite. My father on the other hand said that we control our own destiny."

"Which do you believe?"

I shrug my shoulders.

"Your father sounded wise, and your mother was an intelligent woman."

"Yeah, she was. She raised us to be good people, and my brothers taught me how to defend myself. My sister taught me how to be quick and clever. I suppose that I was subconsciously...maybe..."

"Your family has taught you well; they always wanted the best for you."

"Yeah, if my mother wasn't gone, she would have killed me if she heard me say all of that. Tom, Jake, and Ash would have high fived me and taken me out for ice cream, but my mother believed that every human being deserved respect. I guess now it's every living being deserves respect."

"They wanted you to be strong, and how very strong you are."

"Thanks."

We're silent for another moment.

"I just wish people were nicer," I say. "Deonna seems so..."

"Problematic you said, that was a nice one. Totally her by the way."

"I learned from my elders," I say jokingly. "I heard my sister say it once to this one lady and she became shell shocked."

"I can imagine. Your sister sounded very witty."

"She was. My father once said that she was so good with words that she could have convinced Hitler to love Jews."

Frederick started laughing "If your sister taught you everything she knows, then Deonna better look out!"

We are both laughing for a while, and Frederick finally asks me how old I was.

"I will be thirteen in . . . two months, I think."

Page 81

"Just a baby in this world and you already can see how evil it can be," he cups my chin and smiles at me.

Frederick really is a kind person, and it seems that he really does want to help me.

Hey wait, I'm not a baby!

"How much do you know about the ways of magicians?" he asks me.

"I know as a half magician, I can still go in the sun without losing my powers. I don't know my biological parents. I do turn a little red in the sun after a while. I haven't tried doing magic in the sun, mainly because I can't even do it in the dark. Sorry, I'm getting sidetracked. I have to stay active. I know my powers are limited depending on what type of magician I am. I know we protect humanity even though they've forgotten us. And protect the other remaining dimensions. I know we can't eat processed sugar or else we'd die." I couldn't think of anything else.

"We don't die if we eat sugar, just get really sick."

"That explains a lot."

"What can you do with your magic?"

"I can heal and clear away light, but I still don't know much magic. I tried making my own fire, but I can only get a spark. I know I'm not an elemental or physical magician, but I'm still trying to learn some tricks. I could be a mental magician because I'm great at moving things with my mind, but nothing besides that. Maybe I'm a time magician."

"Time magicians are very rare," he tells me.

"How rare?" I ask.

He stands up. "Come, I'll teach you a few tricks. Help you find who you are."

"I already know who I am," I say smiling.

"You are correct. What I meant to say is, let me help you discover what you can do."

"Like what?"

"Every Magician needs to know certain things."

Chapter 12

"Although you're not getting the misdirection, you are progressing fast with everything else, especially object transformation," Frederick tells me.

"Thanks," I say, turning a leaf into a rock. "It's easier to learn when I'm not being attacked with fire all the time."

"That's Audrey for you."

"How come all magicians can change objects, but not all magicians can shape shift?"

"It's easy to change something else into what you want it or them to be. Changing yourself, now that's hard, and not everyone is capable of doing that."

"Are we still talking about shapeshifting or is this a life lesson?"

He laughs, then looks at me in the eye and gets serious. "Don't tell Emma I'm doing this, but I'm going to teach you something else. Something advanced."

I get excited. "What is it?"

"You've been training, what, three months?"

"Yup."

"The trick I'm going to teach you is an elemental magician trick, but some physical magicians can learn this as well. It has to do with the air. Do you know what the air is made up of?"

"Oxygen, carbon dioxide, nitrogen, um, and something else in the atmosphere."

He laughs lightly and shakes his head. "You're being too literal. It contains hydrogen, and oxygen. There is also a little bit of argon."

"Then what about carbon dioxide?"

"That's what we breathe out that plants use for photosynthesis. I am actually going to teach you how to remove an element from the air."

"But isn't air already an element?"

"Technically yes, but I'm talking about elements on the periodic table."

"What good is it to take oxygen out of the air?"

He tried to think "Have you ever lit a candle and covered it with the lid?"

"All the time. My mother hated it. She would always make me relight it and then take the lid away... Oh my gosh! Fire can't sustain its form without oxygen, so it will go out without it!"

"It's a defense mechanism against fire, and Audrey-

"Cool!"

"-And you can also suffocate a person, or a demon."

***

I was sitting inside the cave the next day. At least I think it was a cave. When I first walked through here to the twin's place, it just screamed cave to me. I was practicing a trick that Frederick showed me last night.

Out of my memory, I replicate the spell that Frederick taught me last night, and I start to slowly clench my fists. Little by little, I could feel the oxygen being absorbed into my hands. I had a small fire in front of me, and I could see it slowly dying. I release all the oxygen back into the air, and the fire shot back to life.

"I guess my uncle taught you something last night." I jump and turn around to see Audrey. I really should start paying more attention to my surroundings.

"Yeah, just don't tell your mom."

"I won't," she smiles and sits down next to me. "She freaks about that stuff. I have no idea why. How come you're not asleep with the others?"

"Your one to talk," I say jokingly. "I'm not with the others because I was kicked out, and I'm not asleep because I woke up about an hour ago."

"Ah, so you're just sitting here playing with fire?"

Page 84

I stick my bare foot in the embers. "Yup."

"Get your foot out of there!"

I laugh and pull it out. My foot up to my lower shin was un-harmed. I removed some oxygen around the area so I would not get burned. Audrey realized what happened and starts to lightly punch my arm repeatedly.

"You're an idiot you know that?"

I put my other foot in the embers. "Yup!"

"Bec!" she screams. With her other hand, she yanks my foot out, which wasn't hurt or red either.

"Got you, Audrey! Plus, this is less dangerous than throwing burning rocks at someone."

She stammers for a moment.

I got her!

"Why would you do that to yourself?" she finally asks.

"I like to challenge myself, take risks and do stupid stuff once in a while. I told you I used to do that all the time."

"You're not kidding when you say that, but don't ever let me catch you doing that ever again, got it?"

"Got it."

"Good, and that also means for your hands as well."

"What are you, a mind reader?"

"You're just easy to read, but I know someone who is."

We start laughing. It was nice to laugh and joke around with someone. I usually only did that with Mabel and John, the other John. Sometimes I wonder if they miss me. I wish I could go see them, just to let them know I'm not dead. I will one day.

"Promise me you won't do that foot trick again, Bec."

"I already said I wouldn't," I tell her, half laughing.

"What do you want? Me to engrave it on my arm?"

"Yes," she says, obviously kidding.

"Fine, where's the knife?"

"No!"

"I got you!" I tell her, and we both start laughing again.

"Well, aren't you two having fun?"

We turn around to see Darren and JP standing there.

"Don't you people ever make any noise?" I ask as they sit on the other side of the fire.

"Well, we can't say the same for you two. I heard someone screaming and panicked," JP tells us.

"So he woke me up," Darren says sluggishly.

"Sorry," Audrey tells him. "I screamed because Bec-"

"You don't need to tell them the details!" I say, interrupting her.

"Yes I do!" classic Audrey. "She purposely put her feet in the fire to play a trick on me. I screamed because I thought she was going to hurt herself."

Darren was now fully awake. "Fire? What?"

"It's a long story," I say. "Do you guys want to go walking in the city before the old geezers wake up?"

"Another one of your sneak out attempts?" Audrey asks.

"It's not an attempt, we're actually going to do it," I tell her.

"I'm in," JP says. "It's boring here."

"I can't go out," Darren announces.

"What's the matter?" I say playfully. "Is your sister going to give you a hard time?"

"It's not that," Darren tells me. "The sun's still up."

"Wait, you're a full..."

"Yeah. Why so surprised?"

"It's just...." Every kid magician I've met has been a half. "Nothing."

He can't go out in broad daylight like Audrey, JP and I can or else he will turn red and lose his magic. I take off my hoodie, which was two sizes too big on me, and hand it to Darren. I also grab the fedora that my brothers bought for me and give it to him. He's only a little bigger than me, so he puts it on easily, and still has a lot of room to hide his hands and shade his face. He takes off the hood, puts the fedora on, then puts the hood back on, which looks kind of awkward. He is completely hidden from the sunlight.

"Do you have sunglasses?" he asks me.

"Sorry," I tell him. "I only have one hat, and the clothes that Emma got me are way too big."

"I do," Audrey says, pulling a blue pair out of her pocket.

"Looks like I'm good to go then," he tells me with a smile, and then he puts on the sunglasses.

"Do you have more?" JP asks her.

"Inside. One sec," she stands up and heads inside.

"Do you need one?" JP asks me.

"Naw, I'm good."

***

Once everyone was all dressed up, we headed out. The four of us are sitting inside a Starbucks. JP and Audrey were drinking unsweetened iced tea, and Darren was eating a panini that he gave more than half of to me. I was drinking a vanilla bean, knowing that the sugar was bad for me, but wanting something familiar.

I used to split these Frappuccinos with Ash all the time, that is until Jake noticed and said it wasn't safe for me to drink it. But it tasted too good to pass up, especially the caramel! Jake always wanted me to lay off of caffeine because it would give me bad headaches at my young age, but then again, what did I care? Now I realize that it was probably the sugar that gave me those splitting headaches, not the caffeine.

I'm not sure how Darren paid for these though. He knows this trick where he has a deactivated card, and, well, I'll ask him again. I didn't really understand when he told me. I wanted to know if this was technically stealing, but I'll ask when there's not a huge ton of witnesses around us.

Although I do wish I had Audrey grab me a pair of sunglasses.

"Your turn, JP," Audrey says. "Embarrassing, personal, or random truth."

I taught them how to play truth or dare, but because we're in the middle of New York City, we were just playing the truth categories.

"Personal."

"I have a good one," Darren says moving his hands further under the sweater I let him borrow. "If you had to pick between the one person you'll ever be in love with, or your family, which would you choose?"

"Family," he says, not thinking twice.

Page 87

"Well duh he'd choose family," Audrey says "He's only eleven, he's too young to know about that."

"What would you choose then?" JP asks her.

She thought for a while. Everyone is answering all the questions because we're all getting to know each other better. "I guess love if you only fall in love once. What about you, Bec?"

"I'll say love. My family's gone now." I force a smile.

"What about you Darren?"

He sat looking at his half of the panini, "I have no idea, for now I'll choose family, but I might change later on in life."

"Are you okay?" I ask him.

He looks up and smiles at me. "I'm okay."

I smile back at him. Darren is way too shy. I'll knock him out of it eventually.

"Okay, this is too personal," Audrey laughs.

"Hence the category," I laugh.

"Bec, your turn," Audrey tells me.

"Embarrassing," I have nothing to hide.

"What is the most embarrassing thing you did when you were a baby?"

"My eldest brother told me a story of when we were at the park, and for some reason, I took my diaper off. I sat in the mud, and would scream and throw mud every time someone would come near me."

They burst out laughing.

"Why'd you take your diaper off?" JP asks me.

"I don't know I was eight months old. I didn't talk until I was four, and I would run and do random things. No one remembers stuff when they're babies. What about you JP?"

"I would run around naked with my sister's music box, in public. I would wave it around and dance to the music."

"I remember that," Audrey says. "Do you still have Raven's box?"

"Yeah, it's back in our tree house."

"You have a sister JP?" I ask him.

"Had," he says glumly,

"I'm so sorry, I didn't mean to..."

"That's alright" he says to me, "She was always tough, she said that she would rather go out in a fight than live to be old."

"I know how it feels to lose a sister."

"Thanks, Bec. I'm just glad I have other relatives who I love, and who love me back."

"How'd she die? Sorry, it's just... hearing about other people's losses helps me cope with my own."

"No, it's fine. I don't exactly know," he says, "My father told me that there was a fight one day when she was playing with me, then she was gone. All I know is that it devastated me. I was only six."

There was a long pause. I drink the rest of my drink, and excuse myself to throw my cup away.

"You know you have us, right?" Audrey tells me when I get back to the table.

"Thanks guys." I tell them. "I just felt kind of alone since the attack, but you guys have made it easy."

"What attack?" Darren asks.

"Guess they didn't tell you. About three months ago my entire family was killed by demons while we were at the beach."

"I'm sorry to hear that," he tells me grabbing my hand. "Your family had a hard time fighting them?"

"They were human," I inform him. "They didn't know how to fight."

"How were they human?" then the thinks for a moment. "You were adopted by humans?"

"Yeah," I tell him. "Emma and Audrey were in Miami when it happened, and they told me who I was. It all happened so fast."

Ash's severed hand pops back into my head.

"I'm sorry," he tells me.

They all came one by one to hug me, Darren being last.

We both smiled at each other.

"Thank you," I tell him. "I'm getting tired of telling this to people. Can we try not bring up dead family anymore? Anyways, what's your baby story?"

***

We spent another two hours walking around the city and talking. We told stories, I told corny jokes, and got to know each other a lot more. For once, I felt almost normal again.

It kind of sucked when Audrey mentioned the sunset as we started to walk closer to the Statue of Liberty.

"So your brother really almost took the duck home?" JP asks. I was telling them a story about how Jake and John caught a duck, and Jake tried to bring it into the house. My mother had a heart attack when she caught him sneaking her under his jacket.

"Yeah, but my mom stopped him," I tell them. "She said that he would end up killing it, so he let it go."

"Bec, are you alright?" JP asks me, sounding very concerned.

"Sure I am," I assure him. "Why wouldn't I be?"

"Because you're shaking a lot, and having a lot of quick, sudden movements and twitches," he tells me.

I thought they seemed a little slow. It was the vanilla bean at Starbucks. And I thought caffeine and sugar was bad for me before, but they weren't kidding when they said it was dangerous to magicians.

"Oh man, she needs to sit down!" Darren grabs my shoulders and leads me to the nearest bench. I'm shaking more than I realized. I start to get a really bad headache. I lay my head on his shoulder and close my eyes. I also feel myself getting very hot and hear JP say that I was sweating. At least there was a strong wind blowing on my face.

"Bec," Audrey says, "was there any processed sugar in what you just drank?"

I nod my head.

"We need to get her some water to dilute the sugar in her system." Darren says. "Why would you drink that knowing it had sugar in it?"

"I used to drink them all the time," I tell him. "I used to share them with-"

"You drank the whole thing by yourself just now!"

"I don't see any food vendors," JP says.

"Was there a strong wind a minute ago?" Audrey asks no one in particular.

"No." JP said, getting scared. "Um, Darren, when exactly did Deonna and my dad say the next opening was?"

Page 90

"They were going to find out tonight," he tells them.

"Well they don't have until tonight."

I opened my eyes, and noticed all the wind blowing towards the middle of the busy road.

A portal is opening!

Chapter 13

This is bad!

I am hyper, jittery, feeling very sick, overheated, and I don't have enough training, tricks learned, or spells memorized. I am so not ready for this fight!

"Can we handle this, just the four of us?" Audrey asks.

"Well if we're not ready," Darren says, standing me up, "then we better prepare for it now!"

"What about Bec?" JP asks, sounding scared.

"She'll have to do her best, and we watch each other's backs, including hers," Darren tells him as the first demon appears.

People stop driving their cars, and everyone walking on the sidewalk stops to look at what is happening.

A red demon that looks like a toddler with three eyes was the first to crawl out from the portal. It has a large mouth, and teeth too large to fit inside. The demon looks around at the screaming humans, then it looks directly at the four of us, sensing who we are. The demon turns around and gives some sort of signal. Then seven more appear that look identical to the first one. They must be a family or something.

They took my family.

"We each take two?" Audrey asks really fast.

My father was lying there headless.

"And assist sick girl when necessary," JP says just as quickly.

These fuckers will pay.

"Yeah," Darren says, letting go of me slowly so I could stand on my own. "Time to go, whether we're ready or not."

Without hesitation, the demons start throwing cars around. One rips the door off, revealing a screaming woman inside. It's mouth latches onto her neck. Her three kids in the back open the door and fall out.

Another demon picks up a human toddler as he cries and rips his stomach open with its large claws. The demon then picks the silent kid up and shoves him in its mouth, feet first.

Unlike on the beach, my mind is processing everything that they're doing, and I wish it wasn't.

I see the two I'm going to take. I point to them and tell the others that I'll deal with them. Dizzy or not, I have to do something. I can't let anyone else die in front of me. These two seemed to stay together like they were siblings. The other demons attacked their victims simultaneously and seem to be giving each other looks of encouragement. Also, they looked smaller than the other six. Hopefully, this means they're not as powerful.

When you witness an infant and her young mother turn inside out before being consumed, instincts tell you to act fast, even when sick and are almost about to faint.

After just a few words said, the other magicians quickly pounce on the demons. I on the other hand am slower and use a little more stealth to catch my dynamic duo prey. One of my demons has his razor mouth inside an obese woman's throat, so it doesn't notice me sneak behind it, but its twin partner did. It rams me from the side and is on top of me in a moment's notice.

This demon has a long snake tongue. It uses its tongue to force my mouth open, but JP lifts it into the air with telekinesis before it's tongue could scratch up my uvula.

"Thanks," I quietly call out to JP, and face the other demon. I give it the "come at me" gesture, and it charges full throttle at me. In the last moment, I move to the right, sending the demon into Audrey's battle with two larger demons. She sets it on fire, half melting the demon. She twirls her hand, collecting water. She then turns the water into a sword, and chops off the demon's head.

Note to self: Stay on Audrey's good side.

To help her out a bit, I try to create a plasma bolt that Emma taught me, but I can't seem to make one. I instead pick up a nearby rock, my head spinning on the way back up, sending it at the feet of a demon that was behind her, causing it to slip and fall on its head. I hear what sounds like bones crack in the process.

Audrey sends a quick smile to me, then puts it out of its misery with her hand in its stomach and rips out its guts.

I suddenly remember the way one demon ripped my mother's head clean off her shoulders.

Mommy.

I shake the thought from my head and look around.

Darren is doing fine in his battle, holding down a demon, and there's another dead demon right next to him.

Saying he killed it is too nice a word. He slashed it in twenty different places, revealing bone, demon guts, and a pool of blood under its desecrated body.

JP had already killed another demon, and he is now assisting three kids who are trapped by two other demons.

The demon bit off a little boy's head before JP could lift a car with his mind and crush the two demons.

Looking away in horror, I notice a demon with wings flying straight at me. I jump up as high as I could to avoid being hit, but end up falling right on its back. When the demon notices me, it starts spinning around frantically, flying in every direction to knock me off. I feel like I'm going to vomit. I hold on as hard as I can, but I feel myself slipping. I feel my breathing weakening like there is no oxygen.

No oxygen! That's it!

I recall the spell Frederick taught me the other night, and I put it into action. I start to feel the demon losing its breath.

We start to fall. Luckily, we were over a large body of water.

Splash!

I don't slow down this time. I snap the demon's neck, shattering bone. I then use every ounce of my energy to keep it under water, hoping it doesn't have gills. I stay floating in the water for a few minutes, half asking myself how I did that, half expecting the demon to regenerate itself, but nothing happens.

It dies.

My first kill.

"That was for you, guys."

Page 94

I can't be too happy about it because I feel like I'm going to black out. I lay myself flat on the water. "Please stay afloat," I keep saying aloud, and then my eyelids shut.

***

I wake up on land. How I got here, I have no idea. All I know is that it is dark, I am alone, soaked, covered in throw up (please be my own!), and have no idea where I am. I try sitting up, but a migraine forces me back down. I grab my head and try to ponder what has happened. I am sick, demons attacked, I killed one in a random lake. No, it was a river. Was it brackish water? I don't really remember.

Oh, what difference does it make!

I guess the others weren't sugar coating it when they said too much processed sugar can mess with our systems.

But Darren ate a panini and he didn't get sick. Do paninis even have sugar?

Darren!

I sit up fast, ignoring my throbbing head.

Audrey! JP! Where are they? What happened? Oh my goodness!

I stand on my feet before falling back on my butt. I am way too sick and dizzy to move, but I know I have to do something. I end up crawling and trying to pull myself along. I am dizzy, barely moving, and I throw up on myself more than once.

After half an hour of pulling myself twenty feet, I come to a stop sign. I see that as a signal to stop and I use the sign to pull myself up. I stand at the sign for a while just hugging it to regain my balance. I almost fall asleep on it, but I force myself to stay awake. With the little energy I have, I clean myself off. No one is going to help me if I'm dirty, and I don't like the feeling anyways. I might just be a child, but the people of New York won't help me in this condition.

Plus, I am vulnerable to muggers and other bad people my mother always told me about.

I start walking. I am traveling slowly and am still very weak. I know I have to find Audrey and the others or else I could die, if I'm lucky.

Page 95

Chapter 14

New York isn't as hectic at night. Most of the pedestrians are home, and traffic actually moves on the road, but this city really does never sleep. I can't tell what time it is, but I believe it is after midnight. I know I'm somewhere in Manhattan, but I don't know how to get to the Statue of Liberty.

Suddenly, I hear someone screaming, "Help me!" It sounds like a young boy. Forgetting about my weak state, I rush over to where the scream came from. I find myself in an alleyway, watching three Hispanic thugs in their twenties beating up a twelve or thirteen-year-old dark-skinned boy with the darkest blue eyes I've ever seen.

"And just what do you hoodlums think you're doing?"

They turn around, appalled at first, but when they noticed a baby faced twelve-year-old girl with her arms crossed giving them a threatening look, they start laughing.

The boy looks at me, not sure what to make of me.

"Well aren't you cute?" the tallest one says.

"You're going to be cute with my foot shoved up your scrotum!" I threaten him. Good thing Ash taught me how to talk tough. Although I fear I might have overdone it, I don't let anything show on my face, or in my eyes, but they start laughing again.

"Can we keep her boss?" a guy I nickname "Muscles" says to the third one, obviously the leader.

"Let's see if she lives after this," he says, and charges his two cronies at me, both of them pulling out pocket knives.

Fighting humans I'm supposed to protect. Talk about irony.

I'm protecting a young boy.

I try and summon fire, but when it doesn't happen, I quickly throw my hands down in frustration. The thugs start moving very slowly. And I mean very slowly. What did I just do? I look at my hands, and then back up at the charging thugs. They haven't moved much. I look at the leader. It looks like he's saying something, but his mouth is barely moving. I look at the young boy. His eyes slowly close and slowly open, that's when I realize that it was a blink.

Did I just slow down time?

I think I did. I never heard of this happening before, but I don't question it. I'll use it to my advantage!

I wait for the tall one to be near me, then I jump and kick him hard in the side of the head. He fell in slow motion as Muscles came from behind. He tries to punch me, but I grab his slowly moving fist and twist it until his bone popped out of his shoulder. I punch him in the stomach with my other hand, and watch him crouch down in pain.

I turn around and see the tall one standing up. He is putting his hand behind his back, but he is too slow. I approach him and give him another kick in the head. I see the blood slowly sprout from his ear. While he is falling, I kick his head in the other direction. He then falls hard in slow motion.

Muscles is slowly bull charging me, but I obviously have the advantage. I grab his good arm and throw him against the wall. I then flatten him on the ground and punch him in the groin.

I turn around and see the boss with a knife held to the boy's throat. He's speaking to me, but time is too slow to understand. I run up to him, probably looks like a sprint to him. He's about to slit the boy's throat but I knock the knife out of his hand with my foot. There's a small scratch on the side of his throat, but he'll be fine. I sit the boy against the wall and face the boss again.

We run towards each other, and I punch him in the groin. When he bends over in pain, I jump a little to punch him in the face, breaking his nose, and then I punch his ear.

He won't be hearing anything from there tomorrow.

I was about to trip him, but he starts moving faster and he hits me hard in the side. The wind was knocked out of me for a moment and he uses that advantage to jab me in the side of the head. He tries

Page 97

to punch me in the face, but I block him and grab his throat. I push as hard as I can on his vein, I believe it's called a dorsal vein, and he faints. The final knockout.

I walk towards the boy and examine him. He is badly bruised, maybe has a few broken ribs, and a busted lip. Thecut in his neck isn't that deep, but there is a lot of blood pouring out of it.

"Thank you for saving me," the boy says, making me jump.

"Your welcome," I tell him sincerely. "Why were those jerks beating you up?"

"You're obviously new in New York," he tells me.

"Thugs jump anyone here. Where did you learn to fight like that? That was awesome!"

"I had a lot of teachers," I tell him truthfully. "You should probably get home, um... name?"

"Chris," he tells me. "I ran away from home months ago."

"Chris, you should really return home. Are your parents abusive or something?"

"No, but I feel like there's nothing there for me. Why aren't you home?"

"Something happened and I got lost, I'm trying to find them," I tell him truthfully. "You should go home. I'm sure your mother misses you. Do you have a mother?"

"Both parents, and a younger brother and sister."

"Go home, Chris," I tell him while helping him stand. "They're probably worried sick."

"Thanks, miss."

"Bec," I inform him.

"Thanks, Bec," he says and gives me a hug. I hug him back. The scent of his blood is really strong. It's so overwhelming. I probably should have applied pressure to stop the bleeding.

Chris screams and holds me up.

"Chris, what's wrong?" I ask him, but I then realize what happened.

I start to get very dizzy, like, dizzier than I was before.

The area where bossy boots punched me was starting to hurt.

Oh no.... the sugar should have... worn off... by now.

I grab my side for relief, but there was no relief when I felt that my side was wet. I look down to where my hand is, and saw blood, and a knife jabbed in my side.

He didn't punch me... he stabbed me. I was...stabbed. I need to...get help. I... need....to find....I... there's a... knife in my....

"Chris..."

Chapter 15

My eyes open slowly to a migraine and a spinning room. I rub my eyes and my temples for a while until my head seems to clear up.

I slowly take in my surroundings. I am in a light blue hospital gown with pink flowers on it. I'm in a small bed under a thin white blanket in a room with blue walls with fish, sand, and a starfish.

A beach, great.

The room is cold. I feel like I just got out of a jacuzzi and dove into a pool. I only have a thin blanket on me, and I only have underwear under the hospital gown. There is a boy a few feet away from me, a little older than Chris probably. He's a pale black kid with no hair. He's watching a cartoon on a small TV on the corner of the wall.

As I watch it for a few minutes, memories start slowly coming back to me. Jake, Ash, and I used to watch this show all the time. I remember this episode. I'm surprised that they show reruns on TV considering the last episode was made years ago.

"Glad to see you're awake!" the boy shouts gleefully. I am so into the episode that I jump out of shock.

I jump and run my tongue along the top of my teeth. I turn towards the boy to see him smiling at me. "Hello," I say. "Am I in a hospital?"

"Yeah, they brought you in early this morning," he tells me. "You had a knife in your side and were really beaten up. I saw the doctor stitch you up and X Ray you. He even put an IV in you to give you blood."

"They gave me blood!" I scream, meaning to sound a lot less freaked out than I did. I look at my arm and saw a piece of gauze on my vein where the elbow bends. Oh man, oh man! If they tested my blood, they would find out it's not human, and they would call scientists to confirm that I'm a...

"Don't worry, the doctor took care of you himself. A little weird considering the nurses usually do that kind of stuff. You could have died."

I look at my side, mostly because I don't want the boy to see that I'm freaking out, and look at my stitches. It wasn't a wide knife, so I don't have a big scar, but it probably went deep considering the blood loss.

This is really bad!

"I'm Julius by the way."

"Nice to meet you," I tell Julius, only half meaning it.

I'm still a bit in a panic from the blood transfer. I think I should be fine. But what if I have different blood by being a Magician? If so, will my new blood counteract it? I could get sick, I could die, I could go into shock, or I could just get sweaty.

I don't know.

I've been to the doctors before, but I've never had an X- ray done, or had blood given to me, all I had were some shots.

Shit! I've had shots before!

Why am I only now realizing this?

Just then a Hispanic doctor around thirty comes into the room. He takes off his glasses and reads silently from his clipboard.

"I see the young lady is awake," he says, noticing me staring blankly at the television screen. I turned my head to look at him. He's tall, broad, and cleanly shaven. His name tag says JAKE. My brother Jake wanted to be a doctor, a pediatrician to be precise. It's surreal meeting another Jake already living the life my brother can no longer have.

"My name is Jake, I am the nurse who will be taking care of you. While you were asleep, the doctor ran a few X rays on you. You have three broken ribs and a concussion. You will need a lot of rest here to recover."

"How much blood did you give me?" I ask. "And how much rest will I need? Will the cracked ribs harm me more? If I have a concussion, doesn't that mean I can't sleep? Why'd you let me sleep? How did I get in this hospital gown? How did I even get here?"

I know I'll be fine in a few days, but I ask those extra questions to sound like a typical curious kid.

"We had to give you three pints," he tells me. "You lost a lot of blood. If that kid hadn't brought you here a few minutes later, you might have bled to death. The ribs will heal on their own, they won't pierce your heart or anything."

I knew they wouldn't pierce my heart.

"We stitched you up. You should be fine in a few weeks. You're under as a Jane Doe, and we had no way of contacting your family, so the doctor had to make the decision to give you blood and stitch you up. What's your name by the way?"

"Where's Chris? Is he the one who brought me in?"

"Yes."

"Where is he?"

He sighs. "We had to alert the authorities."

"What? Is he a criminal?"

Did I almost die saving a criminal?

"No, he's not a criminal," the nurse tells me. "He was reported missing a few months ago, so we had the authorities pick him up and escort him back to his family."

I sigh with relief.

"He said that you told him your name but he couldn't remember it. What is it?"

Quick, I need a name!

"Greg," I say, looking at a poster on the wall with a list of doctors and nurses. Why I said Greg instead of Louise, I have no idea.

"Greg? Greg what?" Jake asked me.

"Gregory Bro- LEX! I am Gregory Brolex,"

"What a strange name," the nurse says.

"Yeah," I say, trying to hide my bad lie. "I have a guy cousin named Ashley and an aunt named Devin, I have a weird family."

He looks like he's suspicious, but then shakes his head and thinks nothing of it. "You were very lucky, Greg," Jake tells me.

"Thanks," I tell him.

"We need to contact your family," the nurse tells me.

"We need your information on file, can you give me a phone number?"

"Oh... uh... the number's in my cell phone," I lie. "In my bag."

"We only have clothes in a locker down the hall for you, but we didn't see a bag. Do you remember the phone number?"

"Uh...no... but I know my mom's Email address."

He writes down my mother's old Email address. I decided to give him a real one in case he gets a notification saying that the message was not sent.

"Well then, Greg, I'll Email your mother now, and then we need to take another blood sample," Jake tells me. "The doctor will be in soon to talk to you."

"What?"

I need to leave the hospital and find the others, but I don't know how long they'll keep me here.

If I don't find the others and fast, who knows how much trouble I'll be in.

The nurse rolls Julius out of the room.

My heart is racing fast. I don't know what to do.

Another man walks into the room not long afterwards. He's tall with black hair and a straight face.

"You okay?" he asks me.

I nod my head.

He nods his head now. "I'm going to need your mother's number."

"I don't know it. I already gave the nurse her Email."

He just stares at me.

I start to twirl my thumbs.

"You don't have to lie to me," he says. "I know who you are."

"What do you mean?"

He turns his head to look at the door, and then back at me. "Didn't your mother tell you about drages?"

"Drages?"

He sighs. "Humans that help magicians."

I almost fall out of the bed when he says that. Now that I think of it, Emma and Audrey did mention this when I first met them, but I don't think they gave me the name of them. I nod after I get myself situated again. "What did you do to me exactly?"

"I gave you the correct blood. If I didn't kick my nurses out when I did they could have accidently killed you."

I gulp and nod. "Thank you."

"You're welcome," he says with a straight tone. "You have three broken ribs and a concussion. Have you eaten anything with sugar lately?"

"Yes."

"Was it an accident?"

"No, sir."

"That wasn't smart. You have no idea how many magicians I've had to treat for accidentally eating sugar. It gets you guys extremely sick. A little bit will get you dizzy and a headache, but the amount you had in your blood got you on the verge of collapse."

"I know. When will I be able to leave?"

"In a few days with your mother."

That's a problem, for a number of reasons.

***

"So my family brings me all of these movies and TV shows. The hospital even installed a DVD player in here."

"Wow," I tell Julius the next day.

He's been in and out of the hospital since he was seven. Poor kid has had leukemia for over half of his life. The nurses usually room him with kids who they believe will be here awhile. "A young girl with no parents to sign her in, they assumed you'd be here awhile. Sometimes it's not so bad, my family comes by, they bring me more stuff to watch, some stuff to play with, little snacks to eat, as long as the doctors approve of them."

"The longest time I've ever been in the hospital was eight hours," I tell him, "and only because I was having throat problems."

Jake comes in just then to see how we're doing.

"We're good," Julius says.

Page 104

"I'm hungry," I tell him truthfully. I haven't eaten anything since being at Starbucks. Magicians need their calories too after all.

How long ago was that? A day? Two days?

"When was the last time you ate?" Jake asks me.

"What day is it?" I ask.

"I'll bring you both some food," he assures us.

"Anything you allergic to, Greg?"

"Sugar!" I quickly scream a little too loud. I clear my throat and continue, "I'm a vegetarian that can't eat sugary foods."

"I guess steak and ice cream is out of the question then," he says jokingly. "You kids want me to put a movie on?"

"Yes please," Julius pleads.

Jake walks over to Julius's movie pile and selects one,cbut I don't see the cover. He then turns everything on andcputs in the movie. "Be right back," he tells us, "You needcanything else?"

"Another blanket, please," I say.

He smiles then leaves.

"You're a vegetarian?" Julius asks me.

"Yeah," I tell him "A lot of people are surprised by that for some reason. Must be America's obsession with flesh."

Julius starts laughing. He has a very bizarre laugh, but it's definitely better than mine.

***

The next day, a woman comes in to visit Julius. She's sitting on a chair next to his bed, talking to him about some other girl when I wake up.

"Good morning, Greg," Julius says when I'm fully awake. I was never a cheerful person in the morning, but Julius's cheerful mood got me waking up more pleasantly.

My mother used to always make jokes about Ash and Jake transferring their teenage habits into me. "She's rebellious because of you two," and "only teenagers wake up that crabby. I wonder where she got that from?"

"Morning, Julius," I say back, almost forgetting my cover name. I used to say, "what's so good about it?" when my family would greet me in the morning. My philosophy, you don't need the "Good" in front of the

Page 105

morning to greet someone in the morning, they'll be just as cheerful without it.

"My son has told me about you," his mother tells me with a straight face.

"Were they good things?" I ask, rubbing my eyes and trying to be cheery.

"A young lady should not be getting into street fights," she preaches.

"Alright, I'll remember that the next time a defenseless kid is being mugged on the street," I tell her.

"Mommy," Julius calls his mother, shaking her arm, obviously trying to change the conversation. "When is Darrell coming up to visit from college? I haven't seen him in several months."

"Now baby, Darrell said he'd try to fly up before Thanksgiving, but almost every flight is booked for the week."

Julius looks at me and says, "my brother is in Texas for college, he's studying to become a pilot."

"Interesting," I tell him sitting up in the hospital bed. "My dad was a pilot."

"Was?"

"Um, yeah, he was. He's in the air force now," I lie.

He's headless now.

"Cool!"

I force myself to take a deep breath and try to not think of my father.

Saved by the bell, nurse Jake walks in with a bowl of cereal, glass of water, and three pills on a tray and give it to Julius.

"Thank you, Jake," Julius says.

"Your welcome, Julius," Jake said not as happily.

"Isadora, may Doctor Kalis and I speak with you privately?"

"Um, okay," she says uneasily. She gives Julius a tight hug. "Eat as much as you can, Sweetie."

Jake looks at me "You want me to bring you something, Greg?"

"Sure, but you can bring it after your conversation," I assure him.

"Can you put a movie on first, please?" Julius asks.

"Sure thing," the nurse says. He goes to Julius's movie pile and selects one at random. He then leads Julius's mom out of the room.

"Is my little boy recovering, Doctor?" I heard Isadora say when they're in the hallway.

"Not exactly..."

"I love this movie!" I tell Julius, trying not to overhear the conversation outside. "I used to watch the show all the time."

"Me too. My little sister and I used to always watch this together. Sometimes she comes to visit and we watch a whole season together."
"I wish I had time for that."

"No!" I hear Isadora cry. "It can't be only a month!"

"His blood is getting worse by the-"

Just focus on the movie, Bec.

Julius picks up his water and swallows the pills one by one.

"Are you feeling alright?" I ask him.

"A little dizzy and weak actually," he admits to me.

"Are you sure that's all that can be done?" I hear Isadora crying now.

"We're really sorry, we're trying everything we can, we've tried new therapy and medicines, but Julius has about a month left before his leukemia kills him."

What?

I looked at the TV, trying to un-hear what I just heard. I look back at Julius, trying to eat his cereal, and notice his arm shaking. His face is very thin, and his eyes look as if they're losing a bit of focus with every passing second.

***

A week has passed and I am still in the hospital. I haven't found a way out because there are nurses and guards patrolling the halls every night. The doctors have just taken my stitches out, and my wound has healed completely, but there is a faint scar there.

Sweet!

My ribs are healed as well, I felt them snap back into place three days ago, but the doctors still think they are nowhere near fixed, so they haven't bothered with the X rays. I can't say the same for

Julius. He's getting much worse. They inject him with new medicines and chemotherapy and give him different foods. They're trying everything, but it's no good. He has about three weeks left.

I could have healed myself and Julius with my powers a lot sooner, but Julius has a relative with him all the time, mostly his mom, always awake. I was thinking about sneaking off to the restrooms and healing myself. Sadly, the only way you're allowed to go to the restrooms and showers is with an escort, and I can't have them see me using magic. Well, there's the doctor, but I don't know who else knows about me. Tonight's when I make my escape.

I'll think of something to get passed the hall monitors.

I need to find the others. Being just a child in a new dangerous situation, there is no way I can survive on my own. The doctors take my blood pressure every hour or so and are always checking my heart. They also tried emailing my mother again, but nothing. They asked for an address but I said I didn't know it. A lot of kids don't know their information or carry identification, and I'm eleven as far as they know. I'm surprised they haven't suspected anything, but it's only a matter of time before I'm caught.

I'm honestly surprised that I haven't already been caught.

Unless the doctor is doing more than I think.

***

When I'm sure that everyone is asleep, I quietly sneak into the hallway at two in the morning, hoping that no one is watching the security cameras. I can't risk them seeing that my blood isn't human with me still here.

Where should I start?

Well, I should probably get my clothes first.

I sneak to the end of the hall and look around the corner.

I don't see anyone, so I walk down that hall. I peek into all the rooms, but most are just offices. On my seventh door, I see a bunch of lockers, so I decide to go inside.

Thankfully the door isn't locked, but sadly, all the lockers are.

I use my telekinesis and unlock the first locker I see. Inside, are a pair of black basketball shorts, and a dark blue T-shirt.

I check the hall again to make sure that no one is there.

When I see the hall is clear, I change out of the hospital gown and into the clothes. Thankfully, I still have my underwear on. I'm too young for bras, so I was never wearing one in the first place, although Emma has gotten me some training bras a little too large for me.

Emma.

Hopefully I'll find her soon.

In the hall, I see a cart that visitors eat crackers and drink coffee at. I take a handful of honey maid crackers and Smuckers peanut butter. I put the crackers and peanut butter into the pockets I'm so thankful the shorts have. I haven't eaten in a while, so I break open a package of crackers and open a thing of peanut butter, and munch it quickly, looking over my shoulder every two seconds in case someone might walk by.

I'm ready to leave, but I suddenly feel my mouth is so dry and I get really thirsty, so I go to the water fountain.

Luckily there is one in this hallway. When I'm done drinking, I realize that I have to pee.

Will I ever leave!

I quietly make my way towards the restrooms. As I'm walking, I hear footsteps and I open a door and run into a patient's room. As the man walks by, I realize that it's a security guard. I really have to be careful! When he's gone and I come out of the room, I realize that I still have an IV in my arm.

Fuck!

***

I wash my hands with the water, running it very slowly to not alert anyone. It's taking forever to get the soap off, but I'd rather be safe than sorry. The air vents get stronger and I am standing right underneath them. Would it kill them to raise the temperature just a little? When I went to reach for the paper towels, a slight movement behind me catches my eye. I look in the mirror to double check, but I see nothing behind me. I stand still for about a minute.

Quit being so paranoid, Bec!

I walk over and pull the lever slowly a few times to give me a foot-long paper towel. As I'm drying my hands, I hear a small thump and the big bathroom stall slightly opens. I freeze. With my hands still half wet, I turn around as quickly and quietly as I can. The stalls are next to the sinks, so I turn my head to look over, but I don't see anything out of the ordinary.

"Julius," I whisper. "Is that you?" Then I remember that I'm in the girl's bathroom, and most of the late workers are guys. Why would I whisper for Julius?

Get ahold of yourself!

I turn around towards the sinks and throw the paper towel away after I finish drying my hands. One of the lights starts to flicker. It's just an electrical problem, I tell myself, but then they start to blow out one by one. Before the last light goes out, I notice something odd. There was never an air vent above me!

Right before the last light fully goes out, I focus all my energy to light a fire in my hand. Only a few sparks are lit.

Come on, please! Audrey makes it look so easy!

After about ten seconds of being in pitch blackness, a small red flame is in my hands. It's not enough to light up the whole bathroom as it only illuminates the area three feet around me. I smile proudly to myself.

I finally did it!

I turn around to race out of the bathroom, but when I turn to face the door, there is a red, slimy figure right in front of me. Before I could scream in surprise, it grabs me by the throat. I realize this thing was red and slimy because it was covered in blood and puss. It doesn't have a face, but it has one green eye and one blue eye full of hate that was staring into my eyes like daggers. It's shaped like a human being, only it isn't. Is this a demon following me? I try to break free, but the thing grabs me tighter, cutting off my oxygen, and lifts me in the air.

With a hole in the middle of its face for a mouth, this thing spoke to me.

"Hello, sissy," is all it utters mockingly with a wide grin.

I use all of my strength and headbutt the bloody female as hard as I can. Then I use my teeth on its neck and bite down as hard as I can. The thing throws me hard on the floor, and I land on my arm.
Page 110

When I stand up in a fighting stance, the bloody woman is gone, and the lights are back on. The only sign of what happened was that someone else's blood is on my throat, on my hands, and in my mouth. The only thing it said to me is playing over and over between my ears, and I was just standing there listening to it.

"Hello sissy."

I'm not a sissy!

Chapter 16

Without thinking, I rush back to my room. Once inside, I stand by the door to catch my breath.

Why did I come back here?

Great! Now I have to start all over!

I grab the blanket on my bed and wipe the blood off. When I'm done cleaning myself, I notice a little green splotch on the blanket.

Green?

I remove the tape from my IV and slowly pull it out.

Fuckfuckfuckfuckfuckfuckfuck!

I grab a clean part of the blanket and apply pressure.

Julius is fast asleep, his heart monitor beeping very slowly. I watch him sleep for a while, knowing he doesn't have much longer to live. His mother is asleep on a chair next to him. I wish there was something I can do. I drop the blanket back on my bed, walk up to his bed and place my hands over his heart. I feel its slow beat, pumping sick blood through his body. I can smell the disease in him.

Now, concentrate on your nose getting better. Let the energy build until it has nowhere to go but out your fingers.

I smile to myself, focus all my energy into healing him.

At first nothing happens and I start to panic a little. I take a deep breath and try again.

There's an icy feeling emitting from my hands, and I can slowly feel the cancer in his blood dying. I can feel his white blood cells improving, defeating all the maladies.

With every second I'm healing him, his breathing is picking up, and his heart rate is returning back to normal.

It takes me five minutes until he's healed completely.

I just cured a cancer patient! I've never done anything like this with my magic before!

"Have a great life, Julius," I whisper with a smile.

I feel around my shorts to make sure I still have the crackers and peanut butter. I have them, and they were surprisingly undamaged. I start walking towards the door, but then I hear someone.

"Gregory?" it was his mom! She sounds bewildered and surprised! How long was she awake? How much did she see? "Did you just-" but I start running down the hall towards the exit before she could finish that obvious sentence.

Yes, Isadora. I just saved your little boy.

***

I couldn't find any emergency exits so I had to break the lobby's glass door with my fists. The receptionist started screaming when the alarm was sounded. I didn't want to hurt her or anyone else, so I just ran out of the hospital through the sliding doors that thankfully weren't locked.

Once I was out of the hospital, I ran a mile a minute in no obvious direction. I could be running towards the Statue of Liberty, or I could be running to New Jersey or Canada.

I have no idea where I am going. All I know is that I have to find the others.

Do they think I'm dead?

I slow down to catch my breath and find a street sign.

When you're tired, everything in this city looks the same. I don't see any signs nearby, but I hope that I'm not too far off track. Where do I go from here? I look down at my hands and see that they're all cut up from when I broke the glass.

I cup my hands together and heal them, the icy aura it gives off gives me the shivers.

Wait, I can just follow the North Star. Why didn't I think of this earlier?

Page 113

I look up at the sky, but don't see any stars. Damn city lights. I try looking around hoping that I'd find something familiar. I stick my tongue out to see if that would guide me, but I put it back in my mouth and tell myself that I am just being silly.

Focus, Bec! Think!

I don't even know how to find the North Star, so why did I think of that? Should I try and listen for something familiar? I try really hard to listen in every direction, but all I hear is sleeping humans, and cars.

Something hits my leg. I look down and see a wadded up sheet of paper. I study it skeptically and don't pick it up until I've pulled away from it three times with it following me and poked it. I unravel it and see a tourist map of New York City. It's a complicated map, or maybe it's complicated to me because I never learned how to read one.

I turn it around several times to try and make sense of it. The first thing I see is the section of Broadway.

Wait, Broadway? Isn't Broadway in Manhattan? And the Statue of Liberty is in Manhattan! Well, it's on the water near Manhattan, but I could probably find the empire state building from there and find a proper tour guide map. At least I have some kind of lead.

"Give my regards to old Broadway and say that I'll be there-ere long!" I sing.

***

Broadway is not very active at this time of night, not really teeming with performers and theater lovers. When I was really young, I had a dream of singing on Broadway, but I guess Magicians are too busy saving the world to become famous performers. Now that I make it to Broadway, I start questioning why I didn't just look for a better map where I was? It could have been a lot faster.

Too late now!

I don't really hear or see anything familiar. All I see is posters for the Lion King performance.

Oh how I loved that movie, and all the songs. I never did have the chance to see the Broadway show before, but I have to find the others first. Maybe I'll find them tonight and have Darren, Audrey, and

JP come and see it with me tomorrow. It's showing until the end of the week.

I should find them fast; the wind is picking up. I'm really cold, and I don't even have a jacket. I should have tried to-

I notice that all the wind is blowing in one direction, towards the front of the theater.

Shit!

I knew there was a reason I came to Broadway, but can't I ever get a break?

Maybe I can close the portal before it opens! How would I do that? What if I shoot a magic gas into the portal, or throw a rock? What if I blow the wind in the opposite direction? That sounds too simple, but so do math problems that seem hard at first but turn out easy.

I don't even know how to do wind magic. Then again, I didn't know how to slow down time before my last fight. I just extend my arms with my hands up, and focus on the wind, and flick my wrists so my hands point down.

Slow.

The wind tremendously slows down. I start to smile, but I refuse to celebrate half way through the job.

Think Bec, what else can I do?

I walk over to where the wind is meeting, hoping an idea will pop into my head. I need to reverse the energy to send it outward. How will I be able to do that? I start to absorb the energy without even think-ing.

How am I doing this?

It hurts! Ow, this was a bad idea, but I'm going somewhere with this, can't back out now.

Think, Bec! Redirect it. How?

Damn! I can't think!

Deonna's bickering and insults come into my head. I remember Audrey, JP and Frederick who taught me so much in just a single night. I think of Darren, the way he's so loving to me, how he seems so very gentle.

"No!" I scream, and fall to the floor in exhaustion.

Great, I screwed up. The wind will blow again and dozens of demons will pour out and kill me.

Page 115

I suddenly feel nothing. I slowly stand up and look around so see the humans carrying on as normal, except a few who glance at me sideways. Not out of fear, but out of curiosity. They think I'm some kind of street performer, and that's when it hits me. I closed it! I start to laugh, but my victory is bittersweet because one of the demons escaped.

It looks taller than the others I've seen, and it is the color of milk. Its bloodthirsty red eyes look right at me.

How do the humans not see this?

Wait, they do!

A few humans look at the demon, but in wonder, not fear. They think it's a costume! How naive can they be?

Humans...Broadway... right!

It raises its head, and sniffs to its right. I look left and see a man charging the demon. Right before the demon can pounce, another man pounces from above and snaps the demon's neck. Before I can blink twice, it's dead.

A lot of humans cheer on the sides, and I'm the only one running towards the two men. They recognize me before I recognize them.

"Bec!" one of the men screams and appears in front of me and wraps me in a hug before I can blink.

I hug him back. "You have no idea how good it is to see you, Frederick!"

John walks up to us and gives me a hug. "What happened to you, hun? Last we've heard you flew off on a demon and disappeared."

"It's a long story, and I'll be glad to tell it as soon as we find the others."

"But first we have to find the other demons," John tells me.

"What other demons?" I ask.

Frederick puts his hands on my shoulders. "I know you've had a rough several weeks while you were gone, but a portal has opened and we only caught one demon. We have to kill the others, before we can get you back." He looks around. "Where are they?"

"There are no others," I explain. "I saw the portal about to open, so I closed it, but only the one demon got out." I gesture to the dead demon body.

The brothers look at me with mouths agape.

"What?" I ask, feeling suddenly uncomfortable.

"That's...not possible." Frederick utters in a hushed tone.

"Sure it is," I tell him. "I just reversed the winds and unleashed my anger. I think. It wasn't hard. Just took some imagination and concentration."

"You can tell us the rest of your story later," John says "What you've done just now is the real story, and could turn the tides of this war!"

Chapter 17

"Bec!" Audrey is the first to engulf me in a bear hug after John and Frederick take me back to the Statue of Liberty. All the others are there waiting for them, so they were really surprised to see me. Frederick decided the three of us should wait for everyone to return.

I'm glad he did.

I hug Audrey back; I've missed her.

JP isn't too far behind, he turns it into a group hug, I try to put my arm around him but Audrey has my arms pinned to her.

"Little girl needs to breathe!" I shout playfully, and they let go. I give them both a small hug.

Darren slowly approaches me, but he doesn't hug me. He just stares at me like I am a ghost. "Bec?"

"Hey, you," I say with a smile. "Long time no see."

He hesitantly puts his hand on my shoulder, and jumps away.

I laugh a bit at him. "Dude, you're such a spaz," I say and pull him into a hug that lasts as long as my hug with Audrey and JP did.

We separate slightly and smile at each other, that's when I notice he's wearing my black and white fedora. He takes it off and puts it on my head. "I believe this is yours."

I smile at him, fixing the hat so it rests better on my head.

Deonna pulls her brother off of me and gives me a hateful look. "You're supposed to be dead. What happened?"

"I see you're still a little ray of sunshine," I tell her sarcastically.

"Alright you two," Emma says, getting in between us.

She looks at me and puts her hand under my chin. She lifts my face so our eyes can meet. I can tell she's glad I'm alive.

"I knew you were strong," Emma says after a while. She pulls me into a hug and asks me where I've been.

Emma guides me to the couch. I sit on the arm, but she tells me to get off. I slide down on the couch and she sits next to me. Audrey leans over so she can be closer to me, and JP comes to my other side. John and Frederick go to the table and suggest making dinner since I already gave them a small recap. I remind them I'm a vegetarian and they say that they remember. The twins sit on the other chair. Deonna slouches like she's bored, but Darren stares at me like he's dying to hear the story.

I tell them about how me, Audrey, JP, and Darren snuck out to hang out at Starbucks. I said what I ate and Emma said that was a dumb move.

"So I have a bad sweet tooth, cut me some slack!"

"It almost got you killed!"

"And now I know I need to work on that!"

I continue my story of how I got sick right before the portal opened and killing the demon in the water before being separated from them. I didn't say how I killed the demon because I didn't want to tattle on Frederick. I tell them how I went to the hospital after the street fight to save Chris, and healing Julius, but not about my encounter in the bathroom or what happened in the alley with the time slowing down. I don't know why I don't tell them that. It feels almost like it didn't happen at all to be honest.

"You can heal?" Darren asks in amazement. "I can't even do that yet!"

He seems to give me a different look and smiles.

"What?" I ask him.

"Just glad you're okay," he says.

I tell them how I got to Broadway, how I closed the portal and about John and Frederick finding me.

"That's impossible!" Deonna says, getting interested when I mention the portal in Broadway, considering they were all trying to locate it. "No one's ever been able to close a portal on their own before. Why would a half be able to do what a full couldn't?"

Page 119

I'm silent for a little bit. I won't admit it, but what she says makes sense.

"How'd you do it?" Darren asks me.

"Well, I reversed the wind, or slowed it down more likely. I went with my instincts to stand in the middle and reverse the energy. Then, presto, portal closed. It sort of just happened."

"But..." Darren was lost for words, so was everyone else. "How'd you do it? What'd you do?"

I hear Frederick setting the table and John bringing in the food. Macaroni, mixed vegetables, and meatloaf. I'll stick with the pasta and veggies.

"That should have taken a great deal of magic," John announces. "Four fulls once closed a portal, but that was only once and it was a weak portal in Australia."

"I just...used my emotions I guess," I tell them. "I only remember what I did, but I don't remember casting a spell or using great sums of magic. I was just thinking and, poof, it's closed."

"That's amazing!" JP tells me.

"Amazing indeed," Emma agrees, "but impossible."

***

A month has passed since I closed the portal. According to Frederick, there haven't been any openings, so I've mostly been training. Emma has been stepping up my physical fighting, and she's also been strengthening my magical training.

"I won't underestimate you anymore," she told me.

I honestly didn't notice she did.

I wonder if I'm a time magician who can dabble in other forms of magic since I'm able to slow down time and heal, but I don't say anything about it to anyone. I want to learn as much as possible before I'm classified. Instead, I sneak it into training to get a boost. After a few days, I realized that I can't do it too much or else I get really dizzy and sick like with the frappe.

"Do you know any time magicians, Emma?" I ask her one day.

"No one in my family and I have never met one, but I did hear about this one time magician who died four years ago, and I have a friend who's a mental magician who studied time magic, but none I have ever met."

"What, are they rare or something?"

"Extremely."

Considering how rare they are it's going to be hard to find a teacher. I haven't learned how to use my time magic to help out yet. Although I did teach myself to age cheese in three seconds. How can time magic help me kill a demon?

I guess I'll find out in the next fight.

"I already have healing tricks, so how is it that I can also do minor elemental magic?" I ask her in another training session after I created a plasma bolt.

"Some Magicians can do magic outside their section. It's rare, but not impossible."

This catches my attention. It's scaring my a little too. I can heal, make fire in my hand, and do time magic. That's already magic from three categories. I decide to ask someone else to get some more information.

***

"Not all magic is used for fighting," Darren tells me one night while we are helping Frederick make dinner.

"You don't have to tell me twice," I say, remembering the cheese. "But say hypothetically, you can make fire and control wind, but you can also slow down time, and heal. What kind of Magician would you be?"

"Overpowered," he says, not batting an eye.

"Alright, how about just fire and healing?"

"Mixed."

"But Emma told me it's rare to be mixed."

"Not as rare as she makes it to be," he grins.

"Audrey and JP also once told me-"

"I love my cousins," he interrupts me, "but they are very young and don't know much about our ways, or human ways."

"They don't get out much," Frederick agrees, taking the salmon out of the oven, "and I prefer it that way."

Page 121

"But they need to explore." I tell Frederick, defending them. "They never had real adrenaline pumping through them before we met, and Audrey is older than me. They can't spend most of their lives training. They didn't even know what bowling was when I first met them!"

"It's a good thing they do," Frederick, says turning around to face me. "If they didn't, then they would not have been prepared for the fight when you had them sneak out."

That actually pinched a nerve a little. Although he is right, I could have gotten them killed. They take me in, and I endanger them.

"You're right, and I'm sorry, but if I didn't sneak them out, then we would not have known about the opening," I remind him. "So at least something good came out of it, right?"

Frederick turns around and faces the salmon, using the spatula to lift it slightly. "I just can't lose him," Frederick says. It almost sounds like he's close to tears. "Not after losing my daughter." His voice starts to crack, "I never even got to bury her."

Now I pinched a nerve! I forgot JP had a sister. What was her name. Ramon? I don't remember. I didn't realize that JP's sister would have been his daughter too.

"I'm sorry," I start "I-"

"No," he whispers, "I'm sorry. Emma and I are just being over-protective."

I see his knuckles starting to turn red. He's gripping the spatula really hard.

"It's not your fault, Frederick," I tell him. "You're the one who's right. I was the one who..."

"I need to be alone," he says, quickly and quietly. I almost don't hear him.

"Come on," Darren says, grabbing my shoulder gently. We leave the kitchen and he leads me past the living room where Deonna is dusting, and into the cave where Audrey and JP are playing racket ball with a yellow fireball against the door.

"Whoa!" Darren and I scream and duck to avoid getting hit.

"Sorry!" they shout simultaneously.

"See you guys are having a bit of fun," I notice.

"Yeah," Audrey tells me, "We decided to take your advice and loosen up a bit. If my mom asks though, we're still training."

Page 122

"Technically you are, but we really should be more careful. I realize that now."

"You okay, Bec?" JP asks me.

"Not really," I admit. "I think I just made your dad cry."

"Did you make him think of Raven?" he asks.

Raven!

That was her name.

"Yeah. Hey, you guys want to go for a walk?" I ask, "Walks usually calm me down."

"Remember what happened last time the four of us went out?" Audrey asks.

"That won't happen again," I say defensively. "Plus, we're not sneaking out this time. We'll tell the others. I'm sorry about last time."

"It's okay, but if we do," Darren says, "we should put on some jackets, it's been really cold out lately."

"Already?" I ask. "That means...it's already November!"

"Losing track of the days?" Audrey asks in a giggle.

"Apparently," I say with wide eyes. "Aw man! I missed Halloween! I was going to take you guys trick or treating!"

Halloween was always my favorite holiday. Monsters, candy, and creepy stuff, totally my thing! My best friend John used to say that I was in my element every time Halloween rolled around. We would always get huge bags filled with candy that would last us for months. I always gave half of it to him though because I always got sick and vomited eating it.

How I missed those days.

Didn't miss the vomiting though.

"We can't eat candy," Darren says.

"Who says we were gonna eat it?" I laugh. "Do you know what day it is?" I ask.

"It's the third," Darren says.

My jaw drops and I stare at him. He starts to shift from foot to foot uncomfortably. He even doesn't meet my gaze.

"Did you say the third?" I ask him.

"Yeah..." he says, slowly meeting my gaze.

"What's so special about three?" JP asks me.

"It's not the number that's special," I say. "It's the day. What time is it?"

Audrey looks at her watch, "Ten fifty-seven pm."

"What's so special about today?" JP asks again.

"Today...in exactly one minute... I will be thirteen," I tell them. "You mean..."

"Today's my birthday," I announce. "I didn't even notice! Wow! I really am training hard!"

"Really?" JP asks.

"Yeah," I tell him. "Do magicians do anything special on their birthdays?"

"Not exactly," Audrey says.

I hear the door open and close behind me. I turn around and see that Darren has left.

"What do you mean, not exactly?" I ask her.

"It's just that we have so many responsibilities," Audrey explains, "We just don't see any point in celebrating them."

"Which is why you need to celebrate something good when it comes along!"

I'm very bummed to hear that. When I was living as a human, my thirteenth birthday was supposed to be one of the biggest days of my life, right next to my high school graduation and my eighteenth birthday.

I hear the door open and close behind me again.

"Audrey," I hear Darren say, "can you please light this?"

I turn around and see him holding a thin white candle. Three seconds later, the wick has a red flame lit.

"Just because we don't celebrate our birthdays doesn't mean you still can't blow out your own candle."

"Wow," I whisper, getting close to the candle flame. I smile at him and put my hands over his hands, holding the candle. "Thank you."

I close my eyes and make my birthday wish.

I wish to be happy with the magicians!

Then I blow out my birthday candle.

Chapter 18

Now that winter is here, I spend most of my time outside. Winter has always been my favorite season. The lights, the cold, the holidays, the happiness of everyone around me. It never got really cold in Florida, but I loved visiting my grandparents in the winter back when they were alive, with the snow, and the dying trees.

I don't know why, but I'm much happier this time of year. I'm a bit sad that this is my first winter without my family, but I try to not let that put a damper on things.

Still, they'll never see another winter again.

I cry to myself some nights at the thought of never celebrating Hanukkah with them ever again.

During the day, I would take Audrey and JP to Central Park and we would build snowmen, make snow angels, and have snowball fights. I didn't know if it is allowed or not, so we tried to stay out of sight, but we still had a blast.

The only thing I don't like about winter are the holiday songs.

God how I hate Christmas carols!

The worst part is that they're blasted everywhere!

Growing up, my dad would blast some Hanukkah music and a ton of Christmas music all over the house. It would drive us mad. My mother and sister would always yell at him to turn the music down, but he would just turn it up louder.

The only song I like is Silent Night.

I don't know why, but it's the only Christmas song that doesn't make me plug up my ears.

Hanukkah music never really plays, and when it does, it's about a dreidel. News flash! Not all dreidels are made out of clay!

Now I'd give anything and more to hear my father blast Oh Holy Night one more time!

I'm standing at the top of the Statue of Liberty looking out into the city. This is the busiest I've ever seen it.

I remember opening presents with my family on Hanukkah. One small present a day and the big one on the last night.

We would also leave cookies out for Santa, but being half Jewish, I always knew that there wasn't a Santa. Jake and I would plan to eat the cookies every year before our father could.

I remember the feasts, the lights my parents would hang, the desserts I'd help my mother bake.

I start to feel sad again, so I sing Silent Night quietly to myself to cheer me up. I sing the second verse more loudly, my alto voice filling up the area. I start the third verse, but then realize I forgot the words.

Great! The only Christmas song I like and I forget the words!

I smile to myself and shake my head, and sing the third verse on "ooh."

"Wow."

I jump, very startled, and turn around to see Darren gaping at me.

"God dammit! Don't sneak up on me like that!"

I really have to be more alert. Everyone is sneaking up on me! To think I should be used to this by now.

"I'm sorry..." he gazes at me like I'm some kind of treasure. "Wow."

"What?" I ask calming down a lot.

"You have such a beautiful voice," he tells me in a hushed tone. Beautiful?

My voice has never been called beautiful before. Pretty, I've been told countless times. Nice I've been told more than pretty. Beautiful? This is the first time I heard anyone say that!

"Thanks," I tell him, trying to hide my confusion. I look out into the city again.

"Sure is beautiful tonight," he says, standing next to me.

There's that word again.

Beautiful.

"How come you don't sing more often?" he asks me.

"I just don't have the time anymore," I admit. "I used to sing all the time, I was even in choir."

"Really?" he asks amazed.

"Yeah," I tell him. "I even had a solo at the holiday concert. Rudolf the Red Nose Reindeer."

"You did? That's amazing! The whole song?"

"Yeah," I tell him. "I wanted Silent Night though, but that song was given to a soprano, but hey, a solo's a solo."

"Can you sing your solo?" he asks me.

I think for a moment. "Sure," I tell him, "but you owe me a solid."

"A what?" he asks laughing.

"A favor," I translate.

"Deal," he smiles.

I smile back, and I sing my solo for him.

***

"Perfect!" Emma tells me.

I hunch over and catch my breath.

"Twelve seconds!" Frederick shouts from the other side of the island.

Turns out, I can do a lot more when I slow down time.

Just now, I slowed down time and made it from one side of the island to the other! I can also heal while time is slowed down, which has increased my healing time tremendously.

"Whoo!" I shout and throw my arms up. "I'm getting better at this!"

"Perfect technique," Frederick says, coming and standing next to his sister, "but how well can you use it, Bec?"

"Why don't you come and find out?" I say as they both charge me. The fight didn't last long, Emma had me pinned down in two seconds.

"Are you teleporting or something?" I ask.

"You know, we can teleport short distances too," she informs me.

Page 127

"And by we you mean..." I ask while she helps me up.

"Me," she states.

"Ah," I say.

"You have to get faster at defending yourself," Emma lectures me. "It can mean life or death. Techniques are good, spells are important, but no matter how good your offensive is, if you can't defend yourself then the fight is over."

"I know."

"I'm serious, Bec." she says.

"I know, and we'll work more on it for the next training lesson. I promise, but that's enough training for the day," I state, walking toward the door.

"Not yet it's not, young lady," Emma snaps at me.

"But I have a thing," I tell her.

"What are you planning?" Frederick asks me.

"You'll see," I smirk.

***

Earlier in the week I had Darren teleport me into the city so I can buy some things, fulfilling the solid he owed me. I didn't tell in what I bought though, or what they were for.

I set the table with a variety of breads, cheeses, and fruits. Not much of a feast, considering what I'm used to this time of year, but it'll do.

I grab the Shamash and light the wick with a match, then I levitate it and light the first candle on the menorah. I have been doing a lot of practicing with telekinesis, and I have been improving immensely. I then place it back in the holder. I turn to get some refrigerated white wine, but I see Darren standing in the doorway.

"How long have you been watching me?" I ask, a bit uncomfortable.

"Long enough to discover that you can levitate objects and set a table."

We stare at each other for a moment, and then he asks, "What's the dinner for?"

"Tonight is the first night of Hanukkah," I explain to him. "It's usually celebrated with lighting the menorah," I gesture to the menorah on the table, "having a dinner and opening presents, but I have no presents this year."

"I'm guessing this is what you wanted me to teleport you into the city to get," he says, walking towards me.

"Uh, yeah."

"Why are only two candles lit?"

"Because it's the first night, so only the first one is lit."

"But there are two?"

"The Shamash is always lit."

"The what?" I turn around and see Audrey walking in while giving JP a piggyback ride.

"Sit down!" I tell them happily. "Tonight's the first night of Hanukkah and we are going to eat!"

"The four of us?" JP asks.

"No," I tell him smiling way too hard. "All of us. go get everyone else."

"But I thought you wanted us to sit?" JP asks confused.

I laugh and grab my waist. "Get the others first, then we shall feast!"

Within ten minutes, everyone was sitting at the table.

They look at the food, which wasn't much of a feast, and stare at the menorah.

"Why are we here?" Deonna asks suddenly.

Of course it'd be her!

"Because tonight's the first night of Hanukkah."

"Why are only two candles lit?" Frederick asks.

"Because it's the first night," I explain.

"But there are two lit," Emma says.

"That's what I said!" Darren laughs.

"Tonight we celebrate!" I exclaim.

"How?" John asks.

I just remember Emma telling me that Magicians don't have a religion, so of course they don't know how Hanukkah works.

"Well, I already lit the menorah," I tell them. "Now we join hands." When we all join hands, I start reciting a prayer that my mother used to always say. After we pray, I tell them we can eat.

"How does the red fruit taste?" Audrey asks me, sitting down next to me.

"You never had watermelon before?"

"Nope," she answers. "Strawberries, yes, but never watermelon."

JP, who is sitting next to Audrey, took a few watermelons from her. "So much water!"

"Well," Darren says next to me, "this is a nice little dinner. Just don't eat too much of the fruit." I thought he was being serious, but he winks at me and I playfully shove him.

"We appreciate you doing this for us," Emma starts.

"But why do it?" Deonna finishes.

"I just thought it'd be something fun and new for you guys since you don't really have holidays." I explain.

"Are we going to do this every year?" JP asks.

I pause to think.

"I'm not sure," I admit. "I haven't thought that far ahead."

I turn to grab some grapes, but I notice Deonna sitting next to JP and John giving me a dagger stare. Emma who is next to John tells her quietly to not be rude. Frederick sits between Darren and Emma and asks me to pass him a few strawberries.

I remember Hanukkah with my family. We would always separate the kids from the adults, and every night a different kid would light the menorah, but an adult always lit the Shamash. The kids would sometimes have a food fight, but usually on the fourth night. On the eighth day, we would always have a big cake. We always had left overs and gave some to my friend John and his family. Sometimes he would join our family. Opening presents during dessert was always the best part. They were small gifts on the first seven days. The way I saw it, small desserts meant small presents, a big dessert meant the big present.

The bigger the dessert though, the bigger my headache that night was.

Even though we can't eat dessert, I can picture us having that big cake I would bring out on the last night. I can picture Audrey scarfing the cake down and JP licking his plate clean. I can see Deonna not being a bitch and laughing with the rest of the kids. I can see the three adults trying to be civil with their cake, but Frederick would use magic to throw cake his two sibling's faces. I can picture myself putting frosting on Darren's nose and giggling as he tries to lick it off and floats my slice of cake away.

Wait, what? I don't giggle.

I notice that I've been blindly eating fruits and vegan gouda cheese. I grab a piece of French bread and I feel full when I finish the slice.

"So, what did you and your family do on Hanukkah?" John asks me.

I smile wide and I tell them my old holiday traditions. I even gave them a little history of how Hanukkah became a big holiday for Jews.

"That sounds very exciting," Emma tells me. "What other holidays did you celebrate?"

Well," I start happily, "my favorite was Halloween, which I sadly missed this year. It was the one night a year where tricksters and freaks like me can show their true colors without repercussions. It was originally the Wiccan New Year and the Festival of the Dead, but it was adopted and altered to be a holiday of monsters and fright. I went trick or treating every year with my friends and brother Jake. We would always bring back so much candy, it lasted for months! I always had a splitting headache so I never ate a lot. When no one was looking, my best friend John and I always messed around with the neighbor's decorations!"

"Why would you do that?" Audrey asks, getting into the story.

I give her a look and say, "I thought you'd know me by now."

"Sorry," she says. "What else would you do?"

"Well," I continue, "every year on the Saturday before Halloween, my mother would throw this huge Halloween party. There were musical chairs, a skeleton piñata, blood punch, not real blood by the way, and my personal favorite, bobbing for apples."

"Sound like a blast!" JP says.

Page 131

"It was," I say, grabbing an apple, trying not to cry.

Wait, I'm full. I take a bite of the apple anyways.

"How do you go bobbing for apples?" JP asks me.

I drop my jaw and laugh. "Well, you fill a large bucket of water, put apples in, and try and get one in your mouth."

"Sounds hard," Darren states.

"Not for me," I smile proudly. "I was the bobbing champion!"

"Did you cheat?" Audrey asks.

I laugh hard uncontrollably and nod my head. "The trick is to bring the apple to the side of the bucket and use the wall to sink your teeth in. I always got soaked, but it was so worth it!"

"What other holidays did you celebrate?" John asks.

"There was New Year's when humans all over the world would light up the night sky with fireworks every hour. There was Thanksgiving when the Americans have a feast-"

"Similar to this one?" Audrey interrupts.

"Yes, but with different food, and only one day," I tell her.

"Like what?" she asks.

"Turkey, mashed potatoes, cranberries, string bean casserole, garlic bread, well, only my family had garlic bread," I explain, "Garlic was my favorite food so my mom tried including it at every holiday. Thanksgiving has an extremely dark backstory, but we celebrate what were thankful for."

"At least it's not on the table tonight," Deonna says.

"It will be tomorrow," I laugh. "What do you guys usually do?"

"Nothing really," Emma admits.

"That's... sad."

"We don't really celebrate anything," Frederick says. "It's just not our way. Although we do go out on lunar and
solar eclipses."

I perk up a bit. "Tell me about that!"

"Well," he starts, "every lunar eclipse, magicians stay up all morning for it to start. We would have mass get togethers with food and music. On solar eclipses we stay indoors, but do the same thing."

"There you go!" I shout, standing out of my seat. "That's celebrating!"

"But it's not a holiday," John informs me, "It's a mini..."

"It's a goddamn celebration!" I tell him. "Holiday or not! I knew magician kind couldn't be totally in the dark!"

They all groan.

"What?" I ask. Then I realize. "Pun not intended!"

"Well, think about it," Darren says in an ax tone. "Do stage magicians ever perform during the day?"

I think for a moment. "Michael Carbonaro."

"He's a half."

"Get out of here!"

"Seriously. A lot of our people become stage magicians. Why do you think most of those performances are at night?"

"Then explain kids parties."

"Wannabees," John adds.

As the dinner went on, we were just talking about random things, with me starting most of the conversations. Deonna even joined in and asked what we'd think would happen if a vampire, zombie, and werewolf bit a human at the same time.

"Werewolves exist!?" I ask.

"No." She laughs calmly.

I didn't even know Deonna could laugh!

After we finish the food, the others, including Deonna thank me for the dinner and leave me and Audrey to clean the table. Tomorrow two other people are clearing the table.

Sunrise came about two hours ago. I guess everyone was enjoying themselves too much to notice the time go by. I didn't notice much because I was stuck in my fantasy, then got caught up in pleasant conversation.

Audrey gives me a skeptical look. "Is there something you're not telling me?"

I give her a look of confusion. "Um, no."

"So you're not going to tell me what was going through your mind?" she winks at me and gestures for me to spill.

Spill what?

"I was just remembering Hanukkah with my human family," I tell her. "I also tried picturing all of us doing similar stuff. Is that what you wanted me to spill?"

She gives me a fierce look, and I know that's not what she wanted to hear. She lowers her voice. "Why didn't you tell me about you and Darren?"

I don't know what she was saying. "Is there something going on with us or something?"

"I saw you giving him looks," she utters in a singsong voice.

"Deonna and your mom give me looks."

That got her quiet for a second. "Do you like him?"

"Of course, he's a good friend and he helped me out a lot. I like him a lot more than his sister, if that's what you're saying."

"Not like that," she says giving me a look, and I knew exactly what she was talking about.

"No. Impossible. Not happening!"

She winks at me and puts the rest of the bread in the cupboard.

"He's just my friend," I tell her. "My cousin now, technically since I'm a part of the family."

"We'll see about that," she smirks.

"I don't have a thing for him," I admit. "I don't even know how to have a thing for somebody."

"Aw," she giggles. "Your first crush! A little weird considering you're thirteen and he's twenty-one-"

"He's twenty-one!" I nearly scream.

She smirks at me again.

I shake my head and say, "I don't have a crush on Darren. Besides, even if I did, he's too old for me, and he's my cousin. You'll feel better once you get your head out of the clouds."

"You'll feel better once you finish cleaning the kitchen," she smiles, and then walks out on me.

Bitch!

I love her, but she's a bitch right now.

Chapter 19

"You never struck me as a Jew," Darren tells me.

He and I were in the kitchen, and Deonna is clearing the table. I was washing the dishes while he was putting away the last of the food. We just finished the last dinner for Hanukkah.

I dry my hands on the towel and pull my necklace out from under my shirt. "You've never seen this before?"

He comes closer to me and stares at the necklace for a few moments. "Can't say I have. Do you always wear it?"

I clutch my necklace, remembering the day I got it. "I never take it off," I whisper while putting it back under my shirt.

"Hey, Bec," he asks. "What's your real name?"

"Rebecca, stupid!" I playfully shout and give him a gentle punch in the shoulder.

"No!" he laughs, "Wait, your last name's stupid?" It's his turn to playfully shove me in the shoulder.

"It's Proenza. Rebecca Proenza."

He takes in my name and thinks. He looks like he's processing something. "That doesn't sound Jewish."

I hear Deonna come in and set some plates next to the sink. I turn around and see her giving me a death stare.

What's her deal!?

"It's not Jewish," I say, watching her walk out of the kitchen. "My mom was Jewish. My dad wasn't. Your name is Paris, right?"

"My mom was Paris," he explains. "My dad was Dean, and Deonna and I took his name."

"Aw!" I say, "That's so cute, Darren Bean."

He starts laughing really hard for a while. After about thirty seconds, he calms down.

Weird.

"I so needed that!" he laughs. "No, not Bean, Dean, with a D."

"Oh," I say embarrassed.

"So you're only half Jewish?" he says, thinking it through.

"Yeah, but the four of us considered ourselves Jewish.

Most religions consider the mother's religion to be the main one."

"The four of us? I thought you only had a sister?"

"I also had two brothers," I tell him while continuing the dishes. "It was my brother Tom, then my sister Ash, then it was my brother Jake, then it was me."

"So you're the baby," he says smiling, then he frowns. "You okay?"

"Yeah," I tell him wiping my eyes with my jacket sleeve. "I just get a little emotional when I think of my family. You'd think I'd be over it by now after six months, but it still hurts sometimes."

I go back to doing the dishes, but he stops me by gently putting his hand on mine.

I look up at him and we lock eyes for a while. He doesn't say anything or smile, he just stares at me.

"I also get emotional when I think of my parents, but after a few years things get better and it won't hurt so much anymore."

I put my hand on top of his. "How'd they die?"

He looked away and clenched his teeth.

"Did I just hit a nerve there?"

He nods.

"I'm sorry," I tell him, squeezing his hand. "I watched my family get ripped to shreds."

He looks back at me and moves closer to me. He gently uses his finger and wipes under my eyes. I didn't even notice that I was crying again.

"All that was left was my sister's hand with a bracelet I made for her."

He swallows hard. "Deonna and I were out with our parents in the Himalayas. We were having a family vacation, just the four of us. During a picnic one night the demons attacked."

He took a deep breath and continued.

"We were outnumbered one to six. The demons were trying to get into the city, and my parents were doing everything they could to stop them, but they failed. I watched helplessly as my father's head was bitten off. Deonna tried running after him, but I held her back. She was almost killed herself. My mother told us to help the humans while she held off the demons, but she didn't make it. We were halfway to the town when we heard her screams."

I pulled him into a hug.

"You must miss them terribly."

He pulls me closer to him. "I do."

"I'm so sorry."

"And to make matters worse, right after our parents died, Deonna and I got stuck in Dimension Five."

Dimension Five, where have I heard that before?

"That sounds so familiar," I tell him, letting go of him. "I think Audrey told me about it the night I met them."

"Dimension Five is where the demons originated from. They have control over Dimensions Two, One, and Seven. Dimension Five is where they're the strongest."

"And you two were stuck there? How'd you make it out?"

"We were trapped there for six months, just wandering around, hiding, and eventually we found demons going through a portal and we ran into it and ended up in Russia."

"Whoa, I can't believe you survived that." I say amazed.

"I've never been so scared in my entire life," he continues. "I hope I never go back."

I pull him back into a hug, and he pulls me closer to him.

"What do I do with the menorah?"

Darren and I stop hugging and stare at Deonna. She stares back at our wet faces and has a questioning look.

"What?" she asks us.

***

"That's it!" JP shouts taking four cards from the main pile. "I hate this game!"

"Come on!" I exclaim. "It's fun!"

"For who? The person winning?"

I decided to teach Audrey, JP, and Darren how to play Uno. This used to be my favorite card game when I was living as a human, and I see it still has its charms. We were sitting at the kitchen table in a circle. The three of them are highly annoyed, probably because we're twenty minutes into the game.

"It's alright," Darren says, putting down a card. "Not something I'd do in my free time though."

"Well, I have other things planned for us as well," I exclaim happily.

"Like what?" Audrey asks.

I smirk at her. "It's a surprise."

"Enough with the surprises, Bec!" JP snaps. "Just tell us!"

"I don't always throw surpris-"

"Yes you do!" Audrey interrupts. "Just tell us so we can prepare!"

"Why do you need to prepare?" I ask.

"If it's outside, we need to know to dress warm. If we're eating, we need to know whether or not to eat. if-"

"Alright." I admit to defeat. "Do you guys rememberme telling you about New Years?"

"Yes," JP tells me.

"Well," I tell them, "tomorrow night is New Year's Eve, and I want to take you guys to see the ball drop! I already talked to Emma about it. She wants us home by two."

"Can't wait!" Audrey shouts.

"Can I bring my sister?" Darren asks.

"Uh, I don't think-" I start, but he shyly interrupts me.

"Maybe this can be a chance for her to get to know you better," he explains. "I know she's been a bitch to you, but you haven't tried to like her either."

I think about his words for a moment, and sigh. He's right. She has been very mean to me, but I should at least try to get along.

Page 138

"Alright," I sigh. "She can come."

***

"So how long is this going to take?" Deonna snaps at me, "We've been here for hours!"

The five of us left the statue of liberty right after sunset, and we walked to Time Square. The spots we got weren't too good. We were far from the ball, but it wasn't hard to see it. There were so many people. Hundreds, maybe thousands, of humans and at least five magicians were gathered here tonight.

"Just another eight minutes and we can leave," I assure her with my hand in my pocket, playing with my bag of mixed nuts.

Since I can't carry around garlic mostly because Emma won't buy it for me, I started keeping peanuts, cashews, almonds, and raisins in my pocket. Darren bought me a whole garlic yesterday, but he told me to ration it, so I only have three cloves in my pocket. The nuts have the same crunch as garlic cloves and the raisins have a strong taste. It makes sense.

When I was younger, I've always wanted to come here on New Year's Eve. My brother Tom went one year with his friends and said some parts were a blast and some parts were kind of boring. I guess it depends on where you were.

Right now I'm having fun hanging with Audrey, JP, and Darren. It was cold outside, and I mean cold. We were all bundled up. I had on the black and white fedora my brothers got me, so my head wasn't really kept warm. Before we left, I almost wore a green cotton hat, but decided against it. Now I'm starting to regret it. I take off my brown scarf and wrap it around my face, but now my throat is getting cold. I sigh and put the scarf back around my throat, but now my face is cold again.

I can't win today! I lift up my glove and blow hot air onto my hand, and I do the same for the other.

I feel little arms wrap themselves around my waist. "I'll keep you warm, Bec!"

"Thanks, JP!" we have to talk very loudly in order to hear each other.

Page 139

"This is actually fun!" Audrey announces. "Cold, but fun!"

"I'm glad you like it!" I tell her.

Deonna just rolls her eyes at us and checks her watch.

"We've got five minutes!"

Time is going by very quickly.

"Admit it!" I mock her, "You're having fun!"

"No!" she snaps, "I'm-"

"Try and enjoy yourself, sis!" Darren interrupts her, "Bec is doing a special thing for us, sharing another of her customs with us and-"

"We shouldn't be here!" she snaps at him. "We should be training! We don't know when-"

"Exactly! We don't know when! Which is why we should enjoy ourselves while we can so we can-"

"She's gotten into your head! Hasn't she?" Deonna shoots a death stare at me. She pushes Audrey out of the way and is in my face. I can feel JP's arms tighten around me. "Quit filling my family's heads with your ideas! You can't change them!"

Change?

I'm just trying to show everyone a good time, take a break from always training and fighting. I'm not trying to change anyone.

Am I?

Suddenly, I wasn't having fun anymore because Deonna the bitch once again ruined something for me.

"Deonna, stop!" Darren shouts pulling her away from me. "She's not trying to change us!"

"Yeah!" JP lets go of me and then stands right in front of me, "She's just helping us have fun, something you need to learn how to do!"

Deonna stares at her young cousin, mouth agape.

"He's right," Darren says. "I shouldn't have asked Bec if you could come! You're ruining the night!"

Deonna stares at her brother. She's obviously hurt.

"She can stay!" I'm going to regret this later.

"Are..." he says something, but I can't hear him over everyone talking loudly.

"I'm sorry?" I ask.

"Are you sure?" he asks again loudly this time.

Page 140

"Yeah!"

I look over at Deonna. She looks less hurt, but she also refuses to look at anyone, including me. She doesn't look thankful, but her features did become a little softer.

"Besides," I say, lightening the mood, "We got three minutes!"

"Already?" JP asks.

"Normally, we make New Year's resolutions!" I say, trying to have everyone forget about the mini fight that just happened. "I'll go first! My resolution is to become better with my powers and be the best magician I can be!"

"That's two!" Deonna says.

"You can have more than one!" I tell her. "What do you hope for next year?"

She thinks for a moment. "To not lose anyone else."

"That's great!" I congratulate her. "Don't worry, this is the last outing for a while."

Everyone else thinks for a few moments.

"I want to master air!" JP says.

"I want to try and heal!" Audrey says. "I know I have it in me!"

"But you're elemental," I say.

"I can try."

"I'd rather not say mine out loud!" Darren says.

"Boo!" I mock him. He gives me a hurt look, then I hug him to show him I'm joking. The wind gets stronger as I start to laugh.

I sure hope no one can hear our conversation.

"Ten! Nine! Eight!"

"The countdown begins!" I shout. "Come on guys!"

The four of them look scared, then I realize something.

The wind got stronger and it's rushing towards the ball.

"Not again!"

"Three! Two!" Half of the humans scream the "one", and the other half just scream.

Chapter 20

Humans near the front of the ball start to run towards us to escape the demons, but it takes a few seconds so I have time to act.

How the hell did we get separated?

"Bec!" yells Darren.

What do I do?

"Bec!" Audrey shouts.

They're looking for me, I have to get to them!

I concentrate hard, bring my hands to my chest, think about the slow seconds, and I throw them down. Time is immediately slowed down. As fast as I can, I look left and right, and I see JP desperately trying to push humans aside.

Everyone is moving slowly so it gives me an advantage. I gently push the humans aside and quickly make my way towards JP. I grab his arm and look around again.

Most of the humans are terrified. Some have a confused looks on their faces. They all run though, even the ones that don't know why they're running.

I spot Audrey desperately trying to calm humans down. At least that's what I think she's doing, it's hard to tell while everyone is moving so slowly.

I quickly make my way to her, which isn't a far distance, and I hook her arm in my free arm. Not far away are Darren and Deonna who are looking around.

While pulling Audrey and JP, I make my way to them as fast as I can, which isn't very fast because now I'm going to where the humans are coming from. When I find them, I hook Darren in the same arm as JP, and I hook Deonna in the same arm as Audrey. I locate the nearest building and I make my way toward it, pulling the four of them with me. I use my telekinesis to move the humans who are in my way.

It's all happening so fast for them they probably don't even notice.

When I reach the building, I face the four of them.

They're all trying to say something to me, but I can't understand them because they're speaking way too slowly.

I put my hands to my chest, and throw them down. Time returns to normal.

"-moving that fast!"

"-going to stop them!"

"-you do that!"

"Okay!" I shout. "One at a time!"

"Forget that!" Deonna shouts. "We have to stop the demons first! Where are they?"

"By the front!" Audrey tells her.

Deonna looks at her brother "Think you can get us over there?" "Sure thing!" he tells her. "Hurry!"

Deonna, JP, and Audrey all put a hand on Darren's shoulder. I follow suit. The second I get a grip, I feel the whole world get ripped out from under my feet, and I'm sucked into a new area. We're right next to the ball, and I don't like the sight of it. There are maybe thirty demons. I was never very good at estimating. There are maybe fifty or sixty dead humans lying in random places. The demons are charging at the humans. One by one, the humans fall. The demons move so fast.

Audrey is the first to spring into action. She forms balls of fire in both of her hands and runs to the nearest demon.

I don't see what the others do. I run to the stage and grab a metal microphone pole. I don't know how much it'll help me, but I will use it. Once it's in my grip, I look around and see a demon about half my size feasting on a screaming woman's stomach. I run toward the demon, but something pulls me back. I almost fall on the floor, but I catch my footing and turn around. I prepare to face a demon, but there's nothing behind me. I look left and right, just in case I missed something. That's when I noticed what pulled me back. The wires on the microphone.

Idiot!

I take the microphone off the stand and check to see that no wires will trap me on the stage.

I'm good to go.

I hear Audrey scream and I turn around.

She's pinned down by three demons, screaming and desperately trying to use her fire to roast them off of her, but they're determined. I jump off the stage and run toward her.

One bites her throat and I see the blood starting to form.

When I'm close to her, I raise my weapon and swing, sending the demon flying several yards away. I'm tempted to scream "four", but that would be highly inappropriate.

The other two hiss at me, but I don't hesitate. I swing again and knock both of them off her in one blow.

I don't see where they land, I kneel next to Audrey, put one of my hands on her neck, and start to heal it. The other hand is holding the top half of the microphone stand threateningly, making sure other demons don't sneak up on us. I scan the area to see if the others need healing. When her neck is completely healed, I stand up and offer her my hand.

"Thanks!" she tells me after I help her up.

"Thank me later!" I tell her. "We're not out of this mess yet!"

Audrey creates more fire in her hands, and I raise my weapon.

We stand back to back and I look around.

Darren has six demons circling him. He's gasping and looks exhausted.

I see Deonna is juggling three demons with her telekinesis and has her hand outstretched toward another.

She looks very confident. I see her shout something to the demons, but I don't hear what she says.

She's fine.

"Let's help Darren!" I tell Audrey.

"You go!" she yells. "I have to help JP!"

Then I don't feel her on my back.

As fast as I can, I run towards Darren.

Page 144

One demon with four eyes and wings flies right for my head, its sharp teeth shining wickedly. I stand my ground and use my weapon and hit it like a baseball.

"Home run!"

I couldn't resist.

I reach one of the demons circling Darren and swing my weapon over my head. I smash the demon down. I hear a loud crunch and know that I badly injured it. I keep hitting it until the demon is nothing but a pile of blood, bones, and smashed up guts.

I look up and see that Darren has his arms out and his head hung. Slowly, the demons start to inflate until they pop. Demon blood hits me right in the face.

"Oh my god!" I feel like I'm going to puke!

I quickly rip my scarf off my neck and desperately wipe as much of the demon blood from my face as I can.

"Thanks for the save," Darren tells me. "I needed a distraction."

"No problem," I tell him, throwing him my scarf. "But we're not done yet."

"The humans are gone," Darren notices.

I look around and realize the same thing. The only remaining humans are the dead bodies ripped to shreds.

Most of them are children.

I suddenly feel anger, sadness, and rage building up inside of me. How dare they! I suddenly remember my little cousin Aliya's body lying in the sand, and tears threaten to build in my eyes.

I never did get to build that sandcastle with her.

"The demons are retreating!" Deonna yells, running up to us.

"They're not getting away that easily!" I get a tighter grip on the microphone stand and spot the area they're retreating to. I run after them.

"Bec, wait!" Darren and Deonna simultaneously call after me.

I can hear their footsteps behind me. They're trying to stop me. They'll have to try a hell of a lot harder than that!

"Bec, no!" I hear Audrey scream as I rush past her and JP.

I see the demons all cluttered up, running down the street. Where are they running to?

Doesn't matter, I'm almost on them.

Page 145

Someone grabs the hood from my sweater and turns me around. It's Audrey. JP is standing next to her looking very worried.

"When the demons retreat, you mustn't run after them!" she tells me.

"Why?" I ask her.

Darren and Deonna catch up and roughly grab my arms.

"We need to go!" Darren informs me.

"Now!" Deonna agrees.

The wind starts to pick up and they pull me harder, this time moving my feet and forcing me to walk with them.

"Why?" I ask louder this time.

The wind starts to get very strong, and next thing I know, I can't breathe.

Next thing I know, I'm not in Time Square anymore.

I'm standing on a large hill that's covered in yellow grass.

What?

I bend down and feel the grass. It's sharp. It cuts my fingers a little. I put them both in my mouth and suck the blood. I look up at the sky and notice it's no longer night.

It's scarlet red with grey puffy clouds. I look out into the horizon and it's yellow and red as far as my eyes can comprehend. There's two orange suns right next to each other.

What?

Where are we?

"Darren..." I hear Deonna gasp, "Are we..."

I hear him gulp. "Nooo," he says in a hushed terrified tone.

Next thing I know, two hands shove me hard and I fall to the floor, almost tumbling down the mountain.

"You stupid, bitch!" Deonna screams. "We told you not to go after them, and what do you do? You go after them!"

"Hey! Back off! You didn't tell me anything until after," I tell her. "Where are we?"

That's when I notice the fear in Deonna's eyes. I have never seen her look afraid before, but she was terrified right now. She's almost in tears.

JP is clinging to Audrey with desperation. Audrey looks like she's about to cry.

Page 146

Darren looks freaked out, but seems to be the one who's most in control.

"I told you about this place during Hanukkah, how Deonna and I were here once after our parents died," he tells me, a heaviness to his usual gentle voice.

"No..." I whisper piecing everything together. Now it's my turn to freak out.

He sighs, "Welcome to Dimension Five."

Deonna's Biting Theory

<u>This scene was written with the assistance of my good friend Alejandro Vasquez</u>.

(Vampire [female], Werewolf [male], and Zombie [male] are playing Uno on a table)

Vampire: Your turn, Zombie.

Zombie: (slow zombie-like drawl) BRAAAAAAAAAINS ... (normal voice looks at Wolf) are what you don't have, sucka! Draw four!

Vampire: (rolls her eyes at zombie)

Wolf: (roars in anger and draws four)

Vampire: Jeez, you get really cranky right after you transform.

Wolf: You'd get cranky, too, if you had to go through violent physical pain once a month.

Vampire: I'm a girl. I *do* go through that.

(awkward silence)

Wolf: Hmm, if vampires drink blood ... What happens when you -

Zombie: Eww, okay, let's change the subject!

Wolf: Alright, alright. (gives evil laugh)

Vampire: That reminds me, I haven't fed in a while. (looks at zombie) Nice, warm, thick, red blood! (bares her fangs)

Zombie: (shudders a bit. Then pauses) Yeah, I'm hungry. I can go for some brains too.

Vampire: I drink blood, moron. I bite their neck and drink.

Zombie: Yeah, I thought you ate brains because you didn't have any.

Vampire: (gets mad and threatens to hit him)

Page 148

Zombie: Well, I need some flesh.

Wolf: To eat or to wear?

Vampire and Wolf: Oooooooooooooooooohhhh! (high fives each other)

Zombie: (hurt) My skin is not that gross...

Vampire: You're a rotting corpse!

Zombie: Hey, I prefer the term, "Undead-American."

Vampire: Well, it's not like you don't bite humans either, Wolf. You're not much better.

Wolf: Yeah, I do. But not all the time considering that they'd turn into a werewolf themselves.

Zombie: Wait a minute, Wolf ... Vampire, you bite people too, right?

Vampire: Yeah, only to feed, but if I only bite, they turn into a vampire as well.

Zombie: Yeah! And if I don't kill while trying to eat, they turn into zombies

(Brief pause)

Vampire: What would happen if we all bit someone?

Wolf: We just said what happens.

Vampire: No no no, I mean simultaneously.

Zombie: At the same time?

Vampire: (Being sarcastic) Naw! At twenty-year intervals!

Zombie: Ah come on, why you gotta-

Wolf: Woah woah woah, that would actually be very interesting.

Zombie: What? Biting someone at twenty year-

Vampire: No, brainless!

Wolf: Not that! I mean, what would happen if we all bit the same human at the same time?

(All ponder in deep thought)

Vampire: Would it die? Considering the overwhelming sensation of the transformation?

Zombie: I bet it'd turn into a rad combination of the three of us!

Wolf: How would that work out?

Zombie: Think about it. It could be a mix of (points to one at a time) a bloodsucker, a ruthless monster, and a mindless stiff, like ... a lawyer.

Wolf: That won't happen! What if it turns into a creature that is unlike us at all, like a mummy or ghost or something?

Zombie: We would have to take out its brains for it to be a mummy.

Page 149

Vampire: Don't zombies already do that?
Zombie: (Quick pause) True...
Wolf: Or maybe it'd turn into a prettyful unicorn!
Zombie and Vampire: (Give wolf a WTF look) You're kidding right?
Wolf: Maybe.... (Crouches into his seat) Yeah, I am.
Vampire: Okay then... So, no one's ever seen what'd happen then? (pause, then waves hands like she's saying "No way") What am I saying, this is completely idiotic. Who would do such a thing!
Zombie: It sounds kinda cool actually. I want to try it!
Wolf: Dude... let's do that!
Zombie: Yeah! (high-fives Wolf)
Vampire: So, you two want to drag me to go up to a random human, bite them, and possibly ruin their life ... for no reason?
Zombie: (serious face) It's in the name of scientific curiosity.
Vampire: You'll have to do better than that to get me to go along with it.
Wolf: Let's make it a bet.
Vampire: Hmm ... What kind of bet? (Wanting to see where this will go)
Zombie: If I'm right, you both have to see New Moon.
Vampire and Wolf: NOOOOOO!!! (Wolf howls sadly)
Vampire: (Now into the idea and furious) That's it! If I win, (pointing to Wolf) you have to enter a dog show. And Zombie can be your owner ...
Zombie: That's not so bad.
Vampire: ... With a ridiculous suit and having to treat people nicely and everything!
Zombie: ... Oh ...
Wolf: Time to bust your confidence even more, if I win, you two have to... don't kill me.
Vampire: No promises.
Wolf: No hurting either.
Vampire: Just say it!
Wolf: If I win, you two have to go on a date at an Italian restaurant!
Zombie: Hell no!
Vampire: Not gonna happen! Not even on your afterlife!
Wolf: What? You two scared?
Vampire and Zombie: The bet is so on!
Wolf: Excellent. (Laughs evil laugh)

Page 150

Vampire: So now we just have to find someone to test it out on. But where are we gonna find a human outside in the middle of the night? I kind of can't go out during the day.

Wolf: Yeah, it wouldn't work for me either if it was during the day since that's when I turn to my human form again. It has to be during a full moon

(they think for a bit and suddenly a random human

[male] walks in)

Human: (to no one in particular and really happy) Oh, it's so great to be alive and walking around outside in the middle of the night!

(all pause for a moment)

Zombie: Well, that was convenient.

Wolf: Do you not get the scenario we are in right now?

(The three of them follow the human as he walks offstage. Roaring, screaming, and bumping sounds are heard. The trio returns to the stage and stands around, looking at where they killed him)

Vampire: So ... they just die? ... Not that I'm complaining, I won the bet, but ... still.

Wolf: That's boring.

Zombie: I'm still waiting for him to turn into a lawyer.

(Human comes back on stage, but not as a human. Explosive, crazy sound effects accompany it)

(More silence from the trio)

Wolf: He's a ghost! He turned into to something unlike us at all. I won!

Vampire: But technically, he did die...

Vampire and Wolf: (looks at Zombie) We won!

Zombie: (upset) So what do I do?

Human who is now ghost: What did you do to me!? I -I think I'm a freaking ghost! Oh jeez, why did you have to do this?

(Trio stands around awkwardly)

Vampire: Well ... these two idiots made a bet, and they-

Wolf and Zombie: Hey!

Vampire: Okay, the three of us made a bet, and we wanted to see what would happen if all three of us bit you at the same time.

Ghost: You killed a random person you've never met before ... on a bet?

(Awkward silence)

Page 151

Vampire: (Looks at Zombie with sarcasm in her voice) It was in the name of scientific curiosity, eh?
Ghost: WHAT THE FREAKING HECK WAS THE POINT OF THAT?! I had hopes, dreams, a life! I even had a promising career in law!
Zombie: So he was one of them all along ...
Vampire: So we all won the bet ... but nobody lost it.
Wolf: Aww c'mon!
Ghost: WILL YOU ALL SHUT UP ABOUT THE STUPID BET! What am I supposed to do now?!?
Wolf: Girls' locker room (wolf-whistles, gets punched in the arm by Vampire)
Zombie: Do whatever you want to do! You have your whole afterlife ahead of you!
Ghost: You can't tell me what to do!
Wolf: We could have planned this better.
Vampire: You think!? Our only plan was to kill him and see what happens!
Zombie: Well, maybe you can-
Ghost: No! You three are going to pay for what you have done to me!
Wolf: The undead don't carry money...
Ghost: (realization face) Wait ... all three of you are undead?
Zombie: ... Yes.
Ghost: Does that mean you'll live forever?
Wolf: ... Yeah.
Ghost: And I'll be around forever.
Vampire: Where are you going with this?
Ghost: I'm gonna haunt your arses for eternity. And there's nothing you can do about it.
(Quick moment of scarred silence)
Vampire: (mad) I told you idiots this was a dumb idea.
Zombie and Wolf: Uh... No you didn't!
(The trio gets chased offstage)
[Curtain]

Respect for Stephenie Meyer.

Page 152

Book 2

Damnation Land

Part 1: Where I Am

Chapter 1

I've screwed up.

No.

I've fucked up!

Thanks to my immature rage, my emotional instability, and my sudden need for revenge that I never knew I had; I just got the five of us trapped in another world! We're going to be killed and it's all my fault.

"Welcome to Dimension Five," Darren told me.

I'm standing on top of the bladed grass hill with Darren, his twin sister Deonna, Audrey, and JP. All of us have shoes and long pants, so nothing is cutting us.

"Oh no, no, no, no, no, not again, not again!" Deonna starts to cry.

I shake slightly in my shoes, more scared of what my friends will do to me than of the onslaught of demons we're bound to encounter.

"Are you sure that this is Dimension Five?" I ask after what feels like a long moment of silence and panic. "I mean, it could be-"

"We were here for six months!" Deonna yells at me, cutting me off. "Of course we're sure!"

I jump back, afraid she might attack me, but she doesn't budge. The daggers in her eyes certainly show she wants to hurt me though.

I look at Audrey and JP. Audrey is hyperventilating while JP is grabbing his hair and bawling.

"Both of you be quiet," Darren whispers, trying but failing to hide the fear in his voice. "We don't want to attract the demons. We have to get out of here, and the only way we'll get out of here is together, so both of you calm down. Whether we like it or not, we're stuck here. The only way we're getting out live is if we somehow manage to not get noticed by any demons."

Deonna growls and avoids my gaze. "You're lucky my brother's here, or else I'd choke the life out of you."

Deonna is truly terrifying when she's mad. I honestly can't blame her for being angry. I'd be furious if one of them had trapped me in this hell. How can I even begin to make amends for this?

"I need to know what the plan is. How exactly are we going to get back?" I ask Darren, desperately looking around for demons but not seeing any.

"The same way we got here," Darren says, not taking his eyes off his enraged sister.

"How did I get us here?" I ask.

He sighs.

"When you ran after the demons like a complete idiot, they were retreating to their dimension. We were pulled into the portal," Deonna explains through clenched teeth. "That's why we told you not to run after them!"

Strange. I don't remember falling through any portal, but we must have, considering our current location.

"Where are the demons? if we followed them, shouldn't they be close by?"

Everyone else quickly surveys the area.

"I guess they must have scattered?" JP hopes more than suggests, wiping tears from his face.

"Could be," Darren says. "We did have some distance between us and them, and our group was pretty close together. In the meantime, we should calm down and gather our thoughts. Being scared and not thinking rationally could get us killed."

"But Bec closed a portal once," JP says, wiping away his tears as they continued to fall. "Maybe she can open one up to get us back home."

Page 156

"I don't even know how I closed it," I explain to him. "I highly doubt I can open one."

"How do we even know that's true?" Deonna snaps. "How do we know that you didn't lie about it?"

"Frederick and John saw me close it!" I say defensively, not even sure if they did see me close it.

Deonna flares up, "Well maybe-"

"It can't be done," Darren says, holding up a hand. He grabs his sister's arm and starts walking down the mountain. The three of us follow suite. "Even if Bec can or can't-"

"Can," I say with a confident grin.

"Look, nobody even knows how demons can open portals in the first place, or even if they are the ones who open the portals. Bec, you said that you didn't know how you did what you did, right?"

"I have no idea. I just thought about it and concentrated. Also, I didn't even know the demons could open up portals." I say, still casting my gaze to the horizon but not seeing any demons. "Since when has that been a thing?"

"Nobody knows exactly," Darren explains. "Whether the universe itself creates the portals, or some other creatures, or if they are machine made.... the point is they exist and the demons take advantage of that." He sighs. "We must do the same if we want to get back."

Audrey tilts her head in confusion. "But when you guys told us the story of when you two were stuck, you said you went through three different dimensions until you got back?"

I look back at her. She and JP are holding hands and are both scanning opposite sides for demons.

"We did," Deonna says. "We wandered around until we found a portal and went through it, but we didn't return home on the first try."

"And that took six months?" I ask.

"We were here in this hell for six months," Darren reminds me.

"Then how long did it take you guys to get back?" I ask.

The twins simultaneously say "One year."

Oh boy.

Just then a thought occurs to me. "What are we going to do about food, and water?"

"Shit!" Audrey says. "I didn't even think about that."

Page 157

"Relax," Deonna says, reaching in her coat pocket.

It's a bit chilly here so we didn't bother to remove our winter clothing. I personally kept my hat on, but I tied my scarf around my waist like a belt.

"I keep these on me for emergencies," Deonna pulls out three small bottles of water.

I had no idea Deonna was so resourceful! I might not like her, but I am happy she's here and I've gained some respect for her. If we all make it out of here, we'll owe her our lives, but that's a big if.

"We need to ration this," Darren says, taking two bottles from her. He gives one to me and holds up the other one. "At least until we get to a river. Deonna and I will share this bottle while you three share that one." He points to the one in my hand. "The third will be our last resort."

"But what about food?" I ask.

"Every living thing needs food," Darren tells me. "It'll be a lot more difficult to find, but there's food here somewhere. We all did eat and drink before leaving for Time Square, so we should be good for another few days."

"So, should we hunt?" Audrey asks.

"I wouldn't recommend it," Deonna tells her.

I try not to sigh with relief.

"How come?" Audrey asks.

"Their meat smells like poison, so we didn't bother eating any the last time we were here."

"Well, what do they eat?"

"Whatever is lying around," Darren tells her. "Let's not worry about that right now. We can always search for food. In the meantime, we should worry about walking and finding these food sources before we go hungry."

We all jump when we hear growls nearby.

We make a break for it without saying another word.

***

We covered ground by walking until one sun seemingly brushed against the other and began to set, then we stopped to relax. The sun

Page 158

intersection has happened three times since we arrived. As of right now, the second one didn't touch the horizon yet, but the sky is starting to get darker by the minute. We've had time to sit down, but we haven't really laid down to rest.

"How big is this meadow?" JP asks.

"We must have appeared in the middle of the meadow when we got here," Darren says, mostly to himself. "We will have to travel a few more days before we have to change locations."

Audrey and JP groan.

I keep my mouth shut. I have no right to speak.

Besides those New York demons we heard earlier, we haven't seen any demons. I still find it odd and a bit eerie that not a single one has appeared. I guess this must be one of those areas where no one goes.

Or we could be walking into an ambush.

I shake that thought from my head.

We're in the Antarctica of Dimension Five. I start giggling to myself at the thought.

Deonna gives me a dark look.

I immediately stop.

"We should probably rest," Deonna suggests. "We haven't stopped since we got here."

"Alright," Darren agrees, "let's stop for-"

Audrey and JP sigh with relief and throw themselves on the floor.

"-the night." Darren finishes.

"Careful with the grass," I tell them.

"A little too late for that," JP says, now with a small gash on his cheek.

I check my shoes and pants. They're torn up at the bottom. It's only a matter of time before my skin looks like that too.

JP starts breathing heavily as if he had just fallen asleep.

"One of us should be on watch at all times," Darren says.

"I'll take first watch," I volunteer.

"Be careful," Darren warns me. "We're in their territory."

"I'm well aware of that. Besides, I can handle a few demons."

"I'm not talking about them. This place does things to people."

Page 159

"What do you mean?"

He shakes his head.

If he's being this way then this must be bad.

"May I ask what happened to you guys?"

"I don't want to talk about it."

I nod as he walks off as I try and imagine what they went through.

Chapter 2

I don't know how long I've been on watch since the second sun fully set. It's so dark that I can't see much of my own hand, let alone the horizon.

There are not many stars in the sky here, and no moon to provide us even a bit of light. It's all so bleak, and scary, like climbing a staircase in the dark. One wrong step and we will fall.

I turn my head and see the others sound asleep. Their stomachs are slowly rising and falling. They're all huddled close together for warmth, still keeping their jackets on.

I wrap my arms around myself.

This dimension must be a lot colder than home. It looks like summer time, but feels colder than a Florida winter. I don't want to know what winter is like here!

I stare at JP for a while. I remember when he said I was the newest member of their family.

I wonder if he still feels that way.

I look at Audrey, well, at least I think I do. It's hard to tell in the dark. Does she even consider me a sister, or a cousin for that matter? If she did, I hope she can still consider me family after this colossal fuck up.

I remember Ash's hand on the beach. I can't bare lose another sister.

I feel so nervous. I start to play with my fingers.

I start on my pinky and count to three, then I go back one and count to three again. I'm getting the hang of it. I count my fingers and look to the horizon; I don't see any movement.

I turn around and look again. Still no demons.

Being in their home dimension, I thought we would have run into thousands of them, but I don't see any. If they are avoiding this area, then what threat is keeping them away? Or maybe I just guessed right about them not coming here.

I take out my only clove of garlic and munch on it. I'd share the clove with them, but that would be just as bad as splitting a grain of rice amongst us. Plus, no sane person eats garlic whole like I do.

My brother Tom used to have to help me peel the garlic cloves when I was really little.

Tom.

I look back at the group.

Darren acts a lot like how Tom used to, minus the spazzing. He may not be my brother, but he sure acts like it.

Do I want him to be my brother?

Maybe not, but I know I can never abandon him.

Is that why I stayed with the magicians instead of going back with my other friends?

What about Audrey and JP; don't I stay for them too?

I never once thought about leaving them, so maybe.

I start to pace.

When in doubt, I just pace around and it helps me calm down. Never been much of a pacer, but ever since I moved in with Emma and Audrey, I find myself pacing a lot.

"Something wrong?"

I jump at the sound of Deonna's voice.

That's it! I need jump scare training!

"Uh... No..." I say, "Nothing wrong... I-I thought you were sleeping?"

"I woke up," she says very point blank.

Well no duh she woke up!

"I can't see much moving out there," I tell her as she casts her gaze out.

Page 162

"Can't really see anything out there," she grumbles, sitting up. JP's head is in her lap, so she gently lifts it and slides her legs out. When she's free, she gently lowers his head.

Then there's Deonna.

I wish I knew why she hated me so much.

I look up at the sky again. There's probably half the number of stars I was able to see in Eagle Lake. I try and find the Big Dipper, but I don't see it. I look for Orion.

When I don't find his belt, I remember we're in a different dimension with different constellations and a different number of stars.

Man, I can be really stupid sometimes! If we weren't in danger of being killed this would be a really cool experience. Everything I know is so far away, but that just means there's lots of new things to explore. I always wanted to travel. Well, travel my home dimension that is.

I never once considered that I could travel to other dimensions.

"You see that circle?" Deonna asks, pointing up and coming to stand next to me.

I follow her fingers and see a fork. I look a little to the right and notice eight stars in a circle. "Yeah," I tell her.

"Last time I was here," she says. "I named it Spherious."

I laugh, but not in a mocking tone. "That's a cute name, how'd you come up with it?"

"It looks like a sphere, and we were in a serious situation, so I just combined the two. Also, there's eight stars in it, so it reminded me of home."

Home.

Where is my home?

"I used to combine names all the time," I tell her. "Every time I shipped something I came up with a combined name."

"So, ship names?"

"Yeah, my favorite was Toxic"

"Toxic?"

"Yeah, my brother Tom and his girlfriend Roxy. At first it sounded like Toxi, so I added the C and said that their relationship was Toxic."

Deonna laughs at that.

I sigh and look at my hands.

Page 163

"You miss your brother?" asked Deonna.

"I miss all of them," I tell her, taking a deep breath. "When I was really young, my brothers used to climb into our beds and tickle us until we woke up."

"My father used to do that to me. I lost the ability to be tickled because of that."

"No kidding. So did I."

"Darren is still ticklish."

"Really?"

"Super ticklish."

"Excellent."

We both laugh lightly for a little bit, not really looking at each other.

"You're lucky you still have a brother that cares about you," I tell her.

"He cares about a lot of people," she says, looking at her sleeping twin. "You especially."

"What do you mean?"

"Uh...forget I said that!" she says in a rush. "Why don't you get some rest, I'll take next watch, but I will say this. We're stuck in this situation whether we like it or not. I know you didn't do this on purpose, but if anyone gets killed because of you, I'll end you."

Not as mean as I thought, but still very scary.

"I understand." I shove my hands in my pockets and turn halfway, but then I feel a plastic bag with stuff inside.

What is this?

I pull it out and take a close look.

"My nuts!" I say, shaking the bag. "I forgot I had these!"

For the first time ever that I can recall, Deonna smiles at me, "Well how about that?"

***

I awaken to find Audrey on my stomach, staring me in the face and JP looking through my pockets.

"Where are the nuts?" she asks me. She sounds desperate. We've only been here a few days and she's already feeling starvation.

Page 164

"Well, good morning to you too," I say.

JP pulls the bag of nuts and raisins out of my pocket and looks at it fully filled.

"Guys," Darren chimes in. "It's all we have until we find more food, so we have to make the most of it unless we want to eat poisoned, demon carcasses." He looks at his sister. "What do you think? Do we split it five ways or use it on an 'as needed' basis?"

Deonna thinks for a moment. "We should do as needed," she suggests. "You and I won't get hungry as often; I don't know about her," she motions to me with her head, "but these two need as much as they can get." She motions to Audrey and JP. "Besides, I don't see splitting evenly going very well."

"As needed it is then." Darren gently grabs Audrey's shoulders and pulls her off of me.

"Does right now count as an 'as needed basis' then?" Audrey asks.

"Yes," he says. "We haven't eaten in days." He extends his hand to me and helps me up. His hand is so warm and his smile is welcoming.

Why am I just now realizing this?

You especially.

What does that mean, Deonna?

I know one thing for sure. I don't want to have another older brother just to lose him.

***

We make it out of the opening the next day and we take shelter in an adjacent forest that stretches for miles.

At least it looks like a forest from the horizon.

I feel drained of all my energy.

I lean against one of the trees and catch my breath. My head rests against the tree, and I realize that it feels weird. I take half a step back and study it for a bit. I rest my hand gently on the pale white bark and notice that it feels like bone. I immediately pull my hand back and wipe it on my pants.

I look up at the top of the trees. The trees are about fifty feet, maybe taller. The leaves on the trees look dead.

In fact, as I look around, everything in this forest looks dead. Even the soil looks extremely dry.

The ground looks like swamp ground, right down to the eerie fog, minus the water. The ground is completely   barren of plants. It oddly smells like that cemetery I walked into once for a dare Jake made me do.

Jake.

Wind starts to blow and it makes me shiver.

Everyone else starts to look every way frantically, but it's not a portal.

JP sighs.

"Where are we?" I ask rhetorically.

"Never been to this part before," Deonna thinks out loud.

We slowly walk farther into the forest, all of us tilting our heads to listen and search for enemies. JP moves closer to Deonna. Every step is sending more and more chills down my spine. In front of me, I see Audrey grab Darren's hand and squeeze it. Behind me I hear JP tripping over rocks and Deonna whispering for him to be careful.

I look out into the forest. Fog, dead trees, and darkness as far as my eyes can see. I just picture a bunch of yellow and red eyes appearing in the distance one by one. The thought freaks me out, so I look at the swampy ground and focus on my footing.

Not even a twig to accidentally step on and snap.

And then I hear it.

Demonic laughter comes from all around us.

I quickly look up and notice everyone's terrified faces.

The laughing stops.

"Please tell me you didn't hear that and I'm just imagining things," I whisper.

The laughing starts again, but they're closer this time.

"Run!" Deonna shouts, and we dash from where we're standing.

Chapter 3

I run out of breath almost the moment I start running.

I feel drained from the lack of rest I've been getting. More panting than breathing, I start to feel my head spin.

Hearing JP running next to me shows that I'm not the only one.

It's so hard not to trip with all the rocks at my feet. My eyes dart down for a few seconds to watch my footing. I then realize I'm not tripping over white rocks.

It's bones!

We wandered into a feeding ground!

I don't hear Darren stop running and I bump into him.

I look up and see what he's staring at.

A demon.

It's a yellow one with random brown lines all over it, one eye, and when it lifts up to show us it's hands, there are two little mouths in them. The tiny mouths open up and laugh at us.

Audrey is the first to act. She throws a blue fireball at it and it falls over, screaming as it's being burned alive.

I hear laughing coming from my right. I turn to see another demon. A blue one with eyes and mouths all over its head.

I lift it up with my telekinesis and bang it against a tree. The blood stain on the tree gets bigger every time I bang the demon against it. When I feel the demon grow limp, I drop it and face my friends, but fear is soon swept over me like a fireproof blanket.

They're not there!

Or anywhere around me.

Oh no!

Not again!

"Darren!" I scream, which I realize is very stupid of me the second the scream escapes my lips. I quickly cover my mouth instantly regretting what I just did.

"Bec!" I hear him call.

I feel a little better.

More laughter is creeping up behind me. I run in the direction of Darren's voice like an Olympic athlete.

I'll beat myself up later.

I have to find them.

Then we need to get out of this wretched place together.

I can hear the laughter following me. I don't dare look in any direction that isn't forward.

The laughter closes in on me.

My heart is racing. My brain is rattling around in my head.

I'm gonna die.

Keep running.

What if I don't find them?

I'll fight if I must.

I've fought demons before, but I've never been this scared in my life.

I think about stopping and fighting them, but I'm alone right now. I don't dare stop until I have to.

Dammit! How far did they get?

My breathing is short and my heart starts to clench.

That's when I fall face first into a body of water.

I'm fully submerged.

I open my eyes and look around. The water stings my eyes, but I force them to stay open. My head starts to spin, but I hug myself.

Stay calm.

Clear my mind.

Stay calm or die!

My head and heart start to slow a little.

The water is red and bunches of small organs are floating on its surface. Some are human, the rest I don't recognize.

I try so hard to keep my distance from the organs, but some brush against my skin.

Oh, God!

I look up and see several figures jump over the small body of water.

Great, I fell into a puddle!

Against the will of my protesting lungs, I force myself to stay underwater for a little while longer to make sure all the demons are gone. I can slowly feel my lungs screaming at me to go up and breathe, they're begging me for oxygen, but I'm at the demon's mercy. I must wait until they're gone. I look forward again and see a human head floating in the water. It turns around and the face takes me completely by surprise.

Ash?

The head opens its eyes. Blue eyes with the eyebrows pointed down, filled with evil.

I scream, a lot of water rushing into my mouth, only for me to realize when it touches my tongue that it's not red water.

Its water mixed with blood.

I push myself away from the head towards the surface and I'm screaming all the while. I can't stop screaming.

Something that looks like a human baby's stomach flies into my mouth and down my throat. I start gagging and choking, and I acciden-tally breathe in some of the bloody water and I go into an underwater coughing frenzy.

I'm going to die here in a bloody puddle.

I feel four hands grab me and pull me out of the pond.

Is this how I die?

I swing my fists around like crazy once I'm out, and it collides with the side of Deonna's head. She falls over due to the force.

"You're welcome!" she snaps.

I stick my fingers down my throat and the blood rushes out of my stomach and onto the ground.

"Bec!"

I keep doing it, but the tiny stomach in my stomach isn't coming out. I'm dry heaving.

"Bec."

Page 169

I do it one last time, and I feel it come up in the back of my throat. I go into a coughing frenzy and spit out the stomach.

"Bec?"

It's Darren calling me.

I stare at him. His concerned face fills me with relief and I immediately start to calm myself, but my body won't stop shaking.

JP hands me my dry fedora that must have fallen off when I fell.

"What happened?" JP and Audrey simultaneously ask behind me.

Then I remember the face and I start bawling. I point to the puddle and try to tell them what I saw, but only wired murmurs come out.

Darren pulls me into a hug and strokes my blood- soaked hair as I cry on his shoulder.

***

This forest is huge, and worst of all almost everything looks exactly the same. We could be going in circles and not realize it. For two nights in a row we had to climb up and sleep in the tops of the trees, each taking turns watching.

"I swear," I whisper loud enough for the others to hear me, "We passed that large pepper shaped rock five times already."

This isn't the first forest I've gotten lost in, so I've been carefully watching my surroundings. I took a special interest in a boulder shaped like a pepper, but I'm not happy about seeing it for a fifth time.

"That's not the same rock," Darren assures me.

"Yes it is," JP protests in my favor as he sits on it.

I smirk at Darren, "See? Even the little boy knows we're lost."

"I'm not much younger than you," JP argues as Audrey shoves him off the rock.

JP pouts and crosses his arms, so Audrey grabs him by the armpits and lifts him off.

"Maybe we should rest for the night," Deonna suggests.

We all then jump at the sound of a deep growl a good distance away.

"Okay," Darren instructs quietly. "Everybody back in the trees."

Page 170

***

Darren is taking first watch, but this tree is so uncomfortable that I can't sleep. Jake, John, Ash, and I used to basically live in a tree next to my house.

Technically, it was the neighbor's tree in between the two houses, but their girls never touched it so they let us have it. We'd bring our Gameboys, snacks, books, pillows, interesting conversations, and we'd be in that tree for hours.

This is not the same!

It's very hard to get comfortable. My stomach is empty, my mouth is dry, I'm shivering in these winter clothes, and on top of that I'm totally creeped out. It wouldn't creep me out so much if this tree wasn't made of bone, or if we were back in Dimension Eight.

Good 'ol Number Eight!

Screw Five!

I lean my head on the adjacent branch, that thankfully passes right by my head, and I just stare out in the distance at nothing in particular.

I start to think.

From what I understand, the plan is to wander around this dimension until we find a portal.

Okay then.

But that might not bring us back to our home dimension. We'd probably have to go through several more, just like the Dean's when they were stuck here their first time.

Instead of wandering, we should try to use our magic and see if we can control opening a portal to bring us home.

The five of us are pretty powerful, even me who's still in training. We can probably pull it off.

I did happen to close a portal before. How hard can it be to open one or redirect it?

Yet again, I did it completely by accident, and they did say it was impossible to do so.

I did it though.

We have to think of something better.

Page 171

Anything will be better than being a nomad!

I look around at the other trees. Dead. All of them. I see Deonna asleep on a tree branch several yards away. JP and Audrey are sharing the tree right next to her. They're not on the same branch, but they're leaning on the same bark. It looks very cute actually.

If they weren't cousins, I'd so ship them!

This place sucks.

I remember I fought a flying demon that separated me from everyone, but these trees are thick, nothing's flying through here.

Also, what was my sister's head doing here? Did one of the demons that killed her bring it over? Did it fall through a portal? Did I imagine that and I'm going insane?

I then look over at Darren. He's sharpening a dead bone branch with a chunk of stone. Or is that bone? I can't really tell from over here. Sharpening a bone with another bone sounds weird.

Then again, dad used to sharpen metal knives with a metal stick.

Darren glances down every once in a while, probably making sure nothing's lurking underneath us. His hair keeps falling in his eyes. He swings it out of his face and continues to sharpen.

I just watch him for a while, alternating between making a tool and checking the ground. I don't know why I'm stalking him right now; I just feel drawn to him.

Technically I'm not being a stalker, am I? Wait, why do I care?

His hair falls in his eyes again. When he swings it out of his face, our eyes lock for a quick moment.

I sit up and turn my head so fast I almost lose my balance and fall out of the tree.

Does he know I was staring at him?

I hope not!

Why was I staring at him anyways?

"Can't sleep?"

I jump at the sound of his voice so close to me. I look back to the branch where I was resting my head to see him lying on it, our faces so close together that I can feel his warm breath on my face.

I want to look away, move to another tree, anything, but for some rea-son I can't move.

Page 172

My body refuses.

"Uh..."

Uh!

Nice going, Bec!

"I don't blame you," he whispers, not taking his eyes off mine, "I have no idea how they're asleep right now."

I feel my face turning hot, and I'm shaking a little. Hopefully he doesn't notice my tomato face. I want to hop to another tree or something, but I can't bring myself to look away from his charcoal black eyes. I don't know how long it's been, but we both just keep staring at each other.

"Something on your mind?" he whispers to me, then I feel something gently grab my hand.

I look down and realize that it's his hand, gently caressing mine.

I feel my heart start to pick up speed. It hurts a little, but it also feels nice.

"Something on your mind?" he asks again. I'm surprised by how soft his voice is.

Just like how Tom used to be with me, but somehow different.

"Uh... I was thinking."

Why am I so nervous? I've always been able to talk to Darren. He's supposed to be the spastic, nervous one, not me! And why is he holding my hand. Stop! Wait, don't stop. Why do I want to hold his hand?

Gah!

Calm yourself, Bec. I take a deep breath. "I was thinking, is there another way to get home?"

He blinks a few times. "What do you mean?" He shifts on the branch and rests his arm and hand under his head.

This moves himself a little farther from me, but his hand is still on mine.

Good.

Good? What is wrong with me?

I sit up a little more and flip my hand over so our fingers are interlocking.

Page 173

His hand is so warm. My heart is beating like crazy. It feels nice, but I'm scared at the same time. I swallow a lump building up in my throat and focus on talking.

"I mean, we're just wandering around waiting for something to happen like a nomad," I explain quietly. "Couldn't we use our magic and-"

"Not possible," he informs me calmly.

"But think about it," I say defensively. "We're all powerful, and I was able to close a portal, maybe the five of us can control one and take it home. Even if we find one, it won't take us to Eight, we might go to Seven and we'll be like 'Aw, so close, but yet so far' and have to do the same thing all over again, but it's better than wandering around. Focusing on opening is our best shot. Don't you think it's worth a chance?"

"I understand what you're saying, but it's highly unlikely. Portals are extremely unpredictable."

"Can't we try?" I plead. "Anything will be better than wandering Dimension Five forever."

He chuckles a little. "I feel you. Deonna and I were going nuts last time."

He squeezes my hands again, and I feel a huge smile spread across my face.

He smiles back at me, and we're staring at each other again, this time more intensely. I don't know why, but I have the urge to be closer to him. Next thing I know, we're both leaning towards each other. Our noses are almost touching. I feel my heart beating so fast that it might pop out of my chest.

What's happening. Am I supposed to be comfortable with this?

Next thing I know, Darren pulls away and looks very embarrassed.

"I should wake Audrey," he says, looking in her direction. "She's next watch."

He then lets go of my hand and teleports to her tree.

I reach out for him, but then I immediately pull my hands back and wrap them around my waist.

I don't know why, but I'm very sad he's gone and I want him back.

Page 174

Was I comfortable with what was happening though?

I don't know.

What exactly was happening?

I lean back on the tree and look away from him. I notice a red leaf on one of the branches. I pluck it off and look at it. There's this weird pollen on the leaf and I inhale some of it.

Smells like vinegar.

I wonder if Darren noticed the leaf.

What the fuck is wrong with me?

Chapter 4

I'm being pulled off the tree by someone before my eyes are even open. I don't even remember drifting off to sleep.

"Bec, what's this?" Audrey asks as she tries to stand me up.

"Huh?"

One moment I'm singing adult lyrics to "Hakunna Matatta!" with a Jewish banana, and next thing I know I'm walking on the forest ground in Dimension Five.

I have really weird dreams.

"Look alive," Deonna informs us, "we don't want another run in with demons in here."

"No worries," I sing lightly, still half asleep.

For some reason I'm really out of it, because some time later, I don't even remember Darren picking me up and carrying me like a bride.

I don't mind.

I like being carried.

I rest my head on his shoulder and close my eyes again.

Not like it was easy to keep them open anyways.

"I'm next!" JP jokes.

"Is she alright?" Audrey asks.

"You remember the red leaf you found in her hand?" Darren says.

"Yeah?"

I don't remember anything after that because I suddenly black out.

***

My eyes instantly snap open and I sit up fast. The first thing I see is a red waterfall that's falling up into a black cloud and also down into the water.

That's not supposed to happen.

Then I remember where I am.

Unless this is another dream.

Well, if I really was dreaming, demons would be sliding down the falls and having a barbeque or something.

I stare at the black cloud and smile at how strangely beautiful it looks.

"Good!" I hear Audrey sigh with relief. "Guys! She's awake!"

"Sh!" Deonna runs up to her and harshly whispers. She says something else to her, but I'm too mesmerized by what I'm seeing to pay attention.

I'm sitting on a bed of yellow grass next to the red waterfall. It's not red like the water in the puddle I fell in; it's clearer. For some reason, I don't hear any water falling. It's totally silent. The waterfall is really high up. I used to jump off large boats and small bridges into water before, but I have a feeling that I'll die if I jump off here.

Darren is hunched over by the river with his hands in the red water. The only plant life is the grass, everything else is pure rock just like in the forest. Even at the falls, it's a ninety-degree shift, and the wall on the way up is all rocks. This time they're regular rocks, not bone looking rocks.

Deonna leans next to me. "How are you feeling?" she asks me with such a straight face that she might as well have just asked me what I had for dinner last night.

"I'm fine," I tell her worried. "Did something happen to me?"

"We found you yesterday morning with a red leaf in your hand," she explains. "They're very rare here, but they have the ability to put any animal to sleep for days."

I'm freaked out by this, "How long was I out?"

"I told you, yesterday morning," she tells me very nonchalant. "Darren carried you here."

Page 177

I notice that my breathing was picking up. I force myself to slow it down.

Audrey, who is standing behind Deonna, helps me to my feet, "Come drink, the water is safe."

"Where are we," I ask as I stare hypnotized at the waterfall. An army of demons can jump out and ambush us and I'll still be staring at that waterfall.

"According to Deonna, it's a water hole for the demons," Audrey says and we stop. "We had to wait a few hours for some to leave before we could drink."

When I realize we're at the river, I bend down and hesitate a little, but I cup some red water in my hand. It becomes clear in my palms. It really is normal water. I bring it to my lips and take a sip. It tastes just like Aquafina. Considering the last water that flew in my mouth was half blood from who knows what, the taste is a relief.

I drink some more.

"We still have some water," Darren says as he gently places a Ziploc bag with the red leaf I was holding in Deonna's hands. "Thankfully, I was able to refill one of the bottles."

"Where'd you get the bag from," I ask as I stand.

"Your nuts. We put them in your pocket and took the bag for the leaf."

"What do we need the leaf for?" I ask.

"You'll never know when it'll come in handy," he says, shrugging his shoulders.

I sigh.

I then put my hand in my zipper pocket and feel my collection of nuts and raisins. I scoop a handful and look at them. They seem clean, so I offer some to everyone.

"You should drink a little more water," Darren assures me, taking a few and staring blankly at me. "You did inhale some pretty strong toxins."

I nod and take another gulp of water from the river.

I look at Darren after I drink. He's popping a few nuts in his mouth one by one. His eyes lock with mine for half a second, but then he looks down.

That was weird.

Normally he always smiles at me.

I'm about to offer some nuts to JP, but I realize that he's not here.

"Where's JP?" I ask.

"He had to pee," Audrey informs me. "He's just behind those trees."

"Okay. Any idea where we should go now?" I ask.

"We can't stay here long," Deonna explains. "Demons can appear at any moment. From past experiences, portals tend to open where there's a large concentration."

"I thought we wanted to avoid the demons," I ask.

"We want to avoid confronting them," Darren corrects me. "We are in their home dimension, it's impossible to avoid them. The plan is to hide out where there's a lot and sneak through a portal."

"That's a terrible idea!" Audrey shrieks.

"And it sounds like you're contradicting yourselves," I say.

"Worked last time," the twins say in unison.

"What worked last time?" JP asks coming up behind us.

"Getting out of this dimension," Darren tells him.

"You trust us?"

"Completely," JP says.

"Then let's move."

"I think we should still try my idea first," I tell Darren.

"Bec-"

"It can't hurt to try," I argue. "Worst thing that could happen is nothing."

"Or we get ambushed while our backs are turned."

"You guys did say you waited till the area was cleared."

"Bec-"

"What are you two talking about?" Deonna asks.

"Bec wants to try opening a portal back home," Darren tells her.

"Even if we wanted to, it's not possible," Deonna tells me.

"There's five of us, and I closed one in Broadway, best case scenario we go home. There are no demons around so worst case...nothing happens." I say.

She sighs and looks at Darren.

He shrugs and looks at Audrey. "What do you think, cuz?"

Page 179

She stares at her tapping foot. "Honestly, I think trying would be better than walking in circles."

"JP?" Darren asks.

JP stares off like he didn't hear us.

"JP."

"What? Oh, yeah. Right. I think we should."

The twins sigh. They stare at each other, then look at me.

"How do you want to try this?" Deonna asks.

I smile at them. "Alright, everyone in a circle, and join hands."

I grab JP's and Deonna's hands. Darren goes next to Deonna, and Audrey next to JP. Then everyone grabs hands and stares at me.

What did I do last time?

I think I put all my energy into the wind and reversed it.

Okay.

Now to open.

"Close your eyes and let your energy build up."

I feel energy spiraling up my body.

"Now, think about home."

I start thinking about the old neighborhood where I used to live.

"I feel nothing," one of them says, but I can't tell who.

I think about bike riding with John and Jake, being at the theme parks Tom used to take us to.

I feel a slight wind building up.

"Bec?"

I start to slowly release my energy. How do I know how to do this?

"Oh shit."

"Bec?"

Next thing I know, I'm screaming, laying down on the floor, and my head is spinning.

"Bec!"

Two of them help me sit up, and all the spinning starts to slow down.

"What happened?" I ask. "Did it work?"

"No." Darren sighs. "It almost did, but it also almost killed you."

"How? I had it."

"You just fell and stopped breathing," Audrey says.

Page 180

"It was... scary." Deonna agrees. "You good?"

I sit up and shake my head. Nothing on my body feels injured, and the waterfall stopped spinning. "No."

***

When we make it out of forest area, we reach what appears to be an ocean. Instead of sand, there's black jagged rocks. Good thing we're all wearing shoes. The red ocean's waves seem to be moving away from the shoreline instead of onto it. I have to remind myself that the physical properties here are different. The sun is resting on the horizon, the scarlet red sky starting to turn blue, and the grey clouds are turning green. I can't see the second sun, so it must have already set.

"Pretty soon it's going to be too dark to see," I tell Deonna.

She stares intensely at the water with pure hatred, more hatred than she's ever given me, and that's saying something. She looks back towards the forest we came from, and then she looks at Darren. They nod once to each other, then she tells us, "Let's walk along the beach until we find a safer place to rest. Until then, nobody goes near the water."

"Why not rest here?" JP asks.

"The rocks, JP," Darren tells him. "They'll cut us. Besides, there's no sand here to lie down on."

JP rolls his eyes and starts walking ahead of us. I see the twins give each other a nervous look. They then look back at JP who's not even looking back to see if we're following him. I look at Audrey, and she just shakes her head.

We follow JP. Audrey's walking next to the forest, picking up large pieces of wood as we make our way down the beach. She seems to have a little dance in her step. Why is she dancing?

Darren falls back and takes up the rear. Meanwhile Deonna struggles to keep up with JP. I'm not really watching where I'm going, since I'm mesmerized by the waves and the grey sea foam. Between the puddle I fell in, the upside-down waterfall, and now the ocean, water just seems to attract me in this dimension.

Never did care much for water before unless it was a water ride with a big drop, or I was jumping into it from a high altitude.

"Careful!" I hear Darren shout and grab my arm.

I jump at the sound of his voice. "What? Where? Huh, why?"

"You're getting too close to the shoreline," he explains to me. "Oceans here aren't created with salt, they have acid that is dangerous to everyone but the demons."

"Oh," I stare at the water, so innocent looking yet so deadly. "Sorry, didn't realize I was drifting." Then a thought comes to me. "How'd you guys discover that?"

He sighs and his eyes gaze over his sister. "When we were here last time, Deonna wanted to go in the water. She got her feet in and I got them out before they melted away."

"Ouch." I wince. "Is that why she had those long socks on when I met her?"

He nods, "She always wears long socks because of it."

I look to where Deonna is. Like all of us, she has on long pants because of New Year's, but I can picture her knee-high socks underneath, and her burnt feet under that.

I look at Audrey, still dancing and collecting pieces of wood. I wonder why she's grabbing those? Is she okay? Is this place starting to get to her?

I look at JP, so far ahead of us and not even turning back. He was so scared before, not being able to let go of Audrey. Now he's going off by himself.

I wonder what's going on with him?

Chapter 5

The beach and forest seem to go on forever. I know I'm exaggerating, but it feels that way. My feet want to pop off my legs and hide in the forest. I'll have to crawl on the jagged rocks once my legs give up.

I don't know which one is worse.

Right before the second sun fully sets, we find a solitary rock cave coming out of the forest. JP tries running inside, but Deonna holds him back.

"We don't know what's in there!" she snaps at him.

"Well, then we have to check it out, duh!" he snaps back at her.

"There's a safer way to do it," she growls at him. "We can't just barge in, and since when are you so fresh?"

"Get off my back!"

"Shh." I inch myself towards the cave opening and poke my head inside.

"Bec!" I hear Audrey whisper harshly. She then throws a piece of wood at me. I stop it with my telekinesis inches from the back of my head, and I drop it to the floor.

"If there was something inside," I tell them, "it would have heard us by now and come out to kill us all. In case you haven't noticed, we haven't exactly been quiet." I continue to look.

The cave seems dry and empty. No dripping water, no eerie growl. It's a large cave, I can tell by the darkness that goes far back, but I can't see how far back it goes. I try to make a ball of fire in my hands like Audrey does, but I can't seem to spark it.

I did it only once before, but I can't seem to do it right now.

I'm pretty calm right now.

How the hell am I calm in Dimension Five?

Audrey peeks her head over and sees what I'm doing… well, at least what I'm trying to do. She comes up next to me, lights one of the pieces of wood on fire, and throws it into the cave. It lands about thirty feet away with a loud thump. The cave seems a lot bigger with the light. I notice that the cave bends down and continues. I'm not sure how far though. This cave really is huge.

I don't know what's back there, but I don't think it's demons.

"I think it's safe," Deonna guesses.

I jump at how close her voice is.

God dammit!

JP strolls into the cave and sits against the opposite wall from where we're looking in.

"I'm not sleepy," I announce, surprised myself. "I can take first watch if you'd like."

"Fine by me." Deonna sighs with relief and collapses on the floor near the back.

I walk in after her, but I sit at the opening of the cave.

"You guys get some sleep," JP tells us. "I'll take first watch."

"It's okay," I smile at him. "I got it."

He looks outside and then back at me. "I'll take next watch then." He then lies down. "Wake me in an hour."

Audrey throws down her six large pieces of wood in the center of the cave. She stretches her hand out and the burning piece we threw in first flies into the pile she made.

Slowly, all the other pieces catch fire.

It feels much warmer in the cave. I take off my outer jacket and move closer to the fire. I put my hands up to it.

I really wish I had brought gloves to the New Year's celebration. I didn't bring a warm hat either, which I also regret.

Before walking in, Darren whispers in my ear, "Wake me instead of him after your watch."

I don't have the chance to ask why because he teleports next to Deonna and lies down next to her.

***

I'm not sure how long it takes for my eyes to refuse to stay open. I use the last bit of energy I have to move down and wake Darren up like he asked me to.

He looks around the cave at everyone sleeping. "Thanks." He stands up and then teleports to the cave opening.

I wanted to ask him why he wanted me to wake him, but my eyes close, I lay my head on Deonna, and everything around me disappears.

***

I'm back on the beach in Miami.

I'd recognize this place any time. I'm standing in the middle, completely alone. The sun is in the middle of the sky, shining happily on while I'm standing in the gruesome site of a mass murder. I hear laughing behind me. I turn around and cover my gasp with my mouth.

It's my eldest brother, Tom.

He's standing in front of a barbeque, flipping a few burgers. Roxy is standing next to him, holding out some paper plates. They both look up at me and smile.

"Don't worry, Bec!" Tom shouts smiling. "I have a few veggie burgers here for you!"

"And garlic pickles!" Roxy laughs, holding up the jar.

I have to be dreaming. I look down and see that I'm in the same outfit that I was wearing the day they died. Am I going to have to watch that again? There was no grill that day, only coolers, chairs, and umbrellas, so I'm guessing no.

Just then a large, white cooler appears next to me. I lift the lid and see that it's filled with dozens of cans of root beer.

My favorite.

I hesitate before grabbing a can. They used to always give me headaches because the processed sugar inside, but not knowing what or who I was, I drank them anyways.

I open it and hold it to my lips for a few seconds, and take a sip. Sweet, cold, and refreshing. Exactly how I remember it, minus the inevitable headache.

Page 185

Water splashes me in the face. The little bit that fell in my mouth tells me it's salt water.

I'm standing on the shoreline now. My shoes and socks are gone, and the warm waves are splashing against my feet, and a strong breeze is blowing my hair away from my face. I never realized how much I missed the smell of the ocean. I'm crying a little, but mostly from the wind in my eyes.

JP is in the water, holding a water hose. He puts the tip under the water, pulls the stick back, and shoots Ash and Audrey with it. They both laugh and use their hands to splash him.

"Help me, Bec!" JP screams. "Please!"

The girls splash him and he screams again. He's covering his face, but I assume he's laughing.

Jake is holding someone's feet. They're girl's legs with small, black, water socks. The girl flips back over and her head comes above the surface.

It's Deonna.

She whips her long hair out of her face and giggles.

I wasn't aware she was capable of such an action. Yet again, I haven't thought much of her.

Jake lightly pushes her. She pushes him back and he falls under the water.

Dream or not, I've never seen her so happy. I finish off the root beer quickly and the can disappears with a puff of smoke.

I feel someone's hand slip into mine. It's very warm against my cold skin. By the feel of it, it's slightly larger than mine, and softer too.

"You coming in?" the boy asks me.

I turn my head and see him smiling at me, his hair finally out of his eyes.

"I'm not even-" I suddenly feel wind all over my body.

I look down and see that I'm in a green bikini top with a matching bathing suit skirt.

He's wearing a bathing suit too now with a water shirt.

He laughs and pulls me in the water, my head falling below the surface. My eyes are still open, and I see a whole bunch of rainbow fish swimming around me, and the water is surprisingly clear and doesn't sting.

Page 186

My head comes up and I struggle to pull my wet hair out of my face.

"No fair!" Jake yells, "I've been trying for twelve years to get her in the water!"

Ash starts to cheer.

Audrey and JP give each other a confused look. They both look at me. Audrey and JP smile.

Salty hair falls in my mouth and I spit it out. Well, I try to. This strand just doesn't want to leave my tongue.

He swims next to me and moves the hair out of my eyes.

"Need some help?" he asks with a small smile.

"Nah," I smile. "I'm good."

He picks me up like a bride. I panic a little and wrap my arms around his neck.

"Hold your breath," he whispers in my ear. He dunks me under the water for a few seconds and lifts me back up.

My hair is neatly behind my head and out of my face when I'm up again.

"That's better," he whispers to me.

My cheeks hurt from how big my smile is.

I stare into his beautiful black eyes for a while as he stares into mine. Slowly, my smile fades into a thin smirk, as does his. I wrap my arms tighter around his neck, pulling him closer to me. He moves his face closer to mine, and I feel myself start to do the same.

Everything goes quiet except for our breathing. Our noses touch slightly, and then I hear screaming from somewhere else. Our noses are still touching, but the screaming continues.

"Wake up!"

My eyes snap open and I sit up fast.

Demons are forcing their way into the cave opening.

Darren is trying to hold them off with telekinesis, and Audrey is trying to create a fire wall. I don't hesitate.

Deonna is still asleep next to me. I grab her sweater collar, lift her up, and shake her violently.

JP is poking his head around the back of the cave.

"There's tunnels back here!" he shouts. "We can escape through these!"

Page 187

"We don't know where they lead," I tell him. "We might get cornered!" Deonna's 'question everything' logic must be rubbing off on me.

I keep shaking Deonna, but her eyes aren't even fluttering. How can she sleep through this?

"Bec! Look out!"

A demon has entered the cave and is running towards Deonna and me.

I stand up and use my telekinesis to fling the green fucker into my hands. I focus on my tricks. My hands immediately catch fire. I drop the cadaver on the ground.

I hear some large rocks collapse, and several demons shriek. The cave goes pitch black, and they start scratching at the walls. I try to see what's happening, but realize it's pointless.

"Everyone okay?" Darren asks.

"Good!"

"Fine."

"Deonna's still asleep!"

A faint glow starts to illuminate the cave. Audrey must have lit a fire in her hand.

"She okay?" Darren asks, teleporting over and placing his hand on her forehead. He's panting heavily.

"She's out cold," I explain. "Do you still have the leaf?"

"She has it in her pocket in the plastic bag," he tells me. He looks through her jacket pockets, but seems to grow worried. "Audrey, did Deonna give you the leaf?"

She shakes her head. "I thought you had it."

"Where is it?" Darren asks.

"We can worry about that later," I say. "It's just a leaf. If we have it, great. If not, oh well. So where did those demons come from? There sure were a lot of them."

"I have no idea," Darren admits. "They all came at once, and there was no way to see them coming."

"Could they have followed us from the forest?" I wonder.

He seems to ponder my thought as he picks Deonna up like a bride. "It's possible, but... Why would they come to just..." his eyes trail to JP, who is shifting uncomfortably in his shoes. "You said there were tunnels here?"

Page 188

He nods extremely fast. Any faster his head would fly off.

Darren looks back at the wall he and Audrey made. He looks down at his sleeping sister and gently sighs. He then looks at me with worry clouding his eyes. He stares at the back of the cave where the tunnels are, contorting his lips in thought.

"Keep your light on, Audrey. We might be in there for a while."

Chapter 6

I grab a walking stick from the wood pile just in case.

My friends have a worried look on their faces, all except Deonna, who's still at dream base.

Labyrinth!

It's a fucking labyrinth down here!

Watch us come out and realize ten years have passed.

That'll be a wreck.

Not funny, Bec.

Behind me I make dirt trails.

We're really moving like snails.

Audrey is our only source of light.

Can't see more than a few feet behind or in front of me. I just blindly walk and pull the stick behind me in the dirt. Just a good thing we don't have to fight.

It's hard to tell time down here.

Has it been forty minutes?

Two hours?

A week?

Gah!

I would strike up a conversation, but if there is something down here, I wouldn't want to be the one to attract it to us.

Man, this place is a bust.

Step. Step. Step.

Hey, that's a nice-looking rock.

I pick it up, pocket it, and continue walking.

Step. Step. Step.

I really have to pee.

Step. Step. Step.

She wakes up.

Oh, good... Great.

We came down this way already. There's my dirt line.

No need to roll your eyes at me, Deonna. I just saved us some time!

I step on JP's foot a few times. I say sorry, but he just sighs and keeps looking straight.

Step. Step. Step.

Darren says we should go left. Deonna says right.

Audrey shines the fire but it's hard to see.

I suggest rock paper scissors.

None of them have heard of it before.

Of course they haven't!

JP grunts and starts walking right. Reluctantly we follow.

Step. Step. Step.

This area's caved in. Gotta turn around.

God dammit!

Step. Step. Step.

We didn't go down this way before.

Step. Step. Step.

I collapse on the floor. We decide to rest.

Zzz.

My mind is caving in.

Zzz.

Time to walk again.

Step. Step. Step.

I'm hungry.

We eat some nuts.

Can we drink a little?

We all drink some water.

Step. Step. Step.

Dead end. Turn around. We went right last time, let's go left. No one argues this time.

Step. Step. Step.

Page 191

I really need to pee.
Step. Step. Step.
Interesting rock formation.
Step. Step. Step.
I hate this rock formation.
Step. Step. Step.
It is pretty cool looking.
Step. Step. Step.
Never mind.
Step. Step. Step.
They're just fucking rocks!
Step. Step. Step.
I don't know what to think about the rocks.
Step. Step. Step.
I really gotta pee.
Step. Step. Step.
That rock looks like a face.
Zzz.
Step. Step. Step.
If I can slow time down, can I speed it up?
Focus. Focus. Focus.
Nope.
Fuck.
Step. Step. Step.
I know I'm Miss Hide-from-the-sun, but I miss the sunlight now. I don't even care from which dimension it's from.
Step. Step. Step.
I step on JP's foot. I say sorry but he seethes at me.
Step. Step. Step.
Zzz.
Step. Step. Step.
This place can't be that big!
I really want to pee.
Step. Step. Step.
We eat the rest of the nuts.
Mazel Tov! We're fucked!
Step. Step. Step.

I want to break my stick. I really shouldn't break my stick. I need to do something though.

I'm gonna break the stick.

Deonna takes my stick and continues the trail.

Step. Step. Step.

I miss my stick.

Give me my stick.

No.

Give me my stick.

No.

Give me my stick.

No.

Give me my stick.

No.

Step. Step. Step.

Give me my stick.

No.

Give me my stick.

No.

Give me my stick.

No.

Give me my stick.

No.

Give me my stick.

No.

Step. Step. Step.

Give me my stick.

No.

Give me my stick.

No.

Give me my stick.

No.

Give me my stick.

No.

Step. Step. Step.

Give me my stick.
No.
Give me my fucking stick.
No.
Give me my stick.
No.
Give me my stick.
No.
Give me my stick.
I get my stick back.
I wanna eat it, but I don't wanna lose my stick again.
Step. Step. Step.
Audrey's tired of holding a ball of fire.
We need it to see.
Let's use the stick as a torch.
You stay away from my stick!
She protests and turns out the light.
Deonna starts to scream at her.
Audrey cries.
Deonna starts to cry, too.
Zzz.
The cousins apologize.
Audrey's fire is much weaker than last night. I can barely see.
I really should pee.
I feel dehydrated. Let me drink a little water. Everyone drinks.
Bad idea!
I'm really busting to pee.
Step. Step. Step.
Who the hell even made these tunnels?
Step. Step. Step.
When can we eat something again?
Step. Step. Step.
I forgot that I put this rock in my pocket. Why did I put this rock
in my pocket?
I'm falling behind.
Stepstepstepstepstep.
Okay, I'm caught up.

Page 194

Step. Step. Step.

Zzz.

Step. Step. Step.

Everything is starting to look the same. We're gonna die down here! At least I have my stick.

How are you stick?

I'm good.

I'm hungry, but we're out of nuts, and I can't create any out of thin air.

I wood.

Oh, you are so funny, stick.

I should name you.

Borris? Turtle? How does Apple sound?

Ow, my stomach, bad idea naming you.

Step. Step. Step.

Zzz.

Step. Step. Step.

Your name is Stick.

Step. Step. Step.

Aw fuck! We have to walk uphill now.

Give me strength, Stick!

Audrey's fire is really bright.

Wait, that's not her fire.

Oh thank God!

I can finally pee.

Chapter 7

Thank goodness, we're finally out! Sunlight has never felt so good, except on my eyes. They sting like hell. I remove my jacket, throw myself on the ground, and soak up as much sun as I can.

"We did it, Stick!" I say, holding Stick close to my chest. "We made it out!"

Audrey's weeping from pure joy and making an angel on the flowery grass.

JP breaks off running. Where he's going, I don't know, nor do I care. I go behind the cave to pee. When I'm done, Deonna stares out into the distance, with pure disbelief on her face.

When my eyes adjust, I look around. There aren't any trees, but there's a few bushes with what looks like tomatoes along a large river that seems to flow up instead of down. I resist the urge to run to the tomatoes and eat them, just in case they're poisonous.

"Guys," Deonna whispers. "We have to be careful. We don't know where we are."

I sit up and look at her. I open my mouth to tell her to cut us some slack, that we've been in the dark for weeks, but I close my mouth when I see her eyes. Her head barely moves as her eyes follow JP. I see a look on her that I've never seen before.

I grab Audrey and help her to her feet.

She's smiling wide and her eyes are darting everywhere. Her head rocks back and forth as if a bobble head is in slow motion.

Deonna approaches her slowly. She cautiously lifts her hands. When Audrey sees her head motion and locks eyes with her, Deonna snatches Audrey in a hug.

Darren teleports from the cave opening and stands next to me. He scans the surroundings and crosses his arms. His face gives nothing away as the sunlight shines through his black hair.

Wait.

Sunlight?

And he's teleporting?

I take a deep breath, extend my hand, and use my telekinesis to grab Stick. I slowly put him behind me like a baseball bat. I approach him while tiptoeing, but I'm shaking so much he jumps slightly and stares at me.

He looks me up and down. He crosses his arms and takes half a step away from me. "Bec?" His voice is slightly shaking, the first time since coming here he's shown any fear. "What's wrong?"

"The sunlight," I whisper, Stick shaking so much in my hands that I almost drop him.

He blinks his eyes several times and slightly shakes his head. "What?"

"Who are you?"

"Bec?"

I swing Stick. I don't move him more than a foot before I fall to the floor.

"Bec," Deonna snaps with not as much harshness in her voice. "You need to calm-"

Without moving an inch, I send her flying back several feet with my telekinesis.

Darren vanishes. Stick is grabbed from me and is held against my throat from behind.

"Don't make me use the leaf on you," he threatens quietly.

"The real Darren would never do that," I snap. I slam my foot on top of his. "Plus, we don't have the leaf."

He winces but doesn't budge. "Bec, what are you talking about?"

"You know exactly what."

Stick is removed from my throat. I remain where I stand, and so does he. Deonna is slowly sitting up from where I threw her, rubbing the back of her head. Audrey rushes up to her. She grabs her shoulder, but Deonna winces and shoos her hand away.

"You think I'm not myself?"

"I know you're not him," I say with my voice cracking a little. "Where is he?"

I hear a small gasp of breath from behind.

"What makes you think I'm not the real Darren?"

"You're not changing," I say. "Not even a little."

"We're all changing."

"No." I hold Stick like a sword to his face. "Being out here right now would cause the real Darren, and Deonna to turn red and lose their magic. Every Full does!"

"What do you-" and then he chuckles.

I turn around with my arm up, ready to sock his face in, but he just stands there shaking his head.

"You just noticed we have been out in the sun this whole time? Bec, the sun in this dimension can't do anything to us. It's not strong enough to. We even arrived here in broad daylight. Remember?"

"The Labyrinth and this dimension must be starting to get to her," Deonna says, coming up from behind.

"Audrey's starting to lose it too. We need to rest for a few days. Plus, there's a river and food here. We can be here a while and not worry about that."

"I thought we needed to keep moving?" I snap.

"Not today we don't."

***

Sunlight or not, something is definitely up with them. Darren seems to not be as spazzy. A situation like this would frighten people, not relax them. Come to think of it, he hasn't acted himself in a while. Then there's Deonna.

She's not being a total bitch to me, and she's staring at us as if we have demons growing out of our heads. They're sitting together several yards away whispering to each other.

Page 198

I think they're hiding something.

Deonna, Audrey, and I catch some weird spikey balls with eyes everywhere that are swimming in the river.

Man, I think, how many eyeballs do these things have?

Thirty-Two.

Did this thing just talk to me inside my head?

That's it, I really am losing it!

We each catch three of these weird little animals.

Funny thing is, I thought only demons lived here. Then again, not only humans live in Eight.

JP starts a fire.

The warmth of the fire feels nice after the dark coldness of the cave's labyrinth.

A few times we're here, Deonna shields us with a force field from some passing demons. Other times we engage, but those fights never last very long.

Darren collects a handful of the tomato things.

"How do we know they're not poisonous?" I ask.

"They don't look poisonous," Deonna says.

"Neither does poison ivy but that'll mess your skin up," I say.

"Poison ivy looks extremely poisonous," she says.

"No, it doesn't!"

"Either way, one of us will have to test it on skin."

"How will that help?" Audrey asks.

"The toxins can show up on your skin," Darren says.

"Not all the time though," I say. "Plus, the poison affects you on the inside, not the outside."

"JP!" Audrey shouts.

The rest of us all look at him, half way through a tomato.

"I was hungry," he said. "I... I..."

Audrey runs and gives him a hug. "JP, what if this kills you!"

"We can say the same about those," he says pointing to the puff balls.

"I guess we'll just have to wait and see," Deonna says with tears rolling down her face.

We wait about a day. When nothing happens to JP, we all assume it's safe to eat.

Page 199

What a relief that JP is okay!

I bite into one expecting it to be soft, but it's as tough as a carrot, and it's sweet like a carrot cake.

They eat all the puff balls; I'm not eating animals no matter what the dimension is. We eat in silence. Nobody even tries to be civil for the few days we're here.

Are they mad at me for attacking Darren?

Did I mess everything up?

Chapter 8

Before we leave after what feels like weeks, we refill our bottles, drink some more from the river, and collect as many tomato looking carrot cakes as we can carry.

Magicians don't need to eat as much as humans do because we burn less calories, but damn they're grabbing a lot.

Outside of where we were, the river stops at a little intersection that you can easily jump over, and there's nothing but dead white flowers for miles.

"We should rest here for a while," Darren says, being the first to speak in days. "We've been walking for a long time."

"Sounds good," Deonna agrees.

***

Something is wrong with them.

We just rested for a long time, why are we resting again?

Why else would they be acting so secretive and strange?

Come to think of it, everyone is not acting like themselves.

Audrey keeps panicking and acting like a psych ward patient, and JP... he doesn't even seem to be JP. He's more like a moody teen who is bottling everything up. He's just sitting at the river end, not looking at a single one of us.

Guess he's either mad at us, or he reached that rebellious point in his life.

Then there's me. I'm lying down in a field of prickly dead white flowers, staring at a setting sun, clutching a wooden stick I named to my chest for dear life, and thinking these things about my friends. I even attacked Darren. I'm not the kind of person to attack people I care about.

Ah! My mind!

This place does things to people.

Sure as hell does!

I tried so hard not to be thinking of this, and yet that's all my brain wants to do right now.

What about this place makes everyone go bananas?

The physical properties are definitely different: Two suns that aren't strong enough to change the skin of a Full and take their magic; oceans of acid; a leaf that can knock a person out; there was the waterfall falling up and down simultaneously; weird rivers; puddles deep enough for me to almost drown in.

My sister's head.

Could that really have been her, or did I hallucinate that?

Is there something chemical in the air? I mean, a leaf that can knock a person out, and an ocean of acid. Wait, I already thought of those.

All the plants being dead can't just be related to the demon's lust for killing. It's too coincidental. Also, the little eye head puff balls in the river are proof that demons aren't the only animals that live here.

Maybe I'm just overthinking all of this and we're only losing our minds because we're the ones driving ourselves nuts.

We started being too defensive since we arrived in this dimension. Defensive is normal. We're in a dimension where almost everything can kill us and it's difficult to get home.

Crazy, however, is not normal.

Think, Bec. When did we start going crazy?

Angels in the grass?

No, Audrey's bolts got untwisted before that.

Labyrinth? Maybe.

We seemed pretty normal when we got in the forest.

I'll go from there. Demon attack in the forest. I fell in the puddle. Trauma, yes. Losing my mind, I don't think so. I'll come back to that.

Page 202

I did hear something talk inside my head, but I lost my marbles before that.

The strange waterfall when I woke up from the leaf.

That has to be when we started going over.

Why though?

"Bec?"

I jump up to a sitting position and raise Stick. I lower him immediately when I see Audrey jumping back and shielding herself with her arms.

"Sorry." I sigh and set Stick down. "You alright?"

"I just wanted to say sorry."

I cock an eyebrow at her. "For what?"

"For acting like a nut job, and not talking to anybody."

I pat the ground next to me and she sits down. "We've all been acting like silent nutters."

"Not really," she sighs. She hugs her legs and buries her face in her knees. She's taking deep, shallow breaths.

"Girl," I hold up Stick. "I named a stick and carried it around like a sick baby."

She giggles and turns her head to look at me. "If I remember correctly you almost ate the stick."

"I thought of eating it," I correct her.

She gently grabs the end and turns it. "Look! Those are your bite marks from when you were chewing on it!"

I snatch Stick and look closer at where she's pointing.

It looks like the pencil of a bored five-year-old chewed up in the middle of class.

"Holy- I do not remember doing that!"

She starts to laugh as I set Stick down next to me. She lies down flat on her back and I can see the horizon again that I was staring at earlier.

The last sun has fully set, but there's still some light shining above the horizon.

"I know you're a vegetarian, but that's going a little too far," she jokes, with an authentic warmth.

There's no faking that spunk and sweetness. It's definitely her.

I laugh with her, and then lie down by her side.

Page 203

"Guess I was just tired of dirt!" I play along.

I cover my mouth to not laugh too loud. Audrey's just clenching her teeth trying to hold it in.

"When we get back, I'm eating cheesy potatoes," Audrey smiles.

I sigh. "If we get back."

Her smile vanishes and she tilts her head slightly. "What makes you think we won't get back?"

I turn around so I'm not facing her, but I can still feel her eyes burning into my skull.

"Bec?"

I don't say anything. Ignore it and she'll stop.

"Bec."

Guess not.

"Bec!"

"It's just... we've been here for so long and not a single sign of a portal has been revealed, except for when I tried and almost killed myself. We've all been going bonkers, and I'm trying to think when it started."

She's silent for about three seconds, then asks, "When do you think it started?"

I shake my head, not wanting to say.

"When do you think it started?" she asks again with a little harshness in her voice.

"I think... that... I'm the one who started it."

I close my eyes tightly and hug myself, expecting her to agree and blame me.

I don't hear her move though. I don't even hear her breathing quickening. After a while, I feel her hand on my shoulder and I let myself go and relax my eyes, but I keep them closed.

"You know that's ridiculous, right? If anything, I'm the one who started it. I keep spazzing out, and I constantly get paranoid that we're being watched. You seemed to be the sanest until the stick thing."

"Think about it," I snap. I take a deep breath and repeat more calmly. "Think about it, Audrey. I fall in a puddle and see something traumatizing. Did I hallucinate it or was it actually there? We'll never know, but then JP started acting rash, you started going nuts, Deonna became 'not so bitchy,' and Darren... he..."

"He what?"

I shake my head again. I open my eyes, but then tears immediately fall out, so I close them again.

I can't say this to her, but he seems to be very distant from me ever since the forest. What exactly happened back there to make him like that?

"Besides," I say, "it's my fault we're here anyways."

Audrey moves herself right next to me and wraps her arm around my waist. "Blaming yourself won't fix anything. You didn't get us here on purpose, and you sure as hell aren't the reason we're acting strange. We might not know why all this is happening, but I know you'll help us out. Now stop avoiding my question."

I love her, but I hate her right now. "You know, I've always wanted to travel, I've even studied my top five places that I wanted to go. I guess this is the universe giving me what I want in a very ironic twist."

"Darren?"

"Russia, Australia, Japan, Egypt, and Peru."

"About Darren?"

"One country per continent is where I want to go."

"When you're done avoiding my question, answer it."

I sigh. "I don't want to talk about him right now."

"Bec, I've noticed a small change in him too, but he's not letting himself go, if anything, he is more of himself and he cares way too much. Especially about you."

I open my eyes. When no tears come out, I turn to face her. "We must not be thinking about the same Darren."

"Girl, I know my cousin. He doesn't show much emotion-"

"Bull, he spazzes a lot."

"Only around you."

"Huh?"

"He doesn't show much emotion, but he's worried about all of us. Especially you. He always takes a double look at you, walks next to you, hey, he even carried you while you were unconscious. Wouldn't let any of us touch you."

"Probably so you wouldn't get infected."

"That comment right there shows he was worried about the rest of us as well."

She got me there.

"Why does this bother you so much?" she asks.

"Everything is bothering me, and I said I didn't want to talk about this."

"Ah, you've reached that stage."

"What stage?"

"The point is, he's looking out for all of us. Trust me, he'll never stop caring or worrying."

"What stage are you talking about?"

"You remember Hanukkah when I said to you-"

"Not happening."

"You'll never know."

"Oh, I know. Why is that so important to you?"

"You don't have to be a teller to see it."

"See what? There's nothing there."

"Mm hm. You two will be there pretty soon, doing kissy faces, and making lots of babies."

"Audrey! No. He's so much older than me! And I don't even know how to do that!"

"Really?"

"I wasn't allowed to take sex ed."

"Your mom never had conversations like this with you? Talked about being careful, showed you videos, or complained how you ripped her stom.... Oh shit! Sorry! I-"

"It's fine, girl."

Audrey then giggles.

"Hey!" I say defensively. "I'm thirteen! I was never taught this stuff! My dad said that I was too young! I had to wait until eighth grade, but I never made it to eighth grade."

"I guess it's time we talk about the bats and the beatles," she says.

"Don't you mean the birds and the bees?"

"What kind of metaphor is that?" She laughs.

I lie on my back and look up at the sky that just turned completely dark. "I hope you're right and this is all in my head."

Page 206

Something starts glowing green next to me. I turn my head and gasp. The white flowers are standing straighter and are glowing green for two seconds, then they turn blue, then purple, pink, red, orange, yellow, green, and even more colors. They don't change color at the same time. If anything, no two change at the same time. Some even end up taking almost a minute to change, some go through all
the colors in a second.

"Wow," I whisper after a few minutes. "It's so beautiful."

"How's this for hope?" She asks me.

"How are you doing this?" I ask her without taking my eyes off the regenerated flowers.

"I'm not," she admits with the same tone I just had. "Must be something that happens here."

I hear her lie down and shift around for a bit. She doesn't say anything else. She either fell asleep or is watching the flowers. I'm glad for the silence at the moment.

I continue to gape at the flowers. I stare at the one right in front of my face. This one seems to be the most active, changing colors faster than the other flowers in the field.

I reach for it and rub its stem. It's smooth.

The flower seems to jump up and down in place as if it's excited. I smile wide at the flower. It starts to shake violently and the colors seem to go through several whole cycles in half a second. It then turns grey and falls dead on my hand, no longer smooth.

There goes my hope.

Chapter 9

Everyone seems to be in a better mood after the flowers in the field.

Audrey's not acting like a basket case, JP's not a grouch, but Darren and Deonna, although calmer, seem to still be a little odd to me.

They seem to have some twin telepathy thing going on, looking at each other once in a while, smiling, and nodding. They're definitely keeping something from us.

They do another glance at each other.

What's going on?

Darren catches me looking at him. He jumps a little and makes a thin smile on his lips.

"You hungry?" Darren asks us.

Busted.

Deonna rolls her eyes at him. "We're all hungry. We have to find a place where we can think. In the meantime, we should drink a little and eat some of our rations."

"Fine."

"Before we do that," I butt in, "I seriously think we should-"

"Out of the question," Darren says.

"But, but you don't even know what I'm going to say."

"You want to retry opening the portal again."

"Okay... so you do know."

"I agree with Darren," Audrey adds. "Bec, you almost died."

"But if I can get you guys out-"

"It's worth a try," Deonna says. "We might all die either way. Plus, if she survives-"

"We're not losing anyone," Darren says.

"People always die. Besides, it's two against two,"
Deonna notices. "JP, be our tie breaker."

"Can we eat first?" JP asks.

"Fine." I go to take some of those funky fruits out of my sweater pocket, but there's only one. "This is all we have left? I put five in here!" Deonna's eyes grow wide and she grabs my wrist to get a better look at our ration. She stares at it with an open mouth. Her eyes nearly pop out of her head. "How can this be all that's left? Who else stuffed their pockets?"

"How much did you eat, Bec?" Audrey asks me.

"Nothing without you guys!"

JP raises his eyebrows, Deonna squints her eyes, and Audrey bites her lower lip and stares sharply at me.

"I'm being honest," I tell them. "The river water actually kept me going so I didn't need much."

"A likely story," Deonna says.

"Hey, hey, weren't we all calm just a moment ago?" Audrey points out. "Let's try and keep our cool or we will loosen our screws like before. The river water did rejuvenate us pretty good, better than the water Deonna brought with her, to be honest."

They give each other another look. Deonna darts her eyes, and Darren nods.

He checks his pockets and his eyes grow. "I had three fruits and now they're all gone!"

"What?"

"Where's our food?"

"Let's drink a bit, and we can refill at the next stream. Sound good?" Audrey offers. "We're not going to find our missing food by yelling at each other."

Deonna agrees despite shaking her head. When she grabs the bottles though, she goes wide-eyed and pale.

"Where's the water?"

"What?" Audrey asks.

She takes out empty bottles.

Uh oh!

"Someone's been stealing rations," Deonna whispers.

Page 209

"But who?" JP asks.

"That's it!" I say. "I'm trying the portal by myself!"

"Bec!"

I close my eyes and focus like before, collecting all of my energy, thinking of Eagle Lake and the tree house.

Then my mind crosses to New York and the Statue of Liberty.

That's when something wraps around my leg.

I instinctively tug on it and it gets tighter. I look down and find one of the flowers is around my ankle.

I start to hear crunching sounds.

We all do, judging by everyone's terrified faces, and eyes darting everywhere.

"JP!" Darren shouts.

"It's not him," I realize, feeling the ground shake.

It's happened to Audrey too. She has a fireball in both hands and she shoots my feet and hers.

I feel a small burn, but it's nothing compared to our training.

Stronger snapping sounds happen and the ground starts to shake more violently. The flowers start to turn back into buds, and the stocks start to grow at an abnormally fast rate.

"Run?" I whisper.

Deonna nods once and we all make a break for it.

I make it several feet before buds force themselves in my face. I instinctively dive underneath them and get back up on the other side.

I hear Darren scream behind me.

I turn around and see his eyes closing. His whole body going limp from a green gas the buds shot in his face.

I run towards him.

Three stalks start to wrap themselves around him and pull him toward the ground.

Deonna extends her arms towards him and closes her eyes.

When I get to him, his feet are already under the ground.

I can't think of anything to do but dig around his feet.

When I get to his ankles, there's a small static shock that goes from my hand to my chest and I start shaking like crazy.

What was that?

I avoid his body and dig around him. It seems to work.

Page 210

Deonna's pulling him out as I dig.

"Why does it only want him?" I ask out loud.

"Don't jinx it!"

The flower buds fight back. They slash at my hands and cut them open. I wince, but I keep digging through the pain.

Acting strange or not, I can't lose him too.

His veins are starting to turn green. I dig up to his foot, but his foot has turned into roots. I yank them off, and Deonna almost goes flying.

Without any words between us, she puts his right arm over her, and I do the same with his left. We move as fast as we can, but the flowers are following us, slithering on the ground after us like water snakes.

I see Audrey and JP in the distance. Audrey is roasting everything she can see, and JP is just standing behind her, looking at the flowers.

I look back down at Darren. His veins are turning a darker green around his face now, and blood from my hand is caking his right cheek.

"Audrey!" Deonna screams.

I look back up and see that she has fallen and flowers start to cocoon her and pull her towards the ground.

"Get him out of here!" I tell Deonna, let go of Darren, and then run to Audrey.

As I run, the flower buds try to grab my ankles, but they never seem to even touch me, although I did see some zipping past the corner of my eye.

The little buds open and close all around me as if they're taunting me. They seem to be saying, "we're gonna get'cha!"

I'm not being fertilizer today, bitch!

I force myself to sprint a little faster.

When I make it to her, she's almost completely cocooned, and her veins are almost black.

Shit!

Instinctively, I throw my arms down and everything around me starts to slow down.

Why didn't I think of this sooner?

I claw at the cocoon, and it rips instantly. I fall on the ground, but I force myself back up.

I manage to rip her out, but she looks awful. She's a lot paler than normal, but her veins are nearly black. Also, up to her knee is now all roots.

I manage to pick her up and put her on my back, piggyback style, and I run faster than I knew I could run.

I pass Deonna and Darren on my way out of the flower field. I don't get a good look at them, but I manage to reach JP at a cliff. I put Audrey down, and I run back for Darren and Deonna.

Buds are making their way up their legs when I reach them. I get in between them and hook both of their arms around my neck.

I don't have a good grip on them.

I run anyways, but not as fast as I was running before.

The flower buds slowly start to come together, which puts me farther in front of them.

I make it back to the edge of the cliff with both of them.

Darren is still unconscious. I notice a dead tree by the cliff.

I lean Darren against the tree and pick up a piece of wood that's next to it. It feels quite nice actually, almost like a-

I don't need to know how to ride a skateboard, it's not going to save my life, or anyone else's!

I find another piece that's bigger than mine and I throw it at Deonna.

I grab Audrey and shout, "We have to skate down!"

When no one moves, I throw my arms down and they move at a normal pace again. "We have to skate down!"

"What!" JP shouts.

I get a better grip of Audrey, look down at the rocks several miles down, and look back at the flowers that have made a wall and are coming after us. Deonna has picked Darren up like a bride and jumped first on the wood I threw at her head where there is now a gash of blood.

"What!" JP shouts again.

I nod to him once, I jump on my wood, get a better grip of Audrey, and I ride down.

Page 212

It's a rocky ride and it's hard to keep my balance, but I soon remember all my skating lessons and get my footing. Having no wheels on this makes this easier.

This being steep, however, does not.

It's just like snowboarding.

It's just like snowboarding.

It's just like snowboarding.

I've never been snowboarding before.

Fuck!

Audrey starts to slip a little. I grab her tighter and pull her toward me. She's starting to look worse.

I look forward again and I have to make a quick sharp turn in order to avoid running straight into a large boulder.

Keep it steady.

I keep my feet at the back and middle of the board so the front doesn't catch on anything.

Left.

Left.

Right.

Feel it in your lower body.

I make small gradual turns, just like on a real board.

A small wall of rocks seems to come out of nowhere.

Jump!

I clear it over the rocks. Audrey nearly slips, but I get a hard grip on her.

Almost at the bottom!

The wind in my face, a board at my feet, I start to laugh. I missed being on a board.

A sharp rock I didn't see catches my board and Audrey and I go flying.

I land on my feet, with Audrey still on me, I break both of my ankles, fall, and hit my head on the ground.

"F-f-f-f-f-fuuuuu!"

I grab both my ankles. I send an icy wave into them, and the feeling travels up my spine. I also put my hands on my head and send the icy feeling there as well.

Page 213

Audrey has a scratch on her face, but nothing seems broken. I grab her head and do the same.

Please work!

Her scratch goes away, her veins slowly turning a lighter green than normal, her legs turn into stumps, everything below the knees are now gone, and then she wakes up.

Oh, thank God my healing is powerful!

"What...." Audrey says.

"Hey, girl," I say cheesily. "Sorry I couldn't-"

"My legs!"

"So, you noticed."

"Where are my legs?" she starts to cry.

"Fuck!" Deonna screams.

The twins make it down now, but they have a very bad stop.

I move to Darren and do the same for him. It takes a lot longer for him to heal, but eventually he wakes up. He's missing a foot now from where it turned into veins.

I guess my healing can't grow back limbs.

I sigh with relief and pull him into a hug.

"What... happened?" he asks silently, grabbing his head.

I just can't lose him.

Deonna's grabbing her leg. It has her bone sticking out of it, and blood is soaking her pants.

I grab her leg to heal it, but she kicks me in the face with her good leg.

"Let me heal you!" I snap. "God dammit! Is this payback for the woods or something?"

"Whatever floats your boat," she sneers.

Bitch!

As she tries to pull her leg from me and I force it still, I hear a thump behind me.

"My foot!" I hear Darren shout.

"Sorry, guys," I tell them, "but those flowers did some irreversible damage to you."

"I'll never walk again," I hear Audrey whine.

"Sure you will," I poorly assure her. "You'll just need some prosthetics."

Page 214

I hear a screech and a stop behind me.

"You okay?" I ask, knowing it's JP, when I just finished healing Deonna.

"What the fuck, JP!" Deonna jumps up and is in JP's face. "You could have gotten her killed!"

"Whoa, Deonna." Darren starts to stand, but he goes back down. "What's wrong?"

"He tried to kill Audrey."

"No I didn't."

"I saw you! You pushed her!"

"It was an accident," JP protests.

"And then you left her to-"

"Well, then it's a good thing Bec was there. Besides, if I didn't leave, I would have been killed myself."

Deonna goes silent. She presses her lips together and glares at him. She then grunts and drops her gaze.

"Lay off him, Deonna," I add, trying to stand, but my head starts to spin. "You're acting like he meant all this to happen. We're all fine now. A little... off.... and.... inj... But... but we're..." my vision spins, "missing limbs," and then everything goes black.

Chapter 10

I wake up laying on a bunch of rocks. I look around and realize that we haven't moved at all.

"How long was I out?" I ask no one in particular.

"About five minutes," Audrey says.

Wow.

Deonna is at her side helping to prop Audrey up. All three of the makeshift boards are gone, and Audrey now has two prosthetic legs under her knees. Darren has a crutch to support his missing foot.

"It's a good thing that didn't happen in the middle of the fight," Audrey laughs. "Then we'd all be dead."

"So... we all good?" I ask. "Besides the missing limbs?"

Deonna grunts and gives JP a look she usually gives me. "For now."

"Should we rest for a bit?" Darren asks. "That was some pretty-"

"No chance in hell am I staying here," Deonna says.

"Audrey and I have to relearn to walk again though," Darren says.

"Well, learn on the way out of here," Deonna says.

***

We walk away from the cliff and enter a canyon of some sort. It's similar to the Grand Canyon, but deeper, redder, and has bizarre rock formations. I'm not sure if the rock that looked like a slice of pizza was actually that, or if I'm just that hungry, but it is weird looking in here. Kind of like pictures of the Mars canyons.

We've been walking for so long that the suns set so many times that I lost count. Have we been in here a month? Damn, that's almost as long as we've been in the labyrinth.

***

Night forty-seven in the canyon, I think.

"Try this," I say, handing Darren a different rock.

He puts both his hands over it and it turns into a prosthetic foot. In order for his transformations to work, the object needs to be the same size, like he can't just take a small rock and turn it into a walking stick.

Deonna helps him attach it.

"It's a little big, but it'll do," Darren says, testing it with the crutch.

I start to grumble. "If only I could of-"

"Don't beat yourself over it, Bec," Darren says to me. "Audrey and I would be dead now if it wasn't for you. We all would."

"You wouldn't have needed me to save your lives if I didn't get us stuck here in the first place," I say.

"True," Deonna says point blank.

"Dee?" Darren says.

"Is she wrong?" she asks her brother.

He sighs.

"I've been meaning to ask you guys something," I say.

They look at me and nod.

"It's about your last trip to this dimension," I say. "Did you guys come to these areas?"

"The first field we were in, yes," Darren says.

"Everywhere else, no."

"Then how do you guys know these places so well?" I ask.

"We don't," they say simultaneously.

I raise my eyebrows at them.

"We don't. We're just guessing," Deonna adds. "Same as you."

I nod slowly.

Page 217

"Also, you know how demons attack and kill?" I ask.

"No," Darren says.

"What?"

He then smiles at me, showing me that he's joking.

I laugh a little. I needed that. Maybe it is Darren. "Do they ever bring people back here?"

They look at each other, then back at me.

"Where'd you get that idea?" Deonna asks me.

"Do they, though?" I ask.

Darren shrugs.

"Not as far as we know," Deonna tells me. "Why? Did you see something?"

Should I tell them what I saw? I didn't even tell Audrey. "I was just thinking about some Bermuda Triangle stuff," I tell them after a few short pauses. "It's nothing. I don't know. I guess my brain just works faster than I do."

They look at each other and say nothing.

I'll have to ask Emma about this stuff when we get back.

If I get back.

***

Day fifty in the canyon.

I think.

We're walking more in the canyon when four demons ambush us. Half of them go straight for Audrey, the other half for Darren.

I'm closer to Audrey, so I use Stick and whack the demons in their heads as if they were baseballs.

I regret this the moment I do because Stick shatters in my hands.

They run up to me again, and I punch one of them square in the face. I take the other one's oxygen away and watch it squirm. The second demon starts to get up when its friend dies.

It runs towards me, but a fireball is thrown at it. It wiggles on the floor until I smell burnt carcass.

I look to my left and see Audrey with her hand out, no longer leaning on her crutches.

Page 218

"Thanks," I tell her. I look to my right and see that Deonna is exploding the last demon. JP is next to her, so I assume he got the other one.

I look down at my shattered friend. He's broken in four different places.

"Maybe I can heal him," I say, knowing it can't be done.

"I'm sorry," Audrey says, patting my shoulder.

I start wiping some tears from my eyes. "We've got to get out of this bloody dimension."

***

"We should stop," JP suggests the next day, shaking a little. He takes off his waist coat and puts it on.

"How come?" Darren asks, raising an eyebrow.

"Uh, we're running out of food and stuff," he tells us. "We wouldn't want to push ourselves too hard and get exhausted. It could kill us."

"But we just rested," I say.

"Speaking of," Deonna snaps, "who was eating our rations without anyone noticing?"

"Wasn't me," JP says, casually shrugging his shoulders.

"And how are we supposed to believe that?" she snaps.

"Dee," Darren whispers.

"Don't Dee me. He's been acting the strangest out of all of us, and you know it!"

Darren sighs and looks at JP. "What's wrong, dude?"

"What's wrong, dude?" I interrupt. "What's wrong? I'll tell you what's wrong, dude! It's you two. You're the ones who haven't been acting like yourselves! The real Deonna would never be considerate towards me and snap at her cousins, and the real Darren would never be this calm, and the two of you are supposed to not have your magic working in sunlight, yet, here you are. You've also been super secretive. What's there to hide, huh?"

"Bec," Darren says calmly. "We are real."

"Then prove it!" I snap.

"The suns affect us differently in this dimension," Darren says. "As for the way we're acting, we have our reasons."

I go to JP and give him a hug, but he doesn't hug me back. The poor thing is scared of us. "Treat him like your cousin, not a demon, and start acting normal."

"You think anyone can be normal here?" Deonna snaps. "You were carrying that stupid stick around like it was a baby!"

"Don't you call my Stick stupid!" I yell despite knowing she's right. "He gave his life for me!"

"It was an inanimate object!" Deonna shouts.

"He would have been useful when the shape shifting demons decide to betray us."

"Bec!" Audrey starts.

There's something sharp pressed against my throat so hard that I start to choke a little.

"JP?" Audrey whispers.

"Surprise!" someone says behind me. "Eh, not really, you kinda knew. Or, well, they knew. You two were clueless as fuck!"

My back is hunched in the wrong direction so I can only see the sun. It burns my eyes, and I can't move without getting scratched.

What the hell is going on?

"You trai-" Darren starts to scream and makes a choking sound.

"What's that black gas coming out of his mouth?" Deonna panics.

"Looks like I'll have to take care of you myself," the voice holding me says. "It wasn't supposed to be this way. Then again, this way is more fun!"

"So you were setting us up!" Audrey screams. "Why!" She starts to sob.

I feel the boy who might be JP, but sounds nothing like him, shrug his shoulders. "Father insisted," he says point blank. "There's no displeasing father, now is there."

Frederick? No, this is not JP.

"Who-" I start, but I stop talking because of the sharp object digging deeper into my throat.

"You'll be coming with me," he whispers in my ear. "Father is excited to meet you."

Page 220

What the fuck! Is it his father? Some sick priest? A codename? Well, whoever he is, I'm not going.

Without moving, I use my telekinesis to grab a rock and fling it at the imposter's head.

When he moves out of the rock's way, I try to grab the object pressed against my throat, but it doesn't budge.

He laughs. "Your misdirection sucks." He slips up his grip a little while he laughs, which is just enough for me to grab the knife on my throat and swing him over my head.

Before he can make an umpf sound flat on his back, I have the knife pointed at his head, and someone else has a spear against his heart.

I don't dare break eye contact with imposter JP.

I hear Darren breathing heavily.

"My misdirection might suck, but my combat skills sure don't."

"That wasn't all you," a girl's voice says next to me. "And that's not JP."

The boy on the floor laughs and turns into a black light, and the light morphs into a taller and thinner boy. When the light fades, a pale white boy who looks eighteen is laying there. He has pale white skin, dirty black hair, and a small nose. He's wearing a brown trench coat. His eyes freak me out a little, for they remind me of the girl in the bathroom, except he has a left orange eye instead of blue.

He looks like a normal magician, except his hands are webbed and he has gills on his neck.

I look at the others while he shifts. JP just shifted into someone else who wants us dead, right in front of our eyes, yet all the three of them can do is gape at the girl next to me, who I can't look at for fear the boy will kill us.

When he looks down, I take a quick glance at her for half a second then look back at the boy, good thing because he shifted a little.
She has on a pair of black shorts, and what I believe is a sweater with some weird device to close it. She has a blue backpack on and no shoes. She has curly red hair, fierce yellow eyes, and freckles. Her face, however, is similar to JP's.

She opens her mouth, and I know who she is even though I've never met her before, and everyone said she was dead.

Page 221

"Now, you're going to tell me where my little brother is."

Part 2: Where I Was

Chapter 1

"Ray!" my little brother calls out, running into my room as I'm setting my music box down on the night table. "Wanna play?"

"In a minute, JP," I tell him. "I'm a little tired."

He sits on my lap and grabs my music box. "You're always playing with this."

I laugh. "Really, because I recall that you used to play with this all the time when you were a baby. Running around the house naked saying, 'chardettle, chardettle,' and annoying every-"

"Okay, okay, I get it."

I laugh again and wrap my arms around his waist.

"Come on."

***

We play with the glow in the dark frisbee out in the front yard. My brother usually leaves it outside during the day for me.

"If you can't see the sun, at least see what it leaves behind," he told me when he first gave it to me.

I send the frisbee soaring over his head, but it lands in the tree several feet behind him.

I extend my hand and use my telekinesis to get it down.

Meanwhile, JP takes out his mother's doll and starts playing with the hair. His mother was a kind human woman, gentle with him, and great with me. It's a shame she got sick. I, on the other hand, never knew my mother.

She died in childbirth.

The wind picks up a lot and the frisbee flies out of my telekinetic grasp.

I hear a growl.

It's close.

"JP, get behind me!"

And then I see them. Four of them. Demons.

I pull JP behind me as I lift one of them into the air and knock the other three down like bowling pins.

"Go inside and get dad!" I shout to him.

"But-"

"Now!"

I feel him jump at the harshness in my voice and hear something fall. When he runs inside, I take a quick glance down and notice he dropped his mother's doll. I pick it up with my telekinesis and put it on my belt as the demons recollect themselves.

Before they can fully recover, I turn invisible.

I sneak up to one of them as they screech amongst themselves. I grab the nearest one and snap its neck. I drop its limp body on the floor as the other three charge me. I turn visible, grab another, and turn it into a rock. I squeeze hard and I crush it as the doll falls out of my belt.

The third demon grabs the doll at my feet and runs off with it.

"Get back here, you little bastard!" I scream.

I go after it at full throttle.

"Raven!" I hear my father scream.

I ignore him.

I've handled these things before. I'm smarter than them and I'm fast on my feet.

I continue sprinting after the demon until I catch up to it.

I manage to grab my brother's doll, but then the fourth demon sinks its teeth into my arm.

I scream.

I punch the demon until it releases its grip on me, but the other demon takes advantage and bites the same spot on my arm.

I scream again.

Page 225

With my free hand, I choke the demon until its jaw is completely loose and it falls limply to the floor. I face the other demon who is charging me. I punch it in the face once it gets close to me. When it's on the floor grabbing its head, I smash my foot into its skull. Its brains splatter against my bare feet.

I sigh with relief as I check the doll.

It's a little dirty, but there's no blood or demon guts on it. The hair is a bit messy, but it's nothing I can't fix.

I turn around to start walking home, but my feet kick water and I sway back and forth.

What the fuck?

I look down and see that I'm submerged in water, but there's no floor. I look up, but I don't see anything that can be the top, or surface.

Where the hell am I?

Chapter 2

I swim for what feels like days, but all that's around me is this accursed water. Thankfully, I can breathe this stuff.

Never run after the demons, that's, like, rule number one, and I totally ignored it!

Gosh! My father and brother must be so worried about me! They probably think I'm dead.

I stop swimming and clutch my chest.

What if I am dead?

I flatten my hand and feel my heartbeat.

Okay, so I'm alive, but why am I here? Where is here?

My stomach starts to growl.

Uh oh.

***

I continue swimming for what feels like much longer, but I get weaker with every stroke. I try swimming up for hours, but I never seem to reach anything. Nowhere else to go, so I continue upwards, but I never seem to reach the surface.

A few times I get tired and rest, but then I slowly start to fall. This method seems kind of redundant, so I move forward instead.

I wish there was some current that I could swim along with to make my life a little easier.

I must be in one of the other dimensions. Solid theory, but which one? Every magician knows there are eight dimensions. We only know about Five and Eight.

Okay, now what do I know?

Demons control three dimensions, plus Five, making it four in total.

I haven't seen a soul since I got here, so I can't say for certain which dimension this is. Also, is this a demon-controlled dimension?

Is this Five?

Oh! Please don't let this be Dimension Five!

My head starts to spin a little. I need some food, and fast. I'm so desperate I'd eat a cupcake!

Focus, Raven.

I take three deep breaths and then I scan around me.

Water.

Water.

Water.

More fucking water.

Some speck.

Water.

Wait! A speck! Could be something living!

Yes!

I turn my body and start swimming toward the speck as fast as my tired body would allow me to.

It grows a little larger with every stroke, and starts developing features. I see one speck turn into several specks. Ten? Ah, who cares, something is better than nothing! Then two arms, and two legs appear on each. Are these magicians? Definitely can't be humans. They appear as different colors, some having horns.

What if these are demons?

Shit!

I quickly stop swimming and turn invisible.

I'm feeling dizzy all of a sudden.

Oh, please body, I need you to work with me!

My stomach growls.

The large specks all turn their heads toward my direction.

Demons. I knew it!

Page 228

They start to swim over, but I don't dare move a muscle.

One of them comes right next to my head. I notice it's gills opening and closing as it breathes.

One versus ten.

In my weakened state, I'd never win. I don't even think I can take out more than two.

Should I just follow them? See if I can find anything out? Maybe get something to eat? It's better than blindly fighting them.

I slowly turn my head and notice a young woman, teenager maybe. Her body looks like that of a normal magician, but she's covered in algae from head to toe. Her bare body isn't what catches me off guard though.

It's her eyes.

Her right eye is green, and her left eye is as blue as the substance I'm trying so hard not to move in.

I've never seen eyes like that before. What's that called? Heterochromia? Ah, fuck, that's not important right now!

Thankfully, she's not aware of my presence. Her attention is on the demons that are bickering around her. She's shouting at them in a language I can't understand, even resorting to grabbing them and forcefully moving them. She then extends her arms out and they all freeze.

They're yanked by an invisible force and are arranged in a straight line in front of me.

She has telekinesis!

Is she a magician?

She must be a half.

Question is, what's her other half?

She makes her way to the front of the demons and faces away from them. She puts up a hand and moves the other one in a circular counter-clockwise motion. A gargantuan sum of currents and energy flow toward the direction she is facing.

What's she doing?

The demons start swimming past the girl.

Curiosity draws me to follow behind the last one.

Next thing I know, I fall flat on my face.

Wait. Fall?

Page 229

My invisible hands are touching solid ground.

I could start rolling around in the orange grass underneath me, but the demons are still around me. I have to stay quiet.

The algae girl didn't follow me, and the demons have already scattered and are nowhere to be seen. I stay invisible for a few more minutes, and then I make myself visible again.

There are jungle plants that seem to spread out for miles on end. Some look like pines, but a majority of them I can't even connect with another plant from home.

What are these?

I'm next to one that I can somewhat describe as a round Venus fly trap that's about the size of the Statue of Liberty. It's blood orange with purple vein-like strands that go all around it. Instead of the mouth having hairs like a Venus flytrap, it has a large purple tongue like object protruding out of the top and it travels all the way to the ground and kind of coils itself in a pile that's almost as tall as I am.

I walk towards the pile and see that there's clean water inside of it.

Is it drinkable?

Will it kill me?

I cautiously stick my index finger inside the water and leave it in there for what feels to be a whole minute. No burning sensation, no tingling, no itching, or rashes.

I cup my hands under the water and bring it to my lips.

I inhale the contents in less than a second, and I stick my hands back under for more. Only when my belly is so full that I can feel the liquid sloshing inside of me do I stop drinking.

I move to the next plant. This plant has orange leaves that are shaped like a six-sided star, and again has the purple veins.

I rip a leaf off, and a purple liquid starts oozing out of the leaf where I ripped it. I touch the ooze. Again, it doesn't burn my skin, so I eat the leaf.

The purple ooze tastes exactly like blood.

I stare at the spot where I ripped the leaf off and purple blood is still coming out of the spot.

I gently touch the stalk.

"I'm so sorry I hurt you," I say to the plant.

Page 230

The stalk seems to move up and down as if it's nodding in agreement. Another stalk with more leaves moves into my face.

"Thank you." I kiss the leaf, and then I carefully tear it off and pop it in my mouth.

Wait!

I'm in another dimension!

Did that girl open a portal and bring me here?

Chapter 3

How could she possibly open a portal?

Has it always been like that?

Are there more people like her doing this on purpose?

Do they control the demons?

Are they the real illuminati?

Holy shit!

Okay, Raven, calm down.

I take a few deep breaths, but it doesn't seem to calm me down at all.

Okay, so I just might be the only magician with this intel. Just another reason why I so desperately need to get home to my father and tell him everything.

Question is, where am I now, and what happened to the demons that crossed over to here?

I quickly do a double take, but I don't see anything.

I try and turn myself invisible, but my head spins too much at the thought of going transparent.

Wait, they would have tried to kill me already if they were nearby.

I relax a little, but I don't completely let my guard down.

I keep an ear listening behind me as I take another leaf.

I can't fight on an empty stomach, but I can't eat knowing there are demons around me.

Gah!

I fucking hate this!

I shove the leaf in my mouth and chew as I grab two more leaves and shove them in my mouth.

I shove leaves in my mouth faster than I can chew them.

Once my stomach is satisfied with my new grass diet, I turn around and scan again for demons.

Still don't see anything.

Still don't hear anything either.

Where did they go?

I slowly walk through the area where I am. All I see are these exotic plants. I look up and see a green sky with a bunch of white dots.

White dots?

Stars.

I'm a fucking idiot.

I go to the nearest white tree and climb up it, grabbing the falling vines to pull me up.

I scan the area again. It's so beautiful. There's a canal not too far from here. I can probably make it there in half an hour. I need to rest after being in that water dimension, but my body for some reason doesn't want to-

***

What just happened!?

There's a light green sky with a giant orange ball near the horizon. Sweat drips down my face, down my neck and back.

Must be, like, a hundred degrees Fahrenheit out here.

Did I fall asleep?

I must have.

Canal!

I jump out of the tree, landing on my feet.

I grab a few more leaves from the bush next to the one I grabbed from yesterday, and start walking in the direction of the canal.

I make it there in no time, though I'm covered in sweat by the time I get there.

The water seems to really sparkle here.

I bend down to take off my shoes, but I realize that I'm not wearing any. Did I really not put on any shoes, or sandals, when I went outside to play with JP?

JP.

I'll be home soon, baby brother.

I hope.

I look around. I haven't seen a single animal since I've been here. Where are they?

Should I take off my clothes? Nah, with this heat they'll dry in no time, and the extra water on me will be refreshing after I get out.

I go to the canal and dip my big toe in.

Fuck! That's cold!

After about a minute when nothing happens, I run in and fully submerge myself.

Never thought I'd willingly go back into water after that other dimension, but damn, it's so fucking hot!

The canal is very shallow, maybe about three or four feet.

There's no fish in here either. Not even a bug to fly around my face. That's so weird. Where are all the animals?

"Gala should have been here with a few of dad's kifomen by now."

I turn myself invisible the second I hear the voice of a boy. Two figures emerge from the trees.

Like, what the hell is a kifomen?

"Ugh! Not now, Trevor. She'll be here soon."

"Shit, Balex, no need to give me attitude just because I'm worried about our sister."

The one named Trevor has a green eye and a hazel eye, and he looks like he is about eight years old. Wait, he's not human. Is he?

Wait.

Humans don't know about the other dimensions and the demons.

Is he a magician?

Well, he said 'our sister' earlier, so the other boy must be his brother.

Page 234

The brother, Balex, looks about thirteen, and has yellow skin, so he definitely can't be human. He also has a green eye too, but his left eye is black.

So they can't be humans, nor magicians. Where are they from?

The yellowed skin brother, Balex, extends his hand toward a tree. Something in the tree snaps, and a pine cone looking object flies towards him. He takes a bite out of it as if it were a pear, and a purple interior is revealed.

He swallows and says, "Gala will be here soon. We're just early."

Who's Gala? Is she the algae covered girl I saw last night? Is she the one who opened the portal here?

Holy shit, can these boys do the same?

"I have a bad feeling about this," Trevor says.

"You have a bad feeling about everything."

"Well, I don't really like what father's-"

"Don't be an Alekai."

"I'm nothing like Alekai!"

"Then prove it," a female's voice says. From the other side of the river where I originally was, the algae girl I saw in the other dimension appears.

Thank goodness I decided to keep my clothes on! If she saw them, they would have known of my presence.

"Gala!" Trevor shouts. "We were just-"

"Ugh!" Balex groans.

Trevor clears his throat and says, "How was Dimension Two?"

"Wet," she snaps. "Don't be an Alekai."

"I'm not being-"

"Did you bring them?" Balex interrupts.

"Yeah, they're here," Gala says, "although there's not much for them to do here."

"I think this dimension is pretty," Trevor says.

"You said the same thing about Dimension Four!" Balex says with a groan.

"I said the living ground there was cool, not pretty," Trevor defends himself. "Dimension Six is actually pretty. There's a lot of nice plants to look at."

Page 235

"And soon it'll all be father's," Gala says.

Balex rolls his eyes. "Yay for father."

Gala crosses the river, almost running into me. "Did you guys bring it?" she says once she's with her brothers.

"Yes, we have the-"

Gala covers Trevor's mouth very quickly.

"What?" Balex says, with Gala's hands still on Trevor.

Gala is staring right at the river. Right where I'm standing.

"The ripples."

"That's a fish!"

"There are no fish here."

"Then that was you crossing the river!"

"Someone's here!"

She lets go of her brother and creates two fireballs in her hand.

I quickly dive under the water, the fire hitting the surface of the water seconds from hitting me, and let the current take me away.

Chapter 4

After letting the current take me for about thirty minutes, I struggle to make my way to the shore because the current became stronger. The water is also no longer shallow. I lie down for another half hour, letting my muscles relax.

I never want to see water ever again.

I'm thirsty.

Fuck.

Well, magicians do need to drink more water than humans do.

I lift myself up and drink from the canal. Once my belly is swishing with water, I stand up.

I walk over to a shaded tree and notice those pine cone looking fruits. I use my telekinesis and grab two like that boy did.

I miss chicken.

Who were those guys anyways?

Who's their father that they were talking about?

Who's Alekai?

What's going on?

What are kifomen? Are they the demons?

Gah! I hate this!

Think, Raven.

I take a bite of the pine pear. It's actually delicious. Juicy and tastes like strawberries.

Focus.

So are demons are called kifomen to them? If they are, what are they doing? How do they fit into this?

They said it'll all be father's soon, or something like that. So
their father is trying to take control?

They don't even look like siblings.

Is this a cult?

What did the boys bring? She asked if they brought something
but she stopped him before I could find out.

What are they collecting these things for?

Sorry, JP, but I have to find out as much as I can from them before I go home.

***

Week eight in Dimension Six. I've been living off of strawberry pine
pears and leaves this whole time. I also haven't been eating as much
as I should be due to there not being many fruits around, so I've lost
maybe twenty pounds. I used to be a little chubby, but now I look
anorexic, and I've lost some muscle mass as well.

I did want to lose some weight, just not this way. I need to get
some meat in my belly.

I haven't run into any of the sibling cultists since that day at the
canal. I've been looking for something, anyone, anything, but there's
nothing but these plants.

Didn't think I'd ever hate plants this much.

Still way better than the water dimension though!

Dimension Two they called it. And this is Six. Home is Eight.
The demon's home, or should I say kifomen's home, is Five.

So much intel I have that I must share. I need to find out more
and escape with my life.

Everything was calm until I ran into a gruesome sight.

This must have been the kifomen's doing.

Plants, trees, and vines were torn up and bleeding all over the
ground.

The ground is broken up, trees are knocked over, everything is
in pieces. All except one plant that looks like the one from the first day I
was here, but a lot smaller.

I rush to the nearest plant and hold it.

It slowly expands, and then contracts.

Page 238

It's still breathing!

There are no animals here because they are the animals!

Oh man!

Oh man!

Oh man!

Wait! There was a much bigger one, the size of a building. This is a baby!

Oh shit! What do I do? I can't heal. Shapeshifting myself won't do anything. Turning invisible won't do anything either! Can I distort the wound? Make it smaller?

No, I tried that once on a fish and I made the fish itself smaller.

I hug the poor thing and feel the water works starting.

I never thought I'd see the day where Raven Paris would cry over a fallen plant.

There's nothing I can do. The baby plant has a vine slowly lift up and stroke my cheek. It drops and the baby stops moving in my arms.

Chapter 5

With the broken ground, I bury the baby plant. I don't know this dimension's customs, but it feels like the right thing to do.

Magicians tend to bury, like most humans, but we don't put religious symbols over the graves.

Reminiscing about all this makes me think of my brother and father. They have to believe I'm dead by now.

Poor father.

He thinks he has nothing to bury.

Poor JP.

He thinks he's lost another family member.

I'll be home as soon as I can.

***

I'm here for about another week when I get the instailk.

Great!

Fucking great! I never thought I'd get this sickness.

Focus, Raven. I need plenty of liquids, warmth, and rest. The creatures here have plenty of water, so that shouldn't be a problem. I can't rest too much because I need to survive on my own. Also, not a single blanket is here to keep me warm.

Maybe I can start a fire?

No.

Bad idea.

These creatures are alive, I can't just kill them and take their wood. Then again, we do that back home.

I really have a lot to think about.

I can't eat much, so I'll be weak tomorrow.

Great.

I lay down against the tree bark and close my eyes. Something touches my shoulder and I jump. I open my eyes and see that the adjacent bushes are wrapping themselves around me, only having my head poke out.

I suddenly feel much warmer.

That's it, when I get home, I'm going vegan!

But these are plants, and they're living. If I go vegan the plants suffer and die.

Gah!

Life was easier when I just ate chicken and didn't think about any of this life stuff.

I close my eyes, pull JP's doll closer to my chest, and try to let sleep overtake me, but then I hear an all too familiar growl that makes my eyes snap open.

There's not much I can do with my sickness, so I hide deeper in the bushes, hoping I won't be spotted. I can't see much, but I can see enough.

Three demons and a green boy with one green eye and one brown eye are visible through the leaves. He lifts his hands and the leaves start to swirl around in the air.

A green magician!

"Quit fooling around, Zigor," another boy says, that I can't see.

"Sorry," Zigor says. "It's not often I get to come to my mother's home dimension."

"So you want to socialize with these plants and the dead plumians over in the town?" the other boy says, stepping into view. He reminds me of the other girl I saw, but instead of algae, he's covered in scales. He also has one green and one yellow eye.

What's the deal with all this heterochromia?

"No, Sax," Zigor says. "I just want to enjoy myself a little before this dimension belongs to father."

Page 241

There's that father person again. They all look different, but they all have mixed eyes, and they seem to be magicians. What were those other names that were said? Gala was the girl, who were the other two boys? Are they all really siblings?

"Let's just move on, okay bro?" Sax says.

Zigor sighs. "Fine."

The two of them kind of do a T pose and I feel the wind starting to pick up a lot.

They're opening a portal!

I can't miss this opportunity!

I jump out of the bushes and run after them, but they seem to be gone. Where did-

I crash into something.

I quickly get my footing and see a brown tree.

Yes! Bitches!

I look around and see the two boys with their backs to me, and five demons running off.

I quickly dive behind the tree I just crashed into.

I look some more and see some weird creatures that have scales. Are these reptiles? The sky is dark blue with three green suns.

"Now you can't tell me that you don't have some empathy for your mother's home dimension?" Zigor says.

Sax bends down and picks up a creature that looks like a lizard, but has two wings and no limbs.

"Dimension Three has nothing on Five," Sax says. "My mother has a nice home, but it can't beat father's."

Five? The demon's home?

"Father's home sucks!"

"But our rooms don't."

"Speaking of father," Zigor says, "let's just find what he sent us here to get, and leave."

The two boys start walking off.

"Alright, alright, but only to avoid a lecture. Plus, the kifomen need to run."

When the two boys and their demons, er, kifomen, are gone, I slump to the ground and bury my face in my knees.

I thought they were going to Eight!

Page 242

Never mind about that now. Their father is having them collect things. Okay, but for what?

Their father is from Five, so they can't be magicians.

Magicians are from Eight. Then how can they have all this power?

I'm in Dimension Three now.

Okay.

One step closer to home, I guess.

Or one step closer to finding out the truth.

I look around and take in Dimension Three while I try to find somewhere to sleep through my instailk.

There are a few flying creatures that look like dinosaurs. It's pretty hot right now. I can't imagine how it'll be during the day. There's a lot of yellow grassy hills, and strange reptilian creatures crawling on them. There's a small city out in the distance. There are also bipedal reptilian creatures that look similar to the boy I just saw, only they have much fiercer facial features, more like a lizard than a magician.

One of them notices me. They grab their friend and point at me.

Uh oh.

I try to turn around and run away, but my head and vision seem to spin, and I fall to the ground.

Chapter 6

My eyes open slowly. The roof is brown and very tall. Sunlight is coming in through the hole on the wall in the shack.

Wait, shack?

I quickly sit up. Something falls off my forehead and onto my lap.

It's a rolled-up damp white towel.

Where am I?

The shack seems to be empty, except for what appears to be straw on the floor, and the straw I'm wrapped in.

How did I get here?

I touch my head. My instailk seems to be gone. Okay, I know I'm fine and alive, but that doesn't tell me how I got here.

I take as much straw off of me as I can manage before I stand up and wipe the rest off.

I hear footsteps behind me.

I try to change myself into a snake, but a bipedal lizard comes in and catches me halfway through my transformation.

It's the same one I saw just before blacking out. I should have gone invisible.

"Ah!" the reptile says, then he says something I can't understand.

Another walks in behind him that looks shorter than the first one, carrying a bundle of what appears to be a six- sided starfruit. Though it's definitely not short considering the taller one is about seven feet tall.

The second one says something in a slightly higher pitch, and the first one points at me and says, "magala, magala, magala!"

"Magala?" the second asks as he or she points at me.

The fuck did they just call me?

They don't seem to be dangerous, or want to hurt me, so I turn back into my original form.

"Magala!" they both chant.

"Mangala?" I ask.

The first one points at me. "Magala."

"I can't understand you," I tell them. "My name's Raven. I'm a magician. What's a magala?"

The taller one says something else, but I can't understand it.

"Raven," I say, pointing at myself. "Raven."

"Gomen," the taller one says, pointing at them self.

"Nawa," the shorter one pointing at them self. Nawa then hands me a starfruit. "Comalan."

I grab the food and smile at Nawa. The second Nawa lets go, the starfruit's full weight hits me all the sudden.

"Whoa! Heavy." I try shaking the fruit with both hands. "Heavy. Very heavy."

"Hempta," Gomen says smiling. "Comalan."

I smile at them, and then I take a bite.

Better hope this isn't poisonous.

***

I spend several months with Gomen and Nawa. I get to know them, and their language. It's a lot like English, so I pick it up fast. Turns out that they're an elderly couple who have seven children, fifteen grand-children, and a great grandson. I've met a few of them too over these past months. They could have me fooled, because the way they move, speak, act, and work, I'd assume they were my age.

Then again, reptiles can live for a very long time.

I help them around the house, and in return, they help me with gathering food, water, and clothing. I do a lot of traveling around the area, but I haven't seen those people or any signs of portals opening.

Until now.

Page 245

I'm in the marketplace buying cashmirals for dinner when I see one of the boys. It's the reptilian one. He looks more magician than the others, so he stands out quite a bit.

Plus, his eyes are the dead giveaway.

He doesn't see me, so I decide to follow him. After about ten minutes, I lose him in the crowd.

***

I go back to the hut with the cashmirals.

"You look down," Gomen says to me in Leptar when I return. "Is everything alright, my little magala?"

"Can I ask you something?" I ask him in Leptar. "Something I probably should have asked you sooner."

"What is it, child?"

"When we first met, you called me a magala, or magician as my people call them."

"Yes, I knew what you were right away."

"But how? Have you seen other magicians?"

"Oh, yes, all over. In the market, by the ruins, in the nature areas, but not many, and only two have looked like you do."

This catches my attention. "What do you mean only two have looked like me?"

"Exactly what I said. Only two have looked like you. The others looked as if they were different species all together. They can do the things you can, and they can even blow the wind and disappear. Sometimes they blow the wind and these little creatures come."

I think back to the reptilian boy. "Have any of them ever looked like you?"

He thinks for a moment. "Only one."

I nod at him. "Thank you, Gomen."

"Raven, is everything okay?"

"It should be soon."

Chapter 7

I'm washing clothes with Nawa when she randomly asks me, "you miss people back home, don't you?"

I sigh. "Yes."

They think I'm dead.

"Why do you not return to them?"

"I'm trying. I have to go through a portal to do so."

"Portal?"

How do I explain what a portal is? I make a spinning circle with one hand, and I shove my other hand through the center.

She nods slowly.

I'm not sure if she fully understands.

"I live in another dimension."

"Oh. Do you know how you'd get back?"

I shake my head and put down the shirt I'm washing.

"Come with me, child."

***

They take me to the area where I first was when I got to this dimension. It's nighttime, the sky is a dark brownish yellow color. There are also several green stars in the sky, and two yellow moons, one a crescent, the other a gibbous.

I pick up one of the strange lizards and put it on my shoulder. It climbs on the backpack Nala made for me. I feel my backpack go up and down as the lizard moves. I've always been a bug girl before, now I'm a lizard girl.

Wait, how old am I now?

The three of us are standing shoulder to shoulder, with me in the middle, looking out toward the city.

"This place is where the magala are a lot," Nawa tells me.

"Are they good magicians or bad?" I ask.

"Batu magala," Gomen says.

I nod. Nice to know what I'm dealing with. "Why bring me back here?"

"The magala often appear and disappear here," Nawa explains.

"I didn't know what was going on until you explained the portal to me. Maybe you can do the same."

I sigh. "I don't know how to open a portal." I turn myself invisible. "This is the only disappearing that I can do." I turn myself visible again.

"So only those kids can open these portals?" Gomen asks.

"Yes, although I don't know how."

"Have you tried?"

"A few times, but nothing ever happened."

He nods.

"I've mostly been getting around by following these other magicians through their portals just as the kifomen do," I explain.

"Evil little things," Nawa agrees.

"Oh, but they're not evil."

The three of us turn around at the sound of a female voice speaking in Leptar.

It's Gala.

"Tell me girl, is a lion evil for killing a gazelle, or is it just nature?"

I stand with my arms up to shield Gomen and Nawa.

She has four kifomen and two boys with her. One boy is dark skinned with a green and white eye, while the other brother I've seen at the river. He looks just like me with a green and hazel eye.

"Trevor, take this," she says in English, and hands a bottle with some dark liquid to the boy with the hazel eye.

"Meet us at the spot in One."

Page 248

He nods, takes the bottle, and runs off. He spins his arms as he runs, and then disappears.

"Now, Bonnie, how should we kill these ones?" she asks, switching back to Leptar.

I fling my concealed knife at Gala, but it stops in midair.

"Kill her with her own weapon," Gala says in a mocking tone. "I love it!"

Their father has to be a magician, but what magician would turn on humanity and the rest of the dimensions?

Bonnie gets near a tree and seems to phase into its shadow.

Uh oh.

"Nawa, Gomen, you guys need to go!" I command them while tightening the straps on the bag that is carrying some food and JP's doll.

"We're not leaving you here," Gomen snaps.

"How touching," a deep male voice says from behind.

I turn my head and see Bonnie popping out of Gomen's shadow.

Gomen sees this too. He jumps out of the way, but Bonnie is inside his shadow, so Bonnie is still attached to him and follows.

I find a large stick on the floor that looks like it can be used as a mini staff. I pick it up with my telekinesis and throw it to Nawa, while making it bigger.

"Catch!" I warn her.

Nawa catches the stick and swings it at the kifoman trying to charge her. She misses him completely and he bites her leg.

I don't go invisible. I can't let them know I have that trick, if they haven't already seen me. I instead extend my hand toward the kifoman at her feet and shrink it.

Nawa stomps on the kifoman and a crunch sound is heard under her foot.

I wish I could shrink her and stomp on her smug ass face, but magicians are immune to that trick.

The remaining three charge Nawa. I'm not able to help her because Gala throws my knife back at me.

"That was pretty stupid," I laugh at her.

"Oh, but I believe in fair fights."

Page 249

"How noble," I say sarcastically.

I swing at her several times, but she dodges every one of them.

I have to find her weaker side, the side she uses less, and exploit it.

She punches me in the face with her left hand and I feel blood come down one of my nostrils.

Right side it is!

I swing for her right side, but she catches my hand with her right hand.

Shit! An ambidextrous fighter!

I break free of her grasp by kicking her.

She comes to punch me again, but I catch her wrist and twist it quickly to the point where her bone pops out of her arm.

"Bitch," she spits at me.

"I know," I say with a smile, and I kick her right in the stomach.

I hear a female scream behind me.

"Nawa!" Gomen shouts.

With Gala several feet away from me, I see Nawa on the floor, unmoving, and with three kifomen digging into her.

"Nawa!" Gomen cries.

Bonnie comes out from Gomen's shadow and stabs him in the stomach.

"No!" I scream.

"Retreat!" Gala says in English to her brother.

I run up to Gomen. I slide next to him and fall to my knees.

"Rav-ven," he stammers, purple blood dripping from his mouth. "G-go."

I shake my head. "I-"

"Now. They're..." he starts to violently shake. "Go."

I stand up and sprint towards the running duo until they disappear. I continue to run until the brownish yellow night sky turns blue.

Chapter 8

My friends are gone! Those bitches will pay!

I don't see Gala, Bonnie, or Trevor when I cross over to the next dimension. Instead I see a giant whale. It swims toward me very quickly and I crash right into it.

Why the hell do I keep crashing into things?

I stand up, the whale continuing to swim through the air, completely ignoring me.

"Sorry!" I yell after it.

Shit! What if those magicians are still around and hear me?

I look left and right for a place to hide, but all I see is an empty beach with a mountain of rocks and a few palm looking trees behind me. I look up at the blue sky and gasp at the amount of swarming fish, whales, sharks, and other marine animals, swimming right above my head.

Am I back in Two?

No, Two was completely empty, and there was water everywhere there. This place is teeming with life. Also, I'm not swimming endlessly, and there's ground to stand on.

Ground.

I look down at the sand I'm standing on, and see a crab scuttle by my feet. Several yards away from me I see a mountain of clams with some fish swimming around them in the air.

I walk towards the shoreline and look at the water. It's blue with white foam. I stick my toe in it. It's cold, but it doesn't seem to melt my skin off.

Meet us at the spot in One.

So this is Dimension One. Where'd they go? What spot in One were they talking about?

Gah!

Alright, new plan. I follow them through the next portal while invisible so I can stay near them.

I take off my bag and look inside it. I have a few vegetables called camdoons from the other dimension to eat, two bottles of water, three four-sided shurikens, a switch blade, a sweater with a glaco strap to close it, a pair of shorts, and the tooth necklace Nawa gave me.

Nawa. Gomen.

What will their children think?

I feel a few tears roll down my cheeks. My friends took me in, and I got them killed. I couldn't protect them.

Their deaths will not be in vain!

In the meantime, I have to find more food. The camdoons won't be good for much longer.

I eat one now, and ponder where I can find more food.

Where'd that crab go?

***

Never found the crab, but there are plenty of other fish in the air.

I make a spear out of one of the shurikens, a long stick I found, and some twine. I used my new weapon to kill some fish and roast them over a fire I had just built.

Sorry, fish, but I need to eat something to live.

The water is very salty, and I have no way to desalinate it, so I have to ration my two bottles.

I kinda miss the lizards from Dimension Three.

They're friendlier than the air-sea life that's here. That one lucky lizard I picked up earlier got away. I would have felt bad for the poor thing if it got stuck here.

I'm taking the scales off of my third fish when I hear a noise that makes me jump. I look up and see a being with webbed appendages. The gills on its neck puff out and its scales stand on end.

We lock eyes. I notice the strange coloration of the oceanic creature's eyes. They're orange irises with yellow sclera.

The creature breaks off, running towards the water.

"Wait!" I call back after them.

The creature runs into the ocean and dives underneath.

I grab my spear, follow the creature, and do the same.

Coldcoldcold!

I force my eyes to open and to take a deep breath.

Water fills my lungs and tightens my chest. The first breath is always the most painful.

I continue to breathe through my mouth until water fills me up to the point where I can breathe normally through my nose.

The salt stings my eyes, but I force them to stay open so I can follow the creature.

It doesn't seem to notice me following it, but it is swimming fast.

After a while of following from a distance, I reach what looks like a floating city under the water.

Wow! A real-life Atlantis!

I swim closer to get a better look.

There are many tall metallic buildings with lights on the tops and bottoms on these suspending blocks. Looking further down below the buildings, it's pitch black. There doesn't seem to be any floors to walk on. Everybody is swimming from building to building. I'm getting a New Yorkish-Tokyo vibe coming from this place.

"Who goes there?" I hear a deep voice asks from behind me.

I turn around and point my spear and the creature, who turns out to be the one I was following, and scowl.

"Is that your business?" I ask.

"It is when ye follow me home and point thy weapon towards me."

What is this? A futuristic city with an old English language?

That's when it hits me.

"You speak my language."

"As ye mine, though a different di-lect. What are thou doith at myne home?"

Okay, now he sounds like he's speaking gibberish with the whole doith thing.

Page 253

"Trying to get to mine," I tell him.

"Ye near?"

"Not even close."

He nods. "Meeteth me back on thy surface. Y will find myne cestra and she and Y will help ye."

His what?

"Outlanders are forbidden in thy city. Ye must hurry and leaveth."

"Thanks, I guess."

I clutch my spear tighter, and start swimming toward the surface.

This is a strange world.

Chapter 9

I'm huddled by the fire, finishing my fish when he comes back with someone about half a foot taller than him.

"This beith her, brother?" the taller one asks with a high-pitched voice.

Cestra. Oh, it means sister. Duh!

"Aye."

I stand up, not sure of what to make of them. Are they even my allies, and if they are, will they be able to help me?

"So ye be one of those dimension hoppers that arrive on thy surface world?"

"If you're referring to the heterochromics, I'm not with them. I'm just a lost girl trying to get home."

"Hetero-what?" she asks.

I point to my eyes.

She nods.

"I fell through one of their portals back in Dimension Eight, my home dimension."

"We can help ye," she tells me, "fer some information."

"About what?"

"We be filling thy gaps about the other worlds. You help us, we show ye thy heterochromos."

I'm not sure if I should trust them, but what choice do I have.

"Sounds fair," I say.

"Brother, call off thy ambush."

"You were gonna ambush me?" I practically shout.

"We hath to be sure of ye intentions."

I can't fully blame her, for I would have done the same thing.

"I'm Raven," I tell them.

"I be Yosha. This beith mi brother, Yohan."

***

I tell them all about my home dimension, and my travels. They were intrigued by our "reverse ocean" as they called it. And they were really fascinated by the water dimension I had to swim in. The siblings already knew about the plants and the reptiles, but they were baffled when I described Dimension Two.

"Used to be life liketh thy ones above our very heads," Yosha explains to me. "Used to have own control. Now kifomen destroyeth everything."

"They're aiming for my home next," I tell them.

"Four too," Yohan says. "Thy kifomen hath been killing their living ground for long time now."

"Living ground?" I ask. "So you mean the ground actually has emotions and feelings?"

"And un appetite," Yosha says.

"So the ground will randomly eat you?" I ask, and shudder at the thought.

"It eats ye, then ye go to Dimension Ten," Yosha says.

"Dimension Ten?" I ask.

"You not knoweth of all ten?" Yosha asks me.

"Dimension Ten is the afterlife?" I ask.

"If that be what ye people call it, then aye," Yosha says.

Amazing. I was always told that there were only eight dimensions.

"What about Seven and Nine?" I ask.

"Seven be a dimension of shadows," Yohan warns me. "It beith very dangerous. Nine is overrun by thy kifomen. Be un place of sadness. Far as Y know, twas similar to ye Eight, except sky be green and plants be blue."

"Wow," I whisper. "I never knew anything about the other dimensions before I fell through that first portal." I sigh.

Page 256

I miss my home.

I need to get back now more than ever and share everything I've learned. Those people with the two- colored eyes and their kifomen, they're collecting things for their father who's the ringleader of all this so he can do who knows what! They're opening portals and causing all this pain, and I somehow feel like I'm the only one who can stop it.

Yohan hands me my spear that was on the ground. "I know not when they open another portal, but we keep ye safe until then."

I smile at him and grab my spear. "Thanks."

***

I spend a few months here with them. Outsiders aren't allowed in their Atlantean city, which is actually called Prage, but they tell me a lot about the development of their city, their way of life, and what they know about the surface world.

I tell them a lot about home, my brother, and what my people are doing to stop the kifomen.

"Our people callith em Lucis," Yohan tells me. "How ye know that's what they be called?"

"It's just something I heard," I say smiling.

I mostly stay on the surface world, but sometimes I take a swim and see the city. I don't go too far, which probably isn't wise. I should be moving soon if I want to find a portal. Then again, I stayed with Nala and Gomen in one place and I found a portal there.

I'll talk to Yosha, see what she thinks.

***

I wait three days to talk to them, but they don't show.

I'm half tempted to go into the city and find them, but I'm not allowed to, and I don't want to find out what'll happen to me if I'm caught. Especially if I'm alone.

I decide to go for a long walk. I get so caught up in the beauty of this dimension that I get lost and wander very far. Good thing I always carry my stuff on me!

"The girl knows their names," I hear a voice say.

Yosha?

"How?" I hear another voice.

I turn invisible and poke my head out from behind a bush with a few fish swimming in front of my face.

I try not to gasp at what I see.

Gala!

And worst of all, Yosha and Yohan are with them.

Traitors!

I can't be too surprised though; I was suspicious of them when we first met.

There's a small boy with her. He looks like a magician, around five years old. I'm guessing he's one of the heterochromic siblings because he has one green eye and the other is purple.

"What else does she know?" Gala asks.

"She's closing in on your plans," Yohan says. "She talks a lot about a younger brother that she has."

Gala smiles. "Interesting." She then looks at the little boy. "Are you taking mental notes, Yulan?"

"Can we go to Four now?" he says in a high voice.

Clearly he hasn't hit puberty yet. "You promised to take me to my mommy's home!"

"Soon." Gala looks back at the traitors. "You have what father asked for?"

Yosha hands her this green liquid inside a bottle.

"People in our city have been working on it for long time."

"Excellent." Gala smiles. "You'll get what was promised to you, but you have to kill the girl first."

Shit! They're still after me!

"Yulan, you try this time," Gala says to her little brother.

"You mean it? Awesome," he says, jumping wildly.

"Yes, but you have to take us to Five first so we can give this to father. Then I'll take you to Four."

The little boy starts cheering and hopping in a circle.

Page 258

"Remember what I told you," Gala says.

I carefully walk up behind them, still invisible.

Yohan and Yosha walk right past me, almost rubbing shoulders with me. That would have been bad!

153

The little boys closes his eyes and moves his hands in a circle.

"Not like that, sweetie," Gala tells him. "You just have to think about it."

"I can't."

"I got it then."

She opens the portal, and I follow them into Hell.

Chapter 10

We get transported into a room with red everywhere. There are four couches, three coffee tables, seven mirrors on the wall, two desks, a giant chandelier on the ceiling, and a fireplace on a wall. The floors and ceiling seem to be the only things that are not some form of red. On the mantelpiece above the fireplace, I notice some trinkets, but I don't get a good look at them.

"We're back, father!" Gala shouts.

"I am right here, my daughter," a man's voice says from one of the couches. He's lounging in fluffy black pants and a T-Shirt "There is no need for shouting."

"Daddy, we got it," the little boy cheers.

"Excellent! My sweet little Yulan, you're learning so fast!"

Yulan giggles and jumps on his father's lap.

This is their father?

Creator of chaos?

The king of what my people call 'the demons?'

"Father! Father!" another boy's voice is heard down the hall. He comes into the room from one of the two doorways on opposite sides of the room. He looks like a regular magician, around thirteen years old. He has one green eye and one hazel eye. "She's here."

"Excellent! My lost daughter will finally come home!"

Gala rolls her eyes.

"Trevor, can you go get your brothers for me, please?"

Trevor, the magician looking one, nods and runs out.

Wait, I've seen him before.

"Family meeting!" he shouts from inside the halls.

"You don't seem happy, Gala?" the Demon King tells her.

She sneers.

"You don't like the fact that you have a sister now, do you?"

"We don't even know if she's our sister. Donna sees a girl with a green and hazel eye and we're supposed to think that-"

"My followers have never steered me wrong," he tells his daughter. "Those two siblings, what were their names again?"

"Yohan and Yosha."

I try not to sneer.

"Did they prove us wrong? Did they not tell you everything? Did they withhold anything from you?"

"Well, no." She hands him the liquid. "They did everything right."

"Then we must have faith in my other children that are helping us put our ancestor's work out there. The kifomen need to expunge the wrongdoings so purity can be spread-."

"So purity can be spread forth throughout the nine dimensions. I know."

Ancestors work?

Kifomen expansion?

Other children?

Is this what they're doing? Wiping out life by using kifomen is what they call purifying it?

"And once I find a way to purify the fallen dimension, all will be well."

Fallen dimension?

"We still need to find a way to get there first," Gala says.

He must be talking about Dimension Ten.

"Hopefully soon," another boy's voice is heard.

Two boys walk in: a yellow skinned boy with a green and black eye, and a regular looking magician with webbed hands with a green and orange eye.

"Balex, can you start the fire place for me?" the Demon King asks.

The yellow boy sighs and gives a thumbs up. He walks over to the fireplace.

"Why not ask me, father?" the webbed boy asks.

Page 261

"Because, Gamma, you'd say 'start it where?' or some other sly comment like that," the Demon King says, rolling his eyes at his son.

Gamma wipes away an imaginary tear and says all emotional, "you know me so well."

In come three familiar faces: Zigor, Sax, and Bonnie. I clearly remember these guys.

"Perfect! We're just missing Trevor and Alekai now," the Demon King cheers.

Apart from Yulan who is practically a baby, and Gala who looks like a young adult, the other boys all look like teenagers.

"What's all this about, father?"

"We'll find out as soon as your brothers come. Ah! Here they are!"

Trevor walks back in with a young man who looks like the eldest child. He has one eye green, and the other red. He looks about twenty-one by magician standards.

"Hello again, my children. Now, as you're all aware, several months ago, our sister Donna has given us information about a long-lost child of mine. Trevor, you're the only one who saw her at the New Year's festivity today, did she look like she could be one of ours?"

Trevor winced, looked at his brother Alekai, and nodded. "She looks just like me, and her green eye is even on the right side."

"Excellent!" the Demon King cheers. "Any questions?"

"But father, she was alone in Miami and we couldn't get her then. Now she has friends with her, how do you expect to get her here?"

"Friends?"

"Yes. Four of them."

Everyone is silent for a moment. I'm extra silent.

"We'll have to pick them off slowly," Gamma says. "Go in as one of them, and have her make her way towards here-"

"What are you saying?" Zigor asks.

"Well, I'm the only shape shifter here. I can wait until the smallest one is alone and take its place in the group."

"Yeah, but they have to be alive for you to change into them."

"Someone else can bring them back. I can lure her here while picking off the group slowly but surely."

Page 262

"You'd have to make them look like attacks or accidents or else they'd suspect something," Sax says.

"Also, one of them is a mind reader, so watch your thoughts!"

Gamma smiles. "I'm already formulating some plans."

"You'd also have to learn their names," Balex suggests.

"Trevor, care to explain?" Gamma asks.

"Well, there's the twins, a boy and girl, Darren and Deonna Dean."

It takes every ounce of energy in my body to hold back from choking.

They're back in Five? Holy shit, this is bad!

"There's a girl with grey eyes and brown hair named Audrey Paris."

Please no!

"And the smallest one is a boy named JP Paris."

I am on the brink of bursting out in tears. My baby brother is here, in this wretched place.

"Bonnie can easily shadow jump JP back here no problem," Gamma says.

Bonnie nods. "That is something I can do."

"Sister!" Yulan says, jumping up and down on the Demon King's lap. "Yay! Sister!"

"Where did they appear?" Gala asks.

"In the razor leaves meadow. On top of the hill," Trevor says.

"What direction are they headed?" Bonnie asks.

"East," Trevor says.

"Think you two boys can handle this little mission?"the Demon King asks.

"Don't sweat it pops, we got this!" Gamma says.

"Yes, father," Bonnie says.

"Bring your sister back here safely," the Demon King warns his sons.

"We'll bring, uh, Trevor, what's her name?"

"Rebecca Proenza, but she goes by Bec."

Part 3: What's Going On

Chapter 1

I'm confused. JP just turned into some strange boy, and a random girl appeared out of nowhere. This is all very overwhelming.

How is she even here?

How did this boy take the place of JP?

What's going on?

Okay, Bec. Just stay calm. Everything can be explained rationally.

"It's funny how you think he's still alive," the boy mocks.

"Oh," the new girl hisses. "I know he's alive."

He smiles. "You're really that sure?"

"I know you need whoever you're shaping yourself into to be alive for the link to work, Gamma."

Gamma's smile vanishes immediately. "My sister was right," he says as nonchalantly as possible. "Someone was watching us."

She gets in his face and hisses, "for far longer than you think."

Gamma smirks, and then looks me up and down. He spends the longest time on my eyes.

I suddenly feel very cold in my winter outfit, but I don't dare shiver.

"Raven," Darren starts, "how-"

"We can talk about this later. Right now-"

Audrey hugs her anyways.

"Uff. Right now we need to find JP before they kill him."

"I say we kill him first," Deonna adds, pointing to the imposter.

"No," Raven tells her, still keeping her eyes on Gamma. "If he dies, so does JP."

"So, what do we do?" Audrey asks, slowly letting go of Raven. "And how do we even know you're the real Raven?"

I didn't even think of that! This could be another shape shifter.

She purses her lips and says. "The music box."

The others start to slowly smile.

"It's Raven," Darren says.

"So... how do we get JP?" Deonna asks.

"I have an idea."

***

Darren turns two large rocks into handcuffs and locks Gamma's arms together.

"The Demon King is what I learned to call him, although he's called Father by his followers." Raven explains to us. "He's the creator of the demons, or kifomen as they're called here. He calls them his children, although he has real children of blended races go out to do his bidding. He seems to have a bunch of them from different dimensions."

"Like this one?" Audrey asks, lightly kicking Gamma's leg.

"Yes. The Demon King also seems to be the one in charge of the whole kifomen expansion across the ten dimensions."

"Uh, there's only eight," Deonna says.

Raven shakes her head. "There's ten, one of which you can only travel to if you die. Dimension Ten."

"Shit," Darren whispers. "This is some heavy stuff."

"He's trying to gain access to it, as well as something else that I wasn't able to find much about."

"How'd you find all this out?" Deonna asks her.

"I've been spying on them, although it hasn't been easy. I've almost been caught several times, and I had a run in with one of them in Dimension Three. They have control over five dimensions so far. Eight is their next target. Portal openings to Dimension Eight have been more common in the past year."

"That explains all the openings," Darren says to himself.

Page 266

I even remember them mentioning it when we first met.

"How have you been staying safe this whole time?" Audrey asks Raven.

"The same way you guys have been," she answers. "Right now, that's not important. What is important is that we storm the castle."

"I'm sorry, you want us to do what?" I ask Raven.

***

Raven runs a dangerous plan by us. "It'll be simple."

"We could all be killed going in like that," I say.

"There's a large outdoor fortress. It's where they live, and where they're keeping my brother. It's here at the bottom of the canyon."

"Ray, Bec's right; we're not storming the castle," Deonna agrees. "How do you even know about this?"

"I stumbled across it."

"Yeah, but how?"

"Completely by accident when I got to this dimension."

"And how do we know you're not working with them?" I ask.

Raven scoffs. "I could ask you the same question, little girl."

"Excuse me?"

She stares into my eyes. "I know who they are, what they are, what they want... and I know about you, and you don't see me questioning you."

"What are you talking about?" I ask.

For the first time that I can remember, I'm too dumbfounded to create a comeback.

"Come on Ray, lighten up," Darren says.

I feel my face start to warm up a little.

She looks me up and down, and then her face becomes a little softer. "This is a conversation for later. Right now, getting JP back and getting home is our first priority."

"How do we return to home?" Darren asks.

"A lot of portals open and close around the fortress because of them. We just have to find the right one."

"And how do we know which is the right one?" Deonna asks. "They're not color coded, and there's no giant sign that'll say 'Dimension Eight this way'."

"I know one way," Raven tells us, "but it's difficult to explain." She looks straight at me.

Gamma starts chuckling behind us while tied up on the floor.

"What are you laughing at," I ask, and then a thought crosses my mind. "I can open portals, can't I?"

He grins at me.

"I can!"

"Zimmer!" he laughs.

"You interfered when I tried to open one, didn't you?"

"So you can open a portal?" Raven asks skeptically.

"It hasn't been confirmed yet," Deonna adds. "Though it would appear so. Also, she might be able to close them too."

Raven raises an eyebrow at me. "Interesting."

"I don't know how I do it," I admit. "I just know I can." I look back at Gamma. "How'd you do it?"

He laughs. "You really have no idea, do you?"

"Idea about what!?" I scream.

"Bec," Darren shushes me.

"Wait a second!" Deonna shouts. She goes behind him and shoves her hand in his coat pockets. After shuffling around through several pockets, she pulls out the leaf.

"You put me to sleep in the cave!"

"And I bet the cave was an ambush!" Darren adds.

"Guilty," Gamma laughs. "Although I meant to put him to sleep, you two are too identical. I couldn't tell the difference."

"And you ate all our rations," Audrey adds before her eyes widen.

"You guys being hungry would have made it easier to pick you off," Gamma laughs.

"You did try to kill me with the flowers!" Audrey shouts. "That fruit should have been poisonous!"

"Technically it was a vegetable," Gamma laughs. "It grew on a bush."

"But there were seeds."

Page 268

"Audrey," Darren says, "are you really arguing with him about this?"

"I can't help it," Audrey says. "He's really getting under my skin."

"We're gonna need a better plan," I say.

"Darren, you ever learn to shape shift?" Raven asks.

"Nope."

She thinks for a moment. "Can you teleport long distances?"

"How far?"

"Over a mile."

"Nope."

She sighs. "Well then that plan can't work."

"Stealth seems to be our best option," Darren says.

"So what do we do about the stalker over here?" I ask.

"Whatever you want," Raven says with a shrug.

***

We get to the fortress the next day. It is just how Raven described. Outdoor, no visible roof, no personality, and at the bottom of the canyon, next to a cliff. She made it seem bigger than it actually is, but it's still large. It looks like one of those St. Augustine forts, except brand new. According to Raven, there's a force field around the place.

"Alright, Bucko," Raven pokes Gamma. "How do we get inside?"

He laughs, laying down on the floor. "Front door. It's how I get in."

"You actually think he'll tell us anything important?" Audrey asks.

"No," Raven says, "but I just got an idea." She looks at me. "You stay out here with him. I don't trust you."

"Just because I'm new doesn't mean I'm useless."

"You know what I mean."

"Uh, no I don't."

She looks me up and down again and then her eyes grow a little softer. "No... you really don't."

"Raven, I know you don't know her, but we can trust Bec." Darren tells her. "Besides, it's going to take all of us to get JP and the rest of us out of there."

Page 269

"True," Raven agrees. "Then again, we have him to worry about." Raven shakes Gamma by his coat collar.

He just smiles.

"I'll watch the Goon," I sigh. "You guys just be careful."

Audrey and Darren both hug me. Deonna nods at me, and shoves something in my sweater pocket. I tap it lightly, and I immediately know what it is.

Raven shakes my hand.

Darren then hands me his crutch.

"Don't you still need it?" I ask.

"I can walk now," he says. "Besides, it'll make a good weapon."

I feel my face start to warm up a little. I take the crutch and look down. "Thanks."

Then they run off, leaving me here alone with Gamma. I keep my eyes on him. He sits there humming a tune. He's so sure of himself.

"Why are you so happy?" I ask him after a while.

"Such a shame," Gamma laughs. "Your friends have no faith in you."

"Yes they do."

"No they do-on't," he sings.

"Can it."

I regret talking to him.

"Well, Pretty Boy likes you enough to-"

"Can it!"

"Why leave you back here if they believed you could help with anything?"

"They know I can help. Someone needed to keep an eye on you, and they have more experience than I do."

"You're so much more than they realize. Think about it."

"Think about what?" I ask.

We'll, I did close a portal, but I'm not going to tell him that. Hope he didn't already hear me tell Raven.

"All you've done," he smiles.

Shit! How much does he know about me? He did say this father guy was excited to meet me.

Why though?

He must need me for something diabolical.

Page 270

What if he needs me to open portals for him?

"You know what I think?" he says while sitting up, his arms still behind him. "They don't trust you at all, and they want to leave you here."

"You're lying!"

"Why would I lie to you?"

"I can think of three good reasons."

"And I can think of three good things we have in common."

"Oh really?" I cross my arms and stare sharply at him with the stink eye.

"You have that look in your eyes that screams you weren't loved much as a child."

I bring my lips inside my mouth.

"I know the feeling, too many siblings, no mother, not enough love to go around."

"My parents loved me, and so did my siblings."

"What about the rest of your family?"

I don't say anything.

"The blush in your face when Pretty Boy stood up for you shows you like him back."

"I do not!" I snap. "Plus, you just said he stood up for me, meaning my friends do have faith in me."

He smiles. "You appear to be smart. I like it, we need more smart people in these worlds. Eight is full of retards."

"Like I care what you think of me!"

"Lastly, you don't believe in yourself, which is why you needed clarification from me." He smiles at me with those creepy eyes. "You're welcome."

I really want to hit him in the face. "I do have faith in myself."

"Then prove it."

"I have nothing to prove to you."

"Not to me, no. But you have a lot to prove to yourself. Go show you and your friends that you have what it takes."

"I have to guard you."

"Says who?"

"Says Raven."

Page 271

"The girl who trusts you the least? That sounds fishy if you ask me."

"Nobody asked you."

"I also know this about you. You're strong, passionate, a rebel, and you have a powerful lineage."

"What's that supposed to mean?"

"It means fighting is in your blood."

In a weird way, he kind of reminds me of Jake. Wow. It's been awhile since I thought of my family.

"You got what it takes?"

I look away from him and out to the fort. Okay, so he knows how to read me, doesn't mean he knows me or the others. Plus, Darren and Audrey would never leave me here. Even Deonna's not capable of that. I know she hates me, but not enough to abandon me.

Just then, the force field on the roof turns red instead of clear.

"What does that mean?" I ask Gamma.

"Several things. The colors are a signal to everyone inside."

"I mean this specific code."

He stands up and takes a peek. "Either 'intruder alert' or 'prisoner escaped,' but there's never a way to tell from the distance because of the shading and the light. Now if I was actually inside-"

"What! So my friends can either be in trouble or in the clear?"

"Pretty much."

Shit! What should I do?

If I go down there and they're okay, I can jeopardize the mission. If I don't go down and they're in trouble, they can die.

"What'll it be?" he asks me.

I don't have to think for another second.

I use the crutch and I smack him in the back of his head as hard as I can. I open the bag with the leaf in it and prop the opening right to his nose. He's asleep in seconds. I might be walking into a trap, a raid, or an execution, but all that doesn't matter right now.

My friends might need me.

Chapter 2

I make it down the cliff and I find an open window. I never tried to break through a force field before.

How did they make it in?

Darren must have teleported them inside.

I need to find an alternative route.

I look along the wall of the hexagonal fort. There are two other windows, but nothing else.

I move to the next wall. There's one door in the middle of the wall. I touch it and my hand goes through. I manage to walk right in.

That was easy.

I turn around and see a faint trace of red in the outline.

They must have just put this forcefield up.

Better hurry. My luck won't last forever.

Unless this is a trap and I'm delivering myself to the enemy.

Can't think about that right now.

Don't be negative.

Gotta stay positive.

I look around the inside. It's barren and dull. This demon king must really be boring. They must also love grey, for all the walls and ceiling I see are all grey. In fact, there's nothing in this hallway.

I listen down one hallway and I don't hear anything. I walk down it.

I see an opening for another hallway and I take it.

I see a few more twists up ahead and grunt.

Great!

Another fucking labyrinth!

This time I don't have Stick.

Most of the hallways I go through are plain. Some have tables with some decoration, some have windows, one has a room that looks similar to the treehouse kitchen.

I go inside. Everything is open. No cupboards, no drawers, no pantry door.

Do these people eat? Where's the food?

My stomach growls.

For some reason apples and peanut butter comes to my mind.

Weird how I can miss something as simple as peanut butter on a Granny Smith.

I hear the sound of a plate rattling behind me and I spin around in an instant.

There on the table is something that makes me think a mind reader is around.

It's a small basket with ten Granny Smiths and a large jar of Jif peanut butter.

My brain tells me to run, but my stomach says 'fuck it, you're hungry.'

I grab the jar.

It's creamy.

I don't care at this point.

Food!

I eat three of the apples and down half the jar. I have never eaten faster in my life before, for fear that someone will walk in.

I feel a soft wind pick up. Seems like a portal is opening in the corner. Raven was right. We should be out of here soon. I should bring them here when I find them.

"Think we'll find-" I hear a boy's voice cut off by another boy's voice coming from the hall where I came in from.

"Of course. Father always gets his way," says another boy.

I grab the jar, pocket two apples, and run out the opposite side from where I came in.

"Who let Yulan eat by himself again?"

"That little boy always makes a mess! Father will blame us for-"

This hallway is a little different. It's still grey, but there's two doors in this one. I put my hand on the knob but get an instant shock.

Okay, not that one!

For a demonic fort in this dimension, this place has a lot of magic.

Focus, Bec!

I hear the voices again.

"Yulan? You by Gala's room?"

I run to the other door and I don't get shocked. I make it inside and close the door. With my ear on the door, I listen for the two boys.

"Zigor, it was nothing," the first boy says.

"Could have sworn that I heard something," he says.

"Ignore it."

"We can't just ignore it, Balex. What if it was-"

"Then we'll find her later."

When I don't hear their footsteps anymore, I lean my head against the door.

Maybe this was a mistake.

Then again, they are looking for Raven and the others. Maybe there's still a chance we can all get out of here safely.

I just have to figure out where I am. I turn around and look in the room. Despite everything I saw before, I was not expecting this.

It's a little girl's room.

The walls are painted green and yellow, the bedspread is blue, the pillows ae orange, and the curtains for the fake window in the back are pink. There's a purple night table with a white lamp, and a red shelf lined with several brown teddy bears.

There's one teddy bear I'm really drawn to. I walk towards the shelf and grab it. It's the softest thing I have ever felt in my life.

I move the fur out of its eyes. Plain black eyes just stare back into mine, begging me to take it with me.

I can't take you home. You belong to someone.

No I don't, it seems to tell me.

I clutch the bear to my chest. It has been so long since I've hugged a plush toy.

I put the teddy bear in my largest pocket, leave the room, and quietly close the door behind me.

Page 275

I go down the hallway where I came from and pass the kitchen.

I go down a few more halls and make a left turn.

The room I reach is huge.

It looks like a family parlor. Compared to the hallways and the room, this place is extravagant. There's red furniture everywhere. Four couches, three coffee tables, seven mirrors on the wall, two desks, a giant chandelier on the ceiling, and a fireplace.

Inside, there's a familiar face, a stranger, and someone I love.

JP, the real JP, lays there tied up in chains, rope, and a third device that I can't identify. His eyes are closed. He's been badly beaten. He has a black eye, and a gash on his cheek. His arms are behind his back, but I see his legs are bent in several places where they shouldn't bend. His face is spotted in blood.

I have to heal him.

There's that puss girl from the bathroom in New York. Now that I look at her with better lighting, I realize that she's not puss, she's algae. She also has gills on the side of her neck. She's rapidly pacing around the room, chewing on her finger.

There's a strange boy on the couch. Probably around seventeen. He's covered in scales so he could be part dragon, part snake, part lizard. I catch a glimpse of his eyes before I hide behind the wall again.

Right green, left yellow.

"Gala, you don't have to guard him so much," the reptile boy says.

"What if he escapes again?" she snaps. "I don't want father to think we can't handle one little magician."

"If it worries you so much, we can have Alekai help you."

"I'm capable of watching a child without him, Sax."

"Suite yourself."

Raven was right. This guy does have a lot of kids.

Unless they're regular followers.

Gah! Now I'm confused.

Focus, Bec!

So, JP escaped once before. Was that the red thing on the roof's force field?

I look back into the room.

Page 276

JP shifts and rolls over where he lays. We lock eyes for a quick moment, and I see that familiar sparkle in him.

They start to grow a little.

I nod at him.

The reptile boy lays down on the couch. "Can't wait till we get to Dimension Eight. There's nothing to do here."

"Father will let us know soon enough."

He rolls his eyes and raises his voice a little. "You're such a daddy's girl."

"You're just jealous because I'm father's favorite."

"He has no favorite; he just pays more attention to you because you're the only daughter."

"Said the non-favorite."

"Well, at least for now."

She says something in a language I don't understand. Probably a curse.

I hide behind the wall again.

My siblings and I never talked to each other like that.

Ah! Stop thinking.

Better yet, think about JP. How am I going to get him out of here?

I can probably do a trick to distract and throw them out, then grab JP while they're not looking?

No, that'll raise an alarm.

Plus, I have no idea where Darren and the others are.

I should find them first, but I can't leave JP here.

Gah! Why do I overthink everything?

I know what to do! Let's hope my training paid off.

I have to find something I can use.

I look back into the room and the first thing I notice is JP. The second thing, however, is the chandelier.

That'll work.

I focus all my energy away from JP and onto the light instead. I try and move it to the opposite side of the room with my will alone.

My eyes are closed, but I can hear the chandelier slightly shaking.

"What was that?" the girl asks.

Page 277

"You're just being paranoid," the boy lazily tells her.

I open my eyes and look back into the room. The light I distorted and moved made a second JP away from the fireplace. I did it!

I celebrated too soon.

A hand covers my mouth.

Chapter 3

The boy the hand is attached to moves in front of me. He puts his index finger to his lips.

I immediately calm down and nod.

He nods back, takes his hand off my mouth, and leads me away from the room.

He leads me to another empty room. It only has one large table in the center and an out of breath Audrey. He leans over and whispers, "What are you doing here?"

"I saw an alarm go off. I thought I might need to break you out, but it turned out to be JP."

"That was us almost getting him out." Darren says.

"We had to hide and they put him under watch. Where's the Demon Boy?"

"Unconscious and out of the way."

"Are you sure?"

"Yes. So what's happening now?"

"Deonna's getting him out now," Audrey tells me. "Raven was able to finish your trick and now we have him back."

"Raven what?" I ask.

I hear slight footsteps behind me. Deonna walks in holding a knife that must be Gamma's. Raven is holding an unconscious JP who is still tied up.

"Your misdirection sucks," Raven tells me as she sets JP down on the table.

I extend my hand to JP and focus on his bonds. They're released in seconds. "I'm well aware of that."

"Ray, you said lots of portals open up here?" Deonna asks.

"Yeah."

"One appeared earlier in the kitchen," I tell them.

"We'll have to look around and find a familiar feeling one. Then we're home," Raven tells us.

"A familiar feeling one?" I ask.

"Great," Audrey grunts. "Exactly what we've been doing this whole time."

"You have any better ideas?" Darren asks her.

"Maybe Bec can open the portal now that Gamma isn't interfering."

"How about we leave this place and then try?" I ask.

Raven moves the bonds off JP and checks his pulse. "He's weak. Very . . . very weak." She gently picks him up.

Then everything turns red.

"Shit," Raven whispers. "We took too long."

"Could have been Gamma."

Darren runs to the door and pokes his head out. "No one here. Let's go fast."

Darren goes first, then Raven with JP, then Audrey, then me, and Deonna takes up the rear.

This has bad idea written all over it.

We make three turns and make it to another large near empty room to try the portal. I was about to try it, but we're spotted in the back. I don't see the two of them at first. It's only when the green boy sends out a dry tree branch and wraps it around my hair to pull me towards them that I get a good look at them.

I then notice another boy who is all green and has two different eyes, one brown, the other green. There's also the reptile boy.

"Where do you think you're going?" the green boy whispers to me.

Next thing I know, Deonna is next to me. With Raven's knife, she cuts loose the branch, along with half of my hair.

I fall on the floor.

Two more boys walk in.

Page 280

One of them is dark skinned with a white, and green eye. The other is yellow skinned with a green and black eye. The yellow one kind of has similar skin to the demons.

"Release the kifomen!" The yellow boy shouts in a familiar voice. I must have heard him talking while I was in the kitchen.

A dozen demons come into the room from behind them. They charge at us.

I'm prepared to slow down time, but the demons, kifomen, whatever, crash into an invisible barrier and fall to the floor.

I turn around and see that Audrey has a ball of fire in her hands, and Deonna has put up a force field.

"This won't . . . last . . . long," Deonna pants, falling to her knees.

Audrey puts out her fire.

"Bec," Darren whispers. "Remember how you said you might be able to open a portal?"

"I-I have to try," I stammer.

"Besides, we're out of options," Raven says as the algae girl, Gala I think, walks in the room with a tall thin boy with one red, and one green eye.

He stares at me. He's about in his mid-twenties I believe. He doesn't look angry. He has a sort of puppy dog look and his eyes are on the brink of watering.

The dark-skinned boy jumps into the shadows and disappears.

I close my eyes, and I can hear multiple heartbeats. I close them tighter and think about Dimension Eight, more specifically, Earth.

I remember being in the forest with Emma, my time with Audrey and JP in Eagle Lake, going Hanukkah shopping with Darren, Frederick training me. I think about the mountains of upstate New York, the Statue of Liberty, the Lake in New York, the vast deserts of the Earth-

A strong wind in the forcefield blows my new short hair into my face.

"Shit!" Raven shouts.

"Let's go!" Darren screams.

I open my eyes, and see the boys pounding on the force field.

"Father!" One of them shouts. "They're getting away!"

The force field starts to produce static and crumble.

My hair starts to slowly stand.

All their eyes are on me. For some reason, their eyes creep me out, but I can't put my finger on the reason why.

"Bec!" Raven calls me, and grabs my arm. "Everyone else went through! Let's go!"

She then pulls me away and everything disappears.

Book 3

Disorder Reigns

Chapter 1

My feet hit the ground faster than my mind could process. A light blue sheet takes up my whole vision. I hear crackling electricity, and feel the wind in my eyes making me tear up. Worst of all, I can smell and taste blood.

Negative energy.

Get away from me!

I focus all my crippling energy on pushing it away.

It takes no time for the energy to fade, and my energy along with it. I fall on my knees. My head falls left, but it rests on a warm, hard surface. It smells like dirt, but what my head rests on doesn't feel anything like dirt.

"Bec," the non-dirt whispers.

"Holy crap," I hear another voice.

"How..."

"Is she alright?"

"Bec," the non-dirt whispers again. "Please, wake up."

I shift my head and the blue starts to fade from my vision, more colors like orange and black come into focus. I feel a chilling wind tickling my face. My body starts to shiver a little.

Where am I? Dimension Five?

No. I got us out of there.

Did I?

Yes. I remember now, I think we're back in Dimension Eight, our home dimension. If we are, where in Dimension Eight are we?

I slowly sit up as my vision comes more into focus. The first thing I see is the sky. Oh, beautiful blue sky, it feels like it's been years!

I look around and take in my surroundings. Clay colored soil lies under my bum, and it stretches out far. Little green plants like little bushes cover the soil like a warm blanket.

We're right next to several mountains that seem to stretch on for miles, their peaks just barely tickling the cosmos. Birds sing in a choir that fills my ears.

How would we get back home? It seems like we're in the middle of nowhere. Where is home?

"Can you stand?" Darren the non-dirt asks me.

I nod to avoid looking him in the face. Just now, I realize that he's holding my hand. He stands me up, holding me close because I start to fall over a little.

He bends back down and passes me my hat. I whisper a faint "thanks," as I put it on my head.

"What you just did is impossible for magicians," Raven tells me, raising her eyebrow and glancing at me sideways. Her skin has turned red, probably on the account that the sun is out. After all, Fulls turn in the sun, while Halfs stay the way they are. She's only wearing shorts and a T-shirt. She's trying to keep her body still, but her arms slightly shake and her teeth chatter a little through her closed lips.

"So is your existence," I say as Darren still holds me upright. "Yet, here you are."

God dammit! I wasn't like this when I closed that portal in New York. Why am I feeling this weak all of a sudden?

"Ray, you said you'd tell us later," Deonna reminds her. Her skin is red as well, erasing all my doubts of us being in another dimension. "It's later." Deonna takes off her jacket, revealing a long-sleeved shirt underneath, and hands it to Raven.

Raven sighs, and looks down at her unconscious little brother that she is cradling in her arms like a newborn. She's probably done this several times when he was a baby.

"Maybe I should wait for JP to wake up. His life is my top priority right now."

"You don't have to give details," Audrey tells her. "Just tell us something so we can understand."

Page 285

Raven looks up at the sun. She squints and stares at it for several minutes.

We all start to look at each other and shrug our shoulders.

"We should head South," Raven says when we all look at her.

"Why not North?" I ask. "Or East for the matter?"

"Because, if we're in the Sahara, I don't want to be caught in the North," Raven says, looking down and blinking several tears away.

"And if we're not?" Darren asks. "If we're in the Gobi or Sonoran Desert?"

Raven shrugs her shoulders, still staring at the sun to find its path. "I'm just going on instinct. It's kept me alive this long."

I'm able to stand fully on my own now, so I let go of Darren.

Raven hands JP to Darren and takes the jacket, nodding at Deonna. She quickly puts it on and tries to control her shivering, wrapping her arms around herself. Raven takes her brother back without a look or a word.

She turns around and starts walking while shifting a pale-faced JP around in her arms. Reluctantly, the four of us follow.

"I got trapped there because I chased after some kifomen who stole JP's doll," Raven tells us. "Although, I have no idea how long ago that was. My first dimension, however, wasn't Five, it was Two, and there was nothing but water. Good thing I can breathe underwater."

She continues to tell us her story of how she wandered from dimension to dimension, doing pretty much what we were doing. Finding a portal to take her home. She went to a total of four dimensions, learning about all ten dimensions before arriving in Five. She appeared inside the castle and spied on the Demon King, known only as Father. She then heard them talking about a group of magicians in the dimension. She figured it was people she knew when
Gamma and his dark-skinned brother Bonnie left, and Bonnie came back with JP. She knew Gamma was leading us into a trap, so she tried to look for us.

"Then I found you guys in the canyon. I started to head down to warn you guys, but he had his knife to Bec's throat. She got out of it, and you guys know the rest."

We're all silent for a while. Nobody knows what to say.

"I'm glad you made it out," Deonna finally says after several moments of silence.

Raven smiles at her, the first smile I ever see on her. "Thanks, cousin. I'm glad we all made it out."

"But how did you survive without eating and drinking a lot?" Audrey asks.

"I didn't need it," Raven says while shrugging her shoulders.

"What do you mean?" Audrey asks.

"Well, I did lose a lot of weight. I was a little dehydrated in Dimension Two, but in Dimension Six the plants sustained me. I was taken care of in Dimension Three, but I was thirsty in Dimension One. I ate some air fish there, so I wasn't hungry. When I got to Five, the water was enough, but I wasn't able to eat in Five besides some flowers and leftovers in the castle kitchen."

"We only had a bag of mixed nuts that Bec brought," Darren tells her. "As well as what we could scavenge."

"Good thing she had it then. What about you guys?"

Audrey and Darren take turns telling Raven our story of what happened to us.

"And how did you end up with them?" she asks me.

I sigh and tell her about the day on the beach when my family was killed and how Emma told me who I was.

"So... you were with humans before?" Raven asks.

I nod.

"And you had a family?"

I nod again.

There's still a little doubt in her eyes when she looks at me.

After a long moment of silence, we seem to make it to the edge of the mountain range, dirt and bushes spreading out to the horizon.

I look to my right at the setting sun, painting the sky orange, and some of the clouds pink. The sun is poking through the clouds on the horizon, and just a sliver of it visible. My mother used to say that South Florida had the most beautiful sunsets in the world.

This one comes pretty close.

The sun was almost directly overhead when we started walking. Now it's on the horizon.

My feet are starting to hurt.

Page 287

Water.

Cheesy potatoes. How I miss you!

My mother used to make excellent potatoes. I haven't thought of my family in a while. I'm not as depressed as I used to be, but I don't like talking about them. I miss being home. Although, now that I think about it, where is my home now?

"What's a wallaby doing all the way out here in the middle of nowhere?" Raven asks no one in particular. She gently shakes JP's head and tries to wake him up, to no avail.

I look forward again and notice the animal that seemed to jump out in front of us.

I've got to stop getting lost in my thoughts.

"It's so cute!" Audrey says and starts to run toward it with her arms outstretched.

Darren runs after Audrey and moves in front of her, facing the wallaby.

"Careful, cuz," Darren tells her, "we don't know what it'll do to us. They can be very dangerous."

"Those are kangaroos you're thinking of." I say, taking a closer look at the small animal. "Wait, it's too big to be a wallaby. It could very well be a baby kangaroo. Also, it's fur is not bright enough."

"How do you know this?" Darren asks, not taking his eyes off of the Joey.

"I studied a lot about kangaroos and Australian animals because when I was little, I always wanted to..."

"To what?" Darren asks.

I look around at the terrain. The rocky plateau, the near blood orange soil, and the bushes.

The bush.

"Guys, I think I know where we are," I say. "I believe we're on the opposite corner of the planet, in the Outback."

"What!"

"At least it's not Africa," Raven says.

"Why'd you bring us here?" Deonna shouts. "To this big, country wide desert of nothingness!"

"Yeah, because clearly I did it on purpose," I snap.

"You're always fucking up!"

Page 288

"Well it's a good thing I didn't fuck up the portal."

"You did!"

"We're in the right dimension, aren't we?" I counter.

Deonna just grunts.

"Stop yelling," Raven suggests.

"Why do you hate me so much?" I ask Deonna. "I've never once did anything to you. You don't even know me that well."

"And I intend to keep it that way."

I don't get it, Deonna was warming up to me a little back in Dimension Five, unless it was just her loosening her screws like the rest of us.

"Darren!" Audrey screams. "Look out!"

I turn around and see Audrey backing away from a seven-foot-tall kangaroo. Darren is laying several feet away, not moving. The little joey just hops behind his mother.

"Audrey, get away from there!" Deonna shouts.

All the experts say to run away from a wild kangaroo if you see one, but I run up to Audrey and the mother kangaroo like a dumbass.

I grab Audrey and go next to her. I then move her behind me. I spin, and she disappears. The kangaroo goes left, I hide her. The kangaroo goes right, I hide her again.

"Deonna," I whisper. "Go get Darren."

"Where's Audrey?" she asks.

"I have her."

I hear Deonna scuttle off behind me, and Raven on the other side.

I keep hiding Audrey from the kangaroo who apparently wants to kill her.

"Amazing," Audrey whispers behind me. "You got it so fast."

"What? Misdirection?"

"Sleight of hand."

"Oh."

The kangaroo hops around me, but I still manage to keep her hidden. I can't even see where she is.

The mother does not look happy, standing up very straight. Well, I've never seen a live kangaroo before so I don't know what a happy one looks like either.

Page 289

The little joey hops over and climbs into his mother's pouch. The mother rubs her nose on her baby.

I grab Audrey's wrist and we run after the others, making her visible again.

There's a tall man with dark hair, probably in his forties, with white paint all over his body, standing with the girls and unconscious boys. He did a bad paint job though. I can see a little bit of red skin underneath. He's grabbing Darren's feet while Deonna has his arms, and Raven is holding JP like before.

"Thanks, Alan," Deonna says. "It's good to see you again."

Chapter 2

Alan brings us to his place inside a mountain after about another hour of walking.

"I'm sorry you can't see my children," Alan tells us. "My son is doing his Walkabout and my daughter had to go into town and get us some food. I won't be here for very long though."

Alan's place is protected by magic on the side of the mountain. He lowers the force field and walks in. It looks almost like the trailer in Eagle Lake, except this one is dark like Darren and Deonna's place, and there's not a lot of furniture besides a couch and coffee table. The place goes very deep into the mountain, so there could be more.

"Maybe next time we can see Alan and Alana," Deonna says as she and Alan lay Darren down.

"Are we really in the Outback?" Audrey asks Alan.

"We're at Flinders Range," he explains to her. "On the edge of the Outback, next to civilization."

I place my hands on Darren's chest, shiver at the touch of his blood. A few of his ribs appear to have broken when the mother kangaroo kicked him. There's also a lot of bruises. I feel the tingling sensation of my healing repairing his ribs. Once his chest closes up, the bruising is down, and his bones snap back together, I stop. His breathing gets more even, and now he sleeps with his mouth slightly open. I place the back of my fingers on his chin and close his mouth, but it opens slightly again when I take my fingers away.

"Incredible," Alan says behind me.

I turn around and see him staring at Darren's chest.

"You completely repaired him. Almost as if it didn't happen at all."

"Thanks," I smile. "It's one of my best magic tricks."

He nods slowly, and gives me a curious glance.

"Alan," Raven says, "you and the other telepath mages need to send a telepathic message to as many magicians as possible and warn them that D-Day is coming. Deonna, that means you too."

"D-Day already happened in-"

"I mean a demon doomsday on humanity and magicanity. The Demon King is sending his kifomen here. His kids will take over this dimension if we don't do something. Then he'll move on and own all nine habitable dimensions!"

"I have no idea what you're talking about."

"Alan, please!"

Alan shakes his head, then looks at his watch. He sighs and says, "Look, I'd love to help, and I'm happy you're alive, but you sound nuts at the moment. Also, nine dimensions? I'm supposed to meet with my son at the Victoria Market, and I had to leave hours ago."

"Is that why you were out there?"

"Yes."

"I can go," Audrey volunteers. "You need to hear her story."

"I don't know," he sighs. "Will he recognize you? You've all grown so much."

"I'm sure he will," Audrey smiles.

"But you can't go alone."

"Bec will come with me."

"I will?"

"You did say you've always wanted to come here."

I sigh. "I did."

"Very well, girls. Be careful. Take the Port Augusta bus to Adelaide, then make your way to the airport, and take that to Melbourne. Meet my son in the market in the place where no magician dares to tread."

***

We had to walk a long way, a few hours. I didn't look at the clock.

Page 292

"You have any idea of what he's talking about?" I ask Audrey once we get onto a road in civilization.

"Not a clue."

We walk alongside the road. There are several little buildings along the nearly deserted road and orange sand.

I'm surprised that there are places this close to the Outback.

We reach a sign that says: Port Augusta dry land. No alcohol in public places.

"I think there's another hour to the bus station," Audrey laughs, and then transfers her laugh into a whine. "My feet hurt."

"At least we're home," I say.

"Barely."

"You whine a lot."

"What do you mean?"

***

The long hours on the bus ride were horrible. I vomited twice. The plane ride was calmer, but it didn't stop my stomach from churning. Not being in any vehicle for a while must have really made me develop some bad motion sickness.

When we arrive at the Melbourne airport, the first thing I notice is that there are a lot of humans. A lot more than at the Adelaide airport.

The second thing I notice are the little coffee shops and book stands.

"I wonder what's going on in the world," Audrey says as she walks towards the bookshop. There's a stand of newspapers called The Age. It's about a local girl winning a medal in track. I gasp at what I see.

"Seems like nothing drastic has happened yet," Audrey says as she hands me the newspaper. I'm shaking so much with rage that I crumble the pages I'm holding.

Audrey doesn't notice. She smiles and tells me that we should hurry to the market. When she's not looking, I put the newspaper in the large front pocket of my sweater and follow her.

***

Page 293

I say nothing on the walk to the train station, the train ride to Flagstaff, or the walk to the market. Audrey keeps glancing at me sideways. Her mouth is straight, but her eyes are shaking, well, the eye I can see shakes.

Why couldn't he have said Sydney, the number two city on my list of places to visit. Instead of going to the harbor or the opera house, we're in Melbourne inside an open market.

"Any idea what we're supposed to be looking for?" Audrey asks me.

"A place where we would fear to tread," I say, "but that's the whole market in my opinion."

I stare off into the market at all the people hustling and bustling.

"Focus."

"I am."

"Do you need to vomit again?"

"I hope not."

We come in through the parking lot and I almost get hit by a car. That would have been embarrassing, survive Dimension Five just to be killed by metal. First thing I see is an old woman selling two stands worth of flowers. There are three women gathered around her. One is smelling the white bouquet while the other two are talking to the vendor.

Not our place.

I have never seen a more disorganized mess in my life. And on top of that, there are so many people that you can barely walk.

Spotty Dot kid stuff with a bored looking Asian woman?

Nope.

Shirts, nope. Coats, nope.

Soaps and shoes? Why sell those together?

More clothes. Jewelry. Another stand for kids. This one has two of those hypnotizing ball machines where the little plastic balls move all around on their own. Up the escalator thing, down and around, back up the escalator, down and around, down and around, down and around, down and around, down-

"Bec!"

"Sorry?"

Page 294

"Snap out of it, you've been staring at that for a while now."

"Sorry."

Glasses, jewelry, lots of watches, lots of bored kids watching the stands, shoes, pricey suitcases, wooden logos, who sells China here? More clothes down this hallway.

"Let's keep going straight," I suggest.

Fake nails. Sports stuff. Pet toys and pet clothes.

Oh, pictures.

"Australians really love their pets."

"That's humans in general," Audrey says. "Focus."

"I am!"

"Your eyes keep wandering."

"Because I'm looking."

"Yeah, at parakeets, but that's not what I'm talking about."

"Listen to ya big sista, lil boy," a man looking at a pink elephant says. "She knows what's best fa ya."

I feel my face start to warm up in the cold.

Little boy? Me?

I look at a smiling and blushing Audrey. "What's gotten into you?" She asks me, trying to hide the laugh in her voice when the man walks away. "You've been acting strange since the airport."

"I need some water."

"Don't dodge my question. This just proves that something is wrong."

I sigh and take the front-page newspaper out of my sweater pocket.

"You kept this?" She takes a careful look, reading the content of the front-page article. "I don't see what the big deal is with-"

"Not the story," I interrupt softly. "Look at the date."

She looks a little longer. "They swap the month and the day here," and then she sees it. "Oh... oh, Bec."

"I'm seventeen," I tell her. "More importantly, I made us miss four and a half years of our lives."

"It wasn't all bad," she tries to appease me. "We all survived, we found Raven, and we even found out some important information. If you ask me, those were four years spent wisely."

Page 295

"Really, Audrey? Everyone thought we were dead, JP is almost dead, Darren got mauled by a kangaroo, I'm seventeen and still look like I'm twelve-"

"Well, you did age a little."

"-and this new hair chop Deonna gave me makes me look like a boy, or like I'm one of those stereotypical strong female leads who chop off half their hair."

"But we're all alive, and we have a chance to stop what this Father guy is planning, thanks to you."

I sigh. "I need some water."

"Well," she looks around, knowing that I can't talk about this right now, "there's a nearby sign over there that says Eat. Let's try there."

I look and see the sign, along with an opening towards more of the market selling everything but stuff to eat.

"But we're still surrounded by clothes and jewelry," I say as we start waking, "and tools, and...car stuff?"

She sighs. "This place is confusing. Oh! Tribe cafe!"

"Coffee, can that be what he meant?"

"Maybe."

I notice a pink sign after another two coffee cafes and walk further to it.

My God, this place sells plants too!

Whatever, that's not important.

I look at the sign. Bite size mini food. Cakes, desserts, and yummy things.

Audrey and I look at each other and smile.

This is it.

"It's closed," Audrey notices.

"Did he say we had to go inside?"

"I-I don't think so."

There are a bunch of tables lined up by the cafes, all with a small round table and two chairs.

"I guess we wait," I say.

"Didn't you want some water?"

***

"So, besides Australia, where have you always wanted to go?" Audrey asks me.

I don't even need to think about my answer for this question. "Russia, Japan, the Bahamas, Peru-"

"Why Peru?"

"Machupichu."

"You know, the Bahamas is also very Magician populated."

"Really?"

"Yeah."

"Where else?"

She smiles. "Everywhere they drive left, and the United States."

"Drive left, but... but those are all the old English colonies."

She smiles again.

Are you serious!?

***

"I need substance."

"Me too."

"That river water was quite thirst quenching."

"I know, right?"

***

"Have you ever kissed a boy?"

"No."

"Ever kissed a girl?"

"No."

"Do you want to?"

"What?"

***

"Wanna get a pizza?"

"We have no money."

"True."

Page 297

"Plus, I'm a vegetarian."
"You mean vegan?"
"No."
"You don't eat cheese unless it's vegan, what do you call that?"
"An extremist?"
"Vegan!"
"Technically, vegans don't use anything with animals, that includes their clothes."
"Vegan."
"I wear cotton!"
"Vegan!"

***

"Let's walk around."
"Can't."

***

"Why do they sell plants in front of a cafe?"
"Beats me."

***

I sigh and put my head down.

It's almost three o'clock and we haven't seen him anywhere.

Well, Audrey hasn't seen him. I don't even know what he looks like.

Coming up with things to talk about is starting to get harder.

"Why do magicians go on the Walkabout?"

"To prove they have a sense of direction."

"But I thought they would go home."

"Humans go home. We go to a riddled location to test our wits as well."

I see someone by the plants dressed head to toe in clothing.

"Seems a bit dramatic."

"Those are our ways."

Page 298

The boy didn't cover his face, and when our eyes meet and he starts to run, I know exactly who he is.

"Gamma!"

"What?"

I don't explain it to Audrey. I jump up and run after him. Past the plants, clothes, and strollers. He breaks right and I follow him down a gap where there are a lot of cars parallel parked, and a lot of light bulbs overhead.

He breaks left.

Dog tags and DVDs.

Pokémon plushies?

I follow him past another gap and a bunch of spiritual rocks into a food market.

Why couldn't they just sell the cafe stuff here? Gah!

Focus!

"Whoa!" I crash into a man.

"You a'ight, mate?" he asks me.

He's fast! He cuts right again.

"Yes. Thanks. Sorry!" I resume running. I cut right and run forward.

Where'd he go?

Wine barrels and smoothies?

Where is he?

Wine barrels!

I run towards the wine barrels, but I only see sixteen large barrels and a man with a large tooth smile in plaid.

Crap!

Audrey runs up behind me huffing and puffing.

"What... just... happened?"

"Gamma was here."

"What! Where'd he go?"

I shrug my shoulders. "I don't know. He was just here!"

"I just realized something," she tells me.

"What's that?"

She smiles. "I think we were supposed to be here tomorrow for the night market."

Page 299

Chapter 3

We're walking out of the market when I notice a certain blue car. Their license plates are on the front and back of their cars, but that's not what catches my eye.

"Audrey, look," I say, tapping her shoulder and pointing at the all zero license plate. "Think they might be one of us?"

"Has to be," she tells me.

We wait by the car for about half an hour when a woman around the age of thirtyish approaches the car. She stops when she sees us. She's holding two tote bags that have food inside them.

I am leaning on her car, and I immediately stand up straight when I see her.

"Hello," Audrey says, smiling at her. "Is this your car?"

"Yes," she says, obviously not sure what to make of us.

"We noticed your license plate and-"

"Ah," the woman says, "you're magicians."

"Aren't you?" I ask.

"My husband and I are drages," she says. "I'm Emily."

"I'm Audrey, and this is my sister, Bec."

Sister?

Sister. I have a sister again!

"Nice to meet you. Are you girls lost?"

"Kind of," Audrey admits. "We were supposed to meet a friend here, but it turns out we were supposed to meet him tomorrow night and we don't have a place to stay. Do you know any hostels nearby?"

"Hop in," Emily says. "You girls can stay in our spare room. I'd have to call my husband on the way home though."

"How far is it?" I ask.

"Not far at all," Emily says, "It's it Footscray."

I nod like I know where that is.

***

We get to her place, which is a little house that's near a university and a park, right on the edge of the city. I have to say, it's kind of cute.

She opens the front door and says, "go wash up in the guest room, girls, dinner will be ready in an hour."

"Thank you, Emily," Audrey says.

"Thanks," I say, smiling back.

A young girl around three runs up to Emily. I don't see what happens because Audrey and I go in the spare room.

"Lucky for us, you picked her car out," Audrey tells me.

"Maybe," I say.

"Why so glum?"

"Well, we are in a stranger's house."

"She's not going to hurt us, Bec."

"We don't know that."

She sighs. "It's only for the night. We can leave early and explore the city if you'd like. You've always wanted to see Australia."

"Yeah, Sydney, the Great Barrier Reef, Uluru, I never even heard of Footscray until now."

"It'll be fun."

I sigh. "We can explore tomorrow, but-"

I stop myself mid-sentence because I feel something flow out of me in a place where I've never thought of.

"Bec?"

I ignore her and run to the bathroom, and find out that blood is pouring out of me.

"Bec!" Audrey knocks on the door. "What's wrong?"

"Uh... I'm bleeding."

"From where? You weren't bleeding... Oh! Damn, I was fifteen when I got mine, you're late as fuck!"

Page 301

"Audrey!"

"Okay! Okay!" She starts to laugh. "One second!"

I grab as much toilet paper as I dare and start wiping blood away, but it doesn't come off easily. I have to use water as well.

I lay my clothes out to dry, and I'm standing naked in the bathroom. My training bra is now way too large on me. I used to have little bumps, but now my breasts have doubled in size.

Also, I've lost a lot of weight. My rib cage is visible, my shoulder blades pop out, and my thighs no longer touch each other.

Funny, I grew so much, but I've probably lost some pounds because of how little I was eating.

Audrey comes back and shoves something that looks like a fancy stick wrapped in plastic under the door. "Why don't you take a shower and I'll show you how it works when you're out!"

Oh boy!

***

Emily made spaghetti and meatballs for dinner. It's not what I expected at an Australian table, but they're delicious.

Well, the spaghetti is. Not sure about the meatballs.

"Where are you two from?" Erick, Emily's husband, asks us. "You sound American."

"We are," I say smiling. "We've been gone for a while though."

"How much longer are you planning on staying in Australia?" Emily asks.

"We don't really know," Audrey says. "Our cousins are in Port Augusta right now with some friends, so we have to meet up with them after tomorrow before we do anything else."

"My mate Tanner was the same way," Erick says. "Always met with other magicians, helped out any way he could. Was a good guy."

I can only guess how he died.

"Who was Tanner?" I ask.

"He was my mate, my best friend. The whole reason my wife and I became drages in the first place. He left us his car when he passed."

Page 302

"That explains the license plate," I say aloud without meaning to.

"Yup," Erick says. "Not many drages have the plate. I think they should, it would help out a lot."

Emily's six-month-old son throws a meatball at his sister.

"Mommy!"

"It's okay, Erika, he's only a baby. He didn't mean it."

Emily tells her. She then grabs her son's hands and says a firm, "no, Emil."

"Have you girls ever tried lamington?" Erick asks us.

"No, but I heard it was good," I say.

"You heard right."

"Is it vegan?"

***

We leave early the next morning and travel around the city of Melbourne. Emily gave us some money for food, but we didn't buy any. We regretted that around two o' clock when our stomachs started bothering us. I started craving weird things, like peanut butter and bananas, but Audrey said that was a normal thing to eat. We went to the Melbourne Star, the aquarium, the Eureka Tower, the St. Kilda beach, and the botanical gardens. Such a beautiful city.

Except for everybody smoking all over the damn place at every goddamn hour!

We find Alan's son at the night market. He looks just like his father. Dark skin, dark eyes, like a true aboriginal.

This Alan, however, doesn't paint his body white. He must have been hiding from the sun like a normal magician.

Audrey and Alan hug and catch up. He has money, so he buys us some sandwiches. I don't focus on them, I'm staring at the crowd, seeing if I spot Gamma or any of his siblings anywhere.

Why was he even here?

"So, we'll stay the night here again, and head back to Port Augusta in the morning," Audrey tells Alan and me.

Aw, not the bus again!

***

"So, Audrey tells me you're her sister," Alan asks me when she's in the hotel shower. "That her mom adopted you after your family was killed."

"I am?"

"Are you not?"

"I-I'm not sure," I answer honestly. "I've been with them for a while, and JP did say that I was the newest . . . member to their family."

"You seem uneasy."

"You seem like a mind reader."

He laughs. "Reality."

"What?"

"I am not, but I know someone who is. Why the trouble? Did you lose your family before?"

He's good for a non-mind reader.

"Two, actually."

"Oh."

I look at the restroom door, hearing the water turn off and the curtain getting pulled back. I never once thought of the magicians as my family. I'm supposed to be the last Proenza. Am I turning into a Paris?

Is Darren my cousin now?

***

We leave early to catch a six in the morning flight, and then the bus.

The fucking bus.

I threw up three times.

Walking over three hours to the mountains or riding on the bus? I'll take walking in the middle of the night where anything can kill you over that fucking bus.

When we get back that night, there's a girl around twenty with dark skin and dark eyes. She's also tall and thin with no blemishes on her face. She looks almost nothing like Alan, but I assume that she's his daughter, Alana.

Darren is awake.

Page 304

He's sitting down, no longer purple, in a chair that was grabbed from the table. Alana puts her scissors down on the couch and hands Darren a mirror, and holds another one behind his head. He nods his head and says something to her.

His hair is shorter, but still barely out of his eyes. As he flips it away, he notices the three of us walking in.

I feel my stomach start to act up again when we make eye contact. He gives me a small half smile, and my insides turn into acid.

I smile wide and look to the side so fast I hear my neck pop. It's a good thing he didn't cut all his hair off.

JP is awake as well. He's laying down with his back on the floor and his head in Raven's lap. She's brushing his hair out of his eyes with her hand.

I never noticed how long JP's hair was until now.

"Your turn, JP!" Alana shouts. She has such a loud voice, but it sounds like sticking a hot knife into a stick of butter.

"Yey!" JP jumps off the floor and does one more jump into the chair, the little jumping bean. "Shave it all off. Buzz cut my head!"

"Sure thing!" she looks up and nods at her brother.

"Dad! Alan's home!"

Their father comes out of the middle of the mountain. His skin is no longer red, and the white paint has been removed. He looks a little older here than he did the other day.

Little Alan runs up to his father and gives him a hug.

"How was your walkabout?"

"I saw Ayer's Rock, reality, dad! It was huge! Not as big as people think it is, but it's still pretty big."

His father laughs and pulls him into another hug. "And I'm happy to say that you passed, son." He then looks at me and Audrey. "Thank you, girls."

"It was nothing."

"I need to vomit."

"I'll get you something," little Alan says. "Come." He walks towards the inside of the mountain, and I follow.

It goes on for a while. I see three bedrooms, and another living room before we reach the kitchen. It's a nice redwood kitchen fully equipped with a fridge, microwave, sink, oven, basically every appli-

Page 305

ance but a dishwasher. Several cupboards, and the door is open to reveal a walk-in pantry.

He opens up a cupboard and takes out a small cardboard box. He then pulls out an orange tablet. He then opens the cupboard right next to the medicine one and pulls out a plastic clear cup. He goes to the fridge and gets a glass of water on the door. When the cup is full, he drops the tablet in and hands it to me.

"Drink when the tablet is fully dissolved."

"Thanks," I smile at him.

Alana comes into the room. She and Alan exchange a look. She then grabs a razor from a drawer and walks out of the kitchen.

"What was that about?" I ask him after taking a sip of the tarty orange drink loaded with medicinal products that make me want to spit it out.

"My sister and I are not on speaking terms."

"That's horrible. Why? What happened?"

He looks down at the floor. "Reality."

"You should make an effort to talk to her. Odds are, the life Magicians lead, you might lose her pretty soon, or vice versa." I rest my hand on his shoulder. "Nothing should be more important than family."

"It's not that easy."

"Reality isn't easy."

He smiles wide. "Fine, you got me there."

I bring the glass back into the main living room.

"What do you mean the telepathy didn't work?" Audrey asks.

"Something's blocking our telepathy. We can't reach uncle Frederick," Deonna tells her.

"We might have to go home and warn them by mouth," Raven says. "I need to see my dad anyway. Let him know I'm alive."

"So it's settled, we have to get back to the States," Darren says. "Little Alan, can you help us make fake IDs and passports?"

"Like it'll be hard," he smiles.

"You can stay here for the night," Big Alan says. "Then you will need to catch a bus to the airport, and fly to Sydney."

"Aw, no!" I scream.

"What?"

"Not the bus again!"

Page 306

Little Alan goes back into the kitchen.

"You'll be able to see Sydney though," Audrey smiles.

"Not helping."

Little Alan brings back three of the orange tablets.

"You'll need these."

I really don't want to go back on the bus for a third time. I'm probably going to be scared for life from buses. At least I'll be able to see Sydney. Besides, we have a job to do.

Protect humanity.

Chapter 4

The flight from Sydney to Los Angeles isn't until the next morning, so I get my wish to see Sydney, even if it is only for a day.

Darren bought us some sandwiches with his special card. I used to wonder if using his card was stealing or not, coming from the girl who once stole a paddle boat with John to escape being caught by the police for putting soap in our neighborhood fountain.

At this point, I don't even know what to believe anymore.

Raven stares at her food, her face transitioning between skepticism, and sadness.

Is she alright?

The six of us are sitting across from the opera house in the adjacent park. We're close enough to the opera house to have a good view, sitting on the grass, right in front of the water. We're literally the only group who have not taken a single picture.

I wish I had a camera.

I used to think the Sydney opera house was just one big building, man was I wrong!

"You keep staring at the damn opera house," Raven says to me. "Why?"

"It's just that Sydney is a place I've dreamed of coming to since I was a child."

"You're still a child."

"I don't feel like one."

"Well, technically," Audrey says, butting in, "we're in the summer, so you only have a few months until you're really an adult. At least by human standards."

"We're in the winter," I tell her.

"Eh, it's summer back home, I was going by that logic," Audrey laughs.

"I just hate how we had a four-and-a-half-year long winter, and we come back into another winter," Deonna growls.

"At least going home and feeling the warm summer air will be all the more satisfying, right?" I grin.

Deonna shrugs her shoulders. "Maybe," she says, "or it will be too unbearable for us because we've been in winter for so long."

"I didn't even think of that," I say.

Deonna takes a bite of her sandwich. When she swallows, she asks me, "aren't you going to finish yours?"

I look down at the sandwich that has one bite mark in it. "I still feel a little sick."

"All the more reason why you should eat," JP says.

I force myself to take another bite, but my stomach is begging me to not swallow. I force it down anyways, but I can't eat another bite.

"Maybe I just need some juice," I say. "My stomach can't take any solids right now."

"But we haven't been on a bus or plane for over three hours now," JP says.

I shrug my shoulders. "I still feel weak."

"Come on," Darren says standing up.

"To where?" I ask.

"To get you something to drink. You can use the calories."

"Thanks?"

"We'll be here," Audrey says, smiling. She then winks at me.

I flip her the bird, and then I stand up.

"What was that about?" Darren asks me as we're walking away on the path.

"Nothing."

I try not to look at him. I instead stare at the opera house. The sun is nowhere near ready to set. It has just reached the top of the opera house from where I'm looking.

Page 309

"You really like that opera house."

"Yup."

"Is Sydney everything you expected?"

"Nope."

"Like how?"

I feel my face start to flush.

Please stop talking.

When I don't answer, he doesn't push for one. When we turn the corner on the path and my back is now to the opera house, I stare straight ahead. Or, at least I try to. My eyes keep darting to his face and his hand.

I want to grab his hand and hold it tight, but I also want to push him into the harbor.

Why do I have these conflicting feelings towards him?

Sure, I accused him of lying. Yes, I tried to kill him with Stick... once. Yeah, I did push him away, but I didn't mean to.

Then what am I doing right now?

I sigh out loud.

"Everything okay?" he asks me.

"I just feel like shit," I admit.

We reach the cafe and he opens the door for me. "What kind do you want?"

"If they don't have anything with ginger, then apple juice," I say as I walk inside.

"I thought juice was your first choice?"

"Well, ginger is good for upset stomachs."

"Can't say you're wrong there," he says, smiling at me.

I stare at him and smile like a moron.

I quickly look away and look at the drink selections. "Do you have any tea with ginger?" I ask the young guy behind the counter.

"We got ginger beer," he says. "It's no tea, but it has more of a punch."

I look at the bottle of ginger beer. Bundaberg. Never heard of it. I'd love to try one, but I don't want to tell Darren that.

"Two ginger beers and an apple juice, please," Darren says.

"Thanks," I tell him while still looking at the bottle.

Page 310

As we walk out of the store, I try to open it, but I have to stick my finger in this ring all the way, and I can't seem to pull it off. Why is this so frustratingly hard?

Darren sticks out his hand. I hand him the drink and he opens it for me.

"Again, thanks."

I take a sip, and wow is that the strongest soda I ever drank.

Wait.

Soda!

"This is soda," I say.

Darren bursts out laughing.

I don't know why, but I start to laugh with him. We laugh for a while. I have to admit, it feels good to laugh with him.

He looks at the nutrition label on his bottle.

"Is it safe?" I ask.

"I can't tell. It's in milliliters."

"And how many milliliters are in a bottle?"

"Can't tell." He looks up from the bottle and looks me dead in the eye. "Did I just buy two sodas?"

"Looks like it," I laugh.

He takes my soda and takes a gulp of it.

"Darren!"

"I'm already at a loss," he says pointing to his red face. "Things can't get any worse."

"Sh! Don't say that! Things always get worse when people say that."

He laughs again. "Like you wouldn't drink any?" He holds out the bottle to me.

I can't. Not after the mess I just got us out of.

"I'm already getting a headache!" he laughs. While he's laughing, he pulls me into a hug.

I don't push him away, and I don't hug him back at first. I force myself to laugh, but I don't force myself to hug him back. That comes naturally.

Then my laughing comes naturally. I hold him tightly as I laugh in his shoulder, not sure of what's so funny, but not wanting to stop either.

Page 311

I don't want him to let go of me. I want him to keep holding me, to kiss me, to make me feel this happy always.

What the fuck is wrong with me?

I stop laughing, and so does he.

He clears his throat a little.

I start to chew on my bottom lip, embarrassed by my own thoughts.

"We should, uh..." he starts to say, but then screaming comes from the opera house.

Uh oh!

We start sprinting back.

There are six kifomen around the opera house, about six more that are attacking humans, and three that are dead on the floor.

Raven and Deonna are containing the six around the opera house. Raven is throwing these little stars at their heads, having them fall down dead. Deonna is slashing them with a knife.

How the hell did they sneak those past airport security?

JP and Audrey are close by, flinging rocks and fire to kill some of them.

I don't hesitate another second. I throw my arms down, and everything is slowed down. I rush up to five kifomen that are running around and rip them to shreds. It was exhilarating.

Darren took the last one of the six.

I throw my arms down again and time returns to normal.

I see four dead bodies. Three men and a woman.

"Okay," Audrey says skeptically, "that was a little too easy."

"Hey!" Raven shouts.

I follow her gaze and see that she's looking at a teenage boy with a smart camera phone. I extend my hand, and use my telekinesis to break it.

"My phone!" he screams.

"Uh, guys," JP says.

There are at least ten more people who are on their phones who are videotaping what is happening.

Like an idiot, I stare directly at one of them. More specifically, the one who caught me breaking the other boy's phone.

I feel someone grab my wrist, and we start running.

Page 312

Chapter 5

"Why are people even videotaping anyways?" I rant.

"Why didn't they just run like normal people?"

"What are they even going to do with those videos anyways?" Audrey asks.

"I'll tell you what," I say. "They're going to upload them on the internet, and magician kind will be exposed all over the planet."

We're at a hostel in Sydney. Thankfully, there are six beds per room, three bunk bed sets, and the six of us have our own room. It's night time now. Darren, Deonna, and Raven's skin has returned to normal color, but Darren has a bag of ice on his head. He got a headache from the soda. JP went to the hostel kitchen to eat something, since food is forbidden in the rooms. Deonna went with him. We can't trust him by himself after what happened.

"I think this was planned," Raven says.

"By who?" Audrey asks.

"By the heterochromiacs." Raven's eyes go on me.

"I didn't do that!" I shout.

"I didn't say you did."

"But you're looking right at me."

"Ray, even with what you learned, you have to believe that Bec is on our side," Darren tells her.

"What do you mean, 'even with what she learned?'"

Darren doesn't say anything.

Everyone seems to shift uncomfortably.

"You all know something that I don't," I accuse them.

"Bec-"

"No! There's something that you all clearly know that I don't, and you refuse to tell me what it is."

"It's complicated," Raven says.

"Well, I'm listening."

"Let's just say, there's a reason that you... can...and have... certain...qualities and skills."

"And that reason is?"

"Better left unsaid for now."

"Why!"

"Because, fuck you, that's why," Raven snaps.

"Excuse me?" I say.

"We should discuss getting home," Audrey says.

"The plane leaves tomorrow," Darren says.

"Hello!" I say.

"Yes, but with that video being put out, people might recognize us," Raven says.

"So, you guys are just going to ignore me?" I say.

"So, you're suggesting we separate?" Audrey asks.

"Exactly," Raven says.

The door opens, and JP and Deonna come in panting.

"What happened?" Darren asks him.

"The video's on the news!" he says.

"What?"

"Top story tonight for Australia, and you can bet it's gonna go viral."

"Shit!" Raven snaps.

"And Bec is the main focus point. Come out and look!"

The others run out of the room.

"Do you really think that's such a good idea?" I call after them.

Still ignoring me. God dammit, those assholes!

"At least grab a key!" I call. I grab my own card key off my bed, and chase after them.

The common room is empty, but the TV remains on. I don't pay attention to the woman or the bottom words scrolling past the screen. I only notice the headline.

Is magic real?

Page 314

It cuts to a poorly taken video of Audrey flinging fire at them, but only briefly, because I come on the scene, moving fast like a maniac ripping the kifomen to shreds. Raven is heard off camera. I then look around, stretch out my arm, and the teenager's phone breaks right in his hand. I then look dead at the camera, my eyes being clearly visible.

Shit!

"Shit!" Raven says, taking the word literally out of my mind.

"This is bad," Darren says.

"So, Raven," Audrey says, "you suggested separating?"

Raven thinks for a moment. "We should go in three groups of two. Leave the hostel tomorrow. I need to get home and see my father, tell him and everyone we know what is going on. Our dimension might be another Five sooner than expected. JP and I go first. Darren, you're strong enough, we need you to be the last group and protect Bec."

"Protect me from what?" I ask.

Raven sighs. "I'll tell you soon enough. Right now, you knowing all this will only...we don't know how you'll react."

"And how do I know you're not lying to me? How do I know you're not secretly working with the Demon King?"

"She's not a spy, Bec," Darren says.

"And how do you know?" I ask him.

He looks away. "I just do."

He looks at Raven. She looks back at him. There's a moment of silence, and he hangs his head.

"Is there some kind of telepathy going on here that I don't know about?" I spit out.

"Bec, you'll know everything in time," Raven says. "We can't tell you this one detail yet, but I need you to trust me, because I spied on them, we learned they're trying to cleanse all the dimensions, including Dimension Ten, but he can't get to Dimension Ten so he has his kids collecting things from all over the multiverse to get him there. They're very powerful, and can do away with us whenever they want. It's going to take all of us to stop them. So, are you going to stop questioning everything I'm doing and work with us to stop him, or am I going to have to kill you where you stand because frankly, I'm still not sure if you're on his side or not?"

"I was never on his side!" I say. "I didn't even know he existed up until you came into the picture. I might have the same eye pattern as them, but I am not one of them. I will stop him!"

"And how do you plan on doing this?"

"With help from my family," I say, smiling at everyone.

Raven smiles. "That's the Bec I've heard so much about."

She extends her hand to me, and I shake it. I smile at Raven, and she smiles back at me.

Those bastards hurt my friend. There will be hell to pay.

"We can trust her," Darren says.

"I know," Raven smiles. "JP and I leave tomorrow. Bec, try not to show yourself around Sydney too much."

"Why?"

"You need to stay hidden."

Again with the secrecy.

Chapter 6

We say goodbye to Raven and JP early the next day. Darren and I go to a hotel, and Deonna and Audrey go to a different one from us.

"One room with two beds please," Darren says.

The woman checks her computer. "I'm sorry, but we only have rooms with one bed available."

Darren looks at me.

"Do what you want," I say, trying not to blush as I steal the counter pen.

Why am I even doing that in the first place?

***

I spend most of our time in the room in the shower, and staring at my body in the mirror.

I can't believe how much I've physically changed and didn't notice.

For one thing, I'm taller.

My rib cage is showing a little, mostly on the account of how little I ate in the other dimension. I've always been slim, but this is ridiculous.

Also, I have breasts now. My training bra was squishing them down. I grab them in my hands.

I let go and put my wet hair behind my ears. It's up to my shoulders now. I hate short hair. Deonna did save my life though by cutting it, so I can't say anything. At the same time though, I look like a guy.

Should this really matter?

No, it shouldn't. I'm happy to be alive.

I look at my eyes.

They all had a right green eye, just like me. Why is that?

Raven said that the videotaping must have been planned by the heterochromiacs, and then looked at me. Maybe-

I hear three knocks on the bathroom door.

"Bec, you've been in there for over an hour, are you okay?"

No.

"Yeah, I'll be out soon."

"Listen, I know being cramped in a room isn't your style, so I was thinking that you might be more comfortable going to the aquarium, or something like that. I mean, if you want to go with me."

I lean my head on the bathroom door. Nothing would make me happier than going to the aquarium and exploring the city I've always wanted to go to. I would love to hang out alone with Darren and just pretend everything is normal for once. I hate being cooped up but we have to listen to Raven and stay hidden. I can't let him risk his life for me.

"That's not such a good idea," I tell him. "You and me, out there, alone, it might-"

"You don't have to say anything more," he says.

I sit down on the bathroom floor with my head still against the door. I hear him walk away and sit on the bed.

Tears start to roll down my face.

I now see what is wrong with me.

***

Darren's unconscious body is spiraled on the couch early the next morning. I watch him sleep a little.

Man, I really am a creep.

I go over to the nightstand where he left his wallet. I grab it and look for something to write on. When I find nothing, I grab three toilet paper squares and write: *Needed to get some things, be back soon. Bec.*

I knew the universe was telling me to grab that pen.

I put my teddy bear that I've been carrying in my large pocket from that room in the other dimension on top of the note's corner.

I've been wearing the same clothes since I was in New York, and they're tight on me. I need to fix that. Buying clothes with his card will help to blend in more. Besides, I'm sure Darren needs some stuff too.

I grab his hoodie from the chair, put it on, and head out the door.

***

I'm a woman now, so I need women's clothes.

What do women wear today though?

Dresses are always in fashion. Do I like dresses though? I stare at this one simple red dress in the window. It's pretty, but is it me?

I kind of wish Audrey was here, she'd help me pick something out and find a nice style. Of course, she'd make fun of me too.

She called me her sister.

I smile at the thought.

Maybe it's not such a bad thing to be a part of another family. I can have a big sister again. Of course, they can never replace my real family.

Well, they weren't my real family. My real family either abandoned me, or are dead.

I wonder who my biological mother was.

I wish I knew one thing about her.

A wish that will never come true.

Besides, I have a family now. I'm surprised I didn't realize this sooner. My big sister, Audrey; my mother, Emma; my uncles Frederick and John; my loving cousin, JP; my unloving and cold cousin, Deonna; and Darren...

Darren and I can never be together.

Why am I thinking of all this?

I'll just buy the damn dress.

***

I buy the red dress, a black dress, a black winter jacket with a hood, some yellow pants, and black rain boots for myself. I change into the red dress and jacket. When I go outside and feel the cold air on my legs, I put the yellow pants on under the dress.

I look better than my clothes that were four years old, kind of.

I'm not sure of what Darren's sizes are, so I just bought a large black shirt, a big black sweater, some black pants with a belt, and a pair of black sneakers with no laces.

Wait, I need shoes too.

I buy another pair of black shoes, with these also having no laces. I've always hated laces. Waste of time and you can seriously hurt yourself.

I go to a different store and buy some gloves. In the window, I look at a poster of Australia in rainbow colors, and it says: *Vote Yes!*

Is the rainbow still the gay pride symbol?

I think so.

"May I ask what the poster is for?" I ask the woman at the counter.

"The whole country is voting to see if gay marriage should be legal here or not," she tells me.

As I smile at the poster, I see a boy in the reflection who's about my age. Only weird thing is that he has my face and eyes.

I quickly turn around, but there's nobody there who looks like me.

I see adults scurrying by, women laughing, two boys around ten holding hands, a young girl with a teddy bear, and a man on his cell phone.

"You okay?" she asks me.

"Never better," I lie. "Thank you."

Probably my own reflection.

I get rainbow gloves for myself, and black gloves for Darren.

I go inside the next store and get some scarves and winter hats. As much as I love my fedora, it won't help me in this cold. I get a green scarf for me, and a black one for Darren. I also get a green hat for me, and a black hat for Darren.

I put everything on and realize that I do not match at all.

Audrey can help me with all of this later.

Now for food.

I'm looking around in a Seven-Eleven, and putting fruits and sandwiches in a basket when the lights suddenly go out.

Oh, no! Not the dark!

Natural light is coming in from the windows, but it's still kind of dark.

"Some light. There is some light," I tell myself.

The employee says something, but I don't really hear what he says.

All I can do is stare at a shadow that appears to be moving in the back. The shadow seems to come closer and closer to me.

I don't wait around to see what it is. I throw my hands down to slow down time, drop my basket, and book it out of there.

Chapter 7

I never grabbed the key card so I knock on the door.

Darren opens the door and yanks me into the room by my jacket collar before I can say anything.

"Dude!" I practically shout.

"Where have you been, Bec? I've been worried sick!"

"Getting clothes. I left a note, I even left my bear."

"A bear! That's what you're worried about? Not the fact that you took my things, and left without an explanation?"

"We needed clothes! We've been wearing the same thing for years now. Not to mention that there was demon blood caked on your hoodie, and I am not worried about a bear!"

"What if something had happened?"

"Nobody recognized me!"

"I'm not talking about the video, Bec! I'm talking about your s-stalkers."

"My stalkers?"

"The people from the other dimension!"

"Oh, you have got to be kidding me, they don't even know where we are!"

"They can find out!"

"How?"

"The video!"

"But you just said you weren't talking about the video!"

"Ugh! You are being so irresponsible!"

I scoff. "Excuse me? I come up with an idea to keep you out of danger and get what we need, and I'm irresponsible? You willingly drank a soda, you wanted to go to the aquarium. I have been working hard to do what's right and not mess anything else up, and I'm irresponsible!"

"I did that because I thought that's what you wanted!"

"What I wanted? First you act all overprotective of me for my own good like a parent, and now you want to be my fun cousin, are you serious?"

He blinks a few times. "Fun cousin?"

I lower my voice at the sight of his confused face.

"Yeah, all of you say I'm in this family, so you're basically my cousin."

"Well, I never saw you as my cousin."

I pause, I even blink a few times myself. "Good to know," I barely whisper.

I start to walk towards the door.

"Wait, Bec! It's not what you think!"

"I get it. I'm just not your family."

"Bec, it's not that! I was acting like that to get you to like me more."

I turn around and face him. "I already liked you, but not anymore considering you don't even see me as family."

"It's not that."

"Then what is it?" I practically shout, trying to hold in tears.

He starts to shake a little. "Bec. I'm in-"

Just then, the lights go out.

"We're in the dark," I panic.

Just like at the store.

We're in a room with a very thick curtain, so barely any light is coming in. We have it closed for Darren.

I open up my hand and desperately try to strike some fire. I successfully do it on the third try, but there's someone else in the room with us.

I don't get a good look at him because he jumps towards me and we fall into the floor next to the bed.

Page 323

It's extremely dark, and I can't breathe for a good fifteen seconds. I feel squished, but my body is also spreading into the shadows.

Before I have the chance to panic again, my body is back to normal and we're behind the hotel, in the sliver of a shadow of the high noon sun.

Also, we're not alone.

There's two other people there. The puss girl, and Gamma.

"Should have killed me when you had the chance," Gamma smirks.

"Aw, then where's the fun in that?" I say with a smirk.

In reality, I'd never bring myself to kill anyone who wasn't a demon, but I can't let them know that.

I get a better look at the boy who just let go of me. He's dark skinned, with a right green eye and a left white eye. All you really see is a thin black ring and a pupil with everything else being white. A little weird if you ask me, but then again, when is anything normal in my life?

"I like her." Gamma smiles.

"Ugh! Now's not the time, brother," the puss girl says.

"As you wish, Gala," Gamma says, bowing.

"Get up you idiot!" Gala snaps at him.

"Oh, but I'm simply-"

"You're simply being a retard!"

"But don't you want everyone to treat you like a princess?"

The dark-skinned boy and I look at each other, then back at his bickering siblings.

"You're too annoying!" Gala tells him.

"And you're too uptight!" Gamma yells at her.

"Does this happen a lot?" I ask the dark-skinned boy.

"Yup," he says, grabbing my arms again. "Gala, Gamma, enough! We have her, let's go before her friends spot us."

I try to pull away from the boy holding me, but he doesn't budge.

I have to think of a way to get out of here.

Gala laughs when she sees me struggling to break free.

"Silly little Bec, you are not strong enough to escape us all by yourself. Father will have you."

"I think you'll see that my strength quite surpasses all of yours," I say.

I then grab the boy's arms, and I flip him over my shoulder.

He lets go in surprise and I start to run.

"Bonnie!" Gamma screams. "You okay, man?"

"She's getting away!" Gala screams.

The flip took a lot of energy out of me, so I don't run very fast. I make it to the alleyway next to the hotel. That's when a hand grabs my arm and pulls me behind the dumpster. Another hand covers my mouth.

"Where'd she go?" Gala says.

"Do I look like I know?" Bonnie says.

"No," Gamma says. "You look more like a-"

"Finish that sentence and I swear on my mother's life I'll-"

"Now is not the time!" Gala shouts. "Gamma, why must you always start fights?"

"Fight? What fight?" Gamma laughs.

Next thing I know, a strong wind blows, and it's silent.

Where did they go?

"Find your friend, and leave this country today." A masculine sounding voice says behind me. "You'll have to avoid the airports in this country too."

The figure lets go of me and is gone before I can turn around and look at him.

I get out from behind the dumpster and run back in the direction I came from.

I find Darren at the front of the hotel ten minutes later.

"Bec!" Darren shouts, and pulls me into the biggest hug. "What happened to you?"

I push him away from me. "Get the stuff. We have to leave. Now!"

Chapter 8

After I told Darren what happened, we manage to get tickets to go from Sydney to New Zealand by boat. We assumed by the warning that the Demon King's kids would be crowding the airports and didn't want to take any chances.

I would have enjoyed my time more if Darren wouldn't avoid me. I need to talk to him, but I'm also still a little mad at him. I wouldn't even know what to say to him after he straight up said that he doesn't consider me family.

Also, I can't help but think of everyone else. They must be so worried. This boat sure is taking a long time.

Right when we get to Auckland, we go straight to the airport and book the next flight to Los Angeles, and then a connecting flight to Harrisburg, Pennsylvania.

We sit next to each other on the plane. Me in the aisle, and him in the middle seat.

There's a little TV screen in front of me. I touch it where it says English, and the screen changes to show a list: Movies, TV, Games, Podcasts.

I click "Movies", and a list of genres appear. I then click "Kids" and a list of movies appear.

This is so cool!

I look at Darren as he reaches over and pulls the window cover up. He stares out the window. I can't see what he's staring at, but I know he wants to avoid talking to me as much as possible.

"Eighteen-hour flight," he says.

I guess not.

"It won't feel that long," I say looking at him. "We got movies."

He doesn't look back at me. He continues to stare out the window.

"You okay?" I ask him after a minute.

"I don't know," he says. "I can't stop thinking."

"Same. I keep thinking of the others, wondering if they're safe. If they got there okay."

"They're there, wondering where we are."

"And how do you know that?" I ask him skeptically.

"Deonna told me."

"How?"

"Telepathically," he whispers so quietly I'm not sure I heard right.

What?

"I thought you were a physical magician," I whisper.

"I'm mixed," he tells me. Then he looks at me. "You mean to tell me that this whole time, you didn't know that?"

"No. You see, this is what I mean when I say 'nobody tells me anything' because legit, nobody tells me anything."

"Yeah, well, I'm mixed. Physical and mental. Now you know."

"Are you a teller?"

"No."

"Well, what else can you do that's mental?"

"Only one other thing."

"Which is?"

"Only Deonna knows the other thing I can do, well, and now Raven, I guess. I try to keep it a secret."

"Yeah, well, you haven't done a good job of it if two people know."

He smiles at me for the first time since Sydney.

"Who am I gonna tell, Audrey?"

"Yes."

"No, I won't. Come on, tell me."

"Excuse me," a woman next to me in the aisle says. "I need to get by." She points at the seat next to Darren. We both move our feet. She gets by us, sits down, and ends our conversation.

Page 327

***

We land in Los Angeles the same day at Sunrise. Its' weird how time zones and traveling work.

"It took eighteen hours to travel back in time a few hours. These time zones defy time, just like me," I tell Darren.

He gives me a shy smile, but I don't say anything more.

We then land in Harrisburg at sunset, and take a bus to Goldsboro where Eagle Lake is.

Honestly, the bus ride felt longer than the plane rides.

Not because the bus didn't have movies, but because I was lost in my own head.

Why doesn't Darren consider me family?

What is his second mind trick?

Why did he tell Raven about it?

Why do male mammals have nipples if only women breastfeed?

Why did that pop into my head? Did I dream about that recently?

Why do I have weird dreams?

Pickles!

Darren starts chuckling next to me.

"What's so funny?" I ask him.

"Just some thoughts running through my head," he tells me.

Why do I still have these feelings for him since he clearly has none for me?

***

We finally get to the cabin. I didn't check the time, so I don't know how long it took us.

Deonna is the first to run out of the cabin. She wraps her brother in a hug.

"Were you guys followed?" she asks him.

"No."

"Good, because we have enough problems here."

"What happened?"

Page 328

"Come."

She grabs his hand and pulls him inside.

I follow.

Once inside, Audrey comes and gives me a hug. JP isright behind her. I hug them back one at a time.

"Why were you guys gone for so long?" Audrey asks me, no smile on her lips, and no indication of a joke or gesture.

"They almost got her," Darren says.

"Shit!" Deonna whispers.

"They did get me," I tell them, "but I escaped."

"How?" JP asks.

"I... I think I had some help."

"You think?" Deonna snaps.

"Any word from my dad yet?" Raven asks, coming out of the kitchen?

"No," Deonna says. "My connection to him is completely gone. It has been since we got here."

"Try again!" JP says.

Raven closes her eyes and slowly shakes her head. A few tears sneak out of her closed eyelids.

"What does that mean?" I ask, starting to panic. "Does that mean Frederick is dead?"

"It's the only explanation," Raven whispers.

JP starts bawling. Audrey brings him into a hug, crying herself.

My breathing starts to pick up in pace, and my vision becomes blurred from the tears that are forming.

Frederick is dead.

No.

How did this happen? Was he killed by demons? Did the Demon King have something to do with it?

I shake my head. No, that's ridiculous. The Demon King doesn't even know about Frederick's existence. There must have been an attack.

Poor Frederick.

Poor JP and Raven. They didn't even get a chance to see their father, or say goodbye.

I know all too well what that's like.

"I didn't want to believe it either," Deonna says, "but I think he really is gone, and we have no other way of contacting Aunt Emma or Uncle John."

"Wait! Emma and John aren't here either?" I say.

"They haven't been here," Raven says, her eyes still closed. "JP had to climb in through the window."

"Shit," Darren whispers.

Raven opens her eyes. "Contact Allen," she tells Deonna. "See if you can get a connection."

Deonna sits on the floor and closes her eyes.

"I got something," she says in a matter of seconds. "So, uncle Freddy really is dead..."

"See how many magicians he's contacted," Raven says, wiping her tears after a while.

Deonna closes her eyes again. In a minute, she opens them and says, "everyone he knows."

"Did you do the same?" Raven asks.

"I will now."

"Why not before?" Darren asks.

"We were kind of busy finding our family." Deonna says.

"Fair enough," Darren says.

"The endgame of our dimension is coming, we must prepare." Raven says.

"When though?" Audrey asks.

"I have no idea," Raven says, "but we should prepare as if it were coming soon."

"And how exactly do we do that?" I ask. "Magicians are the only ones who can fight those freaks. We need more help!"

Just then the lights go out.

They're coming for me!

I scream, and Darren pulls me close to him.

"It's okay, Bec," he says after a while, stroking my hair.

"It's not them. The power just went out."

"Yeah," Audrey says, "but the generator is not kicking in. So who cut it?"

I resist the urge to scream again.

Think I'd be used to the lights going out. I guess the third time isn't the charm.

At first nobody moves for about a solid minute.

Raven goes by the window and takes a peek outside. Her eyes grow wide, but she doesn't have time to react because a woman wearing black and a mask bursts through the window and stabs her in the eye.

I hear the back door crash open. The front door gets knocked down, and two men come running in.

I get a better look. All three of them are wearing black camouflage and have black masks to cover their noses and mouths. They're all very muscular. The woman has brown hair pulled back in a ponytail, and fierce blue eyes. One thing's for sure, she's not one of the Demon King's children.

A third man comes in the room from the back, muscular as well. I don't get a good look at their faces and eyes though. Before I can ask who they are, all four of them throw knives at us.

I put up my hands and stop the knives with my telekinesis. I was about to fling the knives back at them, but one of the men opens a small glass bottle and throws water in my face. I drop the knives and blink for a second.

When I look again, Darren has punched a man in the face who was about to stab me. The woman is holding a metal cross with Jesus crucified on it.

"I'm Jewish, bitch," I tell her, "that's not going to work on me!"

I then do a high kick in her chest and she falls down.

I hear Audrey scream.

Before I can see what's going on with her, another man pushes me against the wall.

I look him dead in his dark brown eyes that are staring daggers at me, and I say, "do your worst."

His eyes soften with every passing second until there are tears in them.

"Bec?" he says.

The fuck?

He lets go of me and takes a step back.

I know I should do something, but I'm stuck in place.

Page 331

How does he know my name?

The fighting around me seems to slowly stop. In my peripheral, I see Audrey on the floor, Deonna above her, and they're both staring at me with blank looks on their faces.

He takes off the mask he has on and I get a good look at his face. He's young, about sixteen, seventeen, with a small beard. His age isn't what surprises me, it's his entire look.

Last time I saw him, he was a little on the overweight side, and his hair wasn't in a buzz cut. We were talking about going bowling, but I had to go to the beach, and I never had the chance to say goodbye.

"John?"

Chapter 9

I can't believe it!

I quickly throw my arms down to slow time down, and I run around the room and separate our attackers from the others, placing them on opposite sides of the room.

I return in front of my old best friend.

"Bec!" he shouts, when I return time to normal.

"John!"

He embraces me into a hug and lifts me up.

"Is she hugging the humans that just tried to kill us?" Deonna snaps.

"Who is this?" Darren asks.

I look around at everybody.

Audrey looks confused. Her prosthetic legs have been removed, and there's a gash on the side of her head.

Probably should have been a little gentler.

Deonna's trying to get Audrey her legs, but she keeps staring at me with anger and confusion.

Darren is standing next to Deonna. Darren's eyes are going back and forth between the attackers, John, and me.

JP is holding Raven's hands, trying to guide her away from the last man, and the woman, because both of her eye sockets are empty.

The woman starts walking towards me. She takes off her mask and I get a good look at her. She's around seventeen, eighteen. Her eyes that were just fierce are now filling with tears.

"Bec!" she calls me.

I recognize her immediately. "Mabel!"

I pull my old two best friends into a group hug. Mabel's hand is bleeding a lot so my clothes get stained. I don't care.

"John! Look at you! You've lost so much weight! Mabel, you're a young woman now, look at you!"

"Look at you!" John says. "You're alive, and you look like you're fourteen!"

"I know!"

"How did you survive?" Mabel asks. "We heard that your whole family was killed by magicians on the beach."

I stand there with my mouth open, not sure what to say to her.

"Hey, Josh!" Mabel calls, "It's Bec!"

"I can see that," Josh says, taking his mask off. Sure enough, it's Mabel's cousin. He gives me a pathetic wave of his hand. "How are you?"

Still the awkward type.

"What are you guys doing here?" I ask after a minute. "Why are you trying to kill us?"

All three of their faces drop.

"Are you a magician, Bec?" Mabel asks.

"Half, technically," I say. "Why should that matter?"

Their good moods seem to fall as quickly as they arose.

"We have to-" the fourth person says, but John cuts him off.

"No way!"

"They're magicians! They're dangerous!"

"But Chris, we-"

"Have a job to do."

Mabel stands in front of me. "We can't!"

"Why?" Chris says. "Because you knew her in the past? Because she was your friend?"

"Guys, what are you even doing here?" I ask.

"How do you know these people?" Darren asks me.

"Bec was our best friend growing up," John says. "That has to mean something."

"Of course it does," I say. "But why were you trying to kill us?"

Mabel smiles at me and says "We work for Organization Salem-"

"Don't give away the society's secrets!" Chris calls out while Mabel talks.

"-an organization to get rid of a species that controls the creatures that want to eradicate all living things on Earth."

"Wait! Wait! Wait!" Deonna says. "Are you talking about the kifomen and the Demon King?"

"The what?" Mabel asks.

"All we were told was that there are beings from another dimension who want to wipe out life here," John says.

"Those would be the kifomen," I say. "They're being controlled by the Demon King and his followers."

"And that's not you?" Chris asks.

"Hell no!" Raven screams. "We're trying to stop them, you dumb ass fucks!"

"Raven," I say, "they're just-"

"Dumb ass fucks who blinded me forever!"

"Sorry," Mabel pathetically calls out to her.

"Ow! This is really painful!"

"Yeah, that'll happen."

Raven flips her the bird, but she misses Mabel and ends up flipping me off instead.

I go up to Raven and try to heal her eyes. The bleeding stops and the redness goes down.

"Better?" I ask her.

"No."

***

I tell them about that day on the beach and how Audrey and Emma found me and took me in.

Emma.

I hope she's okay.

Probably not though.

I tell the four of them about the kifomen and the Demon King. I tell them about his kids who all have heterochromia, so they're easy to spot. I tell them about magicians and how we fight the kifomen who we once called demons. I also tell them how we found all of this out.

Page 335

Chris keeps looking at me with a confused look on his face. Does he not trust me? Then again, he doesn't know me.

I spot Darren holding Deonna's arms, holding her back.

Smart.

She looks like she's about to pounce.

JP got some ice for Raven. He tries to put the bag on her face, but she just swipes it away and crosses her arms. If she could see, she probably would have killed them by now.

"That's some heavy stuff," John says after we're done.

"I don't know what to say," Mabel tells me.

"I know it's a lot to take in," I say, "but we're telling the truth. Magicians are trying to save the Earth. We're not your enemies."

"You never were," Josh says. "Them on the other hand-

"Are my friends and have done amazing things to help people."

"Okay," Josh says. "I wouldn't believe it coming from anyone else."

"These creatures killed my family!" Chris screams.

"And how do we know you didn't kill ours?" Deonna shouts at him.

"What are you talking about?" Chris asks her while practically screaming.

"Our family just happens to go missing and we can't contact them, then magician hunters come out of nowhere-"

"We just got here yesterday and found you guys!" Chris shouts.

"Oh, likely story," Raven adds, shouting herself.

"Seriously!" John shouts.

"We're just the B team," Mabel shouts.

"So somebody else from your organization killed them?" Deonna shouts.

"We don't know!" John shouts. "We don't know much about-"

"Now before the neighbors call the police for screaming in the middle of the night, everybody calm down," I say.

"Our family was probably killed by these fuckers, and you expect us to calm down?" Deonna asks me.

"My family was murdered by these creatures, and I've been chasing the wrong guys, and you expect me to calm down?" Chris says.

Page 336

"They killed mine, too!" I yell back at him, then I catch myself and lower my voice. "They killed all of our family members. You're not the only one."

Chris grunts and turns away from me. "I return home after being gone for so long, and I find them in body bags."

"I'm sorry to hear that," Audrey says.

Chris grunts and punches a wall. "Fuck!"

"How'd you guys get wrapped up into Salem anyways?" I ask.

"So just to be clear, the children of Father are heterochromiacs?" asks Chris.

"Yeah, so just watch out for them." I say.

Just then, Chris pulls out a knife and throws it at me.

The knife is pulled out of the air, and it flies into Darren's hands.

"What are you doing?" Darren screams at him. "Are you trying to kill her?"

"I should never have taken you to the hospital that day!" Chris screams. "I should have let you die, demon spawn!"

"You think I'm one of them?" I snap.

"Look at your eyes! I know you are!"

"Bec is not on their side," Darren says, standing in front of me.

He just grunts and storms out.

***

How can he think I'm one of them? I do have similar eyes, but that's where the similarities end.

I'm laying down outside on the neighbor's trampoline, thinking of everything that just went down. Raven is hiding something from me.

What though?

I hear footsteps in the grass approach me.

"Do you think my eyes connect me to them?" I ask the person.

"Never really known you to give a shit about something like that," John says.

I sit up to take a better look at him. "A lot has changed about me."

"Can you still win any argument?"

I think for a moment. "Not against Raven."

Page 337

"The redhead with the freckles?"

I nod.

"Wow," he says. "Did not see that coming."

"That's life for ya."

He laughs a little. Not a haha laugh. More like a 'I know what you mean' laugh. He sits next to me on the trampoline.

"Even if you have some connection with them, you're not one of them. Remember the time we went skating with your brother and most of the skaters were being jerks to us?"

"Yeah?" That seems like forever ago!

"Well, we had a common love of skating, but were we jerks like them?"

"No. Where are you going with this?"

"Just because you have something in common with someone doesn't mean you're like them, or have any connections with them."

I smile at him. "Thanks, John. That analogy was terrible, but it made me feel better."

He grabs my hand and leans his head on mine. "I've missed you."

"I've missed you guys, too."

"How come you didn't come back? Why not tell us that you were alive?"

"I wanted to, I even thought about coming back, but as long as those things were out there, I didn't feel safe. So much has happened, I was training to use magic. And when I got stuck in the kifomen's home dimension, I thought I'd never return home. I wanted some normalcy, to see you guys, to tell you everything, but I physically couldn't come back. I was barely able to take care of myself, how could I return alone?"

"I think I understand. Was there something else keeping you here?"

Darren is the first person to pop into my head. I shake the thought from my head.

"The people who took me in."

He nods.

"Yeah, I know what you mean. I wanted to leave Florida so badly after I thought you died, but my whole family was there. Josh is still

Page 338

there and he doesn't want to leave. I travel around only because of Salem, but I can never fully leave Miami."

"What does Josh have to do with anything?" I ask.

"Yeah, Josh and I have been together for five years now, I graduate soon, but then there's college to worry about. We also still have Salem."

"Josh? This Josh?"

"Yes."

"Did not see this coming."

"Us?"

"No, you, being... you know."

"Really? You're the only one. Ash even saw it."

"I guess I don't see obvious things."

"Yeah, I believe it."

We both start laughing. I then stop laughing as suddenly as I started.

"Why did you join Salem?" I ask him.

He stops laughing and looks me dead in the eye.

"Because I believed that magicians killed my best friend."

"Mabel?"

"Same reason."

"And Josh?"

"He was in love with you."

"No, he wasn't."

John looks at me and smiles. "Yeah, you don't see the obvious."

"Hey!"

"It's true."

"How long has this been a thing?"

"Since he met you."

"But he's gay!"

"He's bi. I'm gay, and I won him, bitch!"

"Only because I got cut out from the love triangle by seeming to be dead, beeyotch."

We both start laughing again.

"How long has Organization Salem been a thing?" I ask him.

"Since the Salem Witch Trials."

Page 339

"No, not that, although that should have been obvious. I meant you in Salem."

"I started this Summer with Mabel and Josh. We met someone who was in the organization, asked us if we wanted to protect humanity. Chris was in the same recruitment class as us."

"But magicians are the protectors of humanity."

"We didn't know that then. We were told about it, and we believed it. Well, I didn't at first until I actually saw a magician for myself levitate away from a burning building."

"Maybe they were helping people inside? I mean not everyone who flees a burning building is an arsonist."

He shrugs. "Three people died, but many escaped. Wait." He thinks for a moment. "Shit!"

"Not everything is as it seems," I tell him.

"But everything seems like a joke to you?" asks an angry voice.

I look up and see Deonna standing in front of the trampoline with her hands on her hips.

"How is having a serious conversation with my friend a joke?" I ask.

"They tried to kill us!" she yells.

"That was before they knew everything."

"Other Salem probably killed my family."

"They're my family too!"

"You know what your problem is?"

"My problem?" I ask.

"I'm gonna go," John says, getting off the trampoline and heading back inside.

"You're too trusting," she says.

"Too trusting?"

"You trust that nothing is going to happen, so you go out and do reckless things, you get sick and then get lost, you get us trapped in Dimension Five, you delayed my brother and you coming back to the states, and now you're trusting the people who blinded Raven and might have killed Fredrick! Maybe Emma too!"

"I see your point, I really do, but I was going with my gut. I have to trust my instincts."

Page 340

"There you go again! Trusting something you shouldn't! You're going to get everyone you love killed and then you'll realize how foolish you've been once you're all alone! Left with nothing but your guilt!" Deonna starts to cry.

I pause for a moment before saying, "is that what happened to you?"

She climbs up on the trampoline and sits next to me.

I sit down.

"Years ago, I was out with some friends, some human friends. Three sisters, and a neighborhood boy. I trusted them with the knowledge that magicians existed, they were scared of me and had their family move. A week later some demons attacked in the city where the sisters moved, and I found out that they were killed from Gregory, the boy who didn't run but was still scared of me."

"That's not your fault," I tell her.

"I trusted that my mom could take care of the demons, and they killed her, and my father, and then Darren and I got stuck in Dimension Five."

I hesitate for a second, and then I put my hand on her shoulder. "Do you believe that everything happens for a reason?"

She shakes her head as more tears fall.

"Destiny works in mysterious ways. Sometimes we don't know why things happen to us until much later in life. Jews believe in God-"

"I know about all this, but my mistakes got people killed."

"Is that why you don't trust anyone?"

She nods.

"Is that why you didn't trust or like me when we first met?"

She sighs. "I thought trusting you would get my brother or one of my cousins killed. Plus, you were a naive moron...like I was."

"I care about all of them dearly, especially Darren."

"I know. You'd never do anything to hurt them on purpose."

"Then why still the hostility towards me?"

"Because I didn't know you. Not knowing you was easier."

"Then how do you expect to make new friends and be happy?"

She shrugs her shoulders. "I can't lose anyone else I love. Loving new people means that you'll lose more people eventually."

"Or you could have more people in your life who will have your back."

She sighs. "Darren said the same thing to me before I came out here."

"And? What do you think?"

"I can't lose anyone else. Look at the day and age we live in, any one of us can die at any moment."

"Then let's work together to make sure we don't lose anyone else."

I extend my hand to her.

She stares at it for a bit, and then looks me in the eyes with tears pouring down her face.

She grabs my shoulders and pulls me into a hug.

I hug her back.

She leans her head on my shoulder and whispers, "I'm sorry I was such a bitch. Maybe I can trust you."

"And I'm sorry for getting you stuck in Dimension Five, and for what my friends did."

"That last part wasn't even your fault."

"I know, but still."

I don't know if I can fully forgive Deonna for the way she's treated me, especially since this all came out of nowhere, but a hug is a nice start.

Chapter 10

We go back inside and see everyone sitting in a circle.

"That won't work," Raven says. "If we kill the people in charge, the rest will have no one to follow!"

"Yeah," Mabel says, "but a new leader might arise. Simply killing the leaders will not do."

"And sending them a message will?" Raven snaps back.

"It's the most peaceful way," Josh says. "If we start killing, then your oath to protect humanity is out the window."

"But killing some to protect others is different," Raven adds.

"We'll need Salem on our side," Chris says. "We're not very high up, keep in mind, so we don't really have much of a say in the organization, and we don't know a lot of their secrets."

"What's going on?" Deonna asks.

"We're trying to come up with a way to disband Organization Salem," Darren tells us.

"But the organization can help magicians fight the kifomen!" Chris shouts. "Disbanding them won't do any good!"

"But magicians won't be killed anymore," Audrey says.

"So, what we need to do is get them on our side with as few deaths as possible," I say.

"And how do you propose we do that?" Deonna asks.

"We'll have to think," I say. "Make room for us in the circle. Let's think this through."

***

We spend hours brainstorming ideas. After about four, we finally find one that can work, and a plan B just in case the first one is no good.

We split up into two teams.

The first team consists of me, JP, Raven, and Deonna.

The second consists of Mabel, Josh, Chris, John, Audrey, and Darren.

I originally volunteered for the more dangerous job with Darren, but he said Audrey was a better fit.

We depart at first moonlight. Well, tomorrow night. We need time to recover, and pack.

Salem's headquarters are in Boston, Massachusetts. I would have assumed that it was in Salem, Massachusetts, but I guess that's irony.

Audrey and JP went to the store with John, Mabel, and Josh to get some clothes for everyone when it turned morning. Everyone else went to the treehouse to get some food before sunrise. I guess they're now stuck there until nighttime hits. Well, Chris isn't, but I don't think he'll come back on his own.

This whole plan seems a little much. There are a lot of what if's in it.

I try to change, but I have no clothes that aren't yellow pants or winter clothes. I put one of Audrey's old shirts on.

I'm trying to pack a bag, but I have almost nothing to pack. All my old clothes are too small on me, and my new clothes are too nice.

I should have gone to the store.

I groan and sit on Audrey's bed.

"Everything okay?"

I jump at the sound of Darren's voice.

"Holy shit, dude! Don't scare me like that!"

"Sorry," he says, holding his hands up in defense. "I thought you went to the treehouse?"

"I went looking for a walking stick for Raven. I was closer to here than the treehouse when the sky started changing colors, hence sunrise."

"Understandable."

He comes to sit on the bed next to me. I start blushing the second his leg touches mine.

"What's wrong, Bec?" He asks me.

"Nothing," I lie.

"Thinking about the mission?"

I sigh. "Yeah. Too many variables, too many things that can go wrong."

"I know what you mean, but it's a risk we have to take."

Why does he have to be right? "I wish it wasn't," I tell him.

I wish we could just all stay here and not worry about anything, but even if we didn't have Salem to worry about, we still have the Demon King. I wish I can just be safe with Darren. I wish I can just be with him.

"I wish for a lot of things that can't happen."

"I know," he tells me. "Me too. I wish for a lot of things that seem impossible."

"I know what you mean," I say as I smile at him.

He smiles back at me as we stare into each other's eyes.

"Um, Bec?"

"Yes?"

"We've had a lot of close calls."

I look down at my hands. "I know, and most of them were because of me."

"That's not true."

"Dimension Five."

"Well...we never would have found Raven, or knew what was going on if it weren't for you."

And now she's blind. And Mabel is hurt too.

"That wasn't your fault."

"I'm sorry?"

"True, Mabel's your old friend, and she blinded Raven, but no one knew about Salem until now. You guys didn't know about each other until after, and now we have the chance to save magician lives everywhere."

"I never said anything about Raven, or Mabel," I say as I look up from my hands at him.

"Um, well I, kinda sorta, um, well..."

Page 345

I didn't say anything about Raven, did I?

No, I didn't. It's like he pulled it right from my mind.

From my mind.

"You son of a bitch!" I punch him in the arm.

He sighs as he rubs it. "I don't tell people for a reason."

"That's your other mental trick? Invading people's privacy?"

"I never wanted this trick."

"I call bull."

"Bec, the last thing I wanted to do was hurt you or anyone."

What else has he pulled from my head?

Oh my gosh, does he know how I feel about him?

No, stop thinking!

"So, you can read minds. Everyone's?"

"Yup, everyone."

"Then how come you didn't know Gamma was posing as JP?"

"He kept singing about a red cup in his head. That's how I knew something was wrong, JP doesn't usually like jingles, but I didn't know that he wasn't JP until he revealed himself. He must have somehow known about my trick."

"No wonder his plan failed."

"Probably."

"Is that why you volunteered to go in?" I ask him. "So you can poke around in all their heads?"

He sighs. "Deonna thought it'd be a good idea."

"So she knows too."

"And so does Raven."

"And when I volunteered, you were against the idea!"

"Because you look too young and can get hurt."

"Last time I checked, you didn't care about me!"

"That's not true, Bec!"

"You said that you didn't consider me family."

He gulps. "That's... well, because... I..."

"Don't give a shit."

I feel tears coming to my eyes. I stand up and start walking away so he wouldn't see me crying, but he grabs my wrist and stands up.

He turns me towards him and kisses my lips so fast that I didn't register what happened until it was over. I want to say something to him, curse him out, kiss him back, flick his forehead, do something, but I can't move.

"I love you, Bec," he whispers to me. "I don't want you as my cousin, I want you as my wife."

"B-but... you're eight years older than me."

"What is age but a number?" He grabs my hands. "Let's do this, Bec, let's be together. I've wanted to be with you since we first met. I know you want this too."

"You only know because you invaded my privacy," I tell him.

Tears start to roll down my face.

He opens his mouth to say something else, but I walk out of the room before he could.

Chapter 11

Audrey and the others come back with the clothes. Mostly pants and black shirts. I don't mind. I'm not trying to look good for anyone. Besides, we have a mission.

We all got in two cars and, within the next twenty-four hours, we arrived in Boston, Massachusetts.

I was in the car with Mabel driving, John, Josh, and Chris. I didn't want to be in the same car with Darren. Let them all talk bad about me; I really don't care right now.

As we're driving through Boston to a hotel, I notice a plentiful amount of cop cars, ambulances, people sleeping on the sidewalk, and other people walking along with their eyes on their phones.

"I thought Boston was a historical town?" I ask everyone in the car.

"That's more towards the East," John tells me, putting his arm around Josh. "We're in the West."

"And where is headquarters?" I ask.

"East."

"Not in the ghetto, good, you're quite classy for an organization that kills people."

"It won't be any more if our mission works," Mabel says. "If Audrey and Darren do their parts correctly."

That son of a bitch poking in people's heads. How can you do that to people?

"I hope so too," I say.

***

It's eight in the morning when I hear Mabel waking up Audrey the next day. The three of us, along with Deonna and Raven are in a room while the boys are a floor below us.

"Where are you guys going?" I ask groggily.

"Phase one," Mabel says. "Out of bed, girls." Mabel then throws Audrey a blue shirt and khaki pants, similar ones to the clothes she has on. "Don't forget to tuck it in."

The rest of us dress in black.

Raven puts her shirt on inside out, and Deonna goes to help her.

I give Audrey a hug. "Please be careful."

"Audrey smiles at me and says, "I can't promise that."

I don't smile back. "Audrey."

"I'll do my best."

Now I smile. "See you on the cameras."

"See you when I see you."

I give her another hug, for I don't know when I'll see her again in person.

If I do.

As Audrey is hugging Deonna and Raven, and I'm hugging Mabel, there's a knock on our door. Deonna goes to open it. I duck inside the bathroom and close the door.

"You ready, Audrey?" John asks her.

"Ready as I'll ever be," she says.

"Good luck," Deonna says.

"You too," I hear Darren say. I hear the door open and close, and a few tears start to roll down my face.

***

JP and I are on first watch. We're underneath a Catholic church in a surveillance room. According to Chris, a few years ago, this church was closed for a year and got renovated by Organization Salem.

Saint Leonard Church of Port Maurice Parish.

The name's enough alone to put anyone out of breath.

Page 349

Across from Hannover Street is Paul Revere's house, where the organization has its headquarters. Well, not really at his house, more so in his basement that's closed off to the public.

For obvious reasons.

I thought they were crazy, until I saw all of the cameras and how complex and big the underground system really is.

"It's surprising that all this was built in sixteen eighty," I tell JP.

"I know," he tells me. "Twelve years before the witch trials against us started. I wonder why it was mostly women who were hung though?"

"I thought they were burnt at the stake?" I ask him.

"Chris says that the whole burning thing was a myth, that magicians were actually hung, and one guy was pressed to death."

"And now they've advanced," I say, thinking of how Mabel tore out Raven's eyes. She's going to blame me for that for the rest of our lives.

I watch the monitors as the new recruits, Audrey and Darren among them, are being briefed by a tall buff guy who looks very out of place in the uniform.

"It's good that they're underground the whole time," JP says.

"Is it though?" I ask.

"Well, remember, Darren can't go out in the sunlight."

My heart starts to crush itself at the sound of his name.

"You have a point," I say, turning Darren's buzzer in my hands. Chris is many things, but bad with tech is not one of them. I accidentally push the button and see him twitch on camera. He frantically looks around. His eyes settle on Audrey. When he sees she is fine, he goes back into position.

"Careful, Bec," JP says. "That's the warning buzzer."

It's tempting to shock him again, but I instead hand JP the buzzer.

"It's be nice if our telepath was here to let him know that it was an accident," I point out.

"Yeah, but is Deonna here right now? Her turn is tomorrow."

I just sigh and stare at the monitors.

"If only we had ear pieces," I say. "Then we could actually talk to them when Deonna's not here."

Page 350

"Then it would give them away if someone sees it in their ears, or hears us talking to them."

I sigh again. "You have a point."

"It was Chris's point actually."

"Cool."

"Is everything okay?" JP asks me.

I sigh. "No, it's not."

"Talk to me," he says putting his hand on mine.

"It's multiple things," I tell him honestly.

"Like?"

"Darren playing with my emotions, this mission, the world, and the fact that I can only eat kale and a Dunkin Donuts's vegan sausage biscuit."

"Bec, you can eat fruits and veggies too," he says, starting to laugh.

I punch him in the arm and he laughs again.

"Bec, how is Darren playing with your emotions."

"His mind reading trick!"

He winces. "Yeah, I didn't like hearing that he had that trick either. I can see why he kept it from us for as long as he did."

"Then it turns out that he knew everything I was thinking about him and he showed no indication that he had any feelings for me, but then proposes out of nowhere."

"Wait, what!"

"Yeah."

"He proposed to you?"

"Yeah, well, kind of, I think."

"You think?"

"He said he wanted me as his wife."

"He told me he was going to wait until you were eighteen. I guess he couldn't wait anymore."

"Wait, what?" Now it's my turn to be confused.

"Bec, he fell in love with you the day you guys met."

"So he said."

"He was scared of your age difference getting in the way, so he wanted to wait."

"That's some pretty pedophilic shit."

Page 351

"Bec-"

"I was twelve, JP!"

"I know the age gap is...there, but things change. Just look at today compared to four years ago. People are glued to their phones, more people are becoming homeless as the gap between the poor and third class grows wider, more ambulances show up to the hospitals, people are turning into-"

"Mass hysteria, dogs and cats living together, I know the world is getting worse. We have to help. Aren't we the protectors of humanity?" I ask, desperate to change the conversation.

"We can't help them if everybody's dead," he tells me.

"We can do more after Organization Salem is on our side, after the demon king is dead, after you marry Darren."

I wince.

"Yeah, you thought I wouldn't notice you trying to change the conversation."

I stare at the monitor where all the recruits are now doing push-ups.

"Why are you trying to close yourself off from him? Did you do this with every other guy you liked growing up?"

"I don't think I ever liked anyone else," I say.

I think of Josh, but I never had any feelings for him. I don't remember much about him.

JP slowly nods. "I understand everything now."

"Do you now?"

"You don't know how to deal with your feelings."

I think about that for a moment.

He's right.

***

As the weeks go by, the extremely hot weather turns cooler, and the leaves start changing colors. The four of us take turns being under the church every day and night, watching the cameras, and exploring Boston when we're not in the surveillance room.

Raven and JP are together a lot in the room, and I'm with Deonna a lot. She and I have been talking a lot more. It's nice to say that I don't hate her anymore. I just hope she feels the same way.

***

One day I'm in the room with Raven. I basically tell her what's going on when I'm here with her.

"Is she there yet?" she asks me.

"Almost," I say, freezing the images along the way so Audrey wouldn't be seen by the organization people watching on their cameras.

Audrey looks both ways and enters a door.

"She's in," I tell Raven.

On the next monitor, Audrey rushes to the captain's desk in his room, looking through the drawers. After about thirty seconds, she finds some papers and brings them to the camera.

"She's got something," I tell Raven.

"Well, what is it?"

"Not sure yet," I say as I take a picture of the monitor, which shows the paper that Audrey is holding up to the camera.

She holds a few more papers to the camera as I take pictures of them with my camera phone that Deonna recently bought for all of us with Darren's card. The pictures never come out good. There are always these lines that are present whenever you take a picture of a screen. They're so annoying.

"What did she find?" Raven asks me.

"Let me get her back to the girl's barracks first," I tell Raven. "I didn't look at them yet."

Someone is about to enter her hallway. I push on her buzzer and she dives into a supply closet. When he's gone, I push the buzzer twice and she comes back out.

When Audrey is back in her bed, I lean back into my chair. Hacking is hard. Hacking alone is even harder. I know Mabel taught me all she could before going back, but still!

She also said I couldn't be distracted, but it's still hard even when I'm not.

Page 353

"Hey, what was that commander's name again?" Raven asks me.

I go through the photos that we have already printed until I find the chain of command one.

"Rainsford," I tell her.

"What's Rainsford planning?"

I grab the camera and take a look at the pictures I just took.

"They're going after some magicians here in Boston. Staging a secret ambush at the Boston Common."

"Why a secret ambush? You don't think they know about Audrey and Daren, do you?"

"Not likely, but we can't rule out that possibility."

"When is this ambush happening?"

"Three days."

"Then we better prepare."

***

I'm in the room now with Deonna. Raven and JP went to the Boston Common to see if they can help counter the ambush. Deonna has JP on speaker.

"So, what does this family look like again?" JP asks.

"Don't you have the picture?" Deonna asks him.

"It's a very bad picture," he says. "Too blurry and there is a lot of lines."

"Well sorry I'm not an expert photographer," I spit out sarcastically.

"Ooh, there's a frog pond here," JP says.

I hear a smacking sound and JP grunts.

"Okay, okay, no need to hit, Ray," he says.

"Let us know when you spot any magicians," Deonna tells him, "but lay low. We don't want Salem picking up on you guys."

"I know," he says. "Where are the frogs? I want to see that."

"Uh, guys," I say in a panic.

Deonna looks at the monitor I'm pointing at. Audrey is holding a metal rod and being held at gunpoint.

"How'd they find out about her?" Deonna cries. "Play the audio!"

Page 354

"What's wrong?" JP asks over the phone.

One of the Corporals throws something on the ground, then aims his gun at Audrey again. Deonna types something in and flicks a switch.

"If you're human," the Corporal says, "then explain why electricity just went through you and you're still alive?"

Deonna uses one monitor and rewinds the footage. The corporal and another soldier are standing by a metal rod attached to a metal box. The corporal flicks the switch.

Audrey pushes the soldier away, and she takes the full blow of electricity.

"We have to help her!" I shout standing up. "Raven, JP, meet us in front of Paul Revere's house."

"Uh..." JP says. "I don't think we can."

"Why?" Deonna says standing with me. "This is important!"

"A portal just opened," JP says.

Chapter 12

"There's at least two dozen kifomen here!" JP shouts.

"Shit!" I scream. "They're on the monitors!"

"What?" Deonna snaps.

She looks at the monitors, and there's kifomen on each monitor, Salem humans shooting at them, and Audrey throwing fire.

"Where's Darren?" Deonna panics.

Darren.

I feel my heart start to ache.

Then my eyes dart to the other monitors. John, Mabel, Josh, and Chris are all seen.

Darren.

"We have to go down there," I say.

"We need you guys here!" Raven shouts on the phone.

"Ray!" JP shouts. "Where are you?"

"I'm invisible! I can't fight blind!"

"I can't fight alone!"

A growling sound is heard close by.

They both scream, and then the phone goes silent, and the home screen is returned.

Deonna and I give one look at each other, we both nod, and we burst out of the room.

Deonna's ahead of me up the stairs. The glass doors at the top almost hits me in the face. The priest is at the front conducting mass in...is that Italian?

Focus!

Deonna starts to run, way faster than me I should add.

I run in the same direction, but not to the same place. I run across the street, down the block, break down the emergency exit, and arrive outside the Paul Revere museum.

Okay, so this brick building is the visitor center. That's a big bell. This grey building! That's the house!

I run inside and see his kitchen, a small little area with a fireplace, a small table, chairs, and...is that a bassinet?

Focus! The basement!

There's three people in the second room, one of them is a female employee wearing the same clothes Audrey did on her first day. The other male and female look a lot older. The second room is a little bigger with a round table, chairs, cabinets, another fireplace, and two weird holes in the wall.

Is this how I get to the basement?

I stick my hand in one of the holes. Come on!

"No one is allowed to stick their hands in the ovens," the employee says.

Ovens?

Ah, never mind!

I turn the corner and see a winding staircase, an emergency exit, and another short door that has a yellow note on it. I don't have to read it to know it's the basement.

I kick the door. When it doesn't budge, and the employee yells at me, I shoot electricity at the door and it falls down.

That's new.

The people run away screaming.

I run into the basement. It's all cement, low ceiling, but there's three passageways.

My memory of the footage tells me to go down the middle one. I run as fast as I can until I come across two kifomen. I zap lightning at them and they catch on green fire.

Ooh, it's hot!

I continue running and I come to the main room where the smell of blood punches me in the face like a wrecking ball. It looks a lot bigger in person, but I don't admire it because I throw my arms down and time comes to a creep and crawl.

Page 357

I see three kifomen feeding off three different people. I shoot lightning at them and run to the bodies.

All men.

None of them are my men.

"I'm sorry," I whisper to the bodies, and then I turn around.

I see Mabel with two knives, slicing a kifoman in half.

She's back to back with another woman who also has two knives.

Time comes back to a normal pace.

Wait, what? How?

A kifoman jumps on the other woman's head, and she's down in an instant.

The smell of blood is getting a lot stronger, and kifomen keep coming in.

Where's the portal?

I run around the room until I see the wind coming inside a hall-way.

"Bec!" I hear a familiar voice.

One of my men.

"What are you doing here?" he asks.

"Helping you guys!" I shout back over the noise. "Cover me! I'm gonna close the portal!"

"I got your back!"

He and I both run until we make it to the portal. I stand in front of it and stretch my hands out to it. I focus on the winds and reverse them.

He stays with me, shooting at the kifomen that come out of the portal with his rifle gun.

When the portal is almost closed, I start to smile. I'm faster than last time.

"Yeah, Bec!" he cheers, patting me on the shoulder.

We're celebrating too soon.

Three kifomen jump out of the portal at the last second towards me.

"Bec!" he screams, pushing me out the way and they jump on him, ripping into his throat.

Page 358

"No!" I scream, extending one hand out to him and one to the portal.

I lift all three of them into the air, and the portal starts to open more.

No!

I finish closing the portal as tears stream down my face. When the portal is closed, I snap their necks one by one. I let them fall limp, and I go to him and press my hands to his neck.

No pulse.

Shit!

I have to try!

I send an icy feeling into his neck. It takes a few minutes for his wounds to close, but he doesn't move.

I shake his shoulder and whisper his name.

Nothing.

I press my fingers to his now closed neck.

No pulse.

No.

"Bec!" I hear a male voice I recognize immediately.

No, I can't face you, not yet! I burst out crying when he puts his hand on my shoulder.

"What's wro-" he starts to ask, but then he looks at the body on the floor.

"No," he whispers.

"I'm sorry, John," I whisper. "I tried-"

"Josh!" John screams. "Someone get an AED!"

He puts one hand over the other and starts pressing over his heart. After about a minute, he puts his mouth over Josh's and blows twice, then he starts pressing over his heart again.

"John," I say with tears rolling down my face, "I already tried."

He doesn't listen. After a few minutes, he slows down and looks at his lost love. He rests his forehead against Josh's and then gives him a gentle kiss on the mouth.

"I'm sorry, my love," he whispers before bursting out into tears.

I rest my hand on his shoulder.

He pulls my arm down and wraps me into a hug.

Page 359

We both hug each other and cry, mourning my fallen friend, his fallen partner.

A few more screams and growls are heard in the distance. There are still kifomen here.

People are still being killed.

I wipe my face and stand up.

"We have to help them," I tell John.

He nods, wipes his face, stands up, and cocks his gun.

"For Josh."

We take one last look at him, and then we run off to help everyone else.

Chapter 13

John and I run through the compound. I hold a few kifomen with my telekinesis as he shoots them.

I hear a snarl behind me.

I turn around and see a kifoman running at me. Before I can do anything, it is lifted into the air and set on fire.

When the kifoman falls, I see Audrey putting out her hands. Darren is right next to her, throwing a gun to the side and taking out knives.

I sigh with relief.

I run up to Audrey and wrap her in a hug.

"Thanks, but what are you doing here?" she asks.

"Saw the footage, saw you got discovered and then the attack. This is not the only place in Boston that's being attacked."

"Shit," she whispers.

"Where's my sister?" Darren asks.

"With JP and Raven, handling the other attack," I tell him.

I thought he was dead.

He sighs, "Bec, I-"

I grab his face in my hands and I bring him closer to me. I then give him a firm kiss on the mouth.

"So you don't hate me anymore?" he asks me.

Oh, hush up, I think wondering if he can hear me.

He wraps his arms around me and kisses me back. My heart beats extremely fast as if it's about to burst out of my chest.

Just then an explosion is heard in the distance.

Darren and I stop kissing and nod to each other.

He takes off running.

Before I can go after him, Audrey wiggles her eyebrows at me. We both run after Darren, with John behind us.

Back in the giant room, the sprinklers have gone off. More people and kifomen are dead on the floor, and a small fire is struggling to stay alive.

Audrey extends a hand to the fire and it goes out.

Behind the fire is a woman who is shooting the head of a kifoman. She puts her gun back in her holster and examines the four of us. Her eyes settle on me.

"You're not one of us," she says.

"I can be if you guys listen to me," I tell her. "After we kill these things, I need to talk to Commander Rainsford."

She seems a little surprised. "What do you want with Rainsford?"

"Look out!" Audrey shouts as she shoots a ball of fire at a kifoman about to fall on us.

"I see," she says. "You're one of them."

"We're not enemies," I say. "We have a common goal, get rid of the creatures who want to wipe out humanity. We can actually be great allies."

The kifoman she was shooting starts to get up behind her. I extend my hand and I snap its neck with telekinesis.

She lifts up her gun and shoots.

I turn around and see a kifoman fall behind us.

Slowly, Salem members start coming into the main room. Before there were hundreds of members here, now there's probably only fifty.

"She led them here!" a man says, pointing at Audrey.

The man is the one from before who pointed his gun at her on the monitor before the attack.

"I did not lead them here!" Audrey shouts. "I am not your enemy."

He raises his gun at Audrey.

"Careful, Corporal Castillo," the woman behind us says to the man.

"But-"

"They fought to protect us," she says. "Let's just hear what they have to say. If anything, we can kill them afterwards."

"Yes, Commander Rainsford."

"For now, lock them up."

***

The three of us spend some time in separate jail cells. I'm across from Audrey who keeps alternating between smacking the bars and giving me eyes. We can easily break out, but we want these people on our side, so we decide to not do anything rash.

After what feels like an eternity, a man opens the door to Audrey's cell. She follows him and comes back hours later. He then opens the door to my cell.

"Let's go," he tells me.

"Where?" I ask.

"The commander wants a word with you."

He leads me on a long walk, blindfolded with my hands tied behind my back, to a room. I know it's a room because he opens a door and we walk through a doorway.

The moment he forces me to sit, he takes off my blindfold and I notice I'm face to face with the commander once my eyes adjust. She looks like she's in her mid-forties.

"Quite the powerful little one, aren't you?" she asks me.

There's a small TV in the room that's playing the video from Sydney.

I just nod.

"So, tell me child," she says, "how can someone so powerful be willing to stay in a cell? Why not break out by now and kill us all?"

"Because I'm not your enemy," I say.

"Same thing your little friends said."

"Because it's true."

I think of John and Mabel. Where are they? Are they being imprisoned? We're they kicked out of the organization? Does she not know they were working with us and asking her will get them killed?

"Tell me about this video," she says. "Who are these creatures? They've popped up a few times, but never to this degree. We know little to nothing about them other than they might be your kind's doing."

"The kifomen? They're evil creatures who want to wipe out humanity."

"Tell me about the kifomen."

"Magicians fight the kifomen to protect humanity. They want control over everything. Magicians just want a stable world."

"You call this stable? An underground attack that kills almost half my men?"

"We didn't plan that."

"Then how'd you know about it and come down here?"

How much should I tell her?

"Well," I say, "we had this agenda to see what you guys were planning, and we saw the attack happening."

"Who's we?" she asks.

"Pardon?"

"We saw the attack happening, but only you came down. Who else was with you?"

"Only one other friend," I say.

"One other friend to bring us down?"

"No. If anything, we can build each other up. Fight the kifomen, protect humanity, do some good for the world instead of killing. Have you noticed all the homeless? Instead of investing in guns, you can invest in homeless shelters. You guys clearly have the money and tech to cultivate this potential good, instead of spreading evil across the country."

"We're not the ones who are evil."

"True, but you're spreading it like wildfire."

"A pure magician would know of evil."

"I'm actually half human," I tell her.

She blinks a few times. "I'm sorry, what?"

"Yeah, I'm half human, half magician, so is Audrey, but I was raised by humans for the first twelve years of my life, so I'm technically more human than magician."

"There are half breeds?" she asks petrified.

"Oh, yeah," I say. "Lots of them."

Page 364

"Unbelievable...No wonder some don't turn red in the sun."

"Yeah, but we can still burn if we are not careful. Anyways, humans, magicians, halfs, we can all work together."

"And how do you know of these kifomen?"

"Well, there's this family who controls them and uses them to kill humans." I don't tell her about the multiple dimensions. That can just get confusing.

"A family of what? Humans? Magicians?"

"Half breeds," I say. "Just like there's good and bad humans-"

"There's good and bad magicians," she finishes.

"Exactly. He even has followers that are human."

"Does magician kind have a leader?" she asks me.

"No," I say. "We kind of don't need one."

"That sounds like it can get messy."

"Not for us. We never saw the need to elect one. How did you get elected?"

"I was promoted by my father."

"So...it's kind of like a monarchy system down here?"

"We're getting off topic. How do you summon your kifomen?"

"We don't summon them!"

"Then they just appear for you? To do your dark magic?"

"We. Fight. The kifomen."

She then takes out a photo and slides it to me. "Who is this."

I recognize her immediately, even though she's far away. "Gala. She's one of the demon king's children who will bring doomsday to us all. How'd you snap this picture of her?"

"One of our agents out in the city did when we were attacked. Multiple places throughout Boston were attacked that day. There were others with her too, and others spread out."

"Then it's coming soon."

"How soon?"

"I can't say for sure. Few months, years, maybe tomorrow."

"Your friends told me about the Demon King's Doomsday. Tell me about that."

I tell her what I know, which takes a long time to do.

After a while, she just nods, sits there silently for a few moments.

Page 365

"Why call him the Demon King if he commands kifomen?"

"It's just what we call him."

She nods and calls for Corporal Castillo.

He comes in immediately and salutes her.

"Get the other two," she tells him. "And also get the two privates who brought them in."

"Yes, ma'am," he says, and then is out the door as quickly as he came.

We don't wait too long for everyone to be in here. The whole time, the commander is just staring at me.

John looks horrible, and his eyes are red. Poor guy.

She looks at Mabel, John, and Chris first.

"You three disobeyed an order," she tells them.

They all hung their heads.

"You were supposed to kill any magicians the A team missed. Instead you bring them all to Boston. In the end...you kids just might have saved us all."

"Commander?" Chris asks.

"Commander!" Castillo shouts.

"I've been observing this past week." Rainsford says.

"These kids did not break out of jail and kill us, all the attacks that happened on the same day with reports of people with magic saving them, the Sydney incident, all three of your stories adding up. Maybe times are changing."

"We can all stop the Demon King and his followers," Audrey tells her. "Magicians, Salem, and humanity all working together, we won't be able to fail."

"Commander," Corporal Castillo says, "you can't possibly believe this."

"It is strange, yes, but everything these past few months has been adding up to something we didn't believe in before. Also, I haven't been the only one saying these things. Some members in our ranks have been talking about all this too. Most were tried but treason, but now...I'm not so sure."

She then stands up. "There can't be one hundred percent trust yet, but I'll consider what you said. If you really are not our enemy, then you must prove it."

Page 366

"We'll do whatever it takes," Darren says.

Commander Rainsford smiles at him. "Now that's what I wanted to hear." She gets up and starts walking out.

"Commander!" Castillo shouts going after her. "What about years of history!"

"So..." Darren says after a moment of silence. "What do we do now?"

***

Audrey, JP, Deonna, and Raven in the apartment living room Rainsford put us in. "From what I've gathered," Darren says, briefing me, "Salem hasn't always known about kifomen's existence. They recently became known to them and they had no idea what they were. They were deciding to keep them secret."

"So, it made sense she believed you on that," Deonna says, using her good arm to clean Raven's empty eye sockets. She broke it by helping Raven last week. She accidently goes in a little too deep, making Raven wince.

Even though Raven wears glass eyes, Deonna still cleans her eye sockets every so often.

"Careful!" Raven shouts.

"Sorry!" Deonna shouts. "I'm not a lefty."

"There have been doubts in some people's heads about magicians in Salem since the Australia video," Darren continues.

"So, they saw it from the beginning?" JP asks.

"Yes."

"Then how come they just now discovered Audrey?"

"They only paid attention to Bec," he says. "Audrey really isn't seen that well."

"Someone in command just happened to recognize me when they did," Audrey adds.

"So what now?" I ask. "What's our next plan?"

"The world is learning of our existence," Deonna says.

"We should show it that we mean no threat or else the burning of the witches will happen again."

"Hanging of the witches," JP corrects her.

Page 367

"Whatever."

"Ow!" Raven shouts.

"Okay!" Deonna shouts. "You wanna clean it yourself?"

"I can't!" Raven shouts back.

"Well, alright then! Let's try doing this in the bathroom where the lighting is better."

The girl girls get up, Deonna behind Raven telling her where to walk.

Audrey looks at me and smiles. "Bats and beetles."

"What?" I ask.

She then looks at JP. "Hey, JP? Can we go to the kitchen? Let's see if there's anything there."

"Okay?" he then looks back and forth between me and Darren. "Oh! Okay. Sure thing. No problem-o. Not a-"

"JP!"

"Okay, let's go."

JP then walks off with Audrey a little behind him on crutches. Her left prosthetic barely hanging on.

"Poor John and Mabel," I say after a small silence. "I can't believe Josh is gone."

"Were you guys close when you were little?" Darren asks me.

"Honestly, I don't remember us being super close, but we hung out a lot. Is it bad that I feel bad about us not being close?"

He moves closer to me on the couch and grabs my hand. "It's okay to be hurt or have survivor's guilt. You just can't let it eat you alive."

I sigh. "You're right."

He squeezes my hand a little tighter, and I smile at him.

"I thought about you every day while I was down there," he tells me. "I even remembered your birthday."

"I didn't even remember my birthday," I laugh. "Oh, it was last month."

"I often think about it, the day that I asked you to be with me."

"I still think you're a pedophile for falling for a twelve- year-old at twenty-one," I say laughing.

"Well, what about now?"

I move closer to him and kiss his nose. "We will need a lot of work."

"Of course!"

"No looking at little girls," I laugh.

"I wouldn't do that."

"You did with me."

"Okay, fair, but no more pedophile jokes."

I laugh. "Agreed. We need to have trust and open communication. No mind reading!"

"Okay. How do you know all this?"

"My sisters. Ash and Audrey."

"Fair enough."

We smile at each other. We then rest our foreheads together.

"Bec," he whispers, "I love you. Will you marry me?"

"How about we be boyfriend and girlfriend first for a bit?"

"Fair enough."

We then give each other a gentle kiss. I feel my chest exploding as if fireworks were set off inside. We then rest our foreheads against each other and smile.

I have a boyfriend.

Chapter 14

Two years go by with Magician kind working with Salem. Well, some of Salem. The groups who didn't agree have left the organization to fight us. The Salem that has remained has grown into a worldwide organization that drages all over have been joining. Mental magicians and tellers have been working out in the field to prevent catastrophic deaths. With the whole world knowing about magicians and kifomen, people have been being careful, arming themselves with weapons, supporting any way they can, and growing together.

Salem branched out a little more with becoming a charity organization as well as a fighting organization. Lots of people have been making donations to Salem, and we have been making more homeless shelters, helping low-income areas, and recruiting those very people so they can give back to the world. We even started cleaning the oceans too! I never knew of a plastic island in the Pacific. It'll take more time, but it'll be worth it!

The Demon King and his children have not been spotted since that time. What are they planning? Did they have to restructure their whole plan because of what we're doing?

Was it never supposed to happen as soon as we thought it was going to happen? Well, whatever it is, we'll be ready for them!

The world is slowly becoming a better place to live in, and I'm glad to be a part of it.

We're still in Boston. We work one on one with Salem headquarters, but they all got us a place to live here. I do miss the Pennsylvania trailer park though.

Emma, Frederick, and John have not been seen, and we can't contact them. Either they fell into another dimension like we did, or they're dead. It was nice having another mother while it lasted. I'll really miss her.

***

Audrey is putting a white veil on my head. I'm wearing a small white dress that goes up to my knees.

"Aw!" Audrey squeals and wipes some tears away. "You look so pretty!" She then pulls me into a hug that lasts almost a full minute.

"Thanks," I tell her as she hugs me.

Deonna then comes in. "Are you ready?"

"It's been two years," I say. "If I'm not, then there's a problem."

Deonna smiles.

Audrey pulls on my arm as the violin song starts to play from the stereo.

She then lets go of me when we reach the big room.

The first person I see is Darren standing at the end. His eyes grow wide, and I see him mouth, "wow."

I start to tear up a little myself.

JP and Raven are there too. They're standing at the sides, along with Mabel and John. The rabbi is also there.

The only other person in the room. Deonna and Audrey run to the front, and I start to walk.

I clutch my pink roses tighter with every step I take.

When I reach the front, Darren grabs my hands and whispers, "you look beautiful."

"You look great too," I say.

The rabbi speaks for a bit, but I don't really process what he says. My heart is beating way too fast.

"Rebecca Proenza," Darren says, the first time ever saying my full name, "I vow to always be true to you, and honest with you."

"Darren Dean," I say. "I vow to always be kind to you, and there for you."

"You have the candles?" the rabbi asks.

Page 371

Deonna hands Darren a long white candle, as Audrey hands me a similar one. There's a third wick that is not lit, but we light it together with our two candles.

Darren then passes his candle to Deonna, and gently grabs my left hand.

I hand my candle to Audrey as Darren slips a ring on my finger.

I don't see who passes me a ring, but I do the same to Darren. I look up at him and see tears rolling down his cheek and a smile on his face.

We then each pick up a pen and sign the document.

"I now pronounce you man and wife," the rabbi says.

We squeeze each other's hands.

"You may now kiss the bride," the rabbi says.

Darren pulls me close, and I wrap my arms around his neck as we kiss. The others cheer.

When we're done kissing, I smile at him, then I let go of him, and I break the glass under the cloth with my foot.

***

A year after our wedding, I'm throwing up in the toilet while Darren is holding my hair back. It is almost back to its original length before Deonna had cut it.

"You've been getting sick a lot," he tells me. "Are you sure you don't want any medicine?"

"No thank you," I tell him. "Maybe just some carrots with ranch."

I hurl again.

"You're thinking about food at a time like this?" he asks me.

That is weird.

***

I walk into headquarters and find Deonna on the video com talking with Alan Junior and Alana.

"Get back to us once the Sydney base finishes taking care of it," she tells them.

"Don't worry," Alana says, holding a fist to her brother who bumps it. "We got this!"

"Yeah," Alan says. "Reality rocks!"

I laugh and Deonna jumps.

"Always whimsical," I tell Alan. "Stay safe!"

"You too!" he says, then the picture goes black.

"You scared the hell out of me!" Deonna tells me.

"Now you know how I felt during my training," I tell her, laughing. "Everything good in Sydney?"

"Yup."

"Hong Kong?"

"They're still being stubborn about joining."

I sigh.

"Don't worry," Deonna says, "if anyone can get through to them, it's Commander Rainsford."

"I hope you're right."

Just then, a human woman around Deonna's age walks in. It throws me off because she has red eyes. "Your shift's over," she says.

"Perfect!" Deonna says. "Try and see if you can reach the Cape Town base about the malaria infestation in its other cities."

"Will do."

Deonna then looks at me and smiles. "I'm hungry."

"But it's morning," I tell her. "You should get some rest."

"Yeah, but I'm still hungry. Let's go order take out."

"If you say so." I look at the young woman and say, "I like your eyes."

"Thanks," she says. "Only family members of mine have them though."

"A magician family with an eye color all to themselves? That actually sounds cool!"

"Yeah, we used to wear sunglasses all the time. Now we don't have to."

"Nice! Does it mean anything?"

"Well, we're very strong, but that's about it."

"Cool!"

***

"You barely touched your sandwich," Deonna tells me at the Dunkin Donuts an hour later.

"I feel sick," I tell her. "I don't know why."

"Are you getting your period soon?"

"I'd feel pain, not sickness."

"Maybe you should get checked out. I'll even take you."

"Thanks," I tell her. "Maybe I should."

***

Deonna and Audrey took me to the doctor's office the next day.

"You have to tell him," Deonna says.

"I will," I tell her.

Audrey gives me a big hug. "Good luck."

When I get home, Darren is cooking pasta.

"Hey, Hun," he calls out to me.

"Hey, Dare," I say.

I walk into the kitchen. I always stare at our wedding photo. The one picture we have together. The one and only picture we have. We need to take more. He pulls me into a hug and kisses me passionately. How I love coming home to this. I wrap my arms around his neck and kiss him back.

"Everything okay?" he asks me when we pull apart.

"I have some news," I tell him honestly.

His smile disappears. "Is it good or bad?"

"Serious, but it can be either or, depending on how you see it."

"Okay, what is it?"

I take a deep breath, and then I say, "I'm pregnant."

His eyes grow wide and he has a small smile. "What?" he whispers.

"I'm pregnant," I say again. "I found out a little while ago with Deonna and Audrey."

"Bec, this is amazing!"

"Are we even ready?" I ask him.

"No one ever is," he tells me moving some hair out of my face, "but we have nine months to prepare."

Page 374

Well, he has a point there.

"I'm just worried," he tells me. "The world is getting better, but we still live in dangerous times."

"Well, all we have to do is defeat the Demon King."

"You say that like it'll be easy."

"It can be."

"I don't want our child and future children to grow up like we did."

I blink a few times. "What do you mean?"

"I don't want them to grow up as orphans, the way we did."

"Oh..."

"Let's make a promise to each other," he says.

"Okay, what promise?"

"Actually two. One, to protect our children."

"At any cost," I add.

"And two, let's not let them grow up as orphans."

I nod. "Agreed."

I rest my head on his shoulder, and he strokes my hair.

"It'll be okay," he whispers to me, more probably to himself than to me though.

"I believe it will be," I tell him.

We look at each other, and then we kiss again.

Chapter 15

I start showing at three months.

What the actual fuck, body?

"Dang," Audrey jokes. "How many are in there?"

"Not funny, sis," I tell her, stretching out my back.

Raven and JP are also with us. We're outside by the peace garden in front of the church.

"That's hurting you already?"

"Yes!"

"Damn!"

"I love that this is happening, but I also hate it."

Audrey laughs. "Ah, Bec, sometimes when life hands you lemons, you struggle to make orange juice until you realize how stupid you are being."

"Meaning..."

"You fight life until you learn to accept it. This baby won't go away."

"I know, and I'm happy, I really am, I just wish it wasn't so soon."

"You're Jewish, so you should know that it's not when you de-cide-"

I point up and say "-it's when he decides. I know."

"Try and make the best of it."

I nod. "I will."

"Have you thought of any names?" Raven asks me.

"I like Light," I tell her.

"For a boy or girl?" JP asks.

"Both," I say. "I only like unisex names."

Raven feels the ground with her walking stick and lands on my feet. "You know, animals can be unisex names too if you-"

"I'm not naming them Raven," I say. "That'll just be confusing."

She shrugs her shoulders. "Suit yourself."

Just then Darren comes with Mabel and John.

"How's the baby?" Mabel asks.

"Good," I say.

"You know the gender yet?" John asks.

"Nope," I say smiling. "I want to be surprised."

"You'll be surprised alright when five-"

"Audrey!" I shout at her.

"Please," Darren says, "don't let there be five in there."

"There's not five in here."

"Wouldn't that be something," a familiar female voice is heard behind us.

"Gala!" Raven shouts.

There are eight guys with her. They're the demon king's children. I recognize some of them from when we were in Dimension Five. The rest have the eyes. One boy stands out to me, for he looks my age, has my face, and my eyes.

"Won't father be pleased," Gala says, excited.

"Let's get this over with," a moody boy with yellow skin, and a green and black eye says.

"Remember," the one who looks like the eldest says. He has a green and red eye. He looks like a normal magician, except for the eyes. Could he be related to that magician I met? "Father said alive."

"We know the drill, Alekai," Gamma says.

The nine of them charge.

Raven goes invisible.

Where's Deonna with her force fields when we need her?

Next thing I know, a hand grabs me and I'm invisible too.

"It's okay," Raven whispers. "It's me."

Just then, Raven is yanked away from me and I turn visible again.

"Trevor! Now!" The green one says, trapping me in some plants from the garden.

Page 377

"Bec!" Darren screams.

He runs up to me, but so does Trevor, the one with my face.

He's suddenly gone, but then he's behind me.

Darren is on me too in the same instant, both of them grabbing an arm.

Next thing I know, the wind starts blowing hard. Some metal bracelets are put on my wrists.

When my eyes adjust, I realize we're back in the room from four years ago. The fireplace, the red room from the Demon King's castle.

Darren is with me, but so are the Demon King's children.

"Not today!" I scream.

I grab Darren and try to open a portal, but for some reason, the wind isn't working with me.

"Go ahead and try," the dark-skinned boy with the green and white eyes says. "That's blood bound, only one of us can take it off." He then jumps into a shadow cast from the couch and fireplace, and he's next to us. He grabs Darren and they both jump back into the shadows.

"Darren!" I scream. "Where's he taking my husband?"

"Bonnie will keep him safe," Gala says, "in the dungeon."

I try to zap her with lighting, but nothing is coming out.

A boy who seems to be the youngest with a green and purple eye approaches me. "You can't use any forms of magic or open a portal while you have that on."

"How do you know I'm mixed?" I nearly spit out. "How long have you monsters been watching me?"

I look at Trevor, the boy with my face.

"Because we're all mixed," he says. "We can all open portals, we all excel in all forms of magic, all ambidextrous, and we all have heterochromia. Understand now?"

No?

So we have similarities. Big whoop.

I try and punch the youngest one, but he dodges.

"Yulan, stay away from her," Gala says.

"I'll be fine," Yulan says. "She won't hurt me."

"And why not?" I ask harshly.

"Because you value family too much."

"Ah, at long last!" a man's voice is heard from the entrance. He's wearing a dark suit and tie that speaks professional and scary. He has green eyes that match my right one. He also has a red demon with tentacles by his feet. I'd recognize that demon anywhere.

I've never seen the man before, but I know who he is.

"The Demon King," I spit out.

"Ah, my sweet child," he says. His voice is very smooth, which makes me hate it even more. "At long last, my lost daughter has returned home! Come give daddy a hug!"

"You're crazy!" I shout. "My father is dead! Killed by your minions."

He walks closer to me. He has a warm smile that I want to slap off his face. "Weren't you adopted?"

"I was, but what does that have to do with-" I stop myself.

I was adopted!

"You don't know who you are, do you?"

I say nothing. How can I?

"It is time you learned the truth about yourself."

Chapter 16

"Have you ever wondered why you can open portals when no other magician can? About why you excel in more than one area of magic?" he asks me.

My father and I are at a table in the main room. All of my supposed siblings have cleared out except for Trevor. I can't stop staring at him. All of this would sound crazy if he wasn't sitting here next to me.

And yet...

A bunch of food appears on the table, like the apples in the kitchen last time I was here.

There's cheeses, crackers, fruits, vegetables, pasta, rice, and beans.

I give my father a nasty look.

"What? You're not a vegan? Uh, I assumed you were. All my children and I are."

I don't say anything.

I wouldn't eat either, but I have mine and Darren's child growing inside me to think about.

"The cheeses are vegan," Trevor tells me.

I grab some cheese and crackers and put them on my plate.

"So, you got me," I say, putting some food in my mouth and swallowing. "Now what?"

"What do you mean?" he asks me, smiling.

Ugh! How is he so calm right now?

"What are you going to do with me?" I ask more mad than scared. "Take my blood to open a portal into the tenth dimension?"

He starts to laugh. "My child, I just simply wanted you home. I would have liked this to be a family dinner, but I want to get to know you a little bit before I invite the rest of your siblings to join in."

"What?"

"You're my daughter, did you really think that I was going to kill you?"

"Yes," I say without hesitating.

"Nonsense. You're powerful but you still don't pose any threat to me. I want you by my side as we purify the rest of the dimensions, my dear."

"Purify?"

"Yes."

"Is that what you call sending your kifomen to murder children?"

"They only target evil beings. Creatures, such as humans, born with evil intentions."

"Then why don't they target you?" I spit out.

He laughs.

"Ah, you're quick witted and make jokes," he laughs, "just like your brother Gamma."

I take a deep breath. I don't want him to know he's getting to me. It's possible he already knows if he can read minds like Darren.

Darren.

I have to get us out of here.

I look down at the cuffs on my wrists. I look back at the Demon King, my father. Maybe I can find out some information before Darren and I escape.

"So how are we able to open portals and excel in multiple areas of magic?" I ask him.

"We have a powerful lineage," he tells me.

Powerful lineage! That's the same thing Gamma said to me several years ago! Ah, I'm such an idiot! No wonder Raven didn't trust me! She knew all along. Wait, is this what she was hiding from me? What everyone else knew? Darren knew and he still loved me.

Oh, Darren.

I still wish he had told me something, we agreed no more secrets.

Unless this was Raven making him not tell me.

Page 381

"How powerful?" I ask. "I thought that was rare? The last magician seen doing that was-"

He smiles at me.

"You've got to be kidding me," I say.

"We are direct descendants of the mighty Hercules himself," he tells me. "All of his power courses through our veins."

"That makes no sense," I say. "Hercules had eight children that all died."

"Myths and legends can get mixed up," he says. "Some say he had eight children, but he and Megara actually had three sons: Therimachus, Deicoon, and Creontiades. Hercules was called on a mission to help keep peace in Dimension Eight. After he left, some believe that they all died at the hands of humans, but actually Magara and Deicoon lived. Hercules was in a depression, yes. During his depression, Megara, and Deicoon first created the kifomen for peace, to help Hercules with his quests, only attacking the evil."

I look at Trevor. He just nods at me.

"Magicians were against the kifomen, they called them demons. They fled to Dimension Eight and abandoned their home," father tells me.

"Wait wait wait wait wait!" I interrupt. "So you're telling me that magicians and kifomen are both from Dimension Five?"

"Precisely."

When he notices that I'm too shocked to speak, he continues.

"The kifomen did attack evil beings, and also attacked when they were attacked. That's the only reason why they go after magicians, but humans are evil, destroying Dimension Eight."

"So you want to kill all of humanity in the name of peace? That's not peace!"

"You will see it soon," he says pointing to my stomach. "You and my future grandchild."

"I'm not pregnant," I lie. "I'm just fat. Thank you very much for calling out my insecurities."

"You cannot lie to me, child -"

"I'm twenty-one!"

"-although I'm hurt you tried."

Shit!

Page 382

"I believe a congratulations are in order. Is it a boy or a girl?"

"I don't know," I say. I hope he never does either.

"Oh! I hope it's a girl!" he cheers. "Too many boys in this family. I want a granddaughter. I'd kill if another boy is born."

I put up my fists.

"I'm just kidding, he'd be my grandson! Of course I wouldn't kill him! But, seriously, I want a granddaughter."

Chapter 17

Trevor takes me on a walk through their home to my room. It's just as cold, dark, and boring looking as I remember.

"What happened to all of our mothers?" I ask him after a while.

He sighs. "They've all been killed," he tells me after a moment of silence.

"By him?"

Trevor nods.

"And he still has custody of all the kids?" I ask.

He chuckles a little. "Funny how that works out."

"So how did I not get taken?" I ask him.

"When our mother gave birth to us, she must have hidden you from him. It almost worked."

"Gave birth to us?"

"Yeah," he says. "We're twins."

"I'll be honest, I didn't see that coming."

"You must be a little oblivious, aren't you?"

"Hey," I shout, and playfully push my twin brother. We both start to laugh a little. I remember who he is and who he serves, and then I stop.

"So father has a child from every dimension?" I ask.

"Yes."

"And he killed all our mothers."

"I didn't want to believe it, all our siblings told me, but when Yu-lan was born and his mother was killed by him..." he sighs. "It would have been nice to know her, and would have been nice for us to have grown up together."

"But how did he find me if our mother hid me?"

"One of dad's followers saw you in a hat shop. She recognized your eyes and immediately knew you were his."

I think about that for a moment. Was that the day I wanted to go inside that shop in Miami city, and my brothers got me the fedora? What ever happened to that fedora anyways?

"Why still serve him after knowing what he did?" I ask.

"He's our father, and he loves us."

"But it's...wrong."

"Heh, Alekai says the same thing, but we all have our marks, and we all owe our lives to our father in a way."

"Marks?"

"Things that distinguish us as siblings. Like, you know, family traits."

"Is there anything else that distinguishes us besides our eyes?" I ask. "Like, something else that we all have that gave me away?"

"Well, we're all ambidextrous. We can all sing. All don't eat meat, being vegan."

Shit, and I was proud of those things about me.

"Power wise," he continues, "we can all open portals to the first nine dimensions, and we excel in all four areas of magic."

"Oh."

"Here we are," Trevor says. "Your room."

"When can I see my husband?" I ask him.

"Honestly, I don't know."

"He-he-hey, Trev!" Gamma calls, running from the end of the hall.

"Quick!" Trevor says. "Hide in your room."

"What will he do?" I ask.

"Something stupid, probably."

I open the door and go inside my room. I gasp at what I see. It's the same room that I found my bear in. It hasn't changed at all.

I lay on my bed, resting my hand on my stomach, and I start to cry.

What am I going to do?

Page 385

There's a knock at the door a few moments later. I open the door to reveal my algae covered sister.

Hello sissy.

Everyone's right, I am oblivious to everything!

"Come," she commands.

"Where?" I ask, not liking her tone, but considering I can't leave while these cuffs are on, I have to play along.

"To eat something," she says. "You've been in there all night."

Shit. I can't deny food.

"Then father wants me to show you something," she continues. "Get dressed."

"I have no clothes," I tell her.

"Check the drawers."

I go to the drawers and sure enough, there are clothes in there. I hold up a shirt and put it up to my chest. It'd be my size if I wasn't pregnant. I keep looking through the drawers and I find a long black dress with short sleeves. I pull on it a little and it stretches a bit.

I guess this will be my maternity dress.

I turn around and see her still standing in the doorway.

She closes the door, and I change into the dress. It's amazingly comfortable.

I open the door and she nods at me.

We walk to the kitchen in silence.

What if I have to fight for my life soon? Maybe the dress was a bad idea.

Once we get there, I notice all the cupboards are empty except for a few plates and cups. There's a boy around thirteen putting a plate back in the cupboard.

"Hey, Yulan," my sister calls him.

"Hi, Gala," he says cheerily. "Hi, Bec." He rushes up to us and pulls us both into a hug.

Well, that just happened.

I tried to attack him earlier, why is he hugging me?

Page 386

What are they planning? Get me comfortable with them, and then they strike?

No.

I won't get comfortable!

I look at the side of my dress. Surprisingly, there's no algae on it. I guess it works as her skin rather than a coating.

"Gala, are you gonna show her the machine? Can I come?" Yulan asks.

"Sure thing, baby bro," she tells him. "We just have to get something in her system first."

I hope Darren is getting fed. Where is he being held anyways?

Yulan starts jumping up and down. "It's so interesting!"

Wait, did they say machine? Nothing good comes out of ominous devices named 'the machine.'

***

The whole walk over, Yulan was asking me twenty thousand questions about my life, where I've been, what my tricks are, and other stuff like that. I kept it as vague as possible.

I didn't tell him all my tricks. Keeping my slowing down time, healing, and electric ones a secret for now until I need to use them. I told him about the fire, the cheese trick I did, sleight of hand, telekinesis, and that time I had a mental conversation with that puff ball in Dimension Five.

They take me to an area of the castle, fort, house. I honestly don't know what to call this place. Two of my brothers were working on it. One had a wrench and was tightening something. The other was looking at what I believe to be the tunnel of the machine.

"Hey, Bonnie! Hey, Balex!" Yulan calls them.

"Hey, Buddy! Balex, how's the end looking?" Bonnie says, turning away from the screws and swinging the wrench.

"Looks fine," Balex says. "Would look better if it would work."

"That's the spirit," Bonnie says.

"Isn't Father almost done collecting?" Yulan asks them.

"Yup," Bonnie says, him and Balex standing in front of us.

"Yippie," Balex sarcastically says as he twirls his index finger in the air. "He would have been done by now if Bec wasn't hiding in Boston."

So that's why Doomsday is taking so long. They were looking for me!

"True, but hey, the machine looks great!" Bonnie says.

I'm almost too afraid to ask, but I ask anyways. "What is this?"

"It'll help us cleanse the tenth dimension of evil," Bonnie says.

"You mean destroy their souls forever," I say.

"Just the evil and impure ones," Gala says.

"Who is it to decide who's evil and who's good?" I ask.

"Everyone has both good and bad inside of them. People sometimes do good things with bad intentions, and bad things with good intentions. It's not all black and white, there's a huge grey area there."

They all laugh.

"You sound just like Alekai," Gala laughs.

"Alekai?" I ask.

I keep hearing them say that.

"Yeah, that traitor is always talking like that?"

"If he's a traitor, why keep him around?" I ask.

"He's family," Balex says.

I have a brother who doesn't blindly follow our father who is still around. Can I get him to help me?

Or is this part of the trap?

I'm on my own here.

Besides, this is my only lead.

Chapter 18

I slowly meet all of my siblings one on one as the months go by. That is, all of them but Alekai. I've seen him, but no one will let me near him. When I try walking up to him, Gala or one of my brothers always grabs my arm and directs me somewhere else.

It's like they're always watching me!

I'm still not allowed to see Darren. At night I sneak out of my room and try to find where he might be hiding, all attempts to no avail.

One day I get the instailk. Trevor and father take care of me. Gamma and Yulan try to put on a puppet show, but it ends with puppet manslaughter.

My stomach keeps growing bigger. Gamma likes to put a giant ball up to his own stomach and compare the sizes.

We all can't help but laugh at his attempts.

I can't get too comfortable; they must be planning on using me or my child for something.

I still haven't forgotten about my other family that took me in. Blood or not, they're my real family! They must be worried sick. Darren and I need to get back to them.

I don't want to give birth here.

***

I'm walking around one day, trying to bite the cuffs off, when I spot Trevor and Alekai nearby the kitchen. They don't notice me at first.

"We'll know what to do," Alekai tells him. "It'll have to be when the baby comes."

"Hey," Trevor says to me. "How are you feeling?"

Horrible. Depressed. I want to leave.

"Fine," I tell him.

"How's the baby?" Alekai asks.

"Good," I tell him. "I wish I knew what I was having. Speaking of my baby, what were you two-"

"Hey! Little sister!" Sax calls out behind me. "Father wants to see you!"

Without warning, he takes my arm and drags me away. He takes me to the living room area, where father is sitting on the couch with Zigor.

"Your control over plants is getting better, son," he tells him. "It seems you can heal them now."

"Yeah, I've been practicing forever."

"I'm very proud of you, son. You show with hard work you can do anything you set your mind to."

Father kisses Zigor on the head and then sees Sax and I standing there.

"Sax, son, don't forget to feed your dragon," Father tells him.

"It's a bearded dragon, dad," Sax tells him.

"I know, but 'dragon' sounds cooler."

Zigor stands up and says, "I'll help you, bro."

"You have a bearded dragon?" I ask.

"Yeah...he was my mother's," Sax says.

"Even the dragon is a boy," Father nearly grumbles.

My two brothers smile at me, then walk out.

I'm alone with the maniac, the Demon King as Raven calls him.

"Come, daughter," he says patting the couch next to him.

I sit down and my father puts his arm around me. I try not to stiffen up at his touch.

"You seem uneasy, my child," he tells me.

"I want to see Darren," I say point blank.

"You will see him soon enough, I promise. I want to see the baby first. Do you know the gender?"

"No," I say. "I haven't been to the doctor."

Page 390

"Is it okay?"

"I believe so," I say honestly. "I feel a lot of movement."

"I really hope it's a girl!" he squeals, getting excited.

I want a boy, but I'm not telling him that. Please be a boy so I can at least disappoint this asshole!

Wait, what if he kills it!

Gah!

"Child, I need your help with something."

"You mean you want to use me for something sinister."

He sighs. "In order for our mission to succeed, I need all of my children with me. True, I need your energies to help the machine open the portal, but we will do this after the baby is born."

"And what makes you think I'll help you?"

"You will," he says. "I see you're getting along with your siblings, so I know you value family."

"How do I know you won't dispose of us when you're done?" I spit out.

"My child, do you really see me as that malicious? I wouldn't do that to my own children. If I haven't done anything to Alekai yet, what makes you think I'll do something to my other children?"

"So, you know about Alekai."

"I know he doesn't share the same views as me. He's the only one who spent too much time with his mother."

"Before you killed her."

"All your mothers' deaths were accidents or natural causes."

Liar.

"Alekai's mother got sick. He spent a lot of time with her, and she filled his head with these thoughts," father tells me.

"Is that why you're keeping him away from me?"

"I'm doing no such thing. If you wish to know your brother, by all means, you can talk to him."

I glance sideways at him.

"You're still skeptical, I can see that. In time, you will see the truth."

"And what truth is that?"

"That your family loves you and we are trying to do good for the world."

Page 391

***

What should I do?

I don't know if I can bring myself to kill him. I know I won't be able to kill my siblings. I've only ever killed kifomen before. I don't even kill animals! I don't even eat them! Can I really kill my father?

I come across Trevor, Alekai, and Gala feeding a group of kifomen.

What they're being fed, I really don't want to know, but I smell blood.

Gala looks at me, then nods her head.

"Wanna feed one?" Trevor asks me.

"Nope! No thank you!" I practically shout.

"They won't hurt you," Trevor says.

"Tell that to all the kifomen who've tried to kill me in the past," I say.

"Were you attacking them?" Gala asked.

"When I was in Miami, one tried to charge me," I tell her.

"You mean that day on the beach when they were trying to collect you?" she asks.

I knew they killed my human family, but I never thought that day was intentional for me to join them.

Who knows what would have happened if they succeeded that day.

One kifoman grabs a piece of food, and gives it to a smaller kifoman. They smile at each other and the smaller one eats.

"Huh," I utter.

"What?" Gala asks.

"I didn't expect kifomen to act this way," I say.

"You just thought they were all evil?" she asks me.

My silence says it all.

"Is a mother killing a man for trying to kill her child evil?" she asks me.

"Well..."

"Kifomen only kill the evil, or kill those who attack them."

Page 392

"But Raven told me that kifomen killed a bunch of baby plants in one dimension."

"Because they were attacked. Would you not defend yourself?"

"Well..."

"I rest my case." She holds out a piece of food to me. I grab the food and throw it to a small kifoman who giggles as it chews.

I can't help but smile at it.

"You okay, Bec?" Alekai asks me.

I smile at him. "I think so."

That's when a sharp pain squeezes inside my stomach.

Uh oh.

Chapter 19

"I'll go get Father!" Gala shouts and runs out.

I look at Alekai and Trevor. There's fear on their faces.

"I need a hospital!"

"We have to act fast," Alekai tells Trevor.

Trevor nods and then opens a portal, the wind blowing hair into my face and mouth not making my current situation any better. Trevor and Alekai each grab my arms and pull me through.

On the other side, we're in a hospital lobby.

"You know the plan?" Alekai asks Trevor.

Trevor nods and says, "stay safe, big brother."

***

About six hours later, after projectile vomiting, screaming, and lots of pain, I give birth to three healthy little babies.

My two boys and my baby girl.

I name my boys Dare, and Light, and my daughter is Brave.

"They're beautiful," Trevor says.

"Thanks," I say smiling. "Kind of sucks though that I do all the work and they look like Darren."

He chuckles a little. "Yeah, that tends to happen."

"Can I see my husband now?"

"It depends on Father. To be honest, I don't think he'll be too happy about two more boys in the family."

"But I had a girl, too."

"Yeah, but still..."

"Do you think he'll kill my boys?"

He doesn't say anything.

"Trev?" I ask.

Just then a gust of wind blows in the room.

I sit up fast, ready to help my children, but I sigh with relief at who I see.

"Deonna! Audrey!"

"Bec!" Audrey shouts. "You're okay!"

"Where's Darren?" Deonna asks.

"I don't know where he's being held," I tell her truthfully.

"Held?" she asks.

"By your father?" Audrey asks.

"So, you guys know?" I ask.

"Raven told us," Audrey tells me.

I guess I understand why Raven didn't trust me when we first met.

"Does Darren know?" I ask.

"Yes," Deonna tells me.

My sweet Darren. I'll get us out of here now that I can fight.

"Where are we?" I ask. "What state?"

"Pennsylvania," Deonna says.

Alekai goes near Light's crib and looks at him. He then looks at Dare. "They have identical faces," he says.

Trevor goes next to him and looks at them.

I don't know how I feel about my brothers being near my children. Then again, they did help me get them here.

"We can't let father have them," Trevor says.

"He will use them like he did all of us," Alekai agrees.

"Trevor?" I ask. "You don't agree with father?"

He shakes his head. "How can I blindly agree with a madman who killed our mothers?"

All this time I thought my twin brother was one of them. Well, bad like father. I guess I was wrong about him. Unless this is still part of our father's plan.

"Father knows about me," Alekai says, "but he doesn't know about Trevor. No one does, and right now, father also doesn't know how many kids you just had."

Page 395

I don't have to think twice. I have to do what my mother did, except in reverse. I look at Deonna and Audrey. "Take my boys."

"Bec?" Audrey asks.

"Father wants a granddaughter; I'll give him one. Besides, she'll have a better chance of not getting killed by him."

Audrey gently picks up Light, and Deonna gets Dare.

Trevor goes in his pocket and takes out a key. I'm no seer, but I can tell it's the keys to take these cuffs off. "We'll know when to use them."

"I thought it was blood magic?" I ask.

"Which is why I have to take them off for you."

I smile at him.

I nod at Trevor and he carefully tries to pick up Brave.

Alekai goes next to Deonna and she gives him an uneasy look. Still a kinder look than the first look she ever gave me.

"We meet back at the trailer," I tell them.

Trevor and Alekai look at each other and say, "What trailer?"

Chapter 20

Trevor opens a portal and takes me back to our father. I didn't know what to expect coming back here, but I didn't expect father to cry at the sight of Brave.

"She's beautiful," he whispers.

It takes every ounce of my being to not pull her away from him.

"Ha, that sucks!" Gamma shouts. "She looks like her father!"

"Speaking of her father," I say, "can I see him now?"

"Of course, my child," he says, and then leaves the room.

"So, what's her name?" Gala asks with a scoff in her voice.

"Brave," I tell her.

"Pay no attention to her," Sax says. "She's just jealous that she's not the only girl in the house anymore."

"I'm not jealous!" Gala screams in his face.

"You want some potatoes with that salt?" Gamma asks her.

I might... I haven't had a potato in forever!

"Yeah," Zigor says joining in. "All these flavors and you choose to be salty?"

I start to laugh a little. Trevor laughs with me and puts his hand on my shoulder.

"You wanna try and hold her?" I ask him.

"I do!" Gamma shouts.

"That would be the worst idea ever," Balex says.

"Yeah," Yulan agrees. "Gamma with kids?"

"Hey!" Gamma shouts.

I start laughing again.

Trevor hesitates for a moment, but then I support her head on his arm and he starts to laugh.

"I have a niece!" Trevor says.

"We all do," Bonnie says. "Er..." he looks at me, "almost all of us. Sorry. You have a daughter."

I laugh again. Maybe my siblings aren't so bad.

Just then I hear a loud thump close to my feet and I look down.

"There," Father says. "You see him."

I know that black hair anywhere, I smile and get to my knees.

Wait... why is he just lying there?

"Darren?" I ask. "Hunny?"

No response.

"Hun?" I put my hand on his shoulder.

It's cold.

I turn him around and move his hair out of his face.

He's pale.

"Darren," I start to cry.

I gently hit the side of his face a few times, but there's still no response.

I slowly move my ear against his chest, almost like a creep and crawl. When I don't hear anything, my whole body becomes numb.

"No..."

Book 4

Family Wars

Chapter 1

My Darren is gone.

I've never felt so murderous and depressed all at the same time. I want to scream, hold him, kill my father, snatch my daughter, and run, but I can't even move. All I can do is stare soullessly at his lifeless body as tears trickle down my cheeks. Even if I was able to move, I still have these cuffs on... I'm still at my father's mercy.

I gently touch the side of Darren's face. Cold - ice cold.

"I'm so sorry, my love," I whisper.

"Father..." Gala says shocked. "What have you do-"

Father says. "I have done no such thing."

He did do this to my Darren.

I'll make him pay.

"So, all our mothers getting sick was a coincidence too?" Trevor snaps.

"Watch your tone, Trevor," father warns him. "I am still your father."

Trevor hangs his head. "Yes, father."

I hear the shuffling of feet behind me from the rest of my siblings. I still can't move. Footsteps enter the room. I don't look up to see who it is because my eyes refuse to leave my fallen love.

"Leader Ro," an elderly woman's voice says, "the eighth dimension is ready."

I look up when she says that, and I nearly gasp at the sight of her. Even though she's on her knees bowing her head, I recognize her. I've seen her before! But from where though?

"Excellent," Father says. "Thank you, Donna, although I expected the news to be delivered years ago."

She gulps. "Well, you did want your daughter with you."

"That I did," he says. "No matter, we will finish up on our end. Wait, where is Alekai?"

"He's not here?" Sax says.

I know he's with Deonna at the cabin with my boys. They're safe.

"Ugh!" Father groans. "That boy is going to be the death of me. I need him here for the plan to go in motion." He then takes a deep breath. "No matter, I will find him eventually. Until then, my children will ready the machine. Donna, go spread the word to my followers in Eight that we will begin shortly."

"Yes, leader Ro," she says. She gets up and walks out of the room.

"In the meantime, Gala, take your sister and niece to her room. I left a little surprise for the baby in there."

"Yes, father," Gala says.

My brothers all nod their heads. I feel Gala grab my shoulders to stand me up.

"No!" I scream as I shrug her off and grab Darren's hands. "No! No! No!"

Then I feel someone's arms go underneath my armpits and lift me up. Another pair of arms then grab my feet and carry me out. I'm screaming and crying the entire time.

We finally get to my bedroom door and Balex and Gamma put me down. I try to run back, but Gala grabs me. Trevor just stands there, wide-eyed, holding Brave.

I look at my daughter, my youngest triplet, fast asleep in her uncle's arms. She's going to need me. All three of them are.

I hope Dare and Light are okay.

"You need to control yourself," Gala tells me.

For my babies.

I take a few shaky deep breaths as I wipe the tears from my eyes. I grab the doorknob and open the door. My room hasn't changed at all, except that there's now a crib in there with a little yellow bear in it.

I sit on my bed and try to control my breathing. Darren really is gone. How am I going to tell the others? How am I going to tell my children when they're older that their grandfather murdered their father?

Their grandfather.

My father.

I still don't know if I can kill him, but he needs to be taken down, no matter the cost, provided that the price isn't my children's lives.

Trevor tries to lay Brave down in her crib, but he doesn't seem to know how to do it. I stand up to help him lay her down. Her little chest rises and falls, and her little hand twitches.

"The last baby I handled was Yulan," Trevor tells me. "But I was too young to actually handle him. The most I did was sit while I held him."

I nod my head. I need to talk to my twin brother in private.

Page 401

"I'm sorry about your husband," Gala says to me. "Are you okay?"

"Of course, she's not," Balex says. "Nobody is."

Gala opens her mouth to say something but then closes it. She looks at Gamma who is standing there, petrified.

"You have a smart comment to say?" Gala asks, sounding like she's hoping for once that he'll say something stupid.

Gamma shakes his head.

"You didn't know?" I ask.

"Know about what?" Gala asks.

"About Darren, my husband?"

"No," Gala says, shocked. "Of course not! I didn't know that he was dead. Must have been a recent suicide."

She'll never believe that our father killed him. Or maybe she's so loyal to father, she wouldn't bat an eye at it. I don't know what to believe about my sister. Gamma shakes his head again.

"I don't think any of us did," Balex says. "Only Father's followers handle the prisoners."

"But Father has a hand in it," I say.

"He has a hand in everything," Gala says.

"Everything evil is doomed," Balex says.

"My Darren wasn't evil," I tell him, tears rolling down my face again.

Trevor pulls me into a hug, and I hug him back.

"I'm so sorry, Bec," he whispers to me.

"Thanks," I whisper back.

I look at my other three siblings, all shifting uncomfortably. If Darren were still here, he could read their minds and tell me what they're thinking.

Oh, Darren. I'm so sorry!

"Do you want us to leave you for a few hours?" Balex asks me.

Do I?

I need these cuffs off so Brave and I can leave, and I can do magic tricks again. Then again, I can't make it look too obvious what my plan is. Also, I don't want to be alone right now, even if my only form of company is my siblings who follow our father who murdered my husband.

I sit on my bed, grab one of my pillows and scream into it. One of my siblings sits next to me and rubs my back.

"I'll stay with her," Trevor says from right next to me.

"Okay," Gala says. "Come on, guys."

"This whole thing sucks," Balex says. "You okay, little brother?"

"Gala," Gamma finally says, "we're the good guys, right?"

Then the door closes.

"We need to stop father," Trevor whispers to me once the others walk away.

"The key is the machine," I say, taking my face out of the pillow.

"The machine was only supposed to be for dimension ten," he tells me. "We were collecting things for him to be able to break through the barrier. He had something else entirely in store for Dimension Eight."

"Which is what?" I ask.

"Well, he was going to use Organization Salem and the kifomen to cleanse it-"

"Wait, wait, wait, Father knows about Organization Salem?" I ask.

"Yeah," Trevor tells me. "Our ancestors founded it to help out the cause." He nearly spits out the last part in disgust.

"Our ancestors founded Salem?" I ask, not sure why I'm surprised.

"Yeah, they were mostly targeting magicians who didn't follow or agree with them. Just persecution if you ask me. Then the humans got more control of it, forgetting how they started out."

"I never knew that."

"How were you supposed to?"

"Does father have followers in Salem?"

"Oh, yeah."

I look down at my hands. This explains a lot in fact. I look back at my brother. "So, by changing most of Salem into a charity organization..."

"You slowed him down. Also, him not knowing exactly where you were, has also slowed him down."

"So, that day on the beach in Miami, Gala told me that one of the kifomen were trying to grab me-"

"To take you here to start his plan, but you were picked up by-"

"Emma and Audrey."

"Exactly."

"So, I've been slowing down Demon Doomsday without even realizing it?" I ask.

"That's what we're calling it?"

I give him a 'now's-not-the-time' look. Raven calls it that. I hope she's okay.

He clears his throat. "Yes, you were slowing it down. He jump-started his plans back up when he found you in Boston."

"How did he find me?"

"You went to the doctor's office and confirmed pregnancy."

"So, that's why you guys just showed up out of nowhere. So, what does Father plan on doing now?"

Page 403

"He's going to use the machine to suck out all the souls in Ten and eradicate them after he finally opens a portal there."

"And with Eight?"

"Use the kifomen, we have enough to start global domination."

"He can do that?" I ask, horrified.

"He's been building this machine for years, over a decade. I don't know if he can do global domination, but it seems highly likely."

"What about everyone there who is half-human?" I say, thinking of Audrey, JP, and my triplets.

"Them too."

"And full magicians?" I ask horrified, thinking of Deonna and Raven.

"Not them. Father says magicians aren't evil, but I'm not sure if he'll kill them or not. Magicians will never follow him though, so who knows what will happen if his plan succeeds. That's probably why he wants all of us here with him, so he doesn't accidentally kill one of us."

"How exactly does it work? Would we have time once it's been activated? Or does it kill everything at once?"

"It slowly sucks a few souls at a time and locks on to creatures with evil in them and destroys them. We've been collecting parts for it over the years. He's bound to turn it on at some point."

"Then we have no time to waste," I say. "We're going to need help."

Chapter 2

I want to bring Darren's body home, but Father probably did something to him by now.

My poor Darren.

I resist the urge to cry again.

"I have to go tell Alekai," Trevor tells me as quietly as he can. "Maybe he and I can sneak your other magician friends over."

"But we have to do more than just destroy the machine," I tell him as quietly as I can. "We still have our father and his followers across the multiverse and the large expansion of kifomen. Blowing up the mothership will not end this. We must take care of all the problems. Not to mention... our siblings." Then I remember what Gamma said walking out of my room. "Do you think there's a chance they-"

"I don't know," Trevor admits, "but we can't rely on them." He looks off into the distance. "The people that follow father need to be stopped, but..."

"You don't know if you can kill our siblings," I finish for him. He nods.

"I know how you feel," I say. "I was thinking the same thing."

"So, what do we do?" he asks.

"We can't kill them, but if they all live without a change of heart, they'll just start this all over again. Maybe we can do both!"

"Kill them and change their minds?" Trevor asks, horrified.

"No! Save them and change their minds for good!" Then I remember what I just said. Why did I say that? "Sorry, I didn't mean to say do both. Hopefully, most of them are starting to question Father now."

"Because of Darren?"

My heart breaks at the sound of his name. "Yes. You saw how they reacted when father threw his body at me, you heard what Gamma asked Gala-"

"But Gala is Father's biggest supporter," Trevor tells me. "She won't be swayed without a struggle, if at all."

"But our brothers-"

"Might be easier to convince now they've seen some proof of father's malice, but we can't rely on it."

"So, killing all our mothers wasn't proof enough?" I ask.

"It was for me and Alekai."

I sigh. This is not going to be easy. "What should step one be then?"

He thinks for a moment. "I need to go tell Alekai what's happening. You can stay here and talk to some of our other brothers... see what they're thinking. I'll try and bring your friends over to help us destroy the machine. Alekai and one of your friends must stay with Dare and Light. If Father knows we're all here, safe and sound, then he'll move forward with his plans. He's delayed them long enough. Then, father... father needs to be handled."

"What about Brave?" I ask, looking at my sleeping daughter. "Dare and Light are safe from father, but she's not?"

"Are they though?"

"What do you mean?"

"If father decides to start his plan even without all of us here..."

I feel all the blood rush out of my face.

"I'm just saying, we can't rule out any possibility," he tells me. "I'm right now ninety-five percent certain he won't until we're all here with him."

"But what if we're all here and my boys are still with Deonna and Audrey?" I ask.

He gulps. "Then you'll have no choice but to tell father about them. Odds are, he'll send one of us to go get them and we can delay his plans a little longer."

"But how much longer can we keep delaying?" I ask, trying to keep my voice at a whisper.

"As long as we can," he tells me. "Father is an evil prick and a ruthless ruler, but he's a damn good father who wants all his kids alive and with him."

"So, we can stall," I say. "We can use his love for us against him."

"Exactly what I was thinking. So, when do we take these off?" I ask, holding up my wrists to reveal the magical chainless cuffs that are still on me. "They've been on me for months now and frankly, they hurt. I need them off to fight."

"When you need to leave, I'll take them off," he tells me.

"When I need to leave?" I ask.

"You know what I mean. When the time is right for you to leave with Brave."

"And when will that be?"

He thinks again. "I don't know, sis. All I know is that you need to talk to our brothers, and you need those cuffs on to do so."

"So, the cuffs will have to be played by ear?" I ask.

"I'm sorry, but it's the only uncertainty I have right now."

"Shit, Trev, I can't do magic tricks with them on though," I tell him. "Or open portals. What if you're not here and I need them off to defend myself?"

It's his turn for his face to go pale. "Let's not think of that right now. If all goes according to plan, you won't need to fight until they're off."

"Okay, twin brother," I say. "But I think we'll save time if both of us talk to our brothers separately. Like, I take three and you take the other three."

"Then they'll know I'm a traitor," he tells me. "That's our secret advantage right now, we can't blow that. You were raised by humans and magicians, not father. They'll expect this talk from you or Alekai, but Alekai is not here, so it has to be you."

"Okay," I say. "I understand."

Trevor then pulls me into a tight hug.

"Be careful," he whispers in my ear.

"You too," I whisper back.

He lets go of me and goes up to Brave's crib. He takes his finger and gently strokes her cheek. Then he looks at me again. "Make conversation subtle and don't push for answers. If you talk to them and get an idea to change in their head, we might win them over. If you show you're pushing to change them, they might alert father."

I nod. "I understand."

"Also, don't tell any of them about the plan."

"Okay."

"Try and remember everything they say and relay it to me. You can be a little oblivious sometimes and I don't want you to get the wrong idea."

"Hey... nevermind, you're not wrong."

He smiles, pulls me into another hug, then he opens a portal and jumps through it to warn Alekai at the trailer.

I sigh and go to Brave's crib. I take her out and hold her.

"I'm sorry you're wrapped into this," I tell her. "If we all work together, it's gotta turn out okay, right?"

I open the door to talk to potential allies or enemies, my brothers.

Chapter 3

Yulan is the first brother I see. He's in the kitchen, finishing up making a sandwich. He looks at it for a while, but pushes it away - his green and purple eyes filling with tears.

My only little brother.

"Not hungry?" I ask him.

He just looks at me.

"Me neither," I tell him.

"Did father really kill our mothers?" he asks me after a long pause. "Like your husband?"

Okay, I know he's the youngest and hasn't fully matured yet, but he could have worded that one differently!

"It seems that way," I tell him, trying to control myself. "It's too co-incidental that they all died right after we were born."

"Alekai told me, but..." he starts to cry. "I didn't want to believe it."

I use one arm to give him a hug. He buries his face in my chest. I remember Trevor's words and choose my next ones very carefully.

"What do you think you'll do now?" I ask him.

"What do you mean?"

Okay, I wasn't careful enough!

Think, Bec, think!

"What do you want to do? That veggie sandwich looks good. Besides, you'll need your strength."

"I don't want it."

"The sandwich or your strength?"

"I can't eat right now anyway. How can I choose between my father and my siblings?"

"Whoa whoa whoa there, little brother, no one is asking you to choose between your family."

"But that's going to happen," he tells me crying. "You'll never fol-low father now. You and Alekai are going to act out against him. I know it! Our brothers will pick sides, Gala will side with father, then I'll be forced to choose. I just know it!"

"I'll never ask you to pick a side," I tell him. "But I will ask this, what do you believe is the right thing?"

He looks at Brave and strokes her forehead. "I don't know any-more. Father didn't have to kill our mothers or your husband, but there is a lot of evil still out there."

"When it comes to good or bad-"

"The grey area, I know," he tells me. "I remember that conversa-tion, but where's the grey area in killing her father?" He kisses Brave's forehead. "He was just a magician. Magicians are supposed to be pure, and humans are to be evil."

"You know, Trevor and I are half-human, does that make us half evil?"

He thinks for a moment and looks up at me. "No. You're not, so the same is probably true for the others."

"Alekai and Father are both full magicians, and they don't share the same views. Father thinks every being with evil inside them should be eradicated, meanwhile Alekai thinks that killing at all is evil."

"What do you think?" Yulan asks me.

"I think everyone is capable of evil and good, but no one should be capable of playing God."

"Playing God?"

"Deciding who should live and who should die. Bad things hap-pened in human history because evil humans tried to play God. Ever heard of Hitler?"

He nods slowly.

"No one should have that kind of power," I tell Yulan, "and no one should tell you what to believe. You just have to look at the big picture, look at every angle, and make a decision for yourself."

"But if Father is wrong, then...everything we've done..." he starts to cry again.

I pull him into a one-armed hug again, kissing him on the top of his head.

"I'm sorry about your husband," Yulan says after he's calmed down.

"Thank you."

"I think I know what I need to do," he says. He walks out of the kitchen but goes back for his sandwich. "I need to talk to Father and Alekai and come up with my own conclusion."

He leaves the kitchen, and I'm alone with Brave.

"I think that went well," I tell her. "What do you think?"

She twitches a little. I don't know what that means, but I hope it's something good.

***

I find Bonnie pacing in one of the hallways.

"Hey," he says and stops when he sees me. "You okay?"

"No," I tell him honestly. "You?"

He sighs. "I'm sorry about your husband."

"Thanks," I tell him. "I didn't think father would go that far."

"He wasn't eating."

"We both know that's not the case."

We're both silent for a while.

"So..." he says, "what are you going to do?"

"About what?" I ask.

"In general. Like, were you going to get something to eat, or going to your room, like, what are you planning on doing now?"

He's too casual. Too calm. Nothing like how Yulan was.

"Oh," I say.

Thankfully Brave starts to fidget a bit.

"I think Brave is hungry," I tell Bonnie. "I'm gonna go try to feed her."

"You want some company?" he asks me, grabbing Brave's little hand, but she can only wrap her hand around his comparatively giant fingers. "You really shouldn't be alone right now."

"I'm not alone," I tell him honestly. "I have her."

"Okay," he says. "He then kisses me on the forehead and starts pacing again as I walk away.

He wasn't eating? Does Bonnie really believe that?

When I turn the corner, I poke my head and look back at my brother. He's still pacing.

"Bonnie?" I ask him.

He stops and looks at me.

"You sure you're okay?" I need to talk to him, but Brave keeps fidgeting.

"I'm just worried about what Father's next steps are going to be," he tells me.

Ugh, I just can't get a read on this guy! Is he on my side or Father's side? I need to give him some time to decide.

I smile at my brother and say, "you'll know what to do when the time is right."

I then walk back to my room to feed my daughter, hoping my boys are being fed.

***

When I'm done feeding Brave and walk down the hallway, I find Balex coming out of his room. He has a bag on his back.

"You okay?" I ask him.

"No," he tells me. "I don't know how anyone is right now."

"I'm not," I tell him.

He sighs. "I know. Sorry about your husband. Gah! I can't keep doing this!"

"Doing what?" I ask.

"Justifying Father's actions and going along with it like I'm okay. Like I'm not fighting depression every second I'm around all this. Why can't we be a normal family with normal problems? Why do we have to be the ones to purify the multiverse? Why does it have to be purified at all? I was dreading that eventually some of us would snap and go against father, but how can I? He's my father, our father, and he's done nothing but love and support me. I can't choose between my family no matter how fucked up it is. I'm going to the kitchen to stock up on some food, then I'm leaving. I'd do the same if I were you."

"I can't leave," I tell him. "I still have these cuffs on that prevent me from doing so, but Balex-"

"My mind won't be changed," he says.

"I wasn't going to say that," I tell him. "Do you have a place to go?"

He shrugs. "My home dimension, nine, is controlled by our father, so I can't go there. I can't go to seven, for multiple reasons. Can't go to eight, for that will be no more soon...I'll figure it out."

"Be careful," I tell him.

I want to tell him to stay, to fight Father because it's the right thing to do, but he seems so dead set on running away. I follow him to the kitchen as he packs food in his bag.

"Balex..."

My brother pulls me and Brave in a light hug, then he kisses both of us on the cheek.

"Goodbye, little sister. Goodbye, little niece."

He then opens a portal, and he's gone.

Page 411

Chapter 4

Looking for my other brothers in the hallways, I wipe tears away while still holding Brave.

"What is wrong, daughter?"

I jump at the sound of my father's voice. You'd think I'd be over jump scares by now. I turn to face him. Is he seriously in his pajamas? Why are his hands behind his back? This can't be good.

"Nothing," I lie.

"I already told you that you can't lie to me, my child."

What should I say? I go with silence. My father sighs. "There's something I want to show you. It's about your dead magician friends."

Oh, shit! Who's dead?

"Yes?" I say, trying to remain calm.

He reveals the orb from behind his back.

"You seriously have a crystal ball?" I ask him. "Like, see the future kind?"

"I suppose if you're a teller, you can see the future with this. I use this to show people the past."

The past?

"Am I able to use it?"

"Only if you have a certain magic trick, but only Balex inherited that ability out of all my delightful children. He has fled, hasn't he? I know him well. Plus...I can feel it." He holds his chest solemnly.

The sound of my brother's name saddens me, but I'm also intrigued. What trick could he possibly be talking about? He waves one hand over the top of it. I see Emma, Magician John, and Frederick in the living room in the trailer. Why is he showing me this? I already know they're dead.

The window tells me it's nighttime. Emma's pacing around the room. Frederick says something to her from the window, but it's inaudible. Emma snaps something back to him, and John stands up from the couch.

They look so sad. They were probably worrying about us when we were trapped in Dimension Five. Emma storms outside crying, and her brothers follow her.

My father waves his hand again to show me what was going on outside the trailer. Next thing I know, Emma's head explodes, and Frederick and John's heads follow suit.

Two humans jump down from the roof. They're wearing the same clothes Mabel and the other John wore when they attacked us.

Salem agents.

"Why show me this?" I ask my father. "I already knew Salem killed them."

"Without warning or mercy. Do you see how cruel humans can be?"

"But one of your ancestors created Organization Salem. That's on us magicians, dad."

"But magicians didn't evolve it into this evil. I didn't create the other evils of humanity either."

I stare at him, unsure of what to say.

"Tell me, my child, why do you wish to protect this evil?"

"Not every human being is evil. I'm half human, am I half evil?"

"Your magician half purifies you wholly."

"No, that credit goes to the parents that raised me."

"They were not your parents."

"But they still treated me like their daughter."

"Even though the rest of their families hated you? For the simple fact that you didn't share blood with them."

Well, he got me there.

"I want a world full of love, safety and generosity. If we have humans and other evil beings there, they will ruin that."

"But isn't murder evil in itself?"

"Do you think it was evil when the Americans assassinated Sadam Hussein?"

"Well…"

"Killing someone evil to make the world a better place? Now imagine that on a much larger scale. Imagine all the dimensions free of evil for eternity. We can do so much good at such a small price. This world will be safe for your daughter and future generations of all beings."

I look down at Brave.

Is my father starting to make sense? I need to get my mind off this. I should continue talking to the others.

"I need some space."

Father touches my chest tenderly. "This wound will heal in time, my dear."

I turn away in tears and leave him as fast as I can.

***

I find Zigor and Sax in the living room.

They're playing with Sax's bearded dragon on the floor.

"Hey, Bec," Zigor says to me when he looks up and sees me.

"Hey, Bec," Sax says. "Sorry about your husband."

"Yeah, same," Zigor says.

I know they're all being sincere, but I wish they would just stop mentioning Darren. It hurts too much.

"Thanks," I tell them.

"How's she doing?" Zigor asks, motioning to Brave.

"She's good," I tell them.

Considering.

See what good we can do for the world. For your daughter.

I do want my children to grow up in a good world, but is this really the right way to go? Genocide can't be the answer, right? My poor children have no idea what's going on. They're so peaceful.

"So where do you think Alekai is?" Zigor asks.

The dragon climbs up Sax's arm and rests on his shoulder.

Dragon. Now I'm doing what my father does by calling the damn bearded dragon a dragon. How could I ever have considered he was right, even for a moment? Darren, I'm sorry. I know Father is wrong and I will stop him!

"I don't know, man," Sax says. "I just want to do something. I'm tired of waiting."

"What do you think you'll do once something happens?" I ask them.

"I don't know," Sax says. "Something."

"Why do you ask?" Zigor asks me.

Just then, the roof flashes purple.

"What does that mean?" I ask, remembering the red that flashed all those years ago.

"Family meeting," Zigor says. "Probably by the machine."

Uh oh!

"Come on," Zigor says, standing up.

Sax does the same. He then rubs Brave's stomach and gestures for me to follow. This is bad! Where is Trevor?

Page 414

***

We rush through the house, me looking for Trevor. When we arrive at the hallway near the machine, I spot him.

I try not to sigh with relief. He's about to walk towards us, but Gamma stops him and starts to talk to him. Trevor and I lock eyes for a fraction of a second. He doesn't seem worried, which relieves me for only a second.

Zigor and Sax stop when I stop. "You okay?" Zigor asks me.

I forgot to talk to Gamma!

"Yeah...I'm fine," I say, even though it's a flat out lie. Gamma pulls Trevor into a hug, then waves at us.

"What's he doing now?" Sax groans.

"Something Gammaish," Zigor says.

"Zigor! Sax! Bec!" Gamma shouts.

"I'll ask again. What's he doing?" Sax asks.

"I don't know. Do you trust him?" Zigor says.

They both think for a second.

"Run," Zigor and Sax say in unison, giggling down the halls.

They take off, and Gamma follows them.

"I just want to love my brothers!" Gamma shouts. He stops next to me for a quick second to wave hello, hugs me out of nowhere, then continues after them.

"Oh, no, you don't!" I hear Zigor scream from the end of the hall. They turn the corner. I smile at the interaction, but the emptiness I feel inside makes me unable to laugh at it.

Trevor comes up to me.

"Any luck?" I whisper after making sure no one is around to hear us.

"Yes," he tells me. "Met them at the trailer. Three of your friends are hiding here. Audrey, Raven, and JP. They're going to help us. Alekai is still with Deonna and your boys, keeping them hidden."

"What about Mabel and John?" I ask.

"The Salem humans, right?"

I nod.

"They're with Deonna."

"Good," I tell him. Then I tell him everything that I was doing and the conversations I had with our other brothers. He's sad to hear about Balex leaving, but happy to hear about Yulan. We stop talking and reach the machine room in silence.

This machine is larger than an elephant and has a shape that makes it look alive. Though I can't really tell what creature it looks like, something with many limbs and a wet metallic surface.

This massive alien machine seems too big to stop. But we've got to try!

When my eyes leave the machine, I notice that we aren't alone here. It's only our father and his kids in here, minus Alekai and Balex.

"She should be sleeping in her crib right now," Father tells me.

"She sleeps better with me," I lie. I'm not leaving her alone for a second.

Father looks around. "Has anyone heard from Alekai?"

Everyone says no, except for Trevor who remains silent.

"He's a full magician, so he'll be safe, but I still wanted him here," father says, almost hanging his head.

Full magicians are safe then. That doesn't relieve me too much, considering everything else that is happening.

"What about halfs?" I ask Father, glaring at him.

Father ruffles my hair. "You'll be safe, rest assured."

"What about my friends?"

"My children," Father says to us all, ignoring my question, "I am so happy to see you here today. Alekai could not make it today, and that breaks my heart, for he is our family. There is nothing more important than family, except for the good we are doing for everyone."

I try not to scoff. I think he knows that we're all talking about what happened. Is he trying to justify murder?

"You must remain loyal to your family, and your family will remain loyal to you, because without it, what do you really have? You have no one. You'll be another orphan, adrift in the cosmos. I know our cause is a noble one, and I will protect this cause and all my children. Does anyone know where Balex went?"

Everyone looks around. I search for him too, knowing I won't find him. As I'm looking, I see Audrey. She's on the beams on the ceiling. She turns visible for half a second, then she turns invisible again.

Raven, please be careful with Audrey!

Audrey, please guide Raven right, you know she's blind!

"He'll be safe from the machine, but if he's in Eight, that's a problem."

So halfs will die. This is worse than before.

"We'll find him," Sax says. "If we found Bec, we can find Alekai and Balex pretty easily."

"Father! Look out!" Gala screams and pushes him out of the way. Gala catches the fireball and throws it back to its original location at twice the speed. Audrey whines and falls to the floor, visible.

When I rush to help, Father grabs my shoulders and steers me away.

"Stay with daddy. Gala will be fine,"

"She's not the one I'm worried about!"

"You should also worry about her," he says, motioning to my daughter in my arms.

I look down at my precious baby, forgetting for a moment that I was supposed to be protecting her. Her brothers will need her.

I look back at my sisters. Audrey brashly stands as Gala is almost upon her. Audrey kicks her in the stomach, causing Gala to stumble a little bit. Audrey uses this opening to send her fist in Gala's face.

"Come on, Gala," Father says, "I know my daughter can handle a mere half-magician."

Gala smiles and kicks Audrey a few times, sending her stumbling back and eventually to the floor.

"That's my girl!" Father cheers, gripping me tighter as I struggle to break free.

Oh no! Oh no! Oh no!

Audrey is panting, struggling to stand back up. She rises to her knees and wipes blood from her nose. Gala laughs and approaches her. "What did you expect was going to happen?"

Father stands back and smiles.

"I still have strength in me," Audrey declares.

Audrey stands and swings a punch but misses. Then she kicks upward. Her foot collides with Gala's jaw, rattling her brain.

Audrey collects herself, but Gala kicks her, sending her stumbling back. Audrey doesn't fall but instead keeps up by firmly planting her feet in the floor.

"You got this, Gala!" Father says, cheering her on in his PJs.

Audrey sends three fireballs at Gala, but she dodges all of them. While Gala is laughing, Audrey kicks her enemy in the stomach, knocking the wind out of her. "Don't look down on us half-magicians, scaley."

Gala falls to her knees. Audrey releases a battle cry. She grabs hold of Gala's hair and twists her neck. A snapping sound is heard.

Gala!

My sister!

Wait, I care?

Gala soon falls limp and doesn't move. Audrey then throws a fireball at her, and she's quickly erupted in flames.

Page 417

Father and Bonnie are on her in an instant, patting her down and rolling her on the floor. The flames go out and it's a horrible sight. Her green skin has turned to charcoal black, and her hair is completely singed.

"Daughter?" Father whispers, tears filling his eyes. "Gala?"

Just then I blink, and Gala's body is back to normal, but she remains motionless on the floor.

What just happened? Father's face turns pale. His hands shake, and he starts to cry. He brings his shaking hands to his face and covers it.

"I'm sorry, daughter," he whispers to her. "I can't resurrect you."

Oh no! She is dead!

Audrey creates a fireball in her shaky hands. "She won't be the only casualty if you don't surrender."

Father lowers his hands and looks at Audrey, slowly standing up. He is on her in an instant, almost as if he teleported to her, not giving her even a fraction of a second to react. He breaks her hand, exploding the fireball and burning her arm.

Audrey stands up fully. Father is then behind her. Audrey tries to conjure a fireball with her working hand, but she doesn't get it out in time. My father is just too fast for her.

He grabs her by the throat and lifts her in the air. Audrey is wildly kicking her feet and struggling to get out of his grasp.

What should I do?

What should I do!?

"You killed my daughter," Father spits at her.

Audrey grips Father's face, burning the flesh on his cheek.

"Don't do it. Please, Father!" I scream.

It doesn't work.

I hold up an arm to try and separate them with telekinesis, forgetting my cuffs, but the second I do that, Father snaps Audrey's neck and she falls limp to the floor.

Chapter 5

I fall to my knees.
My best friend.
No!
I look at Gala's body, then look again at Audrey's. How many sisters is the universe going to make me lose?
Father reverses time on the wound Audrey inflicted on his face. Then he turns his gaze to me. Tears well up in his eyes, but his gaze alone is enough to murder.
Uh oh.
"You see how the human mind can cause such unnecessary violence? Your sister is dead because of them! This is the reason all evil must be purged from existence!"
"Audrey!" Raven screams, then I hear a loud thud. "Ow. Audrey!" She turns visible. She's frantically moving around though, trying to make sense of her surroundings. She grabs one of her throwing stars.
Where are you possibly going to throw that?
"Audrey! Answer me!" Raven shouts.
Father looks at Raven but with a much darker gaze than the one he just gave me.
Raven turns to Father and throws a star in his direction, but he simply catches it with his bare hand. He's not even bleeding. Not even a little!
"Audrey!" Raven screams again.
"Your Audrey is dead, just like you will be soon," Father spits out at her.
"No! Audrey! Tell me he's lying!" Raven shouts.
"He's not, Ray," I tell her.
"No!"

I look around at my brothers. They're all crying, putting their hands up ready to strike. They look uneasily at each other - probably not sure what to do. The only one not doing that is Trevor. He grabs me by the shoulders, trying to steer me and Brave away.

"No!" our father yells at them. "She's mine!"

Most of my brothers sigh with relief.

Father pulls out a knife and charges Raven. He's about to strike her head, but JP appears out of nowhere and blocks the blow with his left arm.

What looks like a gallon of blood comes out from where the knife struck and stain JP's grey jacket sleeve red. Father is taken back for a split second, but JP takes advantage of that second and kicks him back. Father easily regains his footing. JP tries to put up his fists, but his left arm drops down and he winces.

Father is approaching JP leisurely now, knowing he has JP and Raven right where he wants them. JP grabs one of Raven's stars with his right hand and throws it, landing it in the center of my father's chest.

My father stumbles back. Is he okay? Wait, why do I still care about this monster?

The next thing I know, the star flies back into JP's hand, and my father is standing upright. JP is about to throw it but looks confused.

"Why the surprised look? What, did you really think my children are the only ones with magic?" he asks JP with a sly smile.

JP drops the star, grabs Raven's hand, and they make a break for it.

"The machine!" Raven shouts.

"Later!" JP tells her.

"I got them, Father!" Sax yells, handing his dragon to Zigor, and runs after them.

"Brother!" Zigor calls out to him.

"No, son!" Father shouts after him. "Let me handle them!"

He follows my brother at top speed. I lock eyes with Trevor, and we both run after them.

Please no.

Please no.

Please no!

I don't want anyone else to die!

Not my brothers, not JP, not Raven, not my children, not Deonna, nobody else! Only him. He's the cause of this. Sax is almost upon them.

No!

Raven grabs her knife on her belt, then trips and knocks JP down with her. Sax is hovering over them. Raven jabs her knife forward repeatedly, then starts swinging it.

Sax doesn't even move, for the knife never goes near him.

"This is for my sister," Sax says, his scales sharpening, pointing his arms right at Raven.

JP stands up and kicks Sax back – completely ineffectively. Father grabs Sax and throws him to the side. "I told you I will handle them, son."

Raven's crawling, trying to...what is she trying to do? My father throws punches and kicks at JP so fast I can barely see them fly through the air. What should I do?

"Guys, stop fighting!" I shout at them.

JP then falls to his knees.

"JP!" Raven shouts and throws the knife to him.

"Raven, no!" I shout.

Raven misses, and it hits Sax right in his stomach.

"Sax!" Trevor and I scream.

Father doesn't notice Sax's wound. He grabs JP, lifts him and presses him against the wall. Sax coughs up blood. He lifts a hand to wipe his mouth, but then it falls limp to his side. He then removes the knife from his abdomen.

Oh no! That's even worse! Sax then falls to the floor and is motionless.

"Sax?" Trevor asks, more tears filling his eyes.

No answer.

JP and I lock eyes.

My father turns around, sees Sax, and drops JP.

"Son!" my father rushes to him.

Something inside me wants to hate JP and Raven, but I know it's not their fault. It's my father's fault. Everything is his fault!

I mouth to JP for him to hide. He looks at Trevor, then at Sax's body. JP grabs Raven, and the two of them turn invisible. "You need to go," Trevor whispers to me. "Who knows what father will do to you."

I hear footsteps approaching as Trevor reaches for the key. He's fiddling around inside his pockets for it.

"Hurry up," I tell him.

His eyes grow wide. "I can't find the key!"

"What do you mean you can't find it?"

I look down at Brave, who has slept through this whole ordeal. I put my ear on her chest to make sure she's still breathing.

She is.

Page 421

"Sax?" Zigor whispers.

"Zigor," Trevor says, more tears filling up his eyes.

"Sax," Zigor says louder. He kneels next to his fallen brother and bawls for a few seconds. The bearded dragon crawls off Zigor's shoulder and down his arm.

I never did learn that lizard's name.

He looks down at the bearded dragon, who is rubbing his nose on his dead owner.

Zigor then stands, looks at me, looks at Trevor, and turns around.

"I'm sorry, bro," Trevor says with tears in his eyes. "There was nothing we could do! They just…"

"Father said he would protect us," Zigor spits out. "All our lives, he's been telling us that. Now, look at what happened."

Zigor then spins his arms, and a portal opens. He walks through it, and he's gone.

Trevor falls to his knees. "Gala and Sax are dead, and now Balex and Zigor are never coming back."

I start to cry. "We can't let this go on!"

Both sides of my family are fighting and killing each other. After this whole ordeal, I don't think they'll ever work together to take down my father. What are we going to do?

"Sax!" Bonnie shouts behind us. "Trevor? Bec? What happened?"

Trevor quickly stands up, grabs my shoulders, and we make a break for it.

***

We continue running through the house, although we have no idea where we're running to.

Just then, we turn a corner and bump into Yulan. "Follow me," he tells us.

He puts his hand on the wall next and a secret passage opens up big enough for us to crawl through.

"Come on," he whispers and goes through first.

Trevor and I lock eyes for a moment. We both nod. I hand him Brave and go through first. It wasn't a far crawl, so I reach my hands through the opening to grab her so he can crawl through.

I gasp at the sight. It's, for one thing, a lot larger than I expected a hole in the wall to be. Also, I didn't expect it to be filled with pillows and blankets formed into a fort that fills the room.

"Where'd you have time to build this, little brother?" Trevor asks Yulan.

"I've built it over the years," he tells us. "Mostly to hide from Gamma. Gala once took me to my mom's home dimension, Four. Father was saving it for last on the account of how dangerous it is, so I got inspired to build something the complete opposite."

"Why's it so dangerous?" I ask.

"Living ground, and strong-willed people," Yulan says.

"Strong-willed," I say, "just like you."

He smiles at me.

"How'd you build this without Father noticing?" Trevor asks.

"I opened the portal myself," Yulan says.

"So, this is another dimension?" I ask.

"No, it's an extension of my room. Father usually doesn't come in without knocking, so I hide everything from him."

"Cool," Trevor says.

Yulan then looks at him and raises an eyebrow. "So, you're not on the father train anymore?"

"Are you?" Trevor asks him.

Yulan sighs. "You can't do bad things with good intentions to justify anything. Doing bad things still makes you bad." Tears start to fill up in his eyes. "It corrupts you to the core."

Trevor pulls Yulan into a hug.

"This has to stop," Yulan says, using Trevor's shirt to wipe his eyes. He then blows his nose and wipes it with a clean part of Trevor's shirt.

Trevor looks disgusted but doesn't say anything.

"Gala and Sax are dead. Balex and Alekai, who knows where they are. Our family is falling apart, this needs to end," Yulan says. "He said he would protect us, but everything and everyone is dying."

"I agree," I tell him. "But our father will never stop."

Trevor looks at me and smiles. "Then we'll just have to make sure Father can never move forward with his plans ever again."

"I think I know what we need to do," Yulan tells us, letting go of Trevor "but we have to wait till nightfall."

We spend the rest of the day talking about potential plans for Father. We also tell stories about Sax and Gala. I don't have that many stories with them, considering I haven't been with them very long. I cry along with my brother. I really did love my brother Sax. He didn't deserve what happened to him.

I guess Gala was also sweet in her own way. She was the first one to offer me condolences about Darren, and she was with me as a sister when I was first taken here. A demented sister, but still a sister. I'm gonna miss her too.

And now they're gone.

Forever.

And so is my Darren.

Audrey too. My best friend. She threw fiery rocks at me while I was in training, but I still loved her to death.

Then there's Josh. An awkward friend, but still a friend.

Now I know how my old childhood best friend feels. I hope Human John is coping okay. He and I can cope together when this is all over.

Emma is gone too. Frederick and Magician John too. Ash, Tom, Jake, the mother I knew, the father I grew up with who always wore something tacky, my grandparents, my cousins, my aunts, my uncles.

My biological mother too.

No more.

The next death is my father.

My biological father.

That peaceful, vegan, all-life-is-sacred, Jewish girl is gone.

She died with Darren.

All that's left is a warrior with a mission.

Chapter 6

We leave the pillow fort at nighttime but soon find out that not everyone is asleep. We find Gamma standing on the opposite wall from where the door is.

"How long have you known?" Yulan asks with a little shake in his voice.

"About your fort, for years," Gamma says. "You made it obvious that you were building it when you kept asking Father for pillows and blankets. About the three of you plotting against father, I found out this afternoon when Bec's friends killed our brother and sister. You two run off and I figured this would be your go to spot. Speaking of, sorry about your husband kicking the bucket. None of us knew about him."

"And you didn't say anything to Father?" I ask.

"Why would I? It's his secret fort," says Gamma sarcastically.

"Gamma," Yulan nearly snaps.

"Relax," Gamma says, "I'm not telling Father anything."

"Where is he now?" I ask.

"Outside crying," Gamma says. "He had a mini funeral for Gala and Sax. He wanted to be alone and hasn't come back inside since."

"How do we know you're not lying?" Trevor asks him.

"To show I mean my word, I brought a peace offering,"

He takes out the key to my cuffs.

I look at Trevor and his face goes pale. "So, that's where that went."

"Father trusted you with the key, and I thought you wouldn't free her, so I took it to free her later," Gamma continues. "Little did I know what was really up. You shouldn't be locked here against your will, and neither should we."

He approaches me and uses the keys to remove my cuffs on my wrist. I wiggle my wrists as much as I can holding Brave. It feels good to have those fuckers off. I can also feel my magic returning to me.

"Also, there's something I need to show you guys," Gamma says.

"What is it?" Yulan asks.

"Father's secret library."

***

"Why bother with a secret library?" I ask rhetorically as I look around the vast library that has bookshelves filled with books that reach the ceiling. It has the same decor as the living room.

Yuck.

"Who knows," Gamma says, "but get this, I discovered this place almost three years ago and I found books on ancient magician history."

"History books?" Trevor asks with a smile.

"What's so fascinating about history books?" Yulan says.

"For a young mind like yours, probably nothing," Gamma tells him. "However, when you don't know your history…"

"You're doomed to repeat it," I finish.

"Exactly," Gamma smiles. He then goes to the wall next to the secret door we came in through and crouches down to the bottom shelf. He pulls out a red book with a globe containing a supercontinent on it.

"Dimension Five has its own Pangea?" I ask surprised.

"What?" my brothers all ask.

"Never mind," I say. "What does this book say?"

"It talks about the history of magicians, along with a ruling family," Gamma explains.

"I thought magician kind didn't have leaders?" I ask.

"It did a long time ago. This book stops right before papa Hercules rose," Gamma explains.

"So, was he a dictator that took over?" Trevor asks.

"No, that's the thing," Gamma says, "mama Magara was. She got rid of all the evidence of the royal family and erased everyone's memory of them."

"How do you know this?" Yulan asks.

"I read it in her diary," Gama says.

"She kept a diary?"

"Yeah, she was quite a strange woman. You have all these secrets, yet you write them down for…"

"Gamma," I interrupt.

Page 426

"Sorry," Gamma says. "Everything in her diary lines up perfectly with the recent history in this book," he holds up the red book. "Apparently, they were a wonderful ruling family that brought real peace to magicians."

He runs to the couch, and we follow him. Gamma opens the book to the end and turns a few pages until it shows a picture of a stereotypical royal family, only they all have red eyes.

"Red eyes," I whisper.

I remember a young magician woman who looked human back in Salem.

***

"I like your eyes," I said.

"Thanks," she told me. "Only family members of mine have them though."

"A magician family with an eye color all to themselves? That actually sounds cool!"

"Yeah, we used to wear sunglasses all the time. Now we don't have to."

"Nice! Does it mean anything?"

***

My eyes widen.

"Bec?" Trevor asks me.

"I think I know the royal family," I tell my brothers.

"Really?" Trevor asks, amazed.

"Yeah, there was this girl, er, a young woman who recently joined Salem who had red eyes just like the royal family!"

"What was her name?"

"Never got it!"

"That is fantastic," Gamma says sarcastically.

"No no no! This is good!" I say. I then force myself to take a deep breath. "This means I know where to find her. Her family can take the throne and overthrow our father."

"Father's not a king though," Yulan says.

"You know what I mean," I say. "What if we can show them this and convince them to take power again. If father's followers find out about this-"

"Then his followers might be reluctant to follow him," Trevor finishes for me.

Page 427

"Father is probably going to move forward with his plans when he's back, so whatever you're planning needs to go into action soon," Gamma says.

I've never seen Gamma so serious before. I've never seen him serious period. I have to say, I like this side of him.

"If that's the case, I need to get Brave out of here," I say. "Then come back and destroy the machine."

"Talk to this girl," Trevor says.

"Along with Alekai," Gamma adds.

"Alekai?" I ask. Then I remember. "Alekai has one red eye!"

"Father targeted his mother for that sole purpose," Gamma tells us. "To have a kid in the royal line, so he can better control everything."

"How do you know that?" I ask.

"I heard him tell Gala one time I hid here," Gamma tells us.

"That's so sad," I say. "Okay, we show this to Alekai as well. He's most likely related to the Salem girl. I'll get John and Mabel to help us find her. I mean, red eyes are not common. How hard can it be to pinpoint a girl with red eyes?"

"Then we have to deal with Father and his followers," Yulan adds.

"Deal with Father?" Gamma asks. "You mean like..." he then pretends to tie a noose with an imaginary rope, make a hole, put it around his neck, and pulls it back while making a choking sound.

"We don't know yet," Yulan admits.

"Well, we can't kill him, but maybe one of them can," Gamma says motioning to the corner.

Just then JP and Raven come into view. They are holding hands on the verge of breaking down. JP runs up to me and pulls me into a hug. I hug him back. He buries his face in my shoulder and shudders. I can feel my shoulder getting wet.

"She's really gone," JP whispers.

I hug him back with one arm as tears roll down my face too.

"Weird to see him crying," Gamma says. "He tried to kill me earlier when I offered to help them."

"Why shouldn't he?" Raven asks. "Look at what you and your father have done."

JP glares at Gamma. "If I wasn't so weak, I'd kill you monsters."

"Monsters? Excuse me. When did I ever kill anyone? You're the ones that break into our home to kill us!"

I grab JPs hand. "No more fighting...please."

He nods solemnly. "Why are you with these monsters? Did they brainwash you?"

"Gamma is the one who freed me. And Trevor has been against Father long before we were."

"Do you trust them?"

I look at Gamma and feel doubt welling up in my stomach.

"At the very least, Gamma is honest" I say, though partly doubting myself.

Gamma turns to me with shimmering eyes. "You're the first person to ever say that."

"Stay away from her, demon," says JP with a glare.

I stand between them. "We don't have time for this! Father is going to use his machine to wipe out all humans and half mages in Eight. He could find us at any moment. We need to get the fuck over our grudges and plan our next move!"

Everyone falls silent.

"Maybe we should continue this conversation in the fort," Trevor says.

Raven grabs my hand. "We're only going so we can keep you safe from these demons."

We sneak back to the fort with the book and go back through the hole in the wall one by one with Yulan first, and Trevor last.

"Woah!" Gamma says when he sees it.

"The levels of irony are really high right now," Yulan says.

"Oo, irony," Gamma smiles, returning to his Gamma self. "How so?"

"I'm inviting you into the place I built to hide from you," Yulan tells him.

"That hurts, baby brother."

"So, what are we going to do?" Raven asks, grinding her teeth.

"Trevor and I were talking earlier about what to do," I say. "I'll make it brief. The machine needs to be destroyed, our father needs to be taken down, and his followers must be disbanded or dealt with. The kifomen cannot be unleashed on Eight, they must stay here in Five. I need to take Brave to Deonna and help the true royal family to rise again."

"Destroying the machine should be relatively easy, as well as getting your daughter out of here. I'm not sure how hard or easy talking to the royal family will be," Trevor says. "But I do know the hard parts are going to be Father and his armies."

"Why do we need to handle the followers?" Yulan asks.

"To make sure they don't rise up again with a new leader and start this all over again," Trevor says.

"If I'm going to fight, I need to know my kids are safe," I say.

Page 429

"Kids?" Yulan and Gamma ask.

Oops.

"Uh, I meant my child..." I say. "So, yeah, I need to take Brave to Deonna, and talk to the others."

I really hope that I just didn't raise any alarms. Should I trust them with knowing I had triplets, or should I keep this to myself. If I'm going to work with them, I need to show them that I trust them.

"The truth is, I had triplets. My boys are incognito."

"Wow," Gamma says. "No wonder you were so big."

"Hey!"

"You should do that now," Trevor says, as he opens a portal.

I take the book. "I'm going to need this."

I go through the portal and find myself on the inside of the trailer. Deonna and Alekai are in a fighting stance but relax when they see it's me.

"You're okay?" Deonna asks me.

She doesn't know. Neither does Alekai.

Oh no! I can't do this! How do I tell them that their loved ones are dead? I turn around and see that the portal is still open, wind blowing hair into my face.

"I can't stay," I say truthfully and hand Brave to Deonna after kissing her forehead and telling her I love her. I walk over to my sleeping boys and kiss their foreheads. "I love you," I whisper to them.

"Bec?" Alekai asks.

An idea starts to form in my head. I don't like it, it involves me not telling anyone, but it seems to be the only way.

"You guys have to get out of here," I tell them. "Get out of the trailer park, maybe out of Pennsylvania. Deonna, go back to your place in New York. Alekai, you have to find this girl in Salem." I hand him the history book. "Look for the true royal family."

"The what?" Alekai asks.

"The book will explain," I say. "We have to show it to her, maybe true peace can be achieved again. There was once a royal family of magicians all with red eyes. These people might be your family, and they might be able to help depower our father. Let's have John and Mabel help. If they don't know, maybe Rainsford does."

Alekai flips to the table of contents and opens the book and reads about the royal family.

"She works for Salem in Boston," I tell Alekai. "We have to find her."

"This just might work," Alekai says. Then he looks at me. "I have an idea on how to disband the followers if this doesn't get all of them."

Page 430

He whispers a plan to me.

"That's... actually smart, big brother," I tell him. "I can easily incorporate it into my plan."

"Your plan? Bec?" Deonna asks.

I say nothing.

"Just what are you planning?"

"Something dangerous. I don't want anyone else to get killed," I say.

"Anyone else?" they both gasp.

"Who's dead?" Alekai asks.

I start to cry and shake my head.

"Bec" Deonna says, "you must tell us. Even if it's hard, you must tell us. We can take it."

"It'll be worse if you don't say anything," Alekai tells me.

I gulp and look at Alekai. "Gala and Sax are gone."

Alekai covers his mouth and gasps.

I look at Deonna. "Audrey..."

Deonna makes a small squeak and cries.

"... and Darren."

"No!" Deonna shouts.

"I'm sorry," I say, breaking out into tears.

Deonna starts crying. "How?"

"It was so sudden," I say, not wanting to tell them how they died, afraid it might start a fight between Deonna and Alekai. Deonna wipes her face. I walk closer to her, and we hug.

"Darren was always there for me," she whispers, "and I couldn't be there for him."

Alekai wraps his arms around Deonna and I and rests his head on mine.

"Gala was crazy, but she was still my sister," he tells us. "Our sister. I loved her, Sax too. He was my sweet little brother. He didn't deserve this."

"We can't let any more of our family members die," Deonna says. "I'm coming with you."

"If you do, my and Darren's babies will be at risk. They need both of you here to watch over them."

"She looks upset at this, but she wipes her eyes, knowing I'm right.

"I... must go," I say. "I'm sorry."

Each step I take toward the portal sends surges of guilt and makes me worry if I'll ever see them again.

Page 431

Chapter 7

We all sneak over to the machine room. Before we enter though, I talk to Gamma about a change in the plan I'm making.

"You want me to do what?" he asks me.

"Don't show father that you're going against him," I tell him. "Make it seem like you still believe in him."

"Why?"

"Because, when Trevor takes JP and Raven to New York, you're going to tell Father that you followed me to the treehouse in Pennsylvania. You know of it?"

"Yeah, we followed you there once, but what are you going to do?" he asks me, almost scared.

"If I tell you, you guys will try and stop me."

"Okay... so, should I just stop you now without knowing?"

"Stop me and everyone will die. I'll tell Trevor that Deonna and Alekai are in New York. JP will know where to go once they're there."

"So, I'm not going to help you guys destroy the machine?"

"No," I say, pulling him into a hug. "I'm so sorry, big brother, but I need you for this."

He sighs and hugs me back. "Okay."

We let go of each other.

He smiles at me and then leaves.

"Where's he going?" Trevor asks me, coming up from behind.

"He has an important mission," I say, hoping that Gamma really is on our side and not just pretending to be. "When the machine is down, take the others to New York City."

"Why?"

"Because that's where everyone is meeting up. JP will know where to go. To Deonna's place."

"Meeting up? Are you going somewhere?"

"Yes."

"What are you gonna do?"

"Protect humanity, and everyone else."

Trevor smiles at me, then we lock hands and shake.

"Just be careful," he tells me.

"You too," I tell him.

***

Since when did Father have guards protecting the machine? There are about ten of them surrounding the two entrances, five on each side. They don't all look human though, like his other follower I saw earlier. Donna! The hat shop! That's where I know her from!

Focus. Some look like fish, some have webbed feet, and some look like lizards.

"Trevor, and I will take one side. JP, Raven, and Yulan can take the other entrance."

They nod and head off.

Okay, two webbed guys, a lizard lady, and two humans. Should be no problem, right?

Trevor jumps into action, not even hesitating to punch one of the webbed guys.

Dude! We could have come up with a plan!

The two human-magician looking ones and the lizard lady charge at me.

I guess the plan is no plan. I jump and kick the lizard lady in the nose. She stumbles back but stays on her feet. Man, I'm losing my edge. I slow down time and jab the side of her neck. I then turn and face the other two. I punch them repeatedly in their faces until they go down.

Time returns to normal, and the lizard lady grabs me by the neck. Before she can do anything, she falls.

I turn around and look at Trevor in a karate stance. His two guys are down as well.

"Thanks," I tell him.

"No problem."

We walk a little further, but then Trevor stops me and points to the ceiling. There are little boxes there everywhere. Cameras? No, there's a little faint, thin, red line emerging from it to the floor.

Really, dad! Lasers?

I try to use my telekinesis to break the lasers, but nothing happens.

Page 433

"What are these things?" I ask Trevor.

"They're father's fire catching lasers that are indestructible," he tells me.

"Well, this is great, how are we supposed to disable them?"

"We don't. We just can't touch them."

"And we can't move the lasers with telekinesis?"

"It's light, so no we cannot."

"Wonderful!"

Trevor goes first, but I stop him.

"Wait, let me do something first before you jump into action again," I tell him.

"Sorry, sis, it's just that we barely have any time."

"I know, but look," I say as I take out some of the light to make the room darker, revealing the lasers to our eyes.

"Smart," he says and smiles at me.

I tie my hair into a bun by twisting and tucking it. I don't have a hair tie, so this is the best I got.

Trevor goes first. He steps over the first laser and ducks under the second. I copy him.

As we maneuver our way through, my hair comes undone in five minutes and almost touches a laser. I have a hand on the floor, and a hand in the air. I use my hand that's in the air to carefully avoid a laser and put my hair in my mouth.

In about fifteen minutes, we make our way to the end. When we walk into the machine room, JP, Raven, and Yulan are already inside, studying the machine.

"It's making some noise it didn't make before," Raven says.

We all stop and listen closely. It's whirling and humming.

"It's on!" Trevor shouts.

"Shit!" I shout.

"So how do we destroy it?" JP asks, panicking.

"You don't," a deep voice says, coming up from the front shadow of the machine.

"Now's not the time, Bonnie," Yulan says. "This has to stop. This is killing people."

"Evil never stops," Bonnie says, drawing a knife. "It killed our brother and sister."

"And it'll kill more if we don't stop this," Trevor says.

"Oh," Bonnie says, "I will." He holds his arms forward, knife hovering next to his head.

"Bonnie, please," I say, "you're our brother, we don't wanna fight you!"

"I don't want to fight you guys either," he says crying, "but I'm apparently the only one who's doing what needs to be done. Besides, they killed our brother and sister, and you guys are working with them."

"They're just trying to bring true peace," Yulan tells him.

Bonnie looks down for a few seconds, then back up at us. We are sent flying back by his telekinesis. I hit my head on the back wall, and my vision goes blurry for a moment. As I heal my head, I see JP blow a strong wind at Bonnie. Bonnie remains in place.

Raven throws her stars or tries to, but she misses and sends them flying to the sidewall. The few that do go near Bonnie, thanks to JP's wind, he deflects them like nothing, sending them to the ground.

JP stops the wind.

Raven then grunts and charges into Bonnie.

"You killed Nawa and Gomen!" she yells at him, thrashing her hands around with her stars in them. She misses every time as Bonnie dodges her without a struggle.

This must stop. I look around for something, anything!

Yulan is crying while clutching his knife, probably unsure of what to do.

Trevor is already at the machine holding a wrench, trying to take off the bolts.

That'll take forever, Trev! We need an easier way.

I shoot electricity at the machine, but it does nothing.

"Turn off you shit!" I shout at it.

Bonnie sees what Trevor and I are doing and leaves Raven, but JP slams into him and almost knocks him over. Bonnie goes into JP's shadow. I try to use misdirection to form another shadow, but Bonnie goes into Trevor's shadow and pushes him away with telekinesis.

Trevor kicks Bonnie, but Bonnie doesn't even budge. He picks Trevor up and throws him.

Bonnie is then at his side. He stands over Trevor, breathing heavily, eyes darting around, probably unsure of what to do. Bonnie then grabs his knife from the air.

"Is this still for the cause, brother?" Trevor asks Bonnie.

Bonnie's arms then start to shake. He looks around, then our eyes meet.

"What feels right to you?" I ask him.

He shakes his head and starts to cry again. Raven takes out a throwing star. I hold out my arms, hold my breath, and slowly remove the oxygen from the room. Slowly, everyone in the room is going on their hands and knees, struggling to breathe. When the fighting is done, I return it.

"Does anyone want to be responsible for more of our family member's deaths?" I ask.

Everyone hangs their heads. Bonnie does as well. "No." He stands up and holds out his hand and helps Trevor to his feet. I signal to Yulan, and we both walk over to our brothers.

"Does this feel like the right thing to do?" I ask Bonnie.

He shakes his head. JP and Raven shift uncomfortably, not sure what to do. JP starts to open his mouth, but I signal for him to not say anything. He closes his mouth and grabs Raven's hand.

"Doing bad things for a good reason is still bad," Yulan says. "Everything isn't black and white, there's also grey."

Bonnie sighs. "I always thought by ridding the world of evil, we'd be doing it a favor. Now..." he shakes his head. "Now I'm attacking my siblings... Am I becoming evil?"

"Of course, you're not, Bon," Trevor tells him.

"But if our father doesn't stop, we'll lose more family," I tell him.

"But we can't lose father, too," Bonnie says. "He's loved us and-"

"Lied to us," Trevor says. "He also killed all of our moms and Darren because he wanted to have control over us."

Bonnie looks at the machine. "I don't know what to do."

"Remember how Alekai was the only one who grew up with his mom?" I ask.

Bonnie nods.

"She knew father was mad, and all our mothers would have raised us differently if they were allowed to. That's why he killed them all. So, we'd follow him."

"My head was telling me something similar when your husband died," Bonnie says. "But I ignored it, because he's our father."

"What's your head telling you now?" Trevor asks.

He thinks for a moment, then jumps inside the shadow of the machine. In about a minute, the whole thing stops humming and is torn apart and laying on the ground.

"How'd you do that?" I ask him.

"Jump into the shadow and take it apart from the inside? It was not hard," Bonnie says with a shrug.

"We need to get rid of the pieces before Father comes back and rebuilds it," Trevor says.

"Where do we put them?" JP asks. "It's not like we can just throw them in the trash or bury them in the backyard."

Yulan extends his hands outward, and a light wind starts to blow, opening up several portals.

"We just have to throw the pieces in," Yulan says.

Page 436

"Great idea," Trevor says.

"You guys do that. Bec, you come with me," Bonnie says.

"Why?" I ask, a little skeptical.

"I'll show you how to do a trick," Bonnie tells me. "Your misdirection sucks. You're going to need help."

Chapter 8

Bonnie shows me misdirection in the pillow fort for over an hour while the others scatter the machine pieces across all the other dimensions. Bonnie was a little harsh with training, or maybe it's just that I don't understand it and his voice makes everything sound that way.

I focus on the pillow as hard as I can, but it just wiggles.

"I still don't get it," I say. "I never have."

"Focus on both places at once," he tells me.

"Both?"

"Yes."

"Not on moving it?"

"That would be telekinesis," he says.

No wonder I've never gotten it before.

I close my eyes and do as he say, but nothing seems to happen.

"Just try it one more time," he tells me. "You're very close."

"I am?"

"Yes."

I don't feel like I'm close, but okay.

Before I could try again, Raven, JP, Yulan, Trevor, and Gamma come into the pillow fort, huffing, and puffing.

"Gamma's in on this too?" Bonnie asks.

"We finished right as father started coming inside," Trevor explains. "We had to run and hide."

"Did he see any of you?" I ask.

"No," Yulan says, "but we saw him. He's a mess."

"A mess that is now twice as dangerous," Gamma adds. "He's going to the kifomen pen."

"You okay, Bec?" Trevor asks me.

"Yeah," I lie. "I can't get misdirection though."

"You look exhausted," JP says.

"Well, she did give birth not too long ago," Raven says. "Did you even sleep? Like, at all?"

"No," I admit. "I never had time to."

"We all need to rest," Trevor says, yawning. "We've all been up for a while. If we don't want to lose anyone else, we need to rest."

Everyone looks down at their hands.

"I'm down," Yulan says after a minute, grabbing a pillow from the floor.

"No," I say. "We can't. Not while Father is still..."

"Still what?" Bonnie asks.

I don't finish that sentence.

"If we sleep now, who knows what'll happen," Raven says.

"If we don't, who knows what'll happen," Trevor says.

"Half of us take first watch while everyone else sleeps for an hour," JP says. "Then we switch."

"Sounds good," Yulan says, falling on his pillow and knocking out.

"Bec, Trevor, and Gamma, you guys sleep too," Bonnie says. "The three of us will take the first watch."

"This should be interesting," Raven mutters.

"Raven," I say, "can I trust you to not attack my brothers? They're on our side and know we have to end all this."

She sighs. "On my honor."

I look at Bonnie.

"I know," he says. "I won't attack you guys anymore."

"Doesn't mean we have to like each other," Raven adds.

I sigh and look at Trevor, who just shrugs his shoulders.

I look at JP.

"I won't fight them, but I'm not going to like it. We need to succeed, for Audrey," he says resolutely.

I don't want to sleep, but I haven't slept since before giving birth. I am completely exhausted.

Without another word, I grab two pillows and go to sleep.

***

I'm laying in my bed back in Boston, although I'm not alone. My sweet Darren is with me. He wraps his arms around me and pulls me closer to him and I return the embracement. I know this is a dream, but I can practically feel his touch and smell him this close to me.

"Hey, Bec," he whispers.

"Oh, Darren, I'm so sorry," I cry. "I couldn't save you! Our little children will never know who their father is."

Page 439

"You mustn't blame yourself," he tells me and kisses my mouth gently. I can feel and taste his kiss. "And it's okay. Even though the triplets won't know me, they'll still have you. They can know me through you."

"If I live long enough," I say.

He sighs. "Just don't do anything stupid until we can see each other again."

"I can't promise that," I tell him.

"What are you planning?"

"I can't tell you," I say.

"You've always been the stubborn one. I love you."

"I love you too." I go to kiss him, but the next thing I know, he's gone and I'm in the woods.

"You've come a long way from Miami," I hear a voice behind me. I turn around and see Audrey, holding the head of a deer, just like when we first met.

"Audrey, I'm-" I say, but she interrupts me.

"Take this bastard down," she tells me with a smile. "I will!" I say, returning her smile.

Without a warning, I'm in my room. Not my room that my father made for me, the old room that I shared with my brother Jake.

"Looks like middle school turned out to be the least of your worries," my brother Jake says, materializing in front of me.

If only that weren't the case, they'd all still be alive.

"But hey, you finally met your biological family. Too bad your brothers aren't as cool though."

I laugh a little at that.

"I'll avenge you guys," I tell him.

"Don't do this out of vengeance but do this out of love for everyone you lost, and for your love of humanity and all life."

"I'll do it out of both."

Jake smiles at me. "So much more mature you are but still the same old Bec." He approaches me and kisses me on the forehead. "Now, wake up. Your other families need you. Now."

***

I wake up with tears in my eyes, although it isn't Raven or JP or Bonnie waking me up. It's Trevor.

"What happened?" I ask, looking at Raven. "Why are they just waking up instead of waking me up?"

Page 440

"You wouldn't wake up," he tells me. "You were that exhausted, so we let you sleep. You're okay?"

Does Darren really know about the triplets? Is Audrey not mad at me? Does Jake know everything I've been up to, or was that my subconscious talking to me?

Did I really see them, or is my mental state just that fucked up right now?

"I still feel sleepy," I admit, "but it'll be fine."

Gamma comes in huffing and puffing, with a pale face.

"What happened?" Trevor asks him.

"Not good," he tells us. "The kifomen are already in Eight."

Chapter 9

"How do we prevent the kifomen from mass killing and luring Father?" Trevor asks.

"No idea," Gamma admits.

"I'll distract Father," I say, giving Gamma a look.

"Now?" Gamma asks me.

I nod, not sure if I'm ready.

"Okay," Gamma says, rubbing his hands together.

Trevor looks back and forth between me and Gamma. "What's happening here?"

***

I leave Gamma and Trevor and meet with JP and Raven.

"What is the plan?" JP asks me.

"There's something I've got to take care of," I tell him and Raven. "Go meet Deonna after you evacuate Eagle Lake. Bonnie, Trevor, and Yulan will handle the kifomen. Alekai is taking care of the royal family. John and Mabel are dispatching Salem to help my brothers."

"But we can't just leave you alone," JP says.

"Everything will be as it should be," I tell them.

"Are you sure?" Raven asks.

"Positive," I say. "Evacuate Eagle Lake, then meet me at Deonna's. Make sure my triplets are safe before my father realizes what we're doing."

Then I open a portal for them.

"But, Bec-" JP starts, but I use my telekinesis to push them through and close it right away. I don't hesitate. I've got a date with my father, and it's not going to be at a school dance. But first, I need to check on something.

I go with Mabel, Alekai, and John to see Rainsford. It wasn't hard for her to find someone with red eyes, so it only took us a few hours. She joined Salem shortly after it became a charity organization.

Deonna is with my triplets in the other room, while Alekai meets his cousin. Salem is a fortress; my babies should be fine.

Right?

Kaliyah sits in front of us. She looks exactly as I remember her from that one encounter we had. It seems like a lifetime ago. I had my whole future to look forward to.

"You want me to do what?" she asks us when we're done showing her the book and explaining everything that has happened.

"Someone in your family has to retake the throne," I tell her.

"It's the only way to bring real peace," John tells her.

"You're a princess, Kaliyah," Mabel tells her.

"Maybe my parents know more about this," Kaliyah says, "but what can we do to bring peace?"

"You, or someone in your family, should claim the throne," I tell her. "And stop all this violence."

"It can't be me," Alekai tells her. "No one would follow me because of the relation to our father. It must be someone with a pure bloodline. Someone like you."

I close the book and hand it to her.

She hesitates, then grabs it.

"Be the rulers your ancestors were," John tells her. "No more people should have to die."

Well, one more does.

"We'll do it," Kaliyah says. "I'll talk to my family and show this to them. I don't know if we can, but we'll do our best."

Then she stands and goes into her back pocket. She pulls out a green switchblade and hands it to me.

"You'll need this," she tells me.

"Thank you," I tell her as I take it.

Mabel bows her head to her, as do John and I. Kaliyah smiles.

***

I'm standing outside the treehouse by the lake that is next to the clubhouse. I don't even look at the clubhouse though. I stare solely at the tree that is protected with a spell. There's not a soul in sight. Raven and JP did a good job evacuating this place.

I guess I shouldn't be surprised at the calm. This place is just the eye of the storm now. Then I look at the lake. Grass, sand, and lake. Not a beach, but still quite close, just like the saltwater lagoon on that nightmarish day that set me on the path I'm on now.

I take a deep breath. I need to remain calm. I squint at the setting sun. I never understood why I hated the sun so much growing up. It's indisputably beautiful.

I'm holding my father's crystal ball that I took before leaving, even though that's not what he says it's called, that's what I'm calling it. It's reflecting the light of the sun to the point where it looks like I'm holding another star in my hands.

Father can rewind time and use this to look at the past. I can slow down time, so can I use that to look at the present?

I focus on my brothers and the crystal ball. Soon, I see Alekai and Deonna. They're at her place under the Statue of Liberty with my triplets. Deonna is in the two-person chair, feeding Brave. Alekai is holding both Dare and Light. Alekai says something to Deonna, and she smiles.

So, this does work on the present. What else is going on?

Trevor, Yulan, and Bonnie are in the middle of... New York? Miami? I can't tell what city they're in. I can tell though that there's a lot of chaos the kifomen are causing. There's a lot of blood on the ground too with body parts to match. My brothers are opening portals, sending as many kifomen through as they can. They're banged up severely, but they're still standing strong.

Next, I find Sax meditating on a hill. If only I can read his mind like Darren used to do.

My Darren.

I switch the image over to Gamma. He's standing, talking to our father who is laying on the couch. He must be doing what I asked him to do. Everything is going according to plan, so far.

I couldn't just be a normal kid, growing up to be a normal person. Then again, if my father hadn't meddled in my life, I never would have met Darren or had our triplets in the first place. If he hadn't been around, I wouldn't have been born. Deicoon, my however-many-great grandfather, and everything he has done led to me being here. Who knows what our family tree would look like if he and his mother Magara never created the kifomen in the first place? Maybe I wouldn't have been born, or maybe I would have been born as someone else. My father did have at least one child from every dimension. This must have been planned. Would Trevor and I still be twins or just regular siblings? That is if we're siblings at all.

What if I had been born a boy? That's a disturbing thought for me at least. Never thought of myself as a boy before.

I look back by the tree and see a dead brown and white bird on the ground by the trunk. I wonder what this little guy's life was like? Did He take you from this world, or was it someone or something who was playing God and killed you?

No one should have that kind of power. Even if they do, no one should use it. If they do use it, they should be punished for it.

That includes me and my family.

Why am I rambling right now? I guess I'm just scared. What if Father doesn't show? Or worse, what if he does come and I don't have the courage to do what I came here for?

I see a bird fly off the tree and lands by me.

Food? I hear the bird in my thoughts, just like those puffballs in Dimension Five when we were fishing in the river.

I never ate those puffballs with all their little eyes. too cute to eat...plus I'm vegan.

"I'll get you some bread, little guy," I tell him. "But then you have to get out of here."

I climb the rope ladder and grab some bread. I come back down and feed the bird.

"Hey," I ask the bird, "can you alert me when you see a man coming to my tree house?"

Sure.

"Thank you."

I wait for my father inside the treehouse.

***

I forgot how much food was in this treehouse. I ate an apple and vegan cheese before he showed up. Would have been nice to drink a root beer, but I need all my energy for this moment right here, right now.

I'm inside, sitting on the beanbag when he appears right after nightfall hits.

"Father," I say, looking at him dead in the eye.

"What are you doing, daughter?"

"Don't really know," I say. "I lost my husband, my best friend, and some siblings all in a short time span. Also, some other people way before that. I've lost so many, but I won't give into grief. I never even finished middle school. As much of a drag it was, I liked school. I liked learning new things, hanging out with my friends, and having those immature sleepovers. Then again, I gained so much when I lost all of that. I guess if it wasn't for you, I never would have been born, never would have met Darren, and Brave wouldn't be alive either."

"Where is she?" he asks.

"Safe and sound," I say. "Unlike her father you murdered."

My father sighs. "Why are you here?"

He's not confirming nor denying? I guess crazy people never admit they're crazy because they are in denial.

"Why are any of us here? It's the great cosmic question."

"Stop sounding like Gamma. Speaking of, he told me you came here. Why?"

I shrug my shoulders, even though I know why.

"Why kill my Darren? Didn't you know that would just turn me more against you?"

"I needed you to realize something."

"Which is?"

"He was holding you back from your family. If he were alive, you would have gone with him. You belong with us, your true loving family."

"He was my family."

"Not blood. Think of how you were with us when he wasn't around. You were happy."

"I was happy with him. I could have been happy with all of them...even you. You're a crazed killer."

"Daughter, this is ridiculous," he tells me.

"What was ridiculous was killing all our mothers and saying that they got sick."

"They were an influence you kids didn't need."

I knew it!

He did kill them!

Why is this surprising me?

"Gala and Sax are dead," he continues. "Balex and Zigor went who knows where. You can't defeat me on your own. There's no reason for us to fight. We should come together and grieve. Then I hope you'll help me do what must be done, but now you're acting insubordinate." He looks over me. "You're hiding something. You're not your usual self. Something about you is strange."

"I've always been strange," I tell him truthfully. "Imagine if my name was Rebecca Strange instead of Rebecca Dean. That would have been something."

"What game are you playing, my child?"

"I'm not playing your game anymore. As for why I'm here, I'm just, you know, chilling."

"Daughter, please, I can't lose you again, I can't bear to lose another child."

"What about your loyal followers?" I ask. "You sent the kifomen into Eight without moving them to safety."

"My children are what matter to me. My followers may die, yes, but they were created for this purpose. The evil inside of them only has one remedy. They are just another sacrifice I have to make for the greater good of the universe."

I smile. "I'm so glad you said that," using my telekinesis to push the button on my phone, "but your followers won't be."

"What did you do?"

"My camera phone videotaped you saying that, and I sent it to my good friend Deonna to show to the world, and your human followers, and you can't reverse time on this because it's been sent a while ago, and judging by what I saw, you can only reverse time a few seconds back, correct?"

"Why?" he sounds almost petrified, his black hair falling in his green eyes, and his face growing paler.

I just smile. "So, I am right? If you were able to do it longer, my brother and sister would still be-"

"Daughter! This has to stop!"

"I agree," I say standing up and pulling my shirt down, "but you won't stop, so I'm not going to either!"

Chapter 10

I throw a strong wave of electricity at him. Even though he leaps out of the way, the edges of the blast burn his sides. I blink and he's right in front of me, fully healed. He tries to grab me, but I send electricity through my arms, making him release me. I coat my hands in electricity and rush at him with full force, but he deflects them without getting zapped by knocking my arms aside.

"I don't want to fight you! It wounds me deeper than any blade," he tells me.

"Then you'll get over it. It's not like you have a choice," I hiss at him in anger.

He sighs, giving me the opening, I need.

I slow down time, but he reverses it, and time is back to normal. I feel a small wave of nausea come over me. Okay, can't do that if I want to keep my strength up.

"This battle is utterly pointless, my dear."

I use my telekinesis to lift the fridge and throw it at him. He uses his own telekinesis to stop it and drop it to the floor. He's not trying to attack me, just like I thought. I just need to keep weakening him. I don't want to shoot fire at him. I would burn the whole house down.

Think, Bec, think!

He starts to walk towards me and lift his hands. I use my telekinesis to grab him and throw him in the freezer. I quickly grab the lock and reverse time on it until it's shiny and strong. Easy, just like the cheese I reversed when I first learned this trick!

That'll buy me at least three seconds.

Think!

I'm so dizzy I feel like vomiting.

I don't have a lot of time. What should I do?

I got it!

I hope this works.

The lid to the freezer flies off, and Father bursts out. He throws a piece of meat at my feet. "Look, daughter. These fiends who feast on animal flesh for their own pleasure are who you're protecting. Come to your senses."

I use my light trick to make the room darker.

"Fine, we'll play it your way." He picks up things along the floor with his telekinesis and throws them at me in quick succession.

"You want to fight me? You won't win. There are no winners in family feuds, Becky."

I really hate that name!

He's trying to bait me.

Ignore him! Don't lose focus on what's important.

He throws various household objects at me. I deflect some of them back to him and I aim for his head. A lamp and a nightstand make direct contact, wounding his face. I keep barraging him with more things on the floor, so he won't have time to reverse the damage.

He falls to the floor and is gasping.

He's weak?

He's weak!

Now's my chance!

I cover him with the rug, so he can't see what I'm about to do. He's covered for about three seconds, but that was just enough time. I grab the switchblade that was in my pocket that Kaliyah gave me.

He jumps and grabs my wrist, but that turns me into dust.

"What?" he asks. He then turns his head and sees me standing by the button panel with the switchblade.

"Misdirection."

I throw it at him, then I then close my eyes and press the red button.

Epilogue

There's nothing but white when I open my eyes. Thank goodness I'm not in the dark, I've always feared it.

Where am I though?

I try to speak, but my mouth can't open.

Weird.

Am I dead?

I think so.

I had to kill him though, for the sake of everyone else's lives. I look down. I seem to still have my body, although it's very sheer. I hold my own hand, but I don't feel it. I can't seem to feel anything.

I walk forward despite the crushed feeling in my soul. I walk for what feels like days or perhaps minutes. I don't know if it's been a long time or barely any time at all.

Is this Dimension Ten?

Do I have to open a portal to get there?

I close my eyes and try to open one, but it doesn't work.

I open my eyes again.

Wait! I did do something!

I see something small in the distance. I run towards it, watching as the small speck grows increasingly larger, until I get close enough to it to realize that it is a baby tree.

Where am I now?

I look around. All the white has changed. I suddenly find myself in a forest of baby trees in the night. I look down at the one I saw first and notice a tombstone next to it.

I move in front of it and stare at the name on it.

My name.

It also says "Hero to us all" on it.

This must be where I blew up my father, along with myself. I look around at the other baby trees. There is nothing else here. What time is it? Is it even daytime? Does time even exist here? I can't tell.

"Hi, mommy," I hear a young child's voice say behind me.

I turn around and see a young boy around six or seven, holding a bouquet of rainbow daisies running up to me. His right eye is green, and his left eye is black. Before I can do anything, he runs right through me. I turn around and watch as he places the flowers on my grave.

"Dare! What did I say about running ahead of us?" I hear a familiar voice say to him.

"Sorry, aunt Deonna," he tells her. "I just wanna see mommy."

Deonna pulls him into a hug with tears starting to form in her eyes. "I know, Sweetie."

Dare lets go of her and I notice a small bump on her stomach. He runs up to my brother Alekai who is holding hands with another boy whose face is identical to Dare, and a girl who is similar looking, and the same age as the boys.

I'm so happy they're okay, but my soul is crushed knowing I can't be there for them.

Light and Brave are also holding flowers. Light is holding a bouquet of red roses, and Brave is holding a white orchid.

They both let go of Alekai's hands. Light runs up to my grave while Brave walks slowly with tears in her eyes.

Light places the roses while Brave digs a little hole and buries the orchid.

My triplets.

They're beautiful.

"Can you tell us the story again, aunt Deonna?" Light asks Deonna.

She smiles at him. "For lifetimes, magician kind has been battling another powerful family of magicians and their kifomen who were trying to eradicate all those they deemed to be evil. Your mother was born into that family, but she was raised by kind humans, then taken in by my family when they died. Now, your mother's biological family was so powerful that they could open portals, and for the longest time, we could not stop them. That is until your mother joined the fight."

"Yay, mom!" my boys cheered.

Brave just smiled with tears pouring down her face.

"She gave her life to stop her father's plan. It took magicians five years to move the remaining kifomen to their home dimension, and to handle his remaining followers from all the dimensions that didn't believe or care about the video your mother took of her father not caring for their lives. She sent me the video and I played it in Eight, and word slowly spread amongst the followers. They were closely knit and always communicated, so it wasn't hard."

"And here we are, two years later," Dare says glumly.

My babies are seven. I've been dead for seven years.

Deonna sighs.

"Your mother and my brother did everything they could to avoid you guys growing up as orphans," Deonna tells him. "But she saved the world, and you three in the process. Meanwhile, your uncle Alekai was able to bring in the true ruling family back from hiding, and now magicians know peace again, this time with the humans. The kifomen are back in their home dimension, thanks to your uncles opening the portals for them."

"Is it possible to miss someone you've never met?" Brave whispers.

Alekai pulls her into a hug. "Yes, it is. Very much so."

Dare and Light start crying as well. They all bunch up in a group hug.

I reach out to them, but my arms just go right through. I can't even let them know how much I love them.

Deonna takes out a camera and takes a picture of them by my grave. They're finally taking pictures like I've been advising them to do for years.

I'm so proud!

Brave walks over to my grave and gives the top of it a gentle kiss. "Happy birthday, mommy."

Light does the same thing, followed by Dare. Despite the warmth I feel all over, my desire to be with them crushes my spirit with every passing second. Brave takes the orchid, plants it by my grave, and extends her hand. The orchid starts to grow and the buds bloom greater.

Light rolls his hands in the air, and a small ball of water forms. He hovers the water over the orchid and lets it fall into the soil. Dare compresses his hands, and when he opens them, there's a little ball of fire that looks just like the sun. He hovers it next to the orchid, giving it some light.

The three of them smile at each other.

Just then, a ringing song comes from Alekai's back pocket. "Yeah, Trev?" he says answering his phone. "Okay. Thanks, little bro." He closes the phone and looks at Deonna. "We should go before someone tows the van," Alekai jokes, then gets serious. "Besides, my brothers need us. Trevor was telling me that Balex and Zigor need help with Gamma's-"

"But I wanna stay with mom," Dare says crying. "We never stay with her for long."

Light and Brave start crying too. Light has waterfalls falling from his eyes.

"How about we go have lunch, see your parent's wedding picture, and I'll tell you another story about your father," Deonna says.

They all wipe their little faces and whisper, "Okay."

"Your cousins, JP and Raven, will make your favorite," Deonna smiles at them.

"Mac and cheese!" they cheer.

"Last one to the van cleans up after lunch," Alekai playfully shouts, obviously trying to forget all their troubles.

"Not it!" my triplets shout, then all make a break for it. Dare and Brave are neck in neck, with Light not too far behind.

Deonna laughs a little, and Alekai slips his hand into hers and kisses her on the cheek.

"You think they'd be proud?" Deonna asks.

"Of course, they would," Alekai tells her, and they walk after my children.

My poor babies. I fall to my knees and bury my face in my hands. They're growing up without us. Deonna and my brothers are doing so much for our kids, and I can never repay the debt I owe them.

I feel a hand on each of my shoulders.

I look up and see Darren, and my brother Tom.

I pull them both into a hug.

My brother Jake and sister Ash both run up and pull me into another hug. Audrey is not far behind them.

I thought I'd never see any of them again!

My siblings stand on one side of me and Darren, and Audrey stand on the other side of me. Tom holds out his hand to me and nudges his head in their direction.

Darren does the same thing.

I never thought I could be so happy, especially with what I just saw with my babies.

They'll join us when it's their time.

There's no rush. After all, we have an eternity here.

I take their hands, and I leave with them.

The End!

Page 453